W9-CES-365

THE FIRST OF JULY

THE FIRST OF JULY

ELIZABETH SPELLER

PEGASUS BOOKS
NEW YORK LONDON

NEW HANOVER COUNTY
PUBLIC LIBRARY
201 CHESTNUT STREET
WILMINGTON, NC 28401

THE FIRST OF JULY

Pegasus Books LLC
80 Broad Street, 5th Floor
New York, NY 10004

Copyright ©2013 by Elizabeth Speller

First Pegasus Books hardcover edition November 2013

Interior design by Maria Fernandez

All rights reserved. No part of this book may be reproduced in whole or in part without
written permission from the publisher, except by reviewers who may quote brief excerpts
in connection with a review in a newspaper, magazine, or electronic publication; nor may
any part of this book be reproduced, stored in a retrieval system, or transmitted in any
form or by any means electronic, mechanical, photocopying, recording, or other, without
written permission from the publisher.

ISBN: 978-1-60598-497-1

10 9 8 7 6 5 4 3 2 1

Printed in the United States of America
Distributed by W. W. Norton & Company, Inc.

For my grandfathers
and my great-uncle,
all of whom fought in France
in the Great War.
Captain Vivien Moore MC 1887–1958
Lieutenant Bertram Eric Edmonds 1894–1965
Lieutenant Rupert Howard 1885–1916

"The ground where I stood gave a mighty convulsion. It rocked and swayed. I gripped hold of my tripod to steady myself. Then for all the world like a gigantic sponge, the earth rose high in the air to the height of hundreds of feet. Higher and higher it rose, and with a horrible grinding roar the earth settles back upon itself, leaving in its place a mountain of smoke."

Geoffrey Malins, cinematographer,
on the detonation of the mine
under the Hawthorn Ridge Redoubt
at 7:20 on July 1, 1916

Theirs is the hollow victory.
They are deceived.
But you my brother and my ghost, if you can go
Knowing that there is no reward, no certain use
In all your sacrifice, then honour is reprieved.

"To a Conscript of 1940"
by Herbert Read

THE FILM, JULY 1, 1916

Silence

THE FILM WILL BE SILENT, of course: grainy, flickering images of men, machinery, horses, and eruptions of earth and smoke. In a few weeks its audiences will watch it to the accompaniment of stirring piano music; but they, and those still watching a century later, will have to imagine, from the white faces of the soldiers and the sudden crumpling of their bodies, what the real soundtrack might sound like. In the knowledge of where they are headed, these anonymous men, it will be disturbing and embarrassing to look at their faces: too tired, too resigned, too young, too old, too real. Yet somehow it is impossible to look away. What are they thinking, these men, stripped down by the camera to animal fear?

At 7:29 in the morning of July 1, the cinematographer finds himself filming silence itself. One hundred and twenty seconds of silence. After a week of shelling, day and night, the air and the ground and the men trembling and afire: stillness. The massive mines have been detonated; he has, with a certain exultation, trapped the explosion. The moment of a landscape being altered for ever. It will be his most famous image: the convulsion of earth that looks, on film, like an elm tree in full leaf. Clouts of earth and chalk and terror are still falling, but then the barrage lifts, just like that; by coincidence, both sides ceasing fire simultaneously.

What the cinematographer cannot capture on his 35-millimeter film is the particular quality of this silence: silence and a few larks singing, and no one yet aware how significant their song will become. Even the photographer does not know quite what it is he is filming: the last seconds of the old world, with half a war still to run.

Is the camera trembling? It pans over the men waiting, the attack about to begin, the expected victory still ahead. It moves unevenly down the barrel of a howitzer to the puzzled face of a gunner corporal. The man sticks a finger in his gritty ear. The bombardment has stopped on all sides; his ears are ringing with the sudden absence of war. He hears birds: larks that he associates with Lancashire mornings, walking to his early shift, knowing he'll be dancing with his girl come evening. But the camera just catches the gunner looking up, squinting before moving into position; the film will say nothing about the hazy gray blue that suggests a hot day ahead or that the Lancashire sky is coming with him, the larks singing like some unholy miracle.

The camera closes in on a subaltern of the 11th Suffolks, a keen birdwatcher who returns monthly reports to the Royal Ornithological Society. But not today. Not now. He is oblivious that he is being filmed as he watches the waiting men in his section. The camera follows his glance, lingering almost lovingly on the soldiers in the trench. A couple, like their officer, gaze upward at the birds; some look worried, perhaps by the invisible cessation of noise. Some have set their faces, stonily, to the hours ahead and seem unaware of either gunfire or birdsong, tight and frozen with eyes dark and fixed. The young subaltern, prep-schoolmaster for two years, infantry officer for eighteen weeks, thinks that when the time comes he will blow his whistle, climb the ladder, then fling away his helmet, his Sam Browne and his Webley, open his arms wide, lift his face to the sky and feel the sun upon it and the breeze in his hair and run, run across the lush, flat Suffolk fields of the Stour under the pipits, curlews, and lapwings, and Tilly barking ahead of him with the joy of it.

Steadier now, the camera moves along an untidy row of squatting men, half sheltered in a sunken road, and is challenged by a scowling trooper, who stares right back at it. The camera mistakes the expression, under a helmet pushed too far back on his head, for hostility but it is, in fact, impotent terror. He is thinking that something else has obviously gone wrong again, just their bleeding luck. The gunners, useless buggers, have probably stopped for a mug of tea. He looks at the man next to him, his brother actually, but Albert's eyes are narrowed. He's miles away, probably dreaming of sticking Jerry. Albert had grinned when the major had said they couldn't afford to take prisoners. Not, the major said, that they would meet many living Germans. They would just saunter—"saunter like a masher up Piccadilly" were the words he used—across to the enemy lines because the guns would have taken out all their positions. "Blown to smithereens," the major said, and the barbed wire marking the boundary between front lines (never mind that it is clear enough now to see the wire, looking as if it is holding up pretty well) "ripped to confetti." The trooper thinks of all the bad things that have happened. He thinks of Germans and tries to hate them enough to feel his bayonet slice through their uniform, through soft flesh and tight muscle and grate along their ribs, and wonders what it would feel like to be on the receiving end. In all his time as a soldier, he's never yet fired his gun.

How many men are thinking about salvation, the first-aider wonders? The cinematographer, with the first-aider's thoughts inaccessible to him, has to make do with images of hands rolling bandages. They'd rolled enough days ago, but the first-aider, a searcher who will follow the first waves of attack and treat the injured, finds it a soothing task despite the gauze catching on his rough and raw skin. It takes him back to being a child, watching the women roll up used wool. He can hear shouting and the sound of a breeze catching an unsecured canvas tent flap. He can smell fresh earth—the mass grave they'd dug behind the hospital. They are ready for ten thousand casualties, the senior M.O. had explained yesterday. Far greater capacity than would ever be required, but soldiers deserved to know they'd be cared for if they were wounded or worse. A junior M.O. had made a small grimace.

The camera sees nothing of God, who is never far from the first-aider's side. God, who had wanted him to be a pacifist and with whom the first-aider had made a deal, mistakenly thinking it would be easier to be a first-aider than a conscientious objector. Now God is calling in the debt, sending him forward to face the great enemy, death, hauling back victims from death's indiscriminate feast to life.

The camera gathers speed across the small airfields, the tents, the mechanics, the men of the Royal Flying Corps. But once airborne, the filmed planes are nothing more than darting birds. The camera can't follow the pilot upward or see him in his cockpit, unable to hear the silence or the birds or even his own voice singing "Row, row, row your boat, gently down the stream." He is twenty-five hundred feet above the ground in the cockpit of his nifty parasol and what he feels, vibrating through his feet and hands, is the sweet running of the motor. The pilot looks down on the landscape below, bounded by small dark copses, red hamlets, the green-edged River Ancre, and the Somme marshes, and crossed with the busy arcs of trenches.

He is thinking about a dark-haired girl in Paris and a sapper (engineer) captain he'd met in the mess four days earlier. The man's affable face had been creased with dirt, fatigue, and frustration. "William Bolitho," he'd said, putting out his hand. "Digging for King and country." And then just before their fingers touched, he withdrew it and smiled, looking down at his palm. "Sorry—filthy—you wouldn't want to shake it."

As they drank their way through most of a bottle of Scotch, the sapper had explained flaws in their objective, using matchsticks and a pencil. The pilot remembers that the flaws had to do with sightlines and trajectories and didn't seem to involve anything in the air above the level of shells.

Now the pilot looks down on the relief map of Picardy below him, watching tiny convoys of men or horses moving, apparently arbitrarily, from one point to another, of howitzers and field guns and the raw white scars of Hawthorn Ridge and its redoubt, where the earth itself has just been hurled into the air, blowing his frail machine off course. He thinks the sapper might have liked to see the arcs and fans and parallel lines of his labors. It is like a message carved in code to be read by the gods.

Below him, silently, the camera runs on, making history from unknown lives: such ordinary chaps and volunteers every one.

THE FIRST OF JULY

Before, 1913

CHAPTER ONE
Jean-Baptiste Mallet, Corbie, France, July 1913

SOME DAY HE WOULD STEAL a boat and row all the way to the sea. He sat on the bank of the river, where willows trailed on the surface of the water and where carp sometimes basked—a flash of silver just under the surface—and he threw a stone into the tiny scum of broken leaves and twigs caught in the river's slow bend. In high summer, everything here was green—the water, the trees, the bright duckweed—and the smell: the beginning of slightly rotten vegetation, the deep smell of mud and fat eels who lived on flesh, and everything mad with growing. He liked the river here where it broadened, like a man describing the hips of a shapely woman with his hands, and, where the small island was left in the middle, dense with trees.

In the rushes was the boat. It was a small, tidy boat, well kept and covered with a canvas tarpaulin, held down by rocks in case of rain. Inside lay two new oars, and fishing tackle was stowed under the seat. It was called *Sans Souci* and belonged to Vignon, the doctor. When the roads were bad, Vignon sometimes rowed out to patients; but mostly he used the boat to fish. There was never such a man for fishing, Jean-Baptiste's mother said. There was never such a man for Madame de Potiers, either, Jean-Baptiste thought. He had watched the doctor's astonishingly hairy backside moving energetically between Madame de Potiers's white knees and spread skirts, forcing himself down repeatedly as if he was driving in a wedge to split a log, roaring as he went. It was always on Thursdays, Vignon's day off, that the boat would be moored on the far side of the island. Jean-Baptiste had started by swimming across in curiosity to watch the doctor's fishing. The doctor did fish, afterward, as he could always be seen with two or three pike, singing (in Italian, some said) as he walked back to his house. He sang only on Thursdays—and sometimes on Sundays in church, of course. Perhaps he is singing a song about fish, the women said, as Vignon returned, his trouser knees stained green, to the neat red-brick house with its railings and its pear trees on the edge of town.

It was Vignon's boat that Jean-Baptiste planned to row to the sea. Meanwhile he exercised to strengthen his arms and chest. His mother thought he was doing it to join the Army and sometimes felt the muscle of his upper arms approvingly as she passed behind him while he was chopping kindling. A strong son made a widow's life easier. She dreamed that Jean-Baptiste would march away a cuirassier and return a moustachioed sergeant like the picture that had hung in her bedroom all Jean-Baptiste's life. It was more likely that when he turned twenty, he'd be pitched off for three dreary years on the eastern borders with Germany and live on weevils in the rain. That's where most of the conscripted Corbie boys went. They came back with moustaches and harder faces, and they spoke of women. But he and his mother both knew that he was lucky to have been offered a position in the forge of the widower Godet, the blacksmith. Their busybody of a neighbor, Madame Laporte, whose son Lucien's early career had reached its highest point when he was the school bully, had also told anyone who wanted to listen that Jean-Baptiste was lucky to have a handsome mother, and smirked. Lucien was a lumpy, pale boy who now passed his time drawing obscene pictures on walls around town and, rumor had it, was responsible for the number of dead cats and hens that were found, mutilated, on people's doorsteps. Now it was Lucien who was off to be a soldier, which seemed to offer him undreamed-of opportunities to pursue his hobbies.

"Good riddance," Jean-Baptiste's mother had said. "The boy's funny in the head. In a bad way."

Jean-Baptiste offered to take Dr. Vignon on his riverside rounds, hoping that he could learn to row better. Vignon was no great rower and seemed relieved. Once he was sure that the boy could master the currents and use the oars without splashing them both with water, Vignon relaxed and usually sat back and smoked. After a few weeks, Jean-Baptiste couldn't resist asking whether the doctor would like him to row him to the island on Thursdays for the fishing. Vignon's eyes narrowed. He drew hard on his cigarette. "How old are you now?"

"Fifteen."

"You need to see more of the world," Vignon had said, and his gaze never left Jean-Baptiste's face. "There's more to life than Corbie."

Jean-Baptiste had come to like, even admire, the doctor with his singing, his sweet-smelling tobacco, his neat, glistening black beard, his hairy arse, and his possession of Madame de Potiers's perfect, aristocratic thighs, even if he was from Paris; but he couldn't tell the doctor, of course, of his plans to do just that—to see the world by stealing the doctor's boat. But he had made his plans. The river's history was as long as the world's, and it could be relied upon to bear him north but no more: it had its own loyalties. When the curé had been a boy, two Englishmen had found mammoth bones and a huge flint axe in the river bank near Amiens, and they had tried to claim that these monsters and these fighting axe-men had been here before anyone thought God created the earth. Then they had been taught at school that the Duke of Normandy had invaded the English from the harbor at St. Valéry, and the river had played its part, first in beating the English at Crécy but then helping them win at Agincourt. It had let the Spanish advance into Corbie, but seen them beaten off by forty thousand men sent by Louis the Just.

What started as a muddy trickle in the dense forest of Arrouaise wound its way north for many, many kilometers, past Abbéville, St. Valéry, and Le Crotoy. Befitting its changeable nature, sometimes it was a brisk stream, sometimes a deep pool, sometimes a reedy lake. For a stretch, men had tamed it into a canal; he had seen a school map and there was the canal, straight and regular, and there beside it the untidy undulations of the ancient river, its meres and marshland. He had imagined the canal water always trying to seep back to its wild home. At Amiens, the river was a watery maze where black barges tended the garden *hortillonages*; from time to time it was a peat-fen rich in wildfowl; but still it kept going. It took in smaller rivers—Jean-Baptiste had himself been born and lived all his life in the small town where the Ancre met the greater river—and then, the schoolmaster had told them, it mingled with the Avre and the Selle and the Hallue, and with the burden of all this water it got wider and fuller as more streams ran to join it in its rush to the sea, and then it opened into a vast mouth: half sand, half water.

Jean-Baptiste knew two men who had seen this. The curé said the mouth was known to be nearly as wide as the whole distance between Albert and Paris; and then, as if realizing nobody could imagine such a distance, he explained that it was so wide, a man would need a horse to ride from one side to the other and it would take much more than a day. He said it was a wild, godforsaken place of screaming birds, knifing, briny winds, and hills of sand and coarse grass. Vignon said it was an in-between place where the sky saw its reflection in the water, where the sea sometimes drew itself so far back that seabed became shore, where the light turned the beach to mother-of-pearl. If you walked barefoot, the sand felt like carved ripples under your toes and the froth of breakers was like lace as the river fought a little before surrendering silently to the ocean.

The sea of course was salty and Jean-Baptiste didn't know at what point the fresh river water turned to salt, or at what point its greenness would be overwhelmed by the cold slate gray that sailors talked about, but when he rowed away he would find out these things. The boat would not be diverted into fens or lakes; it would find the sea, like a fish returning upriver to spawn, and if he kept rowing he could even reach England. He would see what was to be seen and then come back a strong man with tales to tell, far more extraordinary than those told by boys who had just sat on the border in the rain.

Before then, he would need to learn a few words in English, and he had tried to get Vignon to tell him what might be useful—without giving him grounds for suspicion—but Vignon had been surprisingly vague for a man who had traveled. A man born in an unnamed city rich with treasure left by the Gauls and the Romans and Charlemagne himself. A man who had once lived in Paris. Had seen Monsieur Eiffel's tower.

"Sausage," the doctor had said. And then "God save the King." His lip had curled. "How do you do?"

How do you do what, Jean-Baptiste had wondered, and considered whether he was more inclined to believe the curé's or the doctor's accounts of the meeting of the river and the sea. Soon he would find out the truth.

Now Vignon sat back, lighting another cigarette. He picked a yellow leaf off the sole of his boot. The toecaps shone like a conker; the laces were plump and tidily crossed, and the leather was rarely muddy or wet, except on Thursdays. Jean-Baptiste thought of his own boots. After his father's death, his mother had kept his boots, much repaired though they were, as an earthly relic. If he thought of his father at all, it was only as these boots. He couldn't remember much else of him above the level of the eyelets for the laces and, somewhere above that, a voice shouting. His father sleeping was a pair of empty boots in the scullery; his father dead was two scarred, upturned soles, one at right angles to the other at the bottom of the stairs. His mother had started making Jean-Baptiste wear the boots when he was twelve, stuffing the toes with rags and putting goose fat on his chafed shins. She was still insisting he keep them, even though it was obvious that he was growing into a much larger man than his father, and he had to curl his toes up when he wore them. His nail beds were bruised if he walked any distance and, out of her sight, he returned to his sabots, his wooden work shoes, with relief. But he rowed barefoot, finding that the sensations in his feet and toes responded to the messages the water transmitted through planks and oars. He steered the small boat precisely and gracefully, having left his sabots under a bush.

"Despite everything, this strange region is quite charming." The doctor waved his cigarette toward the lagoon. "I'm surprised you weren't all born web-footed. And how well named your river is," he said, in the tone he sometimes used that made Jean-Baptiste feel less guilty about intending to steal his boat, a gibe that made it clear that Vignon had seen more reliable land and far bigger, probably more patriotic, rivers, including the Seine itself, and that, in the scale of things, this small town, this Picardy backwater, his patients, even Madame de Potiers, were a temporary amusement.

"Tranquility. That's what the name Somme means," Vignon said. "In an ancient language." He waved an arm in the direction of the past. "And here we are, tranquil in our boat. Or at least I'm tranquil and you are sweating like a bull—so we'd better tie her up for the evening or your mother will be around to deal with me, fierce as a tigress."

Giving Jean-Baptiste another of his slow smiles, lines radiating outward from his black eyes, he pulled out a white handkerchief from his creased linen jacket, raised his hat, and mopped his brow.

"One must never be late for a lady."

CHAPTER TWO

Frank Stanton, London, July 1913

THERE ARE THREE RULES YOU can swear by:

1. Never be late.
2. There is a system for everything.
3. You can say what you like about bicycles, but for a young man they are the way ahead.

When I arrived in London in 1910, I was nearly nineteen years old and a carpenter of sorts. I had had a falling-out with my old man, and it was pride that made me spend the little money I'd inherited from my dead mother on a third-class ticket from Totnes to London. That, and an advertisement I had read in a newspaper wrapped around a delivery of brass fittings.

I applied for a manual position in a shop: *"Shelves, counters, and general carpentry. Knowledge of fine woodwork an advantage,"* although in truth all I had knowledge of was building coffins. But shelves and coffins have more in common than most people know or, strangely, wish to. Both can be a work of art or something flimsy that cannot take weight and is fit only for gimcrack. I have known disasters to befall—in other hands than mine—even in the best of stores. You no more want the deceased to reappear through the bottom of a coffin as the obsequies are being read, than you do some young lady, leaning on a counter, to plunge head-first into a display of Belgian lace.

But Dad had trained me in fine work, and the coffin trade is a punctual trade and one that must adapt to whatever life, or death, brings. In my years of beveling and filleting, chamfering and mitering, I was never late for a customer, and I took that habit to London with me. In stories, London is a place where a man's fortunes can change in a twinkling of an eye. There are no such tales told of Devon.

It was at Debenham and Freebody that my chance came. The new director, Mr. Frederick Richmond, found me working at 8:17 P.M. I was recutting a piece of discarded timber that I could see need not be wasted. In coffins we had learned to improvise, refitting wood, and, although it was never pleasant, on some occasions also the deceased if they were of exceptional height. I told Mr. Richmond this (a need not to waste, not the other business) when he asked me a little about myself. I being honest and he being a board man, I told him about coffins.

Mr. Richmond said "No wonder you've got a feel for the work. We'll move you on to counters."

Great slabs of oak they were: wonderful grained wood from Kent.

"I expect you've handled plenty of oak in your sad business," he said.

"Only for the likes of you, sir," I said, and on seeing his face I added: "I mean gentry, sir."

He looked pleased but puzzled, so I said "Oak, fine solid oak like your counters, is for the highest in the land."

I didn't say that mostly all the coffins I ever made was of elm or pine, and that my father had started me off on tiny little pieces for babies where weight counted for nothing and we used mostly offcuts.

So I worked on counters for a while, but that time flew by and the glaziers and gilders in the store were soon done; and just as I was thinking I'd have to find another job, Mr. Richmond returned. He says he'd be sorry to lose me and then, thinking, calls over this grave and sleek party: very upright, of middle age, everything black and white, even dark eyes behind wire-rimmed spectacles.

"Mr. Hardy," Mr. Richmond says. "Here's the man I was talking to you about. Very punctual and reliable. It is highly unorthodox, but perhaps we can find a place on the shop floor for young Mr. —?"

"Stanton, Frank, sir," said I. Embarrassed, not wanting to catch the superior person's eye.

Mr. Hardy seemed cautiously pleased to have me. "You have an opportunity to rise that is granted to few," he said. "I am sure you will repay our trust."

So that's how I became, in time, senior assistant in ladies' gloves, traveling cases, umbrellas, and parasols. Also gentlemen's straw hats and riding crops, although our ladies mostly go else-where for these—usually to where they are fitted for hunting clothes—but there is, as Mr. Hardy tells us often, always the lady who buys on impulse and can be persuaded by a riding crop with an ivory fox head and a sparkling stone for an eye. Not a *real* lady, Mr. Hardy says. But those who are new to the business of being a lady and still attracted by little novelties.

Systems are there to help us, not, as some of my colleagues believe, impede. For instance, I have two decisions to make:

1. Bicycles. When the time comes, should it be Rudge-Whitworth, Humber, or, as I am currently

considering, the new Royal Enfield Duplex Girder? It is £8 15s., although £9 17s. 6d. with an Armstrong three-speed gear. Some say the motorcyclist can get from A to B quicker than the bicyclist; but what will he hear, what will he see, how will he greet other cyclists as he passes them? On a motor-bicycle there is no mastery of machine. The engine does the work. A bicycle is man and machine in harmony. In time, the decision will be made for me by the amount of information and the balance in favor and, of course, my savings. Saving a regular amount from my wages, I estimate I shall purchase a bicycle in August 1914.

2. A wife. Having found a way to choose a bicycle, I feel the system for selection will be as useful for this equally important decision. I need a young woman who will help me in my profession. A girl who is not in a position where she might look down on my efforts but who wishes, as I do, to improve herself. I would like a pretty one, of course. I don't aim for a young lady of fashion, just a decent young woman who seeks a good provider (once I have bought the bicycle). I need her healthy, as I could not take time off and have no money for her to be sickly and, in time, I should like a small family.

Regarding the selection of a wife, at present I have two on my list:

1. *Florence*, who works in millinery.
For: She is, I think, a very fastidious young woman. I don't think she is spoken for, although it is hard to be sure. If I had a bicycle, I could follow her home at a distance and be certain. She has a nice shape, healthy pink cheeks, fair hair, a pleasant way with customers; she is punctual,

always looks smart; and Mr. Hardy once said "That young lady will rise."

Against: I saw her once dancing with three feather boas around her neck. It was five minutes to closing, but it betrayed a frivolous nature or perhaps just youth. She calls herself Flo, but I always think of her as Florence: it's the name on Mr. Hardy's lips and a more dignified name should she ever get to hold the book. She may not be much more than seventeen.

2. *The young lady at the Institute at St. Pancras.* She may be named Connie or possibly Nancy (it is hard to tell, as she is often with her friend and I do not know which is which). She gives out pamphlets on Friday evenings with a man called Isaac, who looks a bit like the gypsies in picture books, although with spectacles, but knows a great deal about international politics. Connie (or Nancy) seems quiet and is tall and has big eyes. I have heard her ask questions of a speaker and they have always been useful, well-thought-through inquiries. She shows care for her appearance even in straitened circumstances. I think she would be careful with money.

Still, there is no urgency to make a decision. Mr. Hardy would look very poorly on a marriage before I am twenty-three. Also, my lodgings at Lambeth are *quite* unsuitable for a wife, but while I am saving for the bicycle I cannot afford more commodious, not to say salubrious, lodgings.

What if Connie/Nancy is a Suffragist? (Because of the boas I do not think Florence would be.) Mr. Frederick Richmond has very strong views on political ladies. Very.

I have been very impressed by the knowledge it is possible to acquire in London if you put your mind to it. I have learned about wireless communication, Esperanto, the works of Mr. G. K. Chesterton, the poetry of Mr. Longfellow,* and the history of the railway. On Fridays the Institute offers a range of political talks. Isaac, for all that he is young, and the only employment he can find is sewing garments in a Spitalfields factory, began a most interesting discussion on conditions for workers in other countries. I had never known that in Russia they still had slaves. Afterward we had tea together. He is very earnest in all he does and spends hours in the Institute reading room, but in time I have come to think him a friend. I do not say much about all this in the store, as I do not think Mr. Richmond or Mr. Hardy would like such things.

I am an Internationalist. I bought a map of England and a map of Europe (1s. 8d.). Now, of a summer evening or on Sundays, I walk and walk. North, south, east, west I go. Sometimes I feel as if I am pushing London outward with each stride or swing of my arms. When I have my bicycle, I plan to go to the Surrey hills and to the Chilterns, south to the Sussex chalk downs and the English Channel, and east along the brown Thames. Then I shall gaze at the great continent of Europe. Then, one day, to France and the greatest cycle race known to man.

---

* Mr. Longfellow, who is an American, has written a poem about bicycles:
  This rapid steed which cannot stand
  Follows the motion of my hand
  An iron Centaur we ride the land.

CHAPTER THREE
Benedict Chatto, Gloucester, July 1913

BENEDICT CHATTO SAT IN THE cold gray choir of the cathedral, waiting. He heard the wheeze and subdued hum as the organ bellows were turned on, Theo, his friend and fellow music scholar, thumping in the loft as he finished some mechanical fiddling. Years ago, he and Theo, eight years old and choir schoolboys together, had been alike in character and musical ability. But Theo had become everything he, Benedict, was not. Theo had grown beyond him. Theo burned and shone; he had a gift where Benedict was competent and industrious; Theo was impulsive, Benedict was merely cautious; Theo had ready charm and wit, Benedict was reserved, and worried he was dull.

Suddenly, above him, music: a run of semiquavers in F-sharp and a sheet of indigo blue flared up—the painted pipes seeming to tremble with it. A yellow chord followed by blue again and then orange as Theo adjusted the flute stops. The piece was melodic but with the potential to explode: something was simmering underneath. Benedict smiled: Theo must be certain Dr. B was out of the building. It was Vierne: modern, innovative, and French; everything Dr. Brewer, their tutor, saw himself as holding out against.

When it came to music, Theo spoke of the organ as a kind of machine to be controlled. Ben liked to imagine it as something living. When he was a boy, he had thought of it as an animal at the heart of the cathedral, one that breathed through leathery lungs. The sheer peculiarity and force of the organ still thrilled him; when he played, he felt part of it. But he was never, would never be, as brilliant as Theo, who felt none of these things.

Benedict often thought the cathedral was more like a village than a place of quiet holiness. The bishop, the mostly absent landowner; congregations gossiping and haggling with God; King's School boys giggling and pushing; the dean rushing about as if there were some structural or theological emergency that only he could resolve, his demeanor proclaiming that he was far too busy to talk. Dr. Brewer, head down, was oblivious to his surroundings, apparently oblivious to God or indeed anything except, intermittently, his organ pupils and, emerging from the bishop's chilly palace from time to time, Mrs. Bradstock, the bishop's wife, Lady of the Close. Her clipped conversation was punctuated by tiny writhings of her neck, and at her side and always in her sight the eighteen-year-old Agnes, the bishop's porcelain doll of a daughter, the village virgin.

"Perfect," Theo sighed, "pristine," every time Agnes passed. "Look!" Theo had said as they watched her proceeding across the Close with her mother, throwing them a half-look over her shoulder. "Even her eyelashes are gold. Imagine your hand on her arm, the tiny dimples left when you let it go. Would she bruise, do you think?"

It seemed to Ben that his own part in all this was as the stranger who had lost his way. Yet he still found delight in the cathedral's

17

euphoric architecture, every inch of its stone decorated or pierced and, in buttresses upon buttresses, the suggestion of a massive failure of nerve. It was as if the builders had fortified it against divine caprice: thunderbolts or fires or high winds. Ben loved the human doubt of it all.

The gulls and pigeons were the bane of the Clerk of Works' life. Visitors arriving in the Close often took him for a holy man, his brows furrowed like an ascetic, his eyes raised heavenward; but it was the birds and his plans of attack that preoccupied him. The pigeons damaged the stonework and covered it in filth, but the gulls destroyed the very dignity of the Close. They swooped down and assaulted passers-by or those leaving Morning Service. Things had come to a head in a recent St. Kyneburgh Day procession when one of them had fouled the mayor's ceremonial hat. The mayor not being popular, the news had spread around the local public houses, and in no time at all there was a ditty being sung in the Pelican. Theo had noted down the rudimentary tune and then composed a set of variations on a theme. He was planning to play it at the following year's service, he said.

"'Fly, heavenly bird, and drop thy bounteous gifts.' Do you think that's a good title?" Theo had asked.

His beaming face was still a schoolboy's, but it was not Benedict's approval he was looking for then, because Novello had still been at Gloucester; this was when he had still been plain David Ivor Davies, before he left for Oxford and London and reinvented himself. He was in on the joke, leaning over Theo's shoulder, adding some marking in pencil.

"We should have caught it," he said, "and had it stuffed and placed on St. Edward's shrine for pilgrims to honor."

But the thing was, the music was good; Theo had made something beautiful out of a schoolboy joke.

Benedict looked dispassionately at Christ on the cross, wondering again why Christ's terrible wounds did not touch him. He had promised himself not to experiment, but tentatively he touched his own side. Nothing. Beyond the Close stood a monument to Bishop Hooper, burned to death in 1555. It was as terrible a death as any martyr's could be. Mary Tudor's incompetent executioners had needed to rebuild the fire three times. The saintly bishop's lower half had been consumed while his body was untouched above the waist. Toward the end, the man's arm had dropped off while he still lived, his other arm stuck to his chest. Yet still he had commended himself to God.

Theo said that clearly Hooper had been long dead by the time his arm fell off, but Benedict had been haunted by Hooper's death. He often walked by the very spot where Hooper had crackled and blistered, his legs bone and ash, his hair eventually bright with fire like a halo. He could imagine the smell, the blood like dripping molasses, the blackened lips still moving. Could there be anything for which *he* would die so horribly, Benedict wondered? He doubted even that his own father, an earnest Devonshire vicar, would choose such a public spectacle to defend his beliefs. His father was very keen on private faith, modest worship.

Years ago, Benedict had tried to explain to his father the entwining of colors and music. That, for him, D major was golden brown, A-flat almost magenta; that musical performances were as he imagined the Northern Lights to be. He had known immediately that this revelation was a mistake; from the anxiety that radiated out from his father's face, he knew there was something shameful about it. His father had busied himself filling and lighting his pipe before lifting his eyes, very briefly, to Benedict's.

"A gift from God," he'd said. "A gift from God, undoubtedly. But better not tell your mother." Benedict had, however, told his sister, Lettie, who touched his arm gently and looked at him with sympathy. For Lettie, the youngest and only other surviving child of the family, everything he did was special.

Benedict looked at the window, the rainbow of music moving between him and the glass rows of saints. He heard copper, which resolved in arcs of silver-white as Theo brought in the odd modal melody with his left hand. Some notes didn't trigger colors, never had, and none manifested themselves in red, never had; but as the blue returned, his eyes sought the window of St. Catherine and St. John: surely these experiences were God-given? When he had doubts, when he had to search to find any faith at all behind the rituals he had known since childhood, he held on to the beauty he had taken quite for granted as a boy.

He had tried to talk about it to Theo a year or more ago, thinking perhaps that it was not something his father could understand, but that musicians were so accustomed to it that they rarely spoke of it.

"Colored music?" Theo had looked amused and, Benedict sensed, a bit wary, as if his friend might suddenly be going embarrassingly mad. "Like a magic-lantern show?"

"It doesn't matter," Benedict had said, as if it was indeed a joke, feeling relieved that he hadn't mentioned the other thing: the physical pain he felt from injuries that were not his.

"But it does. It obviously does to you," Theo said, slowly, his eyes narrowing very slightly. "You looked almost matter-of-fact about it as you spoke, and yet now you're somehow surprised at my reaction." He paused. "But is this—this thing—this aura or whatever you call it—do you call it anything?—in your mind, or is it outside you?"

Benedict shook his head. "No. It's real. Real to me," he corrected. "It's always been like that." Was it possible to love someone, yet not trust them, he thought with fear?

"And does it work the other way around? If you saw chrome yellow, would you hear C-sharp or whatever? Would Van Gogh's *Sunflowers* deliver you a riot of *Chansons d'Auvergne*?"

This time Benedict was able to smile. "Afraid not."

"And it's not like a fit?"

Benedict stiffened. "No. Nothing like it."

Theo had put out his hand and squeezed his arm, leaving his hand there for a few seconds. "I'm not saying you've got some falling sickness," he said, "or that you're infected by some episcopal miasma from the crypt. In fact, it's probably all very holy." And then, and Benedict's heart had sunk, "I won't tell a soul. You're a rum chap, but your secret's safe with me."

Benedict vowed never to mention it to anyone again. Perhaps it was from God; perhaps it was from the devil.

Theo's brief foray into Vierne ended. He clattered about some more, and then Benedict could hear his footsteps on the wooden stairs. "Like it?" Theo said as he emerged. "A bit of green and purple for you." There was only a hint of teasing in the comment. "I'm practicing it for the midweek recital." He picked up the rest of his music. "Come on, let's have a pint at the New Inn."

Without waiting for an answer, he turned back down the north aisle. Benedict, following, watched as Theo walked, oblivious, into the light cast by the stained glass, his face and hands, his white cuffs, moving through a wash of color.

As they passed through the screens into the nave, the Clerk of Works was there, staring at an elaborate tomb. His face was as creased by the extent of his responsibilities as was that of the pious occupant of the tomb, carved in relief. As they approached, he turned and Benedict felt pain in his right arm, a deep, almost nauseating ache, and he touched the rough tweed of his jacket. Mr. Henshall, the Clerk, was wearing a sling, his arm in plaster.

"Fell over a bit of timber a pair of useless apprentices left by the porch," Henshall said. "What they were thinking of, if anything, who knows? I don't know what to make of these boys, I really don't. To break my arm in my own cathedral, well, it's a shaming thing."

Benedict let his arm drop gently. Nerves tingled. The pain made him giddy, but Theo sped up as they reached the west door.

"A drink in the New Inn, yes, but first to the docks," he said. "There's a very fine Dutch schooner in, used to be a barquentine but they cut her down. And I want to see old Camm's *Agnes* and *The Crystal Palace* and *Kindly Light* taking on loads."

Theo's knowledge of ships and his intimacy with their masters, their journeys, and their cargoes both intrigued and disquieted Benedict. Theo kept a list of the week's sailings and drank with captains and harbormasters down by the docks. Benedict had sometimes wondered if Theo gambled in the dock taverns. Recently he'd asked Benedict to lend him money. On the first occasion Benedict had handed over the paltry contents of his pocket, Theo raised a eyebrow at the handful of coins.

"It's a mug's game, this music," he said. "I've a good mind to run away to sea. I could always take an accordion."

A few weeks later, Theo asked whether Benedict had alms for a starving organist. Benedict had, painfully, said no. He had nothing. Theo made a joke of it and turned away before Benedict could explain that, unlike the first time, he'd simply had nothing to give; if he had, Theo could have taken it it all.

CHAPTER FOUR

Harry Sydenham, New York, July 1913

THE FIRST TIME HARRY SYDENHAM had Marina all to himself was at the Aquarium in Battery Park. Long afterward, he thought it had probably been a bad choice; but he had wanted to go somewhere that was outside the usual New York social round. Somewhere any ordinary New Yorker might go, and yet where they would never run into anyone she knew. Even then, he thought it might not have impressed her well-connected family to know that he was escorting their only daughter down to Lower Manhattan.

Once outside, he and Marina leaned over a wall, with the breeze in their faces, looking across to Ellis Island and watching the ferries on the choppy water. The Indians had called the Hudson Mahicantuck—"river that flows both ways," she told him, surprising him with her knowledge. The wind and the screaming gulls were enough to make conversation hard. Eventually they'd found the sort of restaurant she had clearly never entered and which might have been in a back street of Naples. She had been as excited by this as he was every day by aspects of the city she took quite for granted, and her appetite for unfamiliar dishes—oils, rich tomato sauce, rough bread—had delighted him.

Even after he had married her, he never told her of the two places he liked best in New York, fearing that she would think them too ordinary, too vague; not places so much as worrying states of mind. On the far side of the Brooklyn Bridge, he would stand by the waterfront and gaze across the East River, the water obsidian black and glittering with the lights of Manhattan's sleepless nights, or he would walk through Central Park on a misty, frozen winter day, past the menagerie and under a sky of soft pink-blue and a vaulted tracery of bare branches. It was the other-worldliness that drew him back to the far side of the river: observing the electric dazzle from a distance, he was hidden in darkness like an assassin. In the muffled distortion of the icy park, hearing tropical noises from the zoo and footsteps passing on parallel paths, he became, again, invisible.

For him, beauty in New York was a matter of achievement and ambition. The great red stone blocks, the sheer confidence of those buildings and the carved family names of so many from the Old World who must have arrived in a state of poverty and could now proclaim success: Mannheim, Carlotti, Trüdl, Steinbacker.

Marina was herself a Steinbacker on her mother's side and a Van Guyen on her father's. Her blue eyes and silver-gilt hair would have looked at home in Delft or Bavaria, he thought. In England, much that was thought beautiful was simply a matter of its having endured through time. A building that had survived since the Wars of the Roses, a parkland full of medieval oaks, thatched manor houses whose beds had supposedly been slept in by the great Elizabeth. The older and more fragile the substance, the more the English admired it. The more ancient the family, the more profound the inertia that kept it fixed in the very spot it had occupied for five hundred years, the more that family was revered. He liked the whole, unfinished rawness of the New World. He would go out early to draw sketches of the city growing: the girders and electric lighting and the cranes dipping to welcome ships arriving from the Atlantic. The garment factories and the soapy vapor from basement laundries, the motorbuses and the subway from City Hall to Broadway, the trains setting out to cross a continent, and the steam and sparks at Grand Central Station.

If he were honest, he liked noise. Even in the rooms of his apartment, four floors up, looking out over the treetops, with echoes muffled by wooden paneling and Turkish carpets, he reveled in the hum of this city, which had taken him to its heart. On hot nights, with the sashes open, when it was too hot to sleep, he would lie and listen to distant sounds and rejoice at his own anonymity in the great grinding machine. Yet there had been much that had shocked him when he had first arrived: squalor, violence, destitution, things he might never have seen if it hadn't been for his nocturnal walks, or which he might indeed *have* seen if he had ever bothered to explore the industrial cities of his mother country. He even allowed himself to think back to the woman many thousands of miles away, whom he had once thought he loved, and to feel ashamed that his view of her, so romanticized and physically charged, had completely ignored the fact that she was driven by a need to escape the poverty he now saw around him every day.

He had initially bought into a textile factory. It should have been folly—he knew next to nothing about industry, although his late mother's family had made a fortune in brewery; but he wanted to invest in a business he could work in himself, not just profit from. He was fortunate that although his business partner had had little capital, he was honest, knowledgeable, and experienced. What they shared was a wish to use modern methods, to expand but also to provide the usual hostel for the workers, mostly women, mostly immigrants—not so they could live in a virtual prison but so their conditions could be improved. Behind their backs and, indeed, to their faces, heads were shaken. A penniless idealist and a rich and ignorant Englishman, each exploiting the other. The machines would fail, the business would fold, the workers would take advantage: they would, indeed, steal; their competitors would flourish. But instead it was the workers who flourished with basic medical care, adequate food. Some stole, undoubtedly, some may have taken advantage. Some substituted less healthy sisters or friends when it came to medical care. Some smoked cigarettes or got pregnant by strangers. But many thrived. Classes were introduced to teach English to women who spoke only Italian or Yiddish. In time, the best employees became overseers, less brutal than their predecessors. The workers stayed and gained new skills as more sophisticated machinery was introduced. Harry bought better-quality cotton, sent out work to skilled finishers. A few, a very few, other businessmen came to look at their methods.

Then, in early 1911, his partner, who was only in his thirties and had no family, had drowned while ice-skating, and to Harry's astonishment had left him his half of the now-successful business.

A month or so later, in March, came the calamity that had been waiting to happen, falling on one of his competitors whose factory was an old-fashioned sweatshop. One hundred and forty-six women and children, locked into their workplace at the Triangle shirtwaist factory, had burned to death or jumped to meet it on the pavements of Manhattan. The papers were full of pictures of charred and broken bodies: small bundles of rags on the hard New York sidewalk. Suddenly philanthropists and politicians found a useful model of enlightened industrialism in Harry Sydenham. It was a pity that he was British, but at least he had declared no intention of returning to his native land. In spirit, the papers reported, he was an American: a man of innovation and energy, a man of ideals.

One newspaper proprietor had taken a liking to the young entrepreneur with the pleasing energy of youth and the equally pleasing acquisition of wealth. Harry was also a gentleman and so, in due course, the proprietor, William Van Guyen III, had introduced Harry to his daughter, Marina.

To Marina, born in America and shuttling between Fifth Avenue and Long Island, the juddering cogs of the city were invisible. She gravitated toward the parks, the squares, the flower stalls, anything that to her represented the place it had once been, before the coming of its European settlers: the sea, the river, the banks, the marsh and its islands. She believed she liked nature unspoiled, whereas, Harry thought, what she liked best was nature controlled, with all risk and ugliness removed. He, whose roots were so deep in the Old World, roots that still tried to draw him home even now, found passionate joy in industry and commerce and novelty, whereas she, the great-grandchild of immigrants who had mined the New World for all its treasures so that she might now enjoy them, was nostalgic for the pastoral and the unchanging.

She was a competent water-colorist—indeed, *more* than competent—and she painted wilderness, but on a small scale: domesticated, reduced, made manageable. Sometimes he accompanied her to the small galleries that showed her work. They were mostly patronized by her own circle, but that didn't diminish the pride he felt in her careful draftsmanship and technical skill. Her pictures were popular, and those who bought them had mostly made fortunes in commodities or industry: steel, or rolling stock, hotels, brewing, in land development, shipping, or factories. It seemed ironic that her large family, whose origins lay in the flatlands of Europe, its infinite horizons vast above networks of polders and canals, went into raptures over her careful depiction of the towering Rockies.

He rarely thought of his own home. He almost smiled at the notion: he tried so hard not to call it that in conversation, but in

27

his head it was always that. Abbotsgate. There he had been born, there he had grown up, there he was determined not to die. Letters from his stepmother, Isabelle, almost convinced him that not to return would be churlish and unnecessarily unkind, coming close to pulling him back, but it had now been far too long. Her very warmth made the distance between the two continents seem not only greater but even more desirable.

He had never seen his half-brother, Edward, although Isabelle had sent him a studio portrait. A solemn and sturdy little boy stood by a draped table, wearing a sailor suit and holding a small riding crop. He had a similarity to Harry in the way that all little boys in society photographs resembled each other.

Marina, who was very much attached to her remaining family, found his attitude curious when she had first asked him about his home.

"So your mother died when you were young, and you have a stepmother, Isabel?"

"Isa*belle*. She's French."

"Isabelle. And a brother, Teddy?"

He had nodded. "Half-brother. And he's only ten or so."

She made a face, which he read as sympathy for the little boy. "But you seldom go home?"

"*This* is my home."

She had nodded solemnly as if she understood a terrible sorrow. Looking at her, he feared she was constructing some Gothic drama based on the novels she devoured.

"I'm so sorry," she said.

"My stepmother is a kind and good woman. My stepbrother is a healthy and happy child. They live in a lovely part of England. I am very fond of them," he'd added as an afterthought.

"I love your Englishness," she'd said. "You could be very *fond* of a gin and vermouth. Or a day out sailing."

He smiled.

"What business was your family in? I'm not annoying you, am I?"

"Not at all. On my mother's side, brewing. On my father's side, they have always farmed. A small agricultural and sporting estate." This was a partial truth; the land his father owned, though large in England, would not be especially impressive in the American Midwest. "They were all very, very interested in horses."

"Horses," she said, her face contorting in mock despair. She had admitted to him weeks ago that horses were something she couldn't paint. He had then admitted that he drew only as a hobby—a dilettante, he'd said—and when she insisted on seeing his drawing pad, she was silent and solemn as she went through charcoal sketches of men working, of machinery, of untidy areas of the city and gulls over a rubbish dump, then pronounced that he was better than she'd ever be and that, despite this, she loved him.

But he always thought he had begun to love Marina, and be freed of the past, on that late July day by the Aquarium.

1914

CHAPTER FIVE

Jean-Baptiste, France, April 1914

It had all gone wrong because Godet the blacksmith's reactions were too slow. The old man had no right to still be working; he was getting on and had a limp from an injury back in his youth. Jean-Baptiste's role in the forge was to provide the strength that Bernard Godet, although remarkable for a man in his sixties, now lacked.

Godet had a flesh-and-blood nephew, but the man had married a mill-owner's daughter from Amiens and thought himself above the life of a village blacksmith. The mill-owner had built the couple a good-sized farmhouse on rich land near the river on the far bank from Corbie, to make the point that young Monsieur Armand Godet had moved onward and upward. The nephew showed no great skill at farming, Godet had added, and had even been attacked by his own pigs, but no doubt it passed the day.

Godet dealt with the customers, kept the books, chose the metal, kept the fire heated to exactly the right temperature. Jean-Baptiste started by fetching and carrying and holding the horses' heads, then progressed to operating the bellows. What he'd thought would be easy work, just a matter of pumping, turned out to be a matter of skill: a judgment that had taken Godet half a century of gauging the relationship between fire and iron to perfect. It seemed as if Godet could smell temperature. When they visited farms, Godet drove the cart but Jean-Baptiste did the loading and unloading. They went to the nephew's once. Over the front door was set a carved stone, with the couple's initials entwined and the date of their marriage. Bright windowboxes of red flowers made the whole building look like a child's picture. As soon as the cart stopped, Jean-Baptiste thought it looked all wrong. It was the tidiest farm he'd ever known.

Godet was watching him. "You're wondering: where's the shit," he said. And shook his head as if in the presence of a great folly.

Madame Godet waved at them from the front step, her dark hem bouncing on cream buttoned boots. Her hair was a pile of yellow curls and her blouse a froth of white that was tight to the wrist and rose to her chin, but was somehow still insubstantial. She was unlike any farmer's wife Jean-Baptiste had ever seen.

"Uncle," she said, and looked surprised. "Armand's in Amiens with Papa. He never said that you were coming. I thought you were Doctor Vignon. My chest is not good. Not good at all." She massaged the relevant area, gave a musical cough. Looked beyond them, back up the lane.

They left two heavy blades for the plow. "Good as new," Godet said, but she was scarcely listening and didn't invite them in.

Godet was not above grabbing the bigger hammer when a lady came by, although this was uncommon enough not to threaten his health, but mostly it was Jean-Baptiste who battered the glowing pig iron into submission. Godet told him the best metal came from the east. "Lorraine," he said, and spat on the floor. "Don't know what they are: French or Germans, nor which side they're on from one day to the next, but their iron is rightly French iron, dug from French soil."

Despite the talk of newly mined iron, most of the metal Jean-Baptiste used was simply melted-down worn horseshoes, broken farm implements, hoops from rotten barrels. Some odd bits and pieces arrived by night, were exchanged for a few francs and then stored in the lean-to shed at the back. When he asked Godet where they came from, Godet just winked. He had never been much of a talker, Godet, not with human beings, anyway, though he muttered gently at the horses. Occasionally he would embark on a single story and then, as if he'd used up some ration of words, not speak for two weeks.

The one time Jean-Baptiste peered into the lean-to while Godet was relieving himself, it seemed to be mostly railings and some pipes. There was a cross like on a wayside shrine and a small iron gate which, if he hadn't heard Godet returning from the privy, he would have looked at more closely to confirm that it was the de Potiers coat of arms. Doctor Vignon had once explained the crest, which was engraved on the gates to the chateau, the church, the school, and even, strangely, the abattoir. It was a creature with two faces looking in opposite directions and was called a sphinx; this denoted the fact that Monsieur de Potiers's great-grandfather had gained his rank and estate by serving Napoleon Bonaparte in the Armée d'Orient in Egypt and, it was generally believed, saving his life.

"Why does it face both ways?" Jean-Baptiste had asked.

He was rowing at the time, and it was only when he glanced up that he saw Vignon looked amused as he answered. "Perhaps Colonel Clovis de Potiers needed eyes in the back of his head? The sphinx was said to be exceedingly clever but treacherous. Perhaps, even in his moment of triumph, the colonel needed to be alert to betrayal?"

35

"Who was going to betray him? General Bonaparte?"

"Oh, I shouldn't think it was Bonaparte, would you? Bonaparte could just have had him locked up if he wanted rid of him, or sent him off to Russia. The real betrayals are usually much closer to home."

Since he had started work at the blacksmith's, Jean-Baptiste saw less of the doctor. Sometimes he spotted him at a distance, hurrying down the street with his black bag or drinking a pastis outside the Café Desmoulins on a fine day, but he missed rowing him around and he missed the stories. At first, he checked Vignon's boat from time to time to make sure it was still sound. No one else owned a small boat that was in such good condition. What if Vignon sold it? Monsieur de Potiers was home from Paris now, so Jean-Baptiste doubted his wife was free to float about as she wished. Jean-Baptiste tried to fight his growing loyalty to the blacksmith and his pleasure in his work. He tried to hold on to the certainty of the journey he would make, but weeks passed when he didn't get around to walking along the riverbank to check that the boat was still tucked under its overhanging willow.

So when, after a few months, he turned around to find Dr. Vignon just inside the archway to the forge, he had been surprised and relieved. Vignon held out a rowlock, the pin sheared off from the arms. It was a Thursday. Vignon's immaculate appearance was at odds with the heat and fiery grime of the forge, and Jean-Baptiste, his trousers belted tightly, the hems tucked into his father's boots, his chest bare and glistening, felt suddenly naked. He stopped, put his arm up to mop his brow, and smelled his damp armpit as he did so.

Vignon looked awkward. "Was just off fishing when I snapped this off," he said, adding "I've missed your company. But you're a grown lad now; other duties, other sirens call, no doubt? *Den Schiffer im kleinen Schiffe, Ergreift es mit wildem Weh?*"

There was an awkward pause. "Is that English?" Jean-Baptiste asked. He had written down the few English words Vignon had told him early on, but they seemed inadequate for a possible new life in a new country.

"No."

"It's German," said Godet, appearing from behind Jean-Baptiste, with an expression that Jean-Baptiste thought of as his spitting face. But he did not spit this time.

"Heinrich Heine," Vignon said. "A great Romantic poet. A great lover of France."

"German," said Godet.

"Art transcends borders," said Vignon, and Jean-Baptiste thought he had never seen a man so close to spitting, yet not letting fly, as Godet at this second. He didn't know what "transcends" meant, and he was pretty sure Godet didn't either. Godet stretched out his hand and took the rowlock from Jean-Baptiste, running a finger over the broken end.

Vignon nodded to Jean-Baptiste. "Good to see you looking so well. Perhaps . . . the boat, some time . . . ? Fishing?"

When the doctor had gone, Godet finally let fly. The globule landed in the embers with a brief and angry hiss.

"Fishing," he said. "Fishing. Of course he is. With a long line. But not in M'sieur de P's waters, now." It was said with a passion of loathing that the blacksmith normally reserved for the Church.

A few minutes later, Godet went on, "I don't trust the man. Who knows who he is, where he comes from with his per-nickety accent? What's a man like him doing here—apart from fishing? Or poaching, I should say?" He grunted three times and turned to his workbench, putting down the rowlock and picking up a scythe with a bite out of the blade. Felt it with his hand. Grunted again.

Jean-Baptiste jiggled the coins in his pocket. He was paid every week for the journey upriver. He didn't know what to say.

A rather dirty boy was hovering in the yard, holding a piece of paper. The child had a pale, narrow face and hair cropped so closely that his white scalp showed through.

Godet walked over to him, took the note, nodded. "Tell Sister Marie-Joseph that we'll be up in the morning," he said. The boy, with his large, startled eyes and big feet, looked like nothing so much as a young hare, Jean-Baptiste thought. He was already turning away when Godet said, "Do you like pears, boy?"

The child looked wary, as if this might be a test.

"Come on," Godet said. "Let's get you some pears. Jean-Baptiste here can look after the business."

Godet was gone only ten minutes, and when he returned the child was nowhere to be seen.

"Starving hungry and fearing for his life in case he was late back," Godet said, with real anger in his voice. "And they call them holy sisters. More like a coven of witches."

The nuns kept themselves more or less to themselves behind their high wall. The orphans were quiet boys and girls whose eyes slid away from strangers' smiles or the offer of a cake from a shopkeeper. When they grew up, those who weren't funny in the head went to be soldiers or laborers if they were boys, and the girls became servants or did sewing. Death was quite a frequent visitor at the convent.

"They think they're some kind of saints because they tidy things up," said Godet. "And because we don't want children who remind us of our indiscretions and sorrows, nobody asks any questions." He lit his pipe, sucked hard two or three times, his eyes half shut. "Me, I'd rather give a child to a tribe of savages with bones in their noses than the holy sisters."

Jean-Baptiste was used to Godet's ways, but this time he was shocked. Even his mother said her prayers every night, slowly in summer, very quickly in winter.

An hour later, one of de Potiers's men brought in a bay gelding, leading it with a halter.

"It's got the jiggers," the man said, twitching the rein, stepping back a pace. "It's a holy horror her ladyship calls Prince of Araby, but I call it a little bugger that needs the sting of a stick to show it who's master, and now it's gone and shed a shoe."

Godet moved forward to take the rein, but the groom held tight. "It's best I hang on," he said. "You never know what he's got in mind." The horse was rolling its eyes and pawing the ground. Jean-Baptiste took the long way around its rear end to take the money.

Godet was stroking the horse's flank now, murmuring to it, and the beast stopped fidgeting and trying to walk sideways. It exhaled noisily and stood still.

"Well, you've got a way with them, for sure," the groom said and, at the sound of his voice, the horse started up again.

Godet and the horse stood and looked at each other.

"Well, are you going to fix it?"

Godet grunted. He stood in silence, stroking the animal for a minute or so, then ran his hand slowly down the horse's leg and lifted its hoof. He looked down, smoothed it with his hand, feeling for roughness as Jean-Baptiste had seen him do so many times before.

"Well, will you look at that," the groom said. "I've never ever seen him so easy." He stepped closer and the horse shuffled away from him, but Godet held him firm.

Jean-Baptiste handed him a file and he began to smooth the hoof, making no quick movements that might startle the bay, though it occasionally tossed its head to rid itself of flies. The forge always had this problem on warm days. When all was done to his satisfaction, Godet set the foot down.

"They say that there's trouble brewing. . . ." said the groom. "Of course we hear these things up at the chateau, seeing as Monsieur is an intimate of the president. What he says is Europe is a tinderbox. If there's a war, France will be right in the middle of it, he says. They'll need soldiers. Revenge for the last time." He pulled irritably at the halter and the horse did a little sideways step. "But Monsieur de Potiers wouldn't let me go because he likes things just so. He's a stickler. So that's all right then." He shot a glance at Jean-Baptiste.

Godet had turned away and was choosing metal for the shoe. He took a piece down, placed it in pincers, and set it into the fire. As he moved back toward them, the horse shook its head and flies lifted off. The groom's response was to tug hard on the rein.

"Hold still, you bugger," he shouted.

As the horse sheered away backward, the groom caught his foot in the trailing end of the halter rope and fell. The horse reared up. De Potiers's man rolled fast to avoid the animal's hooves, but Godet was slower and perhaps more trusting. The horse kicked out and caught him a mighty clout on the leg. As the leg collapsed under him, Godet grabbed instinctively at the first thing to hand, grasping wildly at the handle of the pincers, which tipped off the forge, and he fell to the floor with a groan. The metal spun in an arc, Jean-Baptiste ducked, and the hot iron hit the horse, which no one had tried yet to recapture. The animal went mad. It whinnied and rose up, its hooves like weapons. Jean-Baptiste jumped back. The groom was already cowering on the other side of the anvil, but Godet was just lying there, stunned, and as the horse's front hooves came down, they landed on the old man's head and chest. Jean-Baptiste moved as quickly as he could, but the horse was crashing into everything now and the noise seemed to enrage it further. By the time he grabbed the rope, it was almost impossible to hold.

He shouted at the groom: "For God's sake, help me. Get it out of here."

Godet seemed unconscious and there was a terrible wound to his head; his temple looked misshapen. Blood trickled out of his nose; the palm of an upturned hand was burned. Jean-Baptiste thought that this injury was going to be a problem for the old man with his work, even as he realized how irrelevant a burned hand was now.

The groom looked terrified, and the horse stood trembling in the far corner. It was only when two other men entered—Lucien

Laporte and smelly Pinchon, the odd-job man—that the groom rose from behind the anvil. Pinchon had a gun under his arm and dead crows and a rabbit in his hand.

He looked puzzled, staring at the horse, and only then did he seem to see Godet on the floor and the fallen tools. The horse was sweating. It had cut its leg, Jean-Baptiste noticed, and its chest was moving in and out like bellows while it lifted its legs up almost daintily as if to avoid the debris all over the floor. All the while, it was making distressed noises and its nostrils flared. Pinchon lifted his gun, pushed in a cartridge. Jean-Baptiste saw a smile cross Laporte's face.

"Don't," he said. Knowing it was all too late.

Pinchon got as close as he could to the bay and fired. The horse stopped, its restless front legs seemed to cross, and it fell to its knees with a crack. Its eyes were staring as it pitched sideways and lay twitching. Despite Godet sprawled on the cobbles, Jean-Baptiste felt sad. His ears were ringing; but as Pinchon walked up to the horse and reloaded, the groom was screaming "What the fuck have you done? What the fuck . . . ?" There was another shot and the horse stopped twitching and was still, a pool of blood growing underneath it.

Jean-Baptiste kneeled down, touched Godet. Stretched out his hand for a pulse in his neck and wasn't sure there was one. Where did you feel? Godet's wiry beard curled around his fingers. The man's half-open eyes were still, his pupils tiny.

"I'll get Dr. Vignon," he said, hoping the doctor had not gone fishing yet. As he stood up, he noticed Laporte taking a thick hunting knife from his belt.

"Don't you fucking dare," the groom was almost crying. "He's my horse. You'll have lost me my job."

Jean-Baptiste ran down the street. He ran until his chest hurt but then, at the far end of the village, he reached the doctor's house, swung open the gate, ran up the path, and hammered on the door. For a minute there was nothing. He banged again with the side of his fist, moved back to peer at the windows. The door opened, but it was Vignon's housekeeper who stood there, pale and unwelcoming.

"The doctor's not here."

"There's been an accident."

He could have sworn she shrugged. Didn't she care?

"Where is he?"

This time she definitely shrugged. "Fishing," she said.

He ran back down the path. He would fetch his mother to help with Godet, although in his heart he knew the old man was beyond helping.

He and his mother lived nearer the river. The house was always damp and the door was usually open in summer, so he was surprised to find it locked. He went around the back where the latch was broken and took off his filthy boots. As he went in, he heard a noise upstairs and, rather than embarrass his mother by calling out because sometimes, he knew, she still wept for his father in secret, he climbed the stairs quietly.

Halfway up, he smelled something unfamiliar, and it was only outside the door to her bedroom that he recognized it as pipe smoke and knew it was Vignon's at the same moment that he recognized the doctor's hairy backside. His mother was on all fours in the tangle of sheets, her hair loose and hiding her face, her breasts hanging downward into points, and Vignon, groaning, was over her, mounting her like a dog.

He went down the stairs even more quietly than he'd climbed them. By the stove was a tin can, where he kept his wages so his mother could use the money as she needed it. He opened it and took out half of what was inside. It was a meager amount. By the front door, Vignon's linen jacket hung on a chair and beside it a pair of fine black boots, polished as if they had been varnished and on which none of the village dust seemed to have dared lie. Jean-Baptiste tiptoed into the scullery, fetched his own boots from the back: his own dirty, much-repaired boots. The boots that had been his father's. He set them down, picked up Vignon's pair, and went out into the street. Only when he was at some distance from the house did he sit on a bank and put them on. They fitted perfectly. It seemed a fair exchange: Vignon could have his mother and he'd have Vignon's boots. Web-footed. Did he think no one had ever made that joke before?

Of course he would have to leave the village—not just because of the boots, but because he never wanted to see either his mother or the two-faced doctor again. He considered taking the boat now, but immediately remembered that it was lacking a rowlock. He could row for a short distance without one, but not as far as the sea.

He stood up—how comfortable the boots were!—and walked toward the school. At the back of the schoolhouse, the schoolmaster's bicycle was propped up against the steps. He and Godet had repaired it only weeks back. He took out the money the groom had given him for the horse and left it on a big stone on the step.

He wheeled the bicycle away, praying that the schoolmaster had oiled it. When he was well clear of the school, on the track leading between the vegetable fields and the river, he got on and almost immediately fell off. He tried again and lasted for longer, but the front wheel began to wobble so wildly that it would inevitably fall over. All the time, he was moving away from town. He still burned from shame for his mother. She was no better than a whore—except much cheaper and older. Didn't she know that Vignon didn't care where he stuck it—or was she so stupid that she believed he'd marry her? He came to a bit of sloping ground and let the bicycle freewheel down it while he sat, his feet hanging down, not attempting to pedal, only steering to keep away from the river.

He was approaching the place where Vignon kept his boat. It was so well disguised under the low branches of a willow that you really had to know it was there to find it. He stopped, dismounted, pulled back the canvas, and stared at it. Vignon had been giving it a new coat of paint. The paint can was in the boat with the brushes. The name *Sans Souci* was newly picked out in blue. He wanted to kick it as hard as he could. Instead, he stepped inside, and the small boat rocked on the mud. He opened the little hatch where he knew Vignon kept his fishing rod, cigarettes, and a small flask of brandy. As the lid slid back, all he could see was a blanket. The blanket, of course—he felt another wave of anger, looking at the dry grass caught in it. He felt under it for the precious rod, intending to throw it in the river, but his finger found a package wrapped in oilcloth. He sat down and opened it: inside he found a small book and a few tightly rolled-up papers. They were yellowing and, even as he held them, the corners curled up over his hands.

The first two were indecipherable official papers with something like Vignon's name on them, or at least his first name, Felix, which he already knew, then Johannes and something that looked like Vignon but wasn't. *Felix Johannes Wiener*, it said, and a small picture of a youthful, beardless but recognizable doctor was stamped with the imprint of a two-headed eagle. The very last document, although still in an unfamiliar language, was, he was almost sure, a birth certificate. He had seen his own, and this one was laid out similarly. There was a birth date, July 1, 1875, a mother, Hilde, a general-surgeon father, Wilhelm-Markus. Then a single word: *Berlin*.

The fact that Godet had been right all along, that Vignon was not what he said he was, had probably never even been to Paris, filled Jean-Baptiste with bitter joy.

"Bastard," he said, aloud. "German bastard."

He glanced at the book. It was expensive-looking with a soft red-leather cover, though worn at the edges. Jean-Baptiste could read well, had been the ablest in his class at school, but he couldn't read a word of the title. Not only the words but the typeface were unfamiliar to him, although *Felix Wiener* was written in brown ink inside the cover. He opened the pages at random, but the queer lettering, very dark and angular, continued.

He was ready to throw the entire contents of the package into the river, but suddenly felt nearer to tears than rage. It was a beautiful book, no less beautiful because it belonged to a shit, and after a short time he replaced it under the blanket. He got out of the boat, taking the can of paint with him, and prised up the lid with his small knife. It came up easily. He dipped a stick in it and, over the carefully painted *Sans Souci*, daubed GERMAN ARSE in large, dripping letters. As he did it, he was shaking, with hurt and with the desire to pass on that hurt. He looked down at his handiwork, let the branches enclose the boat again, and picked up the bicycle. He got on, wearily, and started down the track.

After three further tries, he found that he could balance. Slowly, tentatively, he began to pedal, carefully at first and then, as he realized that if he went faster the machine was more inclined to stay upright, he gathered speed. If he could get to Amiens by evening, then he might catch the last train to Paris.

CHAPTER SIX

Frank, London,
June 1914

I'LL CERTAINLY NEVER FORGET JUNE 28, 1914. It was a triumph for Belgium. Their man, Philippe Thys, set out on his Peugeot-Wolber in the company of six fine French cyclists who had all won the Tour de France before: Lapize, Petit-Breton, Faber, Deffraye, Garrigou, and Trousellier. Heroes every one. I had a map of the course; it was a map of hell, and a burning fiery hell this year. They even stopped the race for a while for fear the heat would kill someone. Thys came through the ordeal a champion among bicyclists.

As they were setting off from Paris, the man who was the Austrian emperor's son and heir was shot by some anarchist in the capital of a country even us Internationalists had to look up in an atlas. In the days that followed, there was practically nothing about the race as the papers were full of headlines hoping for war.

Not that they *said* "hoping," but hoping it was. A coming war's as good as anything for selling papers.

It was all wrong.

We went to the peace meeting, though that set me back further by two shillings. Connie and Nancy sat either side of me. Nancy is inclined to lean on one, so it became very hot. Rays of dusty light shone down on Mr. Tudor Williams on the stage. Fate could not have dealt him a better card than the assassination three days earlier.

The Reverend Williams was an extraordinary man—huge and red in an old-fashioned sort of black suit and with prodigious whiskers. His great hands were scarred as if he had been a fighter. Connie was especially spellbound when he began to speak in the rich melodious tones of his native country.

"We stand on the brink," Mr. Williams said loudly. Nodding in agreement with himself. "On the brink. A few days ago, we saw a young firebrand in Sarajevo murder the heir to a royal house. A decent man, with his wife, struck down in his prime while a visitor to a foreign country. The hot blood of our continental brothers is stirred." He looked about him, to ensure that we were following.

"That lovely Welsh accent gives me the shivers," Nancy whispered.

"We can understand that," said Mr. Williams, all moderation. "Were it our Prince Edward slain, his blood running into the drains of our city, would our people wish to turn the other cheek as the Bible tells us?" He patted the great leather Bible on the lectern. "Would they wish to be called weak for not rising up to avenge their prince?" He looked around, mild-faced.

Suddenly he roared—a great Welsh roar: FOLLOWING JESUS CHRIST IS NOT EASY.

"We look to our leaders," he went on in a more measured tone, "and we see the admirals and generals who have their ear, adorned in their gold and their feathers. We hear our politicians—some are men of peace, but others would send young men to die for their honor at the drop of a pin. We feel the ground slip under our feet as we start, slowly at first, to stumble toward the abyss." His arms went out as if to steady himself. "There is no purchase on this trembling earth. Smell the sulfur." His eyes widened under their sheltering brows. "See the haze of steam and smoke blurring your vision.

"Should war come, they will speak to you of patriotism, they will unfold the flag. But. I. Am. Second. To. No one." Mr. Williams's clenched fist banged on his chest. "To NO ONE in my love for the King. I am shot through with loyalty. Drank it in at my mother's breast."

I could feel as much as see Nancy making a face.

"I would *die* for my King and my country." The reverend paused, and his dark eyes searched the room as if to find a man there who thought he would not.

"But"—a longer pause—"I would not kill. I should not be *asked* to kill. It is against the scriptures." He made far more of the syllables of the word than any Englishman would.

"Did Jesus Christ, our savior, know of frontiers? Of paltry man-made, not God-given, divisions between Austria-Hungary and Germany and Russia and Great Britain, Serbia and France? Are the men of Bavaria not the brothers of the men of Cumberland? Are not Viennese and Berliners and Londoners all one in the sight of the Lord? Do Cornishmen and Welshmen not descend to the mines just as the miners of Essen and the Ruhr? Are ships not built with the same knowledge God gave on the Elbe as on the Clyde?"

"No sisterhood for us girls then," Nancy whispered across me to Connie—who ignored her, so rapt was she at Mr. Williams's vision and, I dare say, his fine red Welsh whiskers.

"Do you want to kill these, your brothers?

"We are members of one great kingdom of God. His children. He gave us the great riches of the world: the mighty oceans teeming with fish, the orchards, the fruiting vine, the fields of wheat"—the reverend rose and walked agitatedly along the stage, then turned and stretched his arms toward us.

"Not in Rotherhithe, he didn't," Nancy said, very quiet, and yawned.

"Reach out to your brothers and sisters."

At this point, Nancy seemed to be weary and had rested herself on my shoulder. I moved sharply to the side and her head bumped on my arm. She shot me a cross look.

"Reach out and grasp their hand. Reach out and embrace your fellow man whatever his nation, however outlandish his tongue."

Nancy made a strange and not very womanly noise through her nose. The reverend's voice was rising, the music of his homeland clear in his passion.

"Does not Isaiah say 'They will beat their swords into plowshares and their spears into pruning hooks. Nation will not take up sword against nation, nor will they train for war'?"

He stopped and looked around as if expecting an answer. Clearly it was yes, Isaiah did say that. But we stayed silent, as did he for many seconds.

"And Micah," Connie whispered. "And the Psalms."

And now Reverend Williams's voice emerged from the silence, but very quietly so that every head moved forward and I had a chance to dislodge Nancy. We strained to hear him.

"You are the true army. The army of Love, of Right, of Brotherhood; the shield against those who lust, LUST for war, who would gorge on blood. Who would let the fruit rot on the trees, the corn in the fields while they harvest corpses." His voice was raised so suddenly, we jumped as one. "Who lay waste to the land, devour our youth, and would store up grief and poverty." He looked almost excited; there was sweat on his brow and his eyes shone. He strode back behind the lectern and braced himself with both hands.

"I hear the thundering of hooves, ladies and gentlemen."

His hand went up to his ear and he leaned a little into it. He stopped talking. The audience were leaning in the direction of his cupped ear, too. There was nothing but traffic outside and pigeons on the roof. You could have heard a pin drop as we listened. I wondered where Isaac was. I'd looked all around and I couldn't see his face anywhere.

"Who are these riders?" the reverend said finally. "Are they heralds of peace? Do they bring news of God's kingdom? NO, they are the four horsemen of the apocalypse and, brothers and sisters, they draw perilously near. The white horse carries the Antichrist, the blood-red steed brings WAR. The black horse is FAMINE, and with famine comes PEST-I-LENCE.

"And then comes the pale horse: the corpse-green-white pale horse of DEATH, its rider armed with a scythe." Mr. Williams cut down a swath of invisible men with an outflung arm.

"Typical cavalry men," said Nancy.

Connie was ignoring her, and I tried to do the same.

"And you—yes, you. You sitting before me are the only defense. You are God's army. You must stand in the main squares, stand across the roads, hearing the thundering hooves, feeling the heat of the fires blister your skin and the clash of hammers on the plowshares, sharpening them into weapons, and you MUST NOT MOVE. 'No,' you must say. 'No.' Clasp your foreign brothers to your hearts. For we are told in Kings: 'And after the earthquake a fire; but the LORD was not in the fire: and after the fire a still small voice.'"

He stopped, his chest heaving. I could see it even through the ladies' hats and from seven rows back.

Then, quietly, he said: "Yours is that still small voice. God's plan for the world will unfold. Surrender to the warmongers and you fight God's plan."

"That's a bit rich," a man muttered behind us, "surrendering," and Nancy turned and gave him one of her little smiles.

Perhaps Mr. Williams sensed a restlessness, because he returned again to the lectern and, speaking in a matter-of-fact way, said:

"To conclude, let us pray for peace and I say to you, God save the King and his people. For now only God can."

Then he said, mopping his mighty brow, "A collection will be taken at the door. Pennies for peace, but even halfpennies will help."

I saw Connie put a sixpence into the bag. She was watching me and I only had a shilling. I tried not to think of my bicycle. Nancy said later she'd put a button in.

Connie and Nancy let me walk them home.

"Where do you think Isaac was?" I said, mostly to stay on safe territory.

Connie looked at me as if I were dull in the head. She did that sometimes when she sensed that we differed. "His kind, they don't go to church."

In fact Isaac had told me he mostly didn't believe in God. It was not rational, he'd said.

"We're supposed to embrace our foreign brothers." Nancy gave what I think she thought was a tinkling laugh.

"He's not foreign," I said. "And he's talking of joining up to fight for King and country—his country—if war comes." Connie looked very put out, though still pretty, and I knew she'd never give Isaac the time of day again.

"And it wasn't a church service," I said, wanting to stand up for him. "It was just a talk."

"My cousin's all for fighting," Nancy said. "He's going for a soldier as soon as his birthday comes."

Connie said in her usual gentle voice, but firmly, "You should tell him what Mr. Williams said."

"There's no telling Stanley anything," Nancy answered. "He's a law unto himself, Stanley Hutton, my ma says."

"Well, then, you should refuse to speak to him. If we go to war, he'll be killing people. You wouldn't go to Wormwood Scrubs and tattle to murderers there, share your tea. It's no different if he is your cousin."

The sun was beating down as Connie looked at me, to see if we were still friends, given that Isaac was more my pal than hers, and Nancy more hers than mine, so we should be evens.

"I pray every night there won't be war," she said. "But if there is, I shall never hold conversation with a soldier—or a sailor, come to that."

"My uncle says if there's a war, our boys won't have no choice."

"There's *always* a choice, Nancy," Connie said. "Isn't there, Frank?"

Even as I said yes, I thought with foreboding of Mr. Frederick Richmond. Mr. Richmond, the kindest, fairest man you could hope to meet, who brought his dog, Bosun, into the store, he loved him so much, Mr. Richmond was such a man for war that you could almost think he *wanted* it to come. He was friends with all the top admirals, the lads said. "Lance the boil" was Mr. Richmond's cry every time some foreign country played up, while Bosun took tidbits from his hand. And there was the Reverend Williams, as fiery a bruiser as you might see in the streets around Seven Dials, and he was furious for peace.

Mr. Richmond addressed us male employees the next week. His subject: duty.

"We are not at war yet," he said; "but mark my words, the clock is ticking. If war comes, I hope to see every one of you single men go forward to serve the King." He looked around benevolently as if he was our father. "And for those who go, I shall, personally, give a parting gift of five guineas. When you return, you may be sure that there will be a place for you here. We shall use ladies to fill your places temporarily until you get back. If it comes to war, of course. Which we all sincerely hope it does not," he added, not very convincingly. We all knew he had conceived a hatred for the German Kaiser, for all that the German monarch was our King's cousin.

Five guineas. Five guineas was half a bicycle. With my savings already, I could have it in six weeks. But by then I would be away, marching up and down and polishing badges and learning how to shoot men, when I had only ever shot crows and rabbits for the pot, and that was back when I made coffins, and even that I'd never tell Connie. I could buy a bicycle, but what was the point if I was off marching?

Thinking of coffins made me think of Dad and how it was an ill wind that brought no good. War would mean dying, and a few extra deaths never came amiss for a coffin maker. Mind you, if it happened, would the Austrians and the Germans come and fight us here, or would we go there? How were such things agreed upon when it was disagreeing that caused war in the first place?

CHAPTER SEVEN
Benedict, London,
June 1914

BENEDICT HAD NEVER REALLY TRUSTED Davies. Always more Theo's friend than his, plain David Ivor Davies had gone to Oxford and then to London in the process of becoming the urbane Novello. He'd left Gloucester ages ago but always seemed to be returning. Benedict suspected it was to remind himself of how far he had risen since he left.

Now here he was again, with them in London.

Dr. Brewer always arranged the choir's triennial trip to London down to the last detail. They were boarding with a Fellow of the Royal College, although Novello had offered to put them up. Brewer could hardly hide his horror, but Novello was undoubtedly just teasing him.

A bus took them northward from Paddington Station. Theo and Novello, heads together, were laughing about people

Benedict had never heard of and he doubted Theo had either. Novello was confiding rather loudly that he and a friend had written a song.

"What a humdinger! It will express the mood of the nation before they even know what mood they're in," he said. "'Till the boys come home.' All we need now is the war to send them away in the first place."

Benedict opened a recent letter from Lettie. She was innocently excited about his trip to London. She seldom left their home town, and he knew she feared that her duties as a daughter were leading her inexorably into a spinster's life. From time to time, Benedict had wondered if he could introduce Theo to his sister, but in the last year Theo had become more and more fixed on Agnes Bradstock.

What had started as a challenge had appeared to have grown into a genuine attraction. Theo wanted Agnes. Wanted to marry her, he said. Possibly it was true; but Benedict hoped, privately and intensely, that Agnes would say no, or the bishop would say no, or Theo's father would say no, or maybe Mrs. Bradstock, who clearly had ambitions for her beautiful daughter, would place somebody more compelling in Agnes's path. At any rate, Theo would have to wait three more years until he could hope to support a wife.

He tried to believe that his dread was entirely a matter of losing a friend's everyday companionship; but as Benedict looked at Novello, now whispering in Theo's ear, hat brim to hat brim, shoulder to shoulder, Novello's bright blazer against the sturdy tweed of Theo's Norfolk jacket, he considered, bleakly, whether he had earned Theo's friendship simply because in Gloucester there was nobody better.

London was sticky: noisier and more chaotic than Benedict remembered it. The noises of the city ignited tiny flashes of color, like sparks from an anvil.

Near their lodgings, the newspaper boys were shouting about the murder of a European duke. Theo borrowed a halfpenny and bought an *Express*. He pored over it as they waited for the bus.

"Stuffy-looking chap. They all look the same in Austria and Germany, don't they? But the emperor's heir?" Theo whistled. "Nasty. The Austrians are acting very threatening."

"Anything about *our* reaction?"

"Nothing much. Still, one way or another, sooner or later, we're heading for trouble somewhere. Dreadnoughts, maneuvers, sabers rattling like tin cans on a string—of course we are. All those antique admirals are in a frenzy of longing, dusting off their uniforms. Terrible smell of mothballs downwind of Whitehall."

Benedict never knew when Theo was joking, or so Theo had often told him. But this time, behind the light-hearted tone, Theo seemed both serious and excited.

"It wouldn't make any difference to us, though, would it?" Benedict said, as they walked slowly along Welbeck Street, and wondered if he wished it might.

"You're such a chump sometimes," Theo said, with a note of irritation. "Of course it would. You'd be girded in a Sam Browne, pips on your cuff, armed and polished to the teeth, not nipping off to play evensong at St. Elfrida's in your drooping gown."

"But I don't know the first thing about soldiering. My people were always church." Realizing he was sounding like an idiot, Benedict ran on: "I get seasick, I'm a rotten shot, and, anyway, I need spectacles to see into the distance."

"I don't think not seeing into the distance is very crucial," Theo said. "In fact, it could be a distinct advantage."

Each day in London, they had an indifferent high tea and took in a concert. The first evening they heard George Butterworth's *The Banks of Green Willow*, which Dr. Brewer pronounced first-class, having "escaped the tyranny of the modern." The following day, it was a crowded organ recital at Temple Church, and the third was a concert that Brewer evidently anticipated with dread. It was only the insistence of his friend Mr. Alcock, a professor at the Royal College, that saw them seated at the Bechstein Hall waiting for the Russian soloist. Theo shifted about restlessly and Alcock's long fingers tapped on the arm of his seat. The composer, a small, ferrety-looking man named Alexander Scriabin, was playing his own work. Benedict knew of him but had not heard any performance of his work. The program notes said he wrote for music and color; Benedict read them, wondering, hoping; it was the first time he had ever heard of a musician exploring such ideas.

The Russian bounded up the steps, bowed abruptly, sat down, ignoring the applause, closed his eyes for a few seconds, and started to play. Tangerine, then blue, filled Benedict's mind, consuming him. Then it was deep purple; the colors rippled outward—like butchers' tripe, he thought—and then broke into fragments as another wave built. He closed his eyes a few times, but the chords of color continued and filled the space: not a strange phenomenon created by his overactive imagination, just *there*.

Benedict was not special; he was a very ordinary man, yet he knew Dr. Brewer would balk at such perceptions in a professional musician. There was an intellectual understanding of music; there was the aptitude and coordination that drew an individual to the organ; there was discipline, which might make a man succeed in his endeavors; even a constrained emotional response and, occasionally, natural genius, such as Theo's; but music was music. Performed for the ears. Now here was someone who knew better.

Helical columns of green and gold-brown rose in front of him; the piece was so strange, so beautiful; every time the Russian touched a note, he created visual as well as sound harmonies. The sensations Benedict had experienced at five or six in his father's church, with Miss Bradshaw playing the tiny parish organ, were what had bound him forever to the instrument long before he knew of the possible size and scope of it, long before he knew that he was different. Listening now, he felt overwhelmed with joy.

That evening, as they walked back to their lodgings, all he wanted to talk of was the music and Scriabin, but Theo could think only of war and Agnes.

"If England goes to war, I shall join a smart regiment immediately. In my uniform, Agnes will find me irresistible. Her father could hardly deny me her hand if I was going off to do my patriotic duty."

He looked to Benedict for agreement; and when Benedict was slow replying, he added: "He couldn't, could he?"

"You wouldn't finish your pupillage?"

"Heavens, no. There's a whole lifetime for fugues, but war is a young man's game."

"I thought if it came to it, you'd join the Navy," Benedict said.

"Why on earth would I do that?"

"Well, you always seem to be in with the captains and ships down at the docks."

"I like their stories, their travels: storms, opium, fights, women—I love it all, Ben. They sail from here out into the world: Shanghai, Alexandria, Odessa: all these illiterate men who know the world far better than I ever can. But I can't think of anything worse than being stuck on a ship. The smell. The same stories repeated, literally ad nauseam. If they were aeroplanes, now, that would be a thing. A machine, your own small kingdom and the sky, huger than the sea."

"So what will you do? Seriously?"

"I think, if war comes—not much of an if, in my opinion—and we're called up, we'll try for the Gloucesters. At least we'll mostly be able to understand what they're saying. I had a cousin took a commission in the Durham Light Infantry. Chaps might as well have been speaking Swahili, he said."

Benedict hardly heard Theo's cheerful running on, because the word "we" was as far as he got. "We."

"It would be very Homeric," Theo went on. "Brothers in arms. You wouldn't want to stay in Gloucester when only the old men were left. A big strong chap like you." He punched Benedict affably on the upper arm. "And I couldn't have you stealing Agnes from under my nose. Anyway, it wouldn't be for long. We'd take the King's shilling. We could always join a military band if the Gloucesters don't want us. Or the artillery, as we can do math." He beamed. "What a shock it would be for Father."

Was a war inevitable? Benedict had never thought so back in Gloucester, which carried on more or less as it had since Roman times; but in London, where the decisions were made, he sensed a tension and an anticipation that he did not recognize.

He slept poorly that night.

On the following afternoon they were expected at the Royal College of Organists, but for now they could explore London on as fine a summer's day as any visitor could hope for. Benedict thought he might go to Hertford House. It was open to the public, and he had read that it had fine instruments on display. Theo was already at breakfast, looking happy and rested. He was sitting with his back to the window, his hair metallic in the light and the tiny hairs on his hands red-gold as he spread butter on his toast.

Theo said, his mouth half full, "Look. We need to go shopping. I need to get something for Agnes that she couldn't possibly get in Gloucester and that will impress upon her what a sophisticated suitor I am."

Benedict's own plans faded away. Theo's ideas, once broached, always seemed so much more insistent than his own. "London's a big place."

"Well, I thought Mayfair or Knightsbridge, but the best stores are all in Regent Street, Novello says." He looked up as if momentarily nervous that Benedict would say no. "We could take a tram or a bus to Piccadilly Circus. Novello told me how to get there. And then we could look around and then walk past the shops. It's a nice day," he added, as if Benedict might not have noticed.

"And we'll easily be back for this afternoon's little musical outing."
He made a face.

Benedict wondered if he could find something to buy for
Lettie. It would have to be a small something, but then so, presumably, would whatever Theo bought for Agnes.

The interior of the bus smelled of sweat, hair oil, and tobacco.
A fat man, who got on the bus just before them, took up the whole
of the last double seat, staring outward defiantly. They hung on
the rail, swaying as the bus made its way between horses, carts,
and motorcars. There was a young man in a boater standing next
to Benedict. In the crush, his outer thigh was pressed against
Benedict's. When a woman and child pushed past to get off the
bus, he turned slightly and caught Benedict's eye. Though Benedict turned away and looked over his shoulder at the other passengers, the stranger's eyes never left him; he could feel it. They
were still on him when he looked back. And now, unmistakably,
the stranger's groin was against Benedict's hip, and Benedict was
sure he was aroused; the man moved a little and rhythmically.
He swallowed and knew he was blushing, looked across at Theo,
wishing he could catch his eye. The young man must have seen
his confusion, yet he made no attempt to move away, and every
movement of the bus made Benedict more aware of this other
figure, this unknown man, so intimately close.

Finally Theo looked up and mouthed "Next stop." But even
as he felt relief and prepared to get off, Benedict realized that the
man's knuckles were against his hip, moving his fingers gently
and watching his face for any reaction. The bus stopped, Benedict
pushed past, burning with shame, and yet, despite himself, excited.
He felt almost sick with it as he stood on the pavement waiting
urgently for Theo, who jumped off the step to join him. He watched
in dread, in case the stranger stepped down too.

"You all right?" Theo asked.

The bus was pulling away and Benedict thought he could see
the man, watching him still. He pulled down the brim of his hat,

as much to hide his shame from Theo as his face from the stranger. He turned away, walking so briskly that Theo, laughing, reached out and took his arm, saying "Slow down, old chap. No hurry," but Benedict pulled away and felt Theo's puzzlement at his silence.

Piccadilly Circus was all movement: the uneven bobbing of straw hats, a few parasols riding above the crowd and the traffic circling around *Eros*, the burnished statue forever poised on one foot, his arrow ready to fly. Two policemen passed through the crowd, a small path opening before them. It was something of a human rookery: the flurries and shouts, a car's horn, the rumble of hansom-cab wheels and the percussion of horses' hooves.

It was already very warm. Benedict scratched his head surreptitiously under his hat. Two brightly dressed girls came toward them, smiling and swaying arm in arm, looking as if they thought they knew them, but Theo shook his head and grinned before they reached him. The girls swerved past, one looking back and winking.

"Just what Dr. Brewer warned us about, I think," Theo said, looking pleased. "On the whole, any warning from Brewer could be seen as a recommendation, but it doesn't seem quite the thing when we're off to find a present for Agnes." He stopped, pulled out his small map, and traced a finger down it.

Benedict's eyes followed the girls as they turned down by the Lyons Corner House and toward a group of laughing soldiers. Household Cavalry, he thought. The slightly frantic, purple bursts of a hurdy-gurdy came from his left. Just yards away, his eye caught sight of three young men cast into the shade of a building, one of them scarcely more than a boy and another lounging back against the shop front, one knee raised. They stood at a distance from each other, unspeaking, looking at the crowd, simultaneously vigilant yet indifferent. Something about them spoke of threat and possibility: the essence of the whole city, he thought.

"Got it," Theo said. "Up here." He raised his head and specks of light filtered through the brim of his straw hat, scattering on his face like freckles. A light sheen of sweat covered his smooth cheeks. He looked wonderfully happy. Wonderfully young and fine and, for once, with no shadow of dissatisfaction.

They crossed the road, Theo stopping him to watch a shiny black beast of a car grumble by.

"My father has a car," Theo said. "Although not one like that. Unfortunately. But popular with young ladies. As is my father. Now—here we are, Regent Street. The center of the purchasing world."

A newspaper seller was shouting over the crowd: "Tensions rise in the Balkans! The prime minister in talks! Read all about it!"

The broad street curved away in a gentle arc. Dark green awnings shaded pale gray stone, with window displays unlike anything Benedict had ever seen. Caves of draped sea-green and carmine silks; exuberant osprey-feathered and flowered hats. Every building was decorated with festoons of red, white, and blue bunting.

"Where do you actually want to go?" Benedict, unsettled, had already decided there was a limit to how long he wanted to traipse up and down.

"Debenhams," Theo said. "It has everything, Novello says. But I need to hit the right note—not too intimate, or Mrs. B will have the vapors. Not too flashy, but not something a chap might give his maiden aunt."

"Handkerchiefs? With lace? Or her initial?"

"For heaven's sake, Ben, I want to transport her to another world—one she might share with me; one far from the Close and the incontinent seagulls and the smell of halibut on the air—not make her think about blowing her nose."

Benedict laughed. Was Theo serious about Agnes? Was Agnes at all serious about him?

"A parasol," Theo said. "A beautiful French parasol for a beautiful girl born in July. That way she'll always associate me with the sun."

"Or the eternal shades."

"What do you think they'll cost?" Theo said, a little anxiously.

They were outside Debenhams now, and the doors were opened solemnly by a commissionaire as stiff and gold-edged as any general.

Then, looking relieved, he said "Gloves," as if talking of precious jewels. "A pair of continental gloves of rare beauty, a present simple in conception, so acceptable to her mama. They will be my proxy: skin against skin; as soft and pale and pliant as Agnes herself."

CHAPTER EIGHT
Harry, New York, May-June 1914

HARRY MARRIED MARINA IN MAY, when blossoming trees lined the wide avenues. The day was unnaturally hot, especially for a man in formal dress. Harry waited inside the crowded Fifth Avenue Presbyterian Church. He had asked her cousin George to be his best man. He knew it would please her, although he thought briefly of his own cousin Jimmy, who should have been at his side. He was glad that the wedding was in New York and James in Tanganyika, so any obligation, and need for deception, was eradicated by geography. The American cousin, a keen yachtsman, looked more nervous than Harry, and his recent haircut had left a white collar of skin below his sea-weathered tan.

But he had told Marina's father a lie. There was no getting around it. It was a terrible, opportunistic lie and he hated himself for it; what Marina had come to mean to him felt like a punishment for a moment's madness.

Two years earlier, ago a business acquaintance in the Deep South had contacted him. The great liner *Titanic* had sunk and, reading through the passenger list, the acquaintance had seen the name of Henry Sydenham as a first-class passenger who had not been saved. He had thought immediately of Harry, and was relieved to find him alive, well, and on dry land.

Some while later, but long before Harry had realized he wanted to marry his daughter, Mr. Van Guyen had invited him to dinner, a dinner at which Harry had drunk much more than was good for him. He was trying to impress upon the older man the importance of working conditions, and with Marina's father talking of investment in his business and trying to find out more about him, Harry had impulsively sent his own father to the bottom of the Atlantic—although in the best of company. He hoped that this would allay Van Guyen's curiosity about his background and motivation for leaving his home country. He had always known his father would not come to America; he would hate being cooped up on a ship. But Marina's father had twice traveled to London. If Mr. Van Guyen wrote to Harry's father, his father would reply and, in his expansive way, invite Marina's father to Abbotsgate. Abbotsgate was where he had left the muddle of his former life. Neither father must ever know of the other. The easiest answer was for Harry's father to be dead. But as soon as the claim was made, he knew that it was a stupid, unnecessarily dramatic story, even for a lie.

Within the year, everything had changed. There was Marina at the center of his life. There, now, were their kind friends, all of whom shared the distress of Harry's tragic loss. One middle-aged woman among them had indeed been on the *Titanic*, but had not, unsurprisingly, met Harry's father on board. He could never now be resurrected. It was not a matter about which there could have been a misunderstanding. His ghost, Harry's lie, would have to accompany him into marriage; the lingering fear of his resurrection.

A year later, he had had two large brandies before plucking up the courage to approach Marina's father and ask for her hand.

"I am well provided for," he said. "My mother left me a substantial sum of money and property in England. I also have a stepmother. On her death I shall inherit considerably more and, of course, I have built up interests here" (how pompous he sounded; a liar and a pompous fool) "but I am confident I can keep Marina as I would wish to and as I am sure you would hope." Her father looked close to tears.

"Your poor step-mama," said Marina's aunt. "Might she come to the wedding, or is she quite an elderly lady?"

"Not old, but not strong, and, given the circumstances . . . I don't feel I could ask her to make a sea voyage." He felt a simultaneous blend of self-admiration and self-loathing.

The aunt had been mortified. "Of course. How foolish of me. I am so dreadfully sorry." She had taken his hand and he had known himself to be a complete cad.

Now he looked across at that kind aunt, taking the place of Marina's dead mother. She beamed at him from under a purple hat, trimmed with tartan ribbon. She had traveled to England and Scotland as a young woman and developed a passion for all things British. She had always been for the marriage.

He and Marina had had one night in the Waldorf before joining their ship the next morning, and then, ahead of them, lay the freedom of a three-month tour around Europe.

She had surprised him. He'd thought she would be a compliant, even quite an enthusiastic, lover; she was no prude, and their kissing had often left her breathless and flushed; but the woman who was now his wife was eager and subtle and adventurous. When they woke, tangled in sheets in the morning, her skin tasted of salt, she and her hair smelled animal, and he looked down at her nakedness with a great leap of joy and a simultaneous delighted surprise and relief that she made no effort to cover herself. She was the one. She was his. He had his life back. Her damp skin had the sheen of pearls. She was, had been, entirely unexpected.

She was as different as could be imagined from the dark-haired, secretive woman who had obsessed him for so long. Less desperate, less hungry, and less knowing. She followed his lead but did not reposition herself to suggest new ways he could take his pleasure as his former lover had. Now Marina smiled sleepily and put up a hand to stroke his face. "I hope you haven't changed your mind after last night," she said. "I hope there's not a first Mrs. Sydenham locked in an attic in England."

He forced himself to smile. "Only my stepmother, as far as I know. And she's usually in the drawing room or the yard."

Was she watching him more closely than usual? He turned and sat on the edge of the bed.

"I wish I could meet her when we're in England," she said. "I know we'll only be there for a day or so, but it's a shame she can't come down to London."

"I'm sure we'll visit again; in better times."

He found himself on the brink of saying that it would be too soon after his father's death and remembered the father of a school friend, a top King's Counsel who specialized in defending murder cases, saying that building a case was confused by criminals coming to believe, simply by virtue of repetition, the lies they told. Was he turning into such a man? He would tell her. Soon he would tell her. Must tell her. Though even then it must be a partial truth.

"We'll probably take a brace of grandchildren with us to see her next time," he said.

"But if she's not very strong—"

"She's scarcely an old lady," he said. "All the more reason not to wait too long to produce Master and Miss Sydenham." He turned and lay facing her. "Who will scandalize her with their American accents." She gazed back at him, unspeaking, her hair untidy on the pillows. He rolled back toward her. Laid his hand on her breast, feeling comforted rather than aroused. "If we didn't have a boat to catch and countries to conquer. . . ."

The journey to Europe had been mostly pleasure. "You're not scared?" she'd said as the great liner pulled away from the waving crowds, the wharves, cranes, and storehouses.

He laughed. "Of course not. I'm British; we have seawater in our veins."

"I just thought . . . after what happened."

Again a shadow. He was not just a liar, but a careless one. Fortunately she mistook his reaction for distress. "I'm sorry. I've no sense of timing. Come on, Mr. Sydenham, let's explore our newfound land."

The journey had been much easier, much more luxurious, than his outward journey from Liverpool. That time he had been driven forward by anger and hurt as well the fear and excitement of starting a new life. He had removed himself from what he believed was an intolerable situation; exchanged his family and friends for a few letters of introduction and that portion of the inheritance his mother had left him that he could get his hands on. Now he had that new life, a better one than he had ever dreamed of or deserved; yet a small part of him harbored misgivings as they journeyed east. In New York his decisions had been clear-cut; as they crossed the Atlantic they became more complicated, more blurred, more tinged with regret.

Their stateroom was unreasonably large and strangely silent. Although he felt little sense of their occupying a cabin, there was, instead, the feeling of being slightly drunk in a country house. It was very quiet, but he was aware of an almost imperceptible tremor around him if he thought about it. He did think about it sometimes, at night, as Marina lay curled up against him, breathing evenly. Beneath them and the first-class warmth of their cabin lay fathoms of water, and his imagination traveled downward into the rocky abysses, getting colder and darker until, finally, all light was extinguished.

His reasons for spending so little time in England were largely valid: he wanted them to have a real honeymoon, exploring new places, sharing experiences they would remember when they were old. He didn't want to be her teacher, to show her; he wanted them to find things together. They had both traveled to the Continent before: she, briefly, to Paris, he on walking tours in Germany and Switzerland after he left school. Marina teased him sometimes that he was a romantic only thinly disguised as a rational man, as he planned not only the places they should see but, sometimes, the time of day at which they should be seen.

"The Colosseum by moonlight is just a tradition," he'd said. "Byron wrote about it. Shelley too." But he even wondered himself why he needed it all to be perfect.

"Fine models for marriage, both men," she said.

He shook his head at her in mock severity. "You're talking about two of my country's greatest poets. Do you hear me cavil about Longfellow? But in Venice, for instance, if we get up early we can feel we're in Italy, not in some outlying territory of the United States. In Paris, we can buy our lunch in the markets. And in the matter of sunsets, you can never be too careful."

She had flung her arms around him and they had fallen back on the bed in their stateroom. She knelt over him, undressed herself, and this time controlled everything that followed. In this too, she was serious and determined.

Two weeks later they arrived in Venice to cold and drizzle. Marina, her fur wrapped around her, was undeterred. That evening, the skies cleared and they had stood on the balcony of their hotel listening to the bells ring and the drift of voices over the canal. The concierge had lit a fire and they had dinner, almost naked, in their bedroom, she with a sky-blue swansdown wrap around her shoulders. She looked, he thought, like a painting of a wanton girl by Fragonard: the fine strands of hair framing her face, pale and dewy but for the pink fading on her cheeks, her soft mouth, her rose-pink nipples and the reddish gold of the triangle of hair between her legs.

"You're like a box of fondants," he said. "Delicious."

She put down her fork and was about to make a facetious riposte, he thought, when suddenly and almost desperately he leaned forward and held her by the top of both arms.

"Don't ever stop loving me," he said. "If one day you think I'm not the man you thought I was: in all the hurly-burly of our lives ahead, don't stop loving me. I don't think I could bear it."

Her irises were a hundred different flecks of color: blue, yes, but violet, gray, green too, and her eyes were filling with tears.

"You're a man," she said. "Just a man. A human being like me. I don't expect you to be more than that. I can't offer you more than that myself, and I don't want you to be more than you are. Together we're better than apart—that's all and everything."

Looking back, he scarcely remembered the details. There was just the relief. That this perceptive, loving woman was his. That he was cured. All the rest, everything they saw or tried, was just a stage set for loving her. His appetite for her shocked and delighted him; and her abandon, which had so surprised him at first, heightened his hunger for her. They might be gazing at paintings of unknown saints, laughing about the smell of the water or buying Murano glass as green and dark as the stagnant canals, but much of the time he was thinking about how it would be back in their hotel.

If he thought of the past at all, it was in disbelief. How could he have imagined for so long that his life was over, that he could never love again? Every young man had rushed into love and behaved stupidly when it went wrong; many men had to watch the woman they desired in the arms of a rival. But few had to accept her as their mother. Few had to live with the consequences of thwarted passion.

They were in Rome by late June. Then, on their last day, they decided to walk into the countryside. A light carriage dropped them at the centuries-old tomb of Cecilia Metella on the Appian Way. Then they were completely alone. Glimpses of ancient cobbled road continued up into hazy hills, deep ruts worn in its surface from the carts and armies of ancient time. They sat on fallen stonework and looked up at the ivy-covered tower. The high-pitched song of larks dipping and soaring was the only sound in the silence, except for the rustle of dry grass as they moved.

Poppies and cornflowers grew untidily around the base of the tower. Marina had brought her paper and pastels, but she made no attempt to start drawing.

"Sometimes memories are better than pictures," she said. "I can't paint sounds or the smell of hay and pines. Anyway, now that we're married you don't have to pretend you think I'm a good artist."

He cleared his throat. "Well, now is the time you've been waiting for." He pulled out a small book with a shabby cover. "Lord Byron," he said with a flourish. "Who, you suggested, was a less than good husband. In fact it was after his honeymoon that his wife went scuttling back to her parents speaking of unmentionable vices."

"What were they?"

"They were unmentionable, Marina. But he was an imaginative man. Or it could have been the poetry."

They were back through the city gates as the sun was setting and the day was beginning to cool. She sat in the carriage with her head on his shoulders. On one side, the palaces of the Caesars were a vast and forbidding cliff; on the other, a wide area of worn turf followed the lines of a chariot track. The sky was fiery and streaked with violet.

At the hotel, the porter was in his office. Raised voices could be heard. He emerged almost immediately, apologizing with a curt nod of the head.

"I am sorry. The events of the day have unsettled the staff."

They took their key. As the lift went up, with an older couple beside them, Marina whispered "What on earth do you think happened?"

He shrugged. The other man said, in an English accent, "Apparently the heir to the Austrian emperor has been assassinated in Sarajevo. Not a young man and it's hardly likely to affect Italy, but I fear there this may well mean more trouble in the Balkans. However, I wouldn't let it spoil your vacation." After a short pause, he added: "Although I believe the waiter is from those parts and is all for taking up arms tonight. The *padrone*, not unreasonably, wishes him to serve dinner first."

"Such hotheads," said his wife, almost affectionately.

The next three weeks had been a leisurely exploration of tiny churches, Renaissance palaces, and bumpy excursions down white roads edged with cypresses. They dispensed with a driver and Harry took control. *"Mia moglie,"* he would say, introducing her, *"la mia adorata moglie." Signor e Signora Henry Sydenham,* he would sign in the register.

In late July, they took an overnight train north to the border at Ventimiglia and onward to Nice, where they had arranged to spend a few days before taking the train to Paris. The French passengers were buzzing over their papers and the scandal and trial of Madame Caillaux, the finance minister's wife.

"Her brief is claiming it was a *crime passionel*," said Harry, picking up a discarded paper. "It looks as if she'll be acquitted. But she did go to the office of the editor of *Le Figaro* and shoot him at point-blank range in the head."

"Her lover?" said Marina.

"Oh, you worldly cynic. She shot him because his paper was attacking her husband. As any decent wife might do."

"Can you imagine it at home?"

He didn't answer, his eyes scanning the inside pages. While they had been preoccupied with each other, the European situation seemed to have been getting worse. Was it posturing? Knife-edge diplomacy? He tried not to show his anxiety.

Marina had a headache and was resting in their room with the shutters closed. Harry went out for a brief walk along the promenade. He knew she had hoped she was pregnant, but it was not to be. Briefly, a more subdued mood took ahold of him. In a matter of days, they would be in England. His London lawyers were expecting him. He would change his will, now that he was a married man, but he had yet to break the news of his marriage to his legal advisers or to those at Abbotsgate. How could he begin to explain himself?

He intended to buy some cigarettes but stopped to read the headlines in *Nice Soir* to see if there was further news on the stories in the paper he'd seen on the train. Even before he paid for it, he was returned abruptly to the world outside the drunken sensuousness of his insular life with Marina, and with that return came unease. AUSTRIA-HUNGARY MOBILIZES, the headline read. He handed over his centimes, took the paper, and read it while standing there. Serbia had been issued with an ultimatum, but imperial troops were already massed on her borders. A grainy photograph showed lines of men in uniform marching to an unknown destination along an unknown road. He wished he could lay his hands on a copy of *The Times*.

He asked at the hotel, and the porter said he would obtain a paper in the morning.

"Do you think it is bad, sir?" the man said. "For France? We have a rumor now that Austria has declared war on Serbia."

Harry shook his head. He had no idea. He didn't want to worry Marina. This was only the Balkans. Austria could suppress Serbia in a day. It seemed as if war was inevitable, but how far could it spread? How many treaties would be honored, how many evaded?

The next morning, he rose early and took into the bathroom the newspaper that had been left outside their room. *The Times* was relatively sanguine regarding British involvement but reported that Germany and Russia had now mobilized. He found he was reading every word, trying to understand the implications of all the commitments that might lure countries into an unwanted war. According to the *Times* leader, France would, inevitably, be attacked if Russia declared hostilities against Germany. While Marina slept and they enjoyed freedom and sunshine, they were thousands of miles from home, and the conflict was creeping outward from central Europe.

They needed to go to Paris, he thought, and, rather than linger there as they had planned, head straight on to England so he could complete his legal business and return to New York. He hoped he was not panicking; if he had been traveling alone he would have stayed, might even have found the situation interesting—there was a terrible inevitability in it all; but he needed to protect Marina. Should things quiet down and the belligerence recede, they could always change their minds once they'd reached the French capital.

He would wake her, explain the situation, and then wire his London lawyers, both to bring forward their August appointment and to ask them to wire more funds. It might be necessary to pay for a berth on a different ship.

Marina seemed sober rather than alarmed. He went down to the desk and told the porter of their change of plans, asked for a maid to help her pack her bags, and had a wire sent to Lincoln's Inn and to her father, announcing their change of plans.

"You are not alone in departing, m'sieur," the porter said with a shrug. "But it may go well. Our troops have been pulled back

from our borders; France does not want a war. Not the wise men."
He was shaking his head. "We had enough of that forty years ago.
We have long memories. I did my military service ten years back.
Now my wife she is about to have a child."

And Harry, looking at him, realized that if France should
become involved in a war, she would inevitably call on all her
able-bodied men to fight.

It was at the station that the reality of the situation, the uncertainty
and the tension, became inescapable and the boundaries of their
comfortable private world were breached. A solid and noisy mass
of would-be travelers, including, Harry noticed, a large contin-
gent of French soldiers, forced their way toward the platforms or
sweltered, resigned, in the heat. It took twenty minutes to find a
porter, then they stood in line for forty minutes to get tickets on
the late-afternoon train and reserve places on the boat train to
London. Every seat was taken, even in first class. In third class,
the conductor was having difficulty closing the door. They didn't
talk much, just exchanged small smiles from time to time. Eventually Marina fell asleep; despite her sea-blue hat, which she had
told him was the height of fashion, her slightly open mouth made
her look very young. For the first hour or so, they cut through
rocky hillsides, pines, small hamlets, and woods of walnut and
chestnut, strips of ripening sunflowers, and then, as the south was
left behind them, cornfields and timbered farms, dark churches
and wide rivers flowing between limestone cliffs.

Across from him, deep in quiet discussion, sat two formally
dressed, hot-looking Frenchmen, civil servants possibly, one with
a very distinguished air, the other, he guessed, a private secretary.
He had to concentrate to follow their conversation while appearing
to look out of the window, but the one sentence he caught clearly
was the older man saying "The troops withdrew to make the
statement that our war would be a defensive war. But a war there
will be, and what difference does it make if we're attacking or

defending? Germany will be over the border and on us in no time at all, mark my words." Then he had laughed, although without warmth. "Better go and sharpen your father's saber. They won't want me, but they'll be knocking on your door."

Would they? Harry wondered again. Would there be war? He remembered his father's favorite poet, Housman. His father was a great man for recitation and had an infinite repertoire. Once he got over his youthful embarrassment, Harry had had to admit that his father was rather good at it.

> *On the idle hill of summer,*
> *Sleepy with the flow of streams,*
> *Far I hear the steady drummer*
> *Drumming like a noise in dreams.*

What war had that been, Harry had wondered, remembering his father's gestures: the hand cupped to the ear, his voice rising on "far" and the sinister threat of the falling last line. As a small boy he'd been quite sickly, and in feverish nightmares had dreamed of the distant drummer, thudding. What far-off threat had over-shadowed Housman? or was that war, like the half-seen country, just a poet's romantic fantasy?

A chink of memory, against which he was usually so fortified, opened. His father. His strong, argumentative, loyal, fearless, and oh-so-charming father. Widowed young, he had been, Harry now realized, an admirable man, but frustrated, trapped on his estate, with an only son who was no great rider and no great sportsman and who looked very like the pretty wife with the fatally weak heart.

They came slowly into the outskirts of Paris. Harry noticed crowds outside the big banks they passed and felt a stab of anxiety.

The train had to wait for an hour outside the station, and they arrived at their hotel late. The female receptionist made it clear that they were lucky to still have a room, indicating a group of weary-looking travelers across the lobby. "They all want a bed, m'sieur. We could charge double the price." As they were about to follow the bellboy pushing a trolley with their cases, she turned and took an envelope from a pigeonhole. "M'sieur. This came for you."

It was a telegram. Harry thought it would be from his lawyers, so he didn't bother to open it, but it reminded him of the need to draw out funds.

"I need to go to a bank," he said. If there were to be any problems on their way home, he should be prepared.

The receptionist made a face. "It is difficult, m'sieur. Many banks have not opened since yesterday." She leaned toward them, suddenly an intimate with drama to convey. "There are rumors, sir. Bad rumors."

"You'll have no joy, sir," said a large American standing nearby. "They believe there'll be war within hours. I have a letter of introduction from Senator Johnson himself, and I hammered on the doors until they let me in. 'I'm an American,' I said, but not a centime could I get out of them. It was all *'je regrette'* this and that."

It was only when they were, finally, in bed and had exhausted themselves speculating on what was happening in Europe, that he remembered the telegram. There had been talk in the hotel in Nice that it had become impossible to find boats returning to New York from Italy or France, but he felt confident that his lawyers would find him a ship either from Southampton or Liverpool. He got out of bed, fetched the envelope, and opened it, but not before he had looked at the name on the outside properly and had a first premonition of dread.

Sir Henry Sydenham, Bt., it said in clear black copperplate. He had not even noticed.

CHAPTER NINE

Jean-Baptiste, Paris, May-June 1914

Jᴇᴀɴ-Bᴀᴘᴛɪꜱᴛᴇ ʜᴀᴅ ɴᴇᴠᴇʀ ʀᴇᴀʟʟʏ ʙᴇᴇɴ alone in his whole life. Now the thought of it was exciting and daunting. Alone, he would become a different person. But there were things he had not considered. In all the tales of the river, it was not just the banks and the weeds that were slippery, the fish and the water creatures, but also the spirit of the river itself; once a river had flowed with blood, it might develop an appetite for it. Most of all, he should have realized that if you leave such a place, you cannot reasonably expect it to wait for you unchanged.

He had made Amiens by nightfall. He had his small savings, and Parisians were puny and often drunk, so he had heard, so he should find work. But still, he could count on nothing. He wheeled the bicycle to a tiny repair shop. He'd once been there with Godet.

The owner was a dour man and certainly didn't remember him, but he offered Jean-Baptiste a fair sum for the bicycle.

"I have a job starting in Paris," Jean-Baptiste lied.

"Oh, yes." The man couldn't have been less interested or less convinced.

Paris had been everything he'd expected in that nothing was as he'd imagined. He had spent the first night sleeping in a park. It was a warm night, but he was damp and aching when he woke up. He washed his face in a fountain and set out to find work and somewhere to live. By the afternoon, having failed in both, he was hungry. He stopped at bar after bar, asking for any job, but the young men already working there, neat in their aprons and white shirts, looked at him disdainfully. One even imitated his accent, he thought, although he gave him half a stale loaf.

He had walked and walked, and his feet, in Vignon's new boots, were tender and blistered. When he sat on the curb and took them off, the fine leather lining was bloodstained. He ended up by the same bushes in the same park, and at dawn he was woken roughly by a park attendant telling him to move on.

He drank bitter chicory coffee from a street stall, then headed toward the great steeple he had seen from the park. He passed a factory that had a notice saying they required hands, but the watchman wouldn't let him past the door. "Skilled men only," he said, hardly bothering to take his cigarette out his mouth.

He emerged from a narrow lane onto a grand boulevard running along the broadest river he had ever seen. You didn't have to be a man of the world to know this was the mighty Seine. It was wider and busier than *his* river, with barges and skiffs, pleasure boats and pontoons, but it was one sheet of choppy gray rather than the Somme's many shades and depths of seemingly slow-moving green.

From everything Vignon had said, he had expected something different of the Seine. But he knew now that the doctor was a deceiver. Back home, his river had cut its way through the landscape, and the villages and towns had had to grow where they could and their inhabitants had to learn its ways. This famous river of Paris seemed to exist only at the service of men: to be allotted a space, no more, in the stone city. It was wide, but it was walled in. Perhaps some waterways were better imagined than seen.

At the near side of the bridge, men were bustling about repairing a stretch of embankment. For a moment his spirits brightened; here he was in Paris, at the center of the world, and surely there were possibilities for a strong young man. He walked on to the bridge and could see the city: its domes and its gray and bright green roofs—and he wondered, fleetingly, what his mother would think if she could see him in this new life. Two of the workmen were struggling with a long piece of timber. The older set his end down and wiped his brow. Jean-Baptiste climbed down the riverside steps and, moving to the center, took some of the weight. The other man, a sturdy fellow with a red beard, indicated the direction with his head. He walked along the shingle river edge and helped maneuver the plank into position. Below him, three men were shoring up the sides of a muddy trench.

The red-haired man grunted his thanks and on the spur of the moment Jean-Baptiste asked: "Do they need men? I'm strong and a good worker."

The man looked impassive, shrugged, but then pointed at two men standing under a tree, studying plans. One was coatless, neat, in a straw hat, the other a worker in a blue cap. Jean-Baptiste walked over to them, trying to look confident but not assuming anything. When the two men looked up, he was about to speak when a voice behind him said "He helped us. He seems like a good lad. We could do with a replacement for Loiret." It was the owner of the fine red beard.

The man in the cap, who Jean-Baptiste thought must be the foreman, scrutinized him. "Any experience?"

"I was a blacksmith. Well, an apprentice," he said in a burst of honesty. "Near Amiens."

"Come to seek your fortune?" said the man with the map, whose Parisian accent was tinged with authority. "And willing to find it in a ditch." He jerked his head toward the diggings. "I gather we've got a man with a broken leg, so his misfortune might be your good luck. What do you reckon, Duval?"

Blue Cap nodded. "Start tomorrow. No drinking, no scrapping, and you show up on time. No second chances. And you'll need decent boots, it's wet down there. . . ."

The man with the smart accent looked up from his plan again as if recalling something, then down at Jean-Baptiste's feet. He leaned forward, pushing his spectacles up his nose as if unsure of what he was seeing.

"Where in the name of St. Joseph did you get those? You look like a pimp."

"He can have Loiret's," said the man called Duval. "Loiret won't be needing them."

And so began his second river life. It was to be a short one, but he didn't know that then and was grateful simply to have work. The men he was working with seemed all right.

"Thank you, sir," he said to Duval, when the other man, who was clearly a boss, had left.

"Pierre," he said. "No sirs here. We're working men, as good as any. Unfortunately, the redhead over there is also Pierre and so is the boy. You're not Pierre, I suppose? No? That's a relief. Can you write your name?"

"Yes. I mean, I can read and write."

"Ah, an intellectual. Well, we only need your name. In case the police come asking."

For a second Jean-Baptiste was tempted to give a made-up name, but he didn't want to start this new life with a lie and hoped Paris gendarmes, with real crimes, bloody, violent ones, to solve, would have little interest in a provincial bicycle and boot thief.

"Jean-Baptiste Mallet," he said.

"Where do you come from, Monsieur Mallet?"

"A village near Amiens," he said. It was true enough.

"And where are you staying in this great city of ours?"

Jean-Baptiste's head dropped.

"Ah, no work, no boots, no lodgings," said Pierre, shaking his head. He picked up a stub of pencil. "I've known several lads lodge here. It's simple and you'll have to behave, and it's a bit of a walk, but it's cheap and if you take this note, they'll do their best for you."

"I don't have—"

"You can work over there for a couple of hours. Stacking timber. When it's time to leave, you'll have earned enough for a bed. Young Therzon can take you." He pointed to a moon-faced lad. "He boards there."

A couple of hours had exhausted him. The red-haired Breton, one of the three Pierres, could lift four times the quantity that he could and talk at the same time. Jean-Baptiste thought that just a week ago, the strength he had gained in Godet's forge would have left him equal to the task, but the last few days had weakened him. He was glad to follow Therzon to the lodgings, have a bowl of fibrous horsemeat stew, and, exhausted, slump onto a narrow box bed in a dormitory full of other men. The smell of them, tobacco and sweat, reassured him; at least he could smell no worse. A notice exhorted the residents to wash, not to sleep in their boots, warned them that alcohol and women were strictly forbidden on the premises, and advised that holy mass would be held at the church of Ste. Clothilde.

He was awake when Therzon materialized at six the next morning and handed him a brown-paper parcel. Inside were well-worn work clothes, clean and adequate.

"From Pierre," Therzon said, his teeth clamped around an unlit pipe.

"Pierre?"

"Duval. Pierre the old." Therzon took out the pipe and grinned. He had very few teeth for such a young man.

"He seems kind."

"Not bad on a good day. His son's our age. In the Army, serving in Africa with the blackamoors. But Pierre's a man of peace." Therzon grinned again; his face was loose and his speech slow. "Any talk of fighting or generals and he'll fly into a rage."

The days went by, then the weeks. He had enough to eat, he slept well enough, he became fit again. He mostly succeeded in not thinking about home.

The men were decent enough. Young Pierre was only fifteen; his sister was married to a bargee who passed by, waving, his boat heaped with coal, once a week. Pierre Duval with the soldier son had a wife and daughter in Valence-en-Brie. Flame-haired Pierre was from Britanny and provided the muscle. The oldest worker was Marcel, an ill-tempered Parisian. As far as possible, Jean-Baptiste tried to keep out of his way. Therzon was an idiot; it hadn't taken Jean-Baptiste long to figure that out. When it got really hot, Therzon took off his shirt to work and revealed "vengeance" tattooed on his arm. Or rather "v-e-n-g-e-n-a-c-e," although the letters were clumsy and the tattoo was inflamed and hard to read at all. Therzon kept picking at it. When old Pierre Duval, though he was not very old, asked Jean-Baptiste about his family one day, he had simply said his mother was a widow.

"She must miss you."

Jean-Baptiste shrugged. "I suppose so."

"Well, at least you're not too far away, eh?" Pierre patted him on the back, his attention already taken by a cart delivering stone.

Usually Jean-Baptiste put up scaffolding on a central pier, alongside young Pierre, on the basis that they were the only two who could swim. Pierre would secure the boat to an iron ring and Jean-Baptiste would climb onto the thick stone base, holding a line. He looked down: the water was drawn into the thick pillar and swallowed, and from time to time it made a great gulping noise. When rivercraft passed by, the water was first hurled upward and then sucked back, exposing the slippery bright-green stone of the footings. He was regularly soaked. Under the arch it was cool, but it stank. There was a marker on the bridge to indicate that beneath the opaque surface, the Seine went down another fifteen meters. What was on the bottom was something he didn't like to think about. If he went into the water, his ability to swim would have little to do with his fate.

Jean-Baptiste tried to forget Marcel's words and not think of his mother, because when he did, he could see only her curved back and Vignon clutching her breasts as if they were handles keeping him steady on a bucking fairground ride. With time, what he hated most was what he had called her as he rode. Vignon the liar, the philanderer. Vignon the German. Now this foreign duke had been murdered and there was talk, among the men and on the headlines of the newspapers he stopped and looked at, that the Germans were wanting war and plenty of good Frenchmen wanted it too. And what if his mother had married the doctor and he, Jean-Baptiste, would have had a German father without even knowing it? What if Vignon had become his patriotic enemy as well as his personal one?

After a few weeks Jean-Baptiste learned to ignore Therzon's crude jokes and Marcel's malign view of his fellow man. But he did take in the discussions about the murder of the duke, who turned out to be a sort of Austrian prince. Pierre Duval had said it was a disaster while Marcel thought he had it coming. He also stopped and listened when Therzon told young Pierre not long afterward that German spies had been arrested in Paris.

"They'll be for the guillotine," said Marcel as he came within earshot. "Or the firing squad."

"But we're not at war," Jean-Baptiste said. "We didn't kill the Austrian."

"Those Germans and Austrians are as thick as thieves, and they hate us French and they'll be laying their plans." Marcel dropped his voice, came close. His fingers holding the pipe were dark yellow.

"They'll be watching and listening. Finding our weak points." His eyes opened wide.

Therzon, who'd been inexpertly rolling tobacco, looked up. "I heard police are doing checks on men working on the river. Rivers being like roads, they say—for armies and spies."

Red-beard Pierre snorted.

"You're the one who likes to know everything. You'd *like* a bit of spying."

Therzon licked the edge of the cigarette paper. "And you're looking a bit pale, red-beard—you not fancying a visit from the gendarmes?"

"I did time," red-beard Pierre mumbled. He had a way of stroking his beard when he was anxious, not to show it off, but rather as if he was checking that someone hadn't taken it. "Way back. A fight. Over a woman. I'm no friend of the law."

Jean-Baptiste thought that was probably why Vignon had appeared among them when their old doctor had died. There he was suddenly, in his pale linen and his neat beard, with his watch chain, his singing, and his laughing contempt for the remedies the old women set so much store by. Learning the river's secrets. Bastard. Worming his way into their trust. Into his mother's trust.

Therzon said "Do you think we'll have a war?"

"He can't wait to get into his red trousers," young Pierre said, but was quelled by a look from the older man.

"Being a soldier is no joke."

"I didn't mean—"

"And if there *is* a war, you'll all be in red trousers. I'll be in red trousers myself."

Pierre Duval looked around, but his eyes fixed on Jean-Baptiste.

"Our leaders need to stand firm. They need to know that the country has no appetite for other nations' wars," he said. "Not us working men, who'll have to face the guns." Now there was unmistakable anger in his voice. "We might not follow where they lead. They have to know that."

There was a very long silence. Nobody ever mentioned Pierre's son, Corporal Duval, Jean-Baptiste thought, but he was there: a ghost of the living if you could have such a thing.

Therzon made a face. "And how are we to tell the president, then? Knock on his door? Trample the carpets of the palace with our Seine mud?"

"We did more than that in the Revolution," Pierre red-beard said.

"We did a great deal *less* than that forty years ago," said Pierre Duval. "What a disaster."

"Revenge," mouthed Therzon, nudging young Pierre.

Pierre red-beard said: "Our armies were a disgrace then, and our generals." He made a throat-cutting motion. "The Prussians ground us into the dirt. They took Alsace. They took Lorraine. They forced good Frenchmen to become Germans." He shook his head as if denying it.

"Revenge," said Therzon, looking pleased with himself, while rubbing his tender tattoo.

"Revenge?" Pierre Duval looked at Therzon as if he were a small child. "For what? The French brought the last war on themselves, and it was a catastrophe. As it will be if they do it again. Tonight," he went on, "there's a meeting. Informal. With Jaurès. He's a Deputy, a powerful man. He's *our* man. A strong, decent man. Now that Caillaux's been out for three or four months, he's our only hope: a man with a zeal for peace. Who speaks for ordinary men. Tonight he'll speak *to* us. Jean Jaurès. He's the only one trying to keep us all alive."

Young Pierre looked puzzled. "My father says he's an agitator," he said.

Therzon muttered, "Politicking isn't for working people. I don't want to go and be lectured to by some gentleman in a tail-coat at the end of a hard day's work. I want a drink." He belched.

Pierre Duval ignored them both. He looked at Jean-Baptiste. "Jaurès is worth listening to—talks sense. He's staking his reputation on peace."

"There might be trouble," said young Pierre. And then, looking awkward, "My father wouldn't like it."

Pierre red-beard's eyes shone and he rubbed his scarred hands together. "Count me in, brother Pierre," he said.

Jean-Baptiste was aware of Therzon's foolish face caught in the beginnings of a sneer. "And me," he said to Duval. "Could I come with you?"

He set off between Laval and red-beard Pierre: the three men, striding down the Boulevard de Montmartre. It was a warm July night and the cafés were busy. There were bright, noisy girls on street corners and beggars on church steps. A bicycle hurtled by, almost colliding with them, and Pierre red-beard shouted some Breton curse upon the cyclist. The thin notes of a fiddle competed with an accordion supported on the vast bust of a middle-aged woman. Her fat hands could hardly reach the keys, yet her fingers were nimble. Pierre Duval laughed, as he almost never did. "Bravo, Madame."

Jean-Baptiste knew *this* was the Paris people dreamed of. Even people at the bottom, like him, were part of it. Yet whom could he tell? Who would be glad for him that he'd made it there at last?

On a street corner, a man was shouting out headlines and several people were trying to read the same paper. "War coming," shouted the vendor. "Read all about it! Will the British fight for France? Will Italy stay neutral?"

Pierre Duval, who had been laughing just minutes ago, looked grim-faced. "Idiots," he said.

Pierre red-beard snorted. "If we're trusting the English to get us out of this, we're really screwed."

Suddenly, from up ahead, they heard some distant shouting, followed by screams. Several men came running down the street; one was carrying his cap and waving it, though at whom it was impossible to say.

"Dead. He's dead. Shot. He's dead. Blood everywhere. Just eating his dinner. Murder, bloody murder!" he shouted as he went on unsteadily down the street. The music wailed to a stop.

Some gendarmes, running, overtook the men. The two Pierres stopped and stood back in the doorway of a cobbler's workshop, the older Pierre pressing Jean-Baptiste back with the flat of his hand. More men ran by, away from whatever catastrophe had befallen, while other men guided their wives from the street. A smartly dressed gentleman was pulling a reluctant priest toward the commotion.

Pierre Duval reached out and caught one of the escaping men by his jacket. "Who's been murdered?" he asked. "What in the name of the Virgin is going on?"

"Shot in the café. By some ordinary young man. With a gun."

"Who?"

"Jaurès."

"He's dead?" Pierre looked stricken, Pierre red-beard unbelieving. "What's all this nonsense . . . this damn fool city and its rumors."

"Go and take a look. Paddle in his blood. Get arrested. Get shot. The whole place is swarming with police. It was probably a German, if you ask me."

The older Pierre was clearly fighting to keep his voice under control. "Jaurès was trying to keep peace with the Germans. Why would they shoot him?" A small spasm crossed his face. "Dead? Are you sure?"

The man tore his sleeve free. "If a man can live with his brains all over his dinner plate, then yes, perhaps he's alive. I'm getting out of here—there may be more Berlin anarchists about."

Pierre Duval looked up the street. A black official car, its horn hooting, trundled over the cobbles.

"Let's take you back, young Jean-Baptiste," he said, his voice flat. "If Jaurès is dead, we'll hear soon enough." He turned and moved off, Pierre red-beard a step behind him. Jean-Baptiste followed forlornly.

At the hostel, two tired-looking workmen were standing against the wall smoking.

"Jaurès has had it," one said in a thick accent. "Some French lad did it. They've already caught him."

"A patriot," said the other.

Jean-Baptiste expected one of the two Pierres to react, but they hardly seemed to have heard and he was left standing on the steps feeling, suddenly, very alone. But as his companions reached the corner, Pierre Duval turned, looked at him, and walked back. He took him by the elbow, speaking low and urgently.

"You need to go home," he said. "Don't stay in Paris. Go back home. It won't be safe here. Jaurès was a small voice, and now that's silent. War is coming, and Paris is where it will come to first. You'll be a soldier within weeks."

Jean-Baptiste couldn't tell him that there was no way he could ever go home again. That his mother was a whore, that the man he had looked up to was a spy, and that he was himself a thief. By now everybody in Corbie would know what he'd done, but only his mother and Vignon would know that he knew what *they'd* done, what *they* were.

A few days later, Therzon was late for work. Eventually he came haring along the embankment, waving a newspaper, which was odd because he couldn't read.

"War! It's war!" he cried, as if it were the best day of his life. "Revenge! Here!" He stabbed at the newspaper with his finger.

Young Pierre scrambled, goat-like, up the half-built steps from the waterside, his eyes sparkling in his muddy face. Red-beard

Pierre just rested on his pickaxe, with an expression that was hard to read, while Pierre Duval's was unequivocal. Grim-faced, he kept working. Yet Jean-Baptiste felt a thrill of something, even though he was ashamed of it: perhaps Therzon's euphoria was contagious.

He was on the top of the bridge as Therzon ran off, shouting the news to anyone who would listen. The bells had started tolling. Who would have thought there were so many churches in Paris? Jean-Baptiste looked up and saw a couple, very elegant, very *rich*, he thought, walking arm in arm and talking to each other. She had a parasol and a pretty hat and, underneath it, hair so fair it was almost white. The man, who was older, was laughing at something she'd said. They came to a halt when they saw Therzon running across the road, shouting to women waiting outside the baker's. A group of road-menders were all putting down their tools, and a trolley actually stopped while a passer-by spoke to the driver. A waiter crossed the street to join in, still carrying his tray.

The couple, clearly foreign, looked puzzled, even nervous. Were they perhaps Germans? Jean-Baptiste ran toward them, the bells and the shouts across the street creating a sort of urgency that made him run too fast and shout too loudly rather than tell them calmly what had happened. The man caught him by the arm and held him for a minute. He didn't know what he actually said to the couple, but he was certain it was as bad as if it had been Therzon.

He expected Pierre Duval to be cross with him, but Pierre went on working until he'd finished what he was doing. Therzon and young Pierre had disappeared. Pierre red-beard had walked a short way down the river and was leaning back against the embankment wall, smoking and talking to two bargees. Marcel was propped against a tree, smoking his stinking pipe. Jean-Baptiste found himself sitting alone.

Pierre Duval reached the top of the steps and picked up the discarded newspaper.

"Therzon's an idiot," he said without malice. "Today's paper only has yesterday's news. He heard it in a bar when he should have been at work."

"Will we be called up, do you think?"

"Go home," said Pierre, much more insistently than he had on the evening the deputy had been murdered. "You'll be a soldier in weeks. It's a hard, filthy life. At least fight with the men you know, your friends, the boys you grew up with. Fight *for* your own and *with* your own. They're the only ones worth risking your life for."

A week later he was in a long, long queue with red-beard Pierre, Marcel, Marcel's brother, a great ape of a man, and young Pierre. Therzon was nowhere to be seen. Pierre Duval had said gruffly that the authorities could come and find him; he wasn't queuing in the sun for the Army's convenience. Nor was he leaving a job uncompleted. He and Loiret, who was back at work though lame now, worked at the bridge the same as ever, and for a week so they all did, but Duval rarely spoke to them. Even with red-beard Pierre, who had always seemed his closest ally, he was merely polite. But when he found out young Pierre was going with them to enlist, he had lost his temper for the first and last time in the many weeks Jean-Baptiste had known him.

"You're under age," he said. "You're a child. You're not even fully grown—one of us always has to cover for you with the heavy work."

Young Pierre looked hurt. He bit his lip and his chin trembled slightly.

"You're no good to the Army and they're no good for you," Pierre Duval snapped. "If you want to be killed, then I'm sure you'll find plenty of opportunities locally." Then he said "Get out of my sight. I'm sick of all of you."

The next time Jean-Baptiste saw him was at Douaumont eighteen months later. He was Sergeant Duval of the Grenadiers by then, an old man with a long, ridged scar across his face. Jean-Baptiste didn't speak to him. He had heard weeks ago that Duval's son was dead and he didn't know what to say.

CHAPTER TEN
Frank, London, August 1914

WAR!

The Reverend Mr. Williams was a prophet, but then it was not hard to see what was coming.

We were all a bit mad with it—excited, frightened; entertained, even. Take your pick.

Isaac didn't hang around waiting for it to be official. He left his books and the Institute and the piecework in the sweatshop, had a blowup with his brother about it, or so I heard, and went to join up. He was a skinny chap, but with the hours he worked he had to be stronger than he looked. I asked him how he felt about killing Germans, given that we were both in the Young Men's International League. He didn't look happy.

"They've gone against the spirit of it, that's the thing," he said. "I expect there are good working men there who don't like it any more than I do: German internationalists. I expect there are plenty of them." He seemed anxious. "Men and women fighting for workers' justice. Mr. Marx himself was a German."

He was shaking his head in disbelief, but whether at his hero Mr. Marx being, in the end, a German, or at the Germans betraying their greatest son, I couldn't tell.

"But then what about poor little Belgium, Frank? Terrible things are happening. I can't turn my back, although I am thinking that I shall act more in the spirit of defense than attack."

But he didn't look very convinced. "And my family—the Army's good pay and regular. Anyway, we weren't the ones who started it." Now he was staring down at his toecap as he rubbed it on the back of his trousers.

Perhaps I'd offended him, because he didn't come to the Institute again, but I missed his company even though I'd never known him well.

At Debenhams, they gathered us together after work for Mr. Richmond to give us another speech.

"As the great Lord Nelson said" (said Mr. R), "'England expects every man to do his duty,' and so do I." His face was lit with fierce joy. "That is the code of Debenhams. God save the King!"

"God save the King," we said, a bit awkwardly. When Mr. R had gone, Mr. Hardy told us all to calm down because for the time being we were still taking the Board's shilling, not the King's.

Some might prosper in all this, but I wouldn't be one of them. It was clear that if I did not volunteer, I could not stay at Debenhams. If I joined up, I would gain five guineas and thus a bicycle I could not ride until we had sorted the war out, and Connie would, I knew for sure, never speak to me again if I went into khaki. I thought about driving an ambulance or being a stretcher-bearer, but I'd still be in khaki, against which Connie had taken her pledge; and Mr. Richmond wouldn't see that as proper soldiering anyway, I was sure.

As we left the room, I heard Reg Singleton say, to Percy from accounts, "I'm going to ask my girl to marry me straight off. She's nice enough and doesn't talk too much. That way I can stay out of this fight. They don't want married men."

"Blimey, mate." Percy looked genuinely shocked. "How'll you feel come Christmas when we've had our fiver, seen off the Germans like heroes, and are back in our beds—and you're stuck married for the rest of your life? Probably have her in the family way by then?" Reg winked. I never did like him.

Ladies came and went; the excitement seemed to loosen their purses. The apprentices were up and down bringing out yellow, camel, and fawn gloves and even shades we carried as a novelty for foreign ladies: green and mauve and eau-de-nil with fringes or cuffs or cut leatherwork delicate as a cobweb. But spread out on one of my oak counters (for I had made the very substance of the counter itself, although I never said as much, obviously), the rainbow fans of fingers looked very fine.

Despite everything, young gentlemen were in for boater ribbons, it being Cowes regatta week. The first two wanted the colors of the Royal Corinthian Yacht Club, and they were larking about but saying soon they would join the Navy and sail for free.

Then in came two quieter types. Gentlemen, but not the loud sort. They paused at the parasols, were charmed by young Ethel, but moved on swiftly to our matinée gloves. The more talkative of the two seemed to want them for a lady friend, and he looked very pleased indeed when I showed him pairs from our middling range, having judged that they were not young men with money to spare, but even so when he heard the price he went very quiet.

I turned to the drawer of cheaper gloves for ordinary wear. But when I pulled them out, they looked a little mean compared to the promise on display. The pigskin ones were too coarse, the fabric gloves looked limp and short in the wrist, the satin ones were really not appropriate for a young lady, and although there were lace ones, they were too white and stiff.

"I could get gloves like these in Gloucester," said the one who had been so keen. His face was all disappointment. I didn't like to say that some of our cheaper gloves, for lady's maids and the like, came from not ten miles from Gloucester.

The two men left, and by now the department looked more like a market in the Orient than London's finest store; and although a very small part of me enjoyed seeing the good cheer of everything we had to offer in bright disarray, I knew there would be trouble if every boater wasn't lined up straight in groups of sennit braid, split braid, panama, and rustic and every glove wasn't back in the hierarchy of glass-fronted drawers.

But as soon as I looked at the glove counter, I knew something was wrong. And two seconds later, I knew what. A pair of delicate cream opera gloves with tiny rosebuds was gone. I lifted up the other discarded gloves, but I already knew I wouldn't find them. What better gift for a young lady than such beautiful gloves? For a second, I think I even felt pride; there were no such gloves anywhere else in London. But then I reflected that there were no such gloves here either now. The gloves, I was almost certain, were on their way to Gloucester. Of course, even in a shop like this and a department like ours, things went missing from time to time, but I had not thought these two were the thieving sort. Still, I was d*****d if I would have my best gloves taken from under my very nose and find myself in Mr. Hardy's bad books. I would be docked pay for sure, when I had only recently been forced to give two shillings to Mr. Williams's Christian peace. The light-fingered customers might as well have stolen my future bicycle.

Pausing only to tell the assistant to put the gloves away and not pausing long enough for her to ask me exactly what she should do, so that I would end up nearly doing it myself but slower, I left the floor. I walked in a dignified way behind Mr. Hardy, whose attention was entirely taken by his favorite customer (though he thinks it a breach of his dignity to admit this), Lady Lostwithiel. But once on the stairs I ran like the wind. I was out on Regent Street, looking up and down; it was a warm day and the street was a dangerous sea of parasols. But just across the road I thought I saw two gentlemen and on the chance they were my thieves I gave chase. Not that I ran now; I sauntered with purpose, thinking if only I had a bicycle, I could have foiled their attempts to get away. As I drew level with them, I started to cross.

It was indeed the culprits, and they appeared to have anticipated no pursuit and were chatting as easy, or as hardened, as you please. Drinking lemonade! I saw two policemen coming slowly along the pavement and for one second I faltered. I was in two minds whether to return to the shop. Was it possible that in my anxiety and haste, I had simply overlooked the gloves? At exactly that moment, the friend of the would-be glove buyer looked up and saw me. He looked puzzled as if he couldn't place me, but not in any way guilty, and as I approached he slowed and said something to his companion in a perfectly relaxed way. I reflected on my position. I could not demand that I search them. I had left the floor without permission and on an impulse. The way I was going, I had put myself in a situation where I stood to lose my job, not just the cost of a pair of gloves from my wages.

I paused as the more talkative of the two men followed his friend's gaze and saw me; and although for a few seconds his face looked blank (people do not, in the main, recognize those who assist them in shops), I knew I had my man. He blushed, his head tipped down so his face was obscured by the brim of his hat, then he turned toward the crowd and would have walked off, I think, had his friend not stayed still. The current of humanity passed to either side of the pair.

In the business of selling apparel, one learns to be an observer. To know when to speak and when to stay silent; to know what a lady may afford or not afford or what she dreams in her heart of having, rather than knowing she needs. In the business of coffins there are dreams too, not just a matter of a good or bad job, of corners cut or corners embellished. It was observation that revealed to me that one man was guilty, his face now displaying every sign of panic, while the other had no idea that his friend had left our store with anything other than disappointment.

He had already gotten them out by the time I reached him. The gloves hung limply from his hand. "Theo?" said his friend, uncomprehending, and then "Theo" again as he caught on. Then, very quickly, he said "It was a mistake" just as he clearly realized that it was not. His look was one of pure mortification. His tone was almost pleading, as much to this Theo as to me, I thought. "We can pay. I can pay," he said, or something like it, looking hot and feeling in his blazer pocket.

I hadn't touched the gloves.

"I'd rather just have them back," I said. Hoping they weren't soiled.

"Well, take a guinea for yourself," said the friend. He was like a man who has had a dreadful shock and although I shouldn't have, I almost felt sorry for the two of them. And then I thought *a guinea!* I could have my bicycle now! Have it without joining up.

I said "The gloves will do." Knowing that Mr. Hardy was a stickler for theft. We had a special code for alerting each other should any pilfering take place on the floor. Mr. Frederick Richmond, if notified, would call the police. "Theft is theft," he would say, "whether a loaf for a starving man or Raffles stealing a duchess's emeralds or a young lady helping herself to a lawn handkerchief." Knowing all this, I simply put my hand out, and he laid the gloves in it. I looked down, folded them, and placed them in my own pocket.

"There's this young lady," the one who was not the thief began, still holding out the guinea.

And I thought there was always a young lady, or a bicycle, or both, but it didn't have to turn us into thieves. If I took the guinea, I would in effect be stealing from Debenhams, because they had their rules and I would be looking away. To look away for no reason other than my own inclination was another thing.

"No, thank you, sir," I said and turned away, already hoping I could get back to the floor and thinking what excuse I might make. That the potted tongue I'd had for tea the day before had disagreed with me, perhaps. But when I arrived breathless on the floor, it was like a fairytale in which time doesn't change, for there was Lady Lostwithiel in a mauve hat now, and her daughter and Mr. Hardy and the entourage and items being carried out and borne away. And there was the assistant looking confused and there was the pile of gloves, hardly smaller in size than when I'd left the counter. And within a minute or two, there were the cream opera gloves, back where they should be.

After the day was finished, I walked down through Piccadilly Circus. Men on boxes were shouting the odds about this and that, and there were people milling around in the early evening sunshine. There were men with their sweethearts and a chap spinning past on an Italian Bianchi, of all things. I walked on toward Trafalgar Square, because I wanted to take a stroll before going back to my room. I went on down Whitehall, under the trees, and looked to the right and left as I came into Horse Guards Parade. There was the Admiralty and the War Office where, no doubt, grave men in frock coats and admirals in gold braid were causing office boys to scurry around, and messages and telegrams were going hither and thither and letters were being written by men of state. Mr. Asquith and Lord Kitchener and Sir John French and the King in his palace, all thinking who knows what. It seemed to me that war must be a very busy undertaking. There were soldiers on parade, looking hot with drums and bearskins, all in bright colors, just the same as they had been when war was only an idea; and there, just across from them, the dark green of St. James's Park, where the young couples and the nursemaids and the white ducks on the lake wouldn't know a German if they saw one. Nor what to do with him.

I thought two things. One was that the code of Debenhams was a fine thing, but it was different from my own. I could not join up and go and fight in foreign lands just because Mr. Richmond wanted me to. I would look for another position, although I could not hope for the status I had at present owing to my irregular beginnings. I considered briefly going back to Devon. War should mean that business would be brisk, and I might do my duty by my country *and* my father. But to go home was to go back to being the son of the family, and he would never accept that my return was other than the failure in my present occupation that he half feared, half hoped for.

The second was the day on which my path had crossed with the gentleman who had stolen my gloves, and for a moment I'd had his fate in my hands, and I'd had to make a choice. It was not the choice Mr. Hardy or Mr. Richmond would have made. Now I would choose for myself what to do regarding the war.

I had reached Westminster Bridge and, not for the first or even the hundredth time, I stood looking back at the houses of our great parliament and the glowing new statue of Boadicea, looking fierce on her plinth. How fine the bronze queen and her chariot looked in the golden London sunlight!

CHAPTER ELEVEN

Harry, Europe, July 1914

THAT LAST NIGHT IN PARIS, Harry had sat on the edge of the bed, perhaps for hours, he had no idea, all the time wondering what to say to Marina.

He stood up, paced across the room, parted the heavy curtains, and opened the shutters as quietly as he could. Soon it would be dawn; there was already a greenish light in the east. He looked over the city spread out in front of him. The great dream of lovers. He could see the illuminated Tour Eiffel, the dome of the Sacré Coeur, and the Seine, only just visible between lime trees. The lights of a river boat flickered in and out of sight. There was the faintest of breezes. And his father was dead. Gone. Suddenly, at the age of only fifty-nine. It was thought his heart had given way, the lawyers had told him. They had been trying to contact Harry for some days. He had felt disbelief, then a brief flare of relief, of freedom, followed by deep shame and a greater pain than he might ever have imagined. He had always thought there would be more time.

He must return home. The lawyers had written—and he thought he detected the very faintest note of condemnation—that they awaited his decisions but that if they did not hear from him, the funeral would be held on August 4. He would understand that any greater delay would be distressing for Lady Sydenham.

He jumped as a hand touched his shoulder. It was Marina. "Isn't it beautiful?" she said, standing beside him, squeezing his arm.

Then she said "What's the matter?" and her eyes dropped to the letter still in his hand. "Have you had bad news?"

"Let's go in."

And so he had sat her down on a chair, sat opposite her, his knees touching hers and holding her hands.

"I'm dreadfully, dreadfully sorry," he said, and watched her expression change from concern to alarm.

"I've done something unforgivable. I want to ask you to forgive me first and to tell me you love me as I do you, but that's a coward speaking. I *am* a coward, and I'm not sure you can forgive me." He was stammering now, and her face showed fear.

"It's my father," he said.

"But he's no longer with us. . . ." She looked momentarily less worried, but puzzled.

"He is no longer with us. He is dead. Dead now. But he wasn't dead when I told you he was."

She drew back very slightly and pulled up her wrap.

"He died a few days ago. Very suddenly. I'm so sorry but, you see, there'd been this misunderstanding. No, this *rift*. With a woman I thought I loved, with my father—and I was too hurt and down-right stubborn to make it up." She bent over and took his hand.

"And I went to America and too much time passed and I lied to your father and then I met you and I wanted to marry you so much but couldn't explain to you and—" his voice was hoarse.

"Harry," she said, eventually, and too calmly, though the silence before she reacted seemed an age, "your father's just died. It's a shock. For me too. All of it. Come back to bed. Try to rest. We're both tired. In the morning we'll set it straight. You, me, everything. It's not that it's all right, but we shall have to live with it."

"I'll have to go back," he said. "I'm sorry."

"Of course *we* will go back."

Later, next to her, comforted by her warmth and the familiarity of her, he still couldn't sleep. He hadn't even told her that she was now Lady Sydenham. Most of all, he had let the bigger lie go untold. By the morning he'd have to provide some better account of the family split and his flight from England, and he already knew that he would contrive some story that would evade the truth. Finally he allowed himself to think of his father, handsome, hot-tempered, loving, impatient, and permitted the realization of what was lost to squeeze his heart.

On the Saturday morning, he had asked the hotel to send a telegram to his lawyers and Isabelle. It was a fine day, and he persuaded Marina to take an early walk along the river. Things had, understandably, changed. There was nothing he could identify specifically: Marina conversed, was sympathetic, looked beautiful, and was a dutiful companion, a wife any man might envy. But he was not sure that she was any more than that. He could not measure the gap that had opened up between them; it might be merely a crack, or an unbreachable abyss. What had been comfortable silences now seemed pregnant with what was unsaid.

Nearby, a church bell started to chime and then, a few seconds later, two more, slightly farther away. Harry looked at his watch—it must be later than he thought, but it was not time for the marking of the hour. As some larger and more sonorous bells began to toll continuously, he guessed it must be some religious festival. Groups of men and women were gathering outside small shops and near boats. He and Marina were crossing over a bridge when a young workman came running around the corner and cannoned into Marina. She stumbled, put out a hand, and crashed into the side of the stonework. Harry, thinking she'd had her bag stolen, caught the young man and held him back against the side of the bridge. He quickly realized his mistake as the boy, wide-eyed, put up both his hands in entreaty.

"Pardon, m'sieur, madame, pardon. . . ."

And then, as if to excuse his haste and carelessness, he said in French, "We have mobilized. France has ordered a general mobilization. It is to be war. With the Germans." And he looked somehow excited and fearful. The bells, Harry thought. The damn bells.

He let the boy go, who backed off a little, still apologizing, then ran off toward a group of laborers working on the bridge footings, shouting to them. They all stopped work, and one yelled *"Vive la France! Aux armes, mes frères!"*

Harry turned to Marina. "They're at war," he said. "Or will be within days." It felt unreal and over-dramatic, as if they were spectators at some show that was not at all the one they had expected to see. Then, more practically, he said: "For every reason, we need to go to England as soon as possible."

Back at the hotel, the elegant foyer, with its thick carpets and heavy flower arrangements, its burnished columns and quietly competent concierge, had turned into a circus of competing voices. Every other British and American guest also wanted to leave immediately. All that time, the bells tolled.

"Is there any answer to my cable?"

The clerk just shrugged.

"It's not the troubles," Harry said. "My father has just died. Please, I need to return very urgently."

"I have a cab waiting," said an English voice. A well-dressed man was standing next to him, looking calm but determined. "Wilding," he said, and held out his hand. "It was taking us to the Gare du Nord, but I've heard it's impossible to catch a train and the driver has agreed to take us all the way to the coast for the boat. He comes from the Pas de Calais and is eager to return home. I'm traveling with my wife and daughter, but we can take you with us if you wish. With only a small amount of luggage, I'm afraid." He turned to Marina and smiled. "No doubt the hotel will store extra trunks until things have quieted down."

The journey had been cramped and uncomfortable, but their companions' conversation had helped pass the time. They, too, hoped for an onward ship to America. Wilding was evidently a very successful businessman with engineering factories across the continent. The family was returning from a holiday on the Swiss lakes. At the docks, a British officer boarded the train with two French gendarmes. They had an incomplete list of passengers and were checking them off by examining papers.

"They want to see if there are any Germans," their new friend said with a shrug. "They won't be welcome in England now." After a brief pause and with a forced naturalness, he added: "I am myself half German, but fortunately not the half that provides my surname. Indeed, my sister was, until her death, married to a very English parson and my nephew is an organ scholar at Gloucester Cathedral." He gave them one of his open smiles. "You can't have better credentials than that, I feel. Nevertheless, I should feel happier to be in America for the duration of whatever is to come, and fortunately I have tickets for our onward voyage." He looked at Marina. "For my wife's sake, most of all. And my boys. Both at Harrow. No good having a father who has a connection with the enemy."

"The Germans aren't *our* enemy," Harry said. "Our King's grandfather was German. The Kaiser is his cousin." But he knew he was being disingenuous.

"Not yet our official enemy. But you know as well as I do that they *will* be, of course. It's been coming for years."

The officer reached them. He was about the same age as Harry. "Do you think there'll be war?" Mrs. Wilding asked, over-hastily. "I mean with us?"

The British officer looked surprised, though she could not have been the only person to ask him this.

"I think it is likely," he said in a matter-of-fact way as he examined their papers. "We are bound to France by treaty." He sounded businesslike, his opinion lacking the drama of every other speculative conversation Harry had heard. But then the man was presumably a regular; war was his profession.

"But we are much more like the Germans than any other nationality," Mrs. Wilding said. "I mean, don't you think?"

The officer only nodded as he eyed both the Wildings for a few seconds before walking on.

"My papers give my birthplace as Bremen," Wilding said.

Later in the journey, Wilding and Harry had stood smoking on deck, watching as the cliffs of Dover seemed to grow a little closer. "It will be difficult for you," Harry said. "You'll have decisions ahead. And none of your choosing. I don't envy you."

"You too," Wilding said. "You may live in America, but you are British. War will break out. Look around you." He gestured out over the black waters. "The British could never let Germany conquer France, not least because they could then control the English Channel and that would cut Britain off. You might yet find yourself taking up arms."

Harry started to laugh but was stopped by the expression on Wilding's face.

"You have been too polite to ask me my business. What I make in my factories," Wilding said. "How I became a wealthy man."

"A British trait." This time Harry did laugh. "In America they'll have no such reticence. They'll want to know how and how much."

"I manufacture arms. It is strange, because I am very much a city man. I do not like shooting game or hunting. I abhor it,

killing things, although in English society I keep that thought
to myself. But arms were my father's business, and now they are
mine. What we are making now—the capacity for slaughtering
men—is beyond even our generals' imaginings."

"Does our Navy have the edge on the Germans, do you
think?" Harry said, conscious of having to make a decision as
to whether Wilding was included in "our" or in "the Germans."

"It won't be a naval war. Whatever the British believe, or rather
hope. Not dreadnoughts. Not cavalry with gleaming swords. This
will be about the land, about earth. About infantry. Most of all,
it will be about guns. New, powerful guns." He looked grave.
"Guns that can fire at invisible targets and men who will be killed
by weapons they cannot see.

"America will keep itself out, I expect, unless its interests
are seriously compromised. President Wilson will see to it.
But you—and I—we can't necessarily count on avoiding it all.
Not because of our possibly ambiguous loyalties, nor where we
choose to live."

Harry thought he was wrong, but Wilding was in the business
and he had no inclination to challenge him. Harry had made his
choices: America, marriage, and Marina. Europe was making its
choices, or being forced to, but he was no longer part of Europe.
His loyalties lay across the Atlantic.

When they disembarked in Dover the customs officer told them,
in some agitation, that Germany had declared war on France. The
country whose great and beautiful capital Harry had strolled in just
a day earlier, the country that lay so few miles to the south, that
was visible across the Channel on a clear day, was under attack.
He thought of the tense clerk at the hotel desk, the affable waiters
who had served them in Nice, the carrier who had borne them
to Calais, and the young workman, hardly more than a boy, who
had told them of mobilization, and he wondered how quickly they
would be scooped up into a war France could never win.

A chauffeur was waiting to take the Wildings to Hampshire, and Harry and Marina were proceeding to London by train. As it carried them north to Victoria, across the timeless chalky sweep of the downs, he was glad Marina was reading. He tried to process a confusion of thoughts. He was returning to England for the first time in a decade, and its very familiarity, and the lack of change in everything around him, suddenly compressed all those years. His chest was tight with emotions he thought he had mastered, and he was conscious of an odd intensity of recognition: of everything from the smell of the train to the landscape about him. Marina, who was his wife and had been so known, was suddenly and unnervingly foreign: she was a New Yorker, visiting the Old World; he was part of this world, and she was not.

The last time he had made this journey, he had been consumed by an urgent hunger for Isabelle and the terror of losing her. It had been only a fantasy of love, and lust that he had believed was love, all so bound up with betrayal that he now recalled it as tainted. Even the thought of her with tangled hair and abandoned limbs, or her sweetness, as it had seemed then, as she rested her cheek on his or stroked his hair, only made him angry with his youth and poor judgment.

They stayed at the Savoy, and there was relief in being free of the febrile atmosphere of Paris. He wondered: would the British honor their promise to France? At what cost to themselves? He found that he still liked to think of Britain as an honorable country.

Yet in the dining room the next morning, leaving Marina to breakfast in their room, he could tell immediately from how the staff held themselves, from the tension and movement of fellow guests, that something new had happened. The Germans had entered Belgium, and now the British government had issued an ultimatum.

He thought of Wilding. This time tomorrow, Britain would be at war, there was no doubt of it, and he would be at his father's graveside in what was, now, his estate. *The old order changeth*, he thought. How dreadfully and appropriately inauspicious the timing was.

He and Marina went to Regent Street, to buy her a black dress, gloves, and hat. London was crowded, more so than he remembered. As Marina looked at black gloves, he tried to grasp the fact that this was for a funeral, his father's funeral. That the handsome, charismatic man who, even unseen, had such a hold on his imagination was now gone forever. He would never be seen again; he was sealed in his coffin, he was history. He found his emotions changing swiftly from sadness to disbelief to humor. On the streets, with the shops draped in Union Jacks and some of the women wearing red, blue, and white cockades on their hats, it felt more as if a vast summer fête was in progress.

From the moment they had woken up on the day of the funeral, he thought that he should simply take Marina's hand in his and tell her everything. A greater catastrophe waited if he did not. Yet, hours later, they had passed through the town nearest to his estate and still he had said nothing. Instead he tried to reassure himself. Isabelle was now the dowager, but, as he had no intention of taking on the house and would return to New York as soon as was decent, much of his life could continue unchanged. Surely it could.

Finally, there was Abbotsgate, appearing far more quickly than it should have. The car was running up the drive, and there on the steps were Hopkins the butler and Mrs. Fawkes the housekeeper.

The hired chauffeur stepped out, opened the door, and, just as he had known he would, Hopkins stepped forward and said, "Sir Henry, Lady Sydenham. Welcome home, sir. We are all so sorry that it is in such very sad circumstances, sir."

Just as he'd known she would, Marina shot him a look of bewilderment, shock, and deep hurt. For a second she stood stock-still, staring at him as if he were a complete and unwelcome stranger. Which, he supposed, he now was. As they moved side by side into the house, he touched her arm, but she made no response.

His stepmother was there in the cool of the Great Hall, and beside her Edward, smiling tentatively. Behind them was a portrait of his father in hunting pink.

"Isabelle," Harry said, first shaking her hand and then kissing her awkwardly. In her black dress, her skin was almost colorless. Inevitably she looked much older than he remembered her, though still beautiful.

She attempted a smile as she stepped forward and then said "We're so very glad you're home." Then, blinking, on the edge of tears, "I'm so terribly sorry. We had no warning—he had complained of indigestion but no more," as if she had failed in a responsibility to look after his father.

Edward looked anxiously from her to Harry.

"This is Teddy," she said, just as Harry said "This is my wife Marina." It was as if both women, both once his, were strangers, not just to each other, but to him.

Marina and Isabelle shook hands. "I'm so sorry for your loss," Marina said, her accent so American and her smile so kind. She turned to Teddy. "My, aren't you the image of your brother. I don't have a brother myself, so I'm very glad indeed to find I have a brother-in-law." Teddy shook her hand, apparently both curious and delighted. He looked lively despite his mother's distress and the loss of his father.

They were shown to their room, large and overlooking the park, by a young maid. Marina had behaved perfectly: friendly, sympathetic, and dignified; but once the door shut, she turned away from him and moved to the window, not speaking.

"Marina. . . ." He had had no idea how to begin to deal with the situation he had known from the minute he had opened the letter. He had known this would happen from the first time he realized he wanted to marry her, at the Aquarium, and yet he had failed to tell her anything about his background except in generalities, which he could never have gotten away with had she been an Englishwoman.

"So how many other lies have you told me?" She spoke in a cooler tone than he'd ever heard from her, although with a tremor that belied her external self-control.

"Not lies—"

"Oh, Harry, I had expected more of you. Lies, omissions, convenient forgetfulness. What else will I find out about my marriage and my husband if I wait long enough?"

"I just didn't want—"

She was staring at him, fierce and unreachable. "I don't know what's going on here. I don't know why you abandoned these perfectly nice people—because clearly that's what you did. Maybe your relationship with your father was difficult. It often works out like that. Maybe you just didn't want to deal with it. But it feels as if you just wanted the easy life. You thought you could come to America with your mother's money, leave any responsibilities behind you, marry an American wife, young enough, knowing nothing about your country home, to accept your vague accounts of your childhood and. . . ." Her thoughts echoed his, but she was shaking her head in disbelief. "One thing is certain. We can never tell my father. He admires you, trusts you, and you lied to him in circumstances where he might have expected total honesty."

"No, that's not how it was—" he began, but it hit him that it was almost entirely how it was. "I'm sorry," he said. How inadequate.

After a very long silence, she said, politely, as if to a stranger, "And your brother—"

"Half-brother—"

"Your *half*-brother," she repeated sarcastically, "he's, what, eleven years old?"

"Twelve."

"He's twelve years old," she said, nodding to herself. "He doesn't have any other brothers and sisters, I assume?"

Harry shook his head.

"So you abandoned him too? He can't know why you vanished out of his life," she said, sounding less angry now, more sad and perplexed. "Maybe he had a hard time with your father too. If he was a difficult man, maybe a big brother would have helped him."

"It wasn't that," Harry interrupted. "It wasn't like that."

"Well, what was it like, *Sir* Henry? Or can I expect that if we go through hard times, you'll run away from me too? Perhaps it's a habit. . . ."

She was close to tears. He desperately wanted to hold her and tell it was all right. But it wasn't.

"I don't want to cry," she said. "It's not my day for crying. It's your father's funeral, and the tears must be your stepmother's and Edward's. I don't want to look as if I've been weeping. But later I need to know. I'm a city girl. If you have some plan of coming back here to be a squire on a horse with yellow teeth with peasants doffing their hats, I need to be told. I liked being Mrs. Harry Sydenham. I don't at all want to be Lady Sydenham."

"Marina—" he said and then stopped. In New York society, most girls would fall all over themselves to gain an English title, and here was Marina, furious at finding herself the wife of a baronet.

"I do so love you," he said.

"Then give me the truth," she said. "Later, after the funeral. Never, ever lie to me again."

CHAPTER TWELVE

Benedict, London,
August 1914

BENEDICT TRIED TO CONCENTRATE ON *The Times* and put everything else out of his mind on the journey home; he was exhausted by his own emotions. Sun shone through the smeared windows of the train and fine silvery dust was suspended in the light. Theo sat, his eyes on his book, *The Riddle of the Sands*, which he'd been enthusing about on their journey up. Benedict noticed how rarely he turned a page and how hot and uncomfortable he looked. In Gloucester, Theo appeared worldly; but in London he had at first seemed younger, excitable yet out of his depth, and then, since the disastrous expedition to Regent Street, subdued to the point of disconnection. He was, Benedict was certain, horribly humiliated by what had occurred, and he wondered which of them most wished it had not.

But where Theo had given in to a moment of temptation, a moment where his longing and his impulsive nature had come together and brought him close to disaster, Benedict was preoccupied with his own, impossibly inaccessible, much more terrible desires. In London he had seen a life of opportunity, of risk. At any point, in a matter of minutes, he thought, he could have vanished out of sight, become a different man. By day he had dwelled on the music and the secret of senses without boundaries, which he was increasingly sure the Russian composer understood perfectly. By night he lay in bed and remembered the youths he had seen hovering about Piccadilly Circus and the man, that man, on the bus.

The newspaper he'd bought at Paddington was a special edition. Things were moving so fast on the Continent that the news was already out of date. Tomorrow, the next day, or next week, they would be at war. He glanced up and the outskirts of London were just the same: small lives, shabby houses, little businesses: the foundations of an empire. He looked down at the tall dark headlines that threatened it all. The printers' ink stained his damp hands.

Theo threw his book aside.

"Look, we're carrying on as if I was a chancer who'd stolen a kiss and you were a well-mannered and very chaste maiden." He was speaking fast as he sometimes did when he was drunk, although he was sober now.

Benedict began to protest but Theo went on determinedly. "I am sorry. I am truly sorry and embarrassed and anything else you want me to be. Perhaps I'm just a bad character, but I can't bear any more of this politeness. I mean, we're chums. We've each been all the other's had in the face of the sheer ghastliness of choir practice and lunchtime recitals and endless pernickety exercises. Of living in Gloucester forever."

Benedict found himself halfway to a smile. "Actually, I wasn't thinking about anything much."

Theo was running his long fingers through his hair. The sun was in his eyes and he crinkled them against the light. Benedict stood up and pulled the blind halfway down.

"It's all right. It really is all right," he said. "Of course we're friends. You made a mistake—"

"Oh for God's sake," Theo said. "You know it wasn't a mistake. I'm a thief. A failed thief. If you're my friend, then that's the sort of friend you've got. And now I'm at your mercy—my reputation, in Gloucester at least, is in your hands."

Benedict inhaled deeply. Sat back. Looked at Theo, uncertain whether he was sincere or acting, whether he was on the edge of tears or laughter, and wanting, more than anything, to take Theo in his arms. To make it all right. To bury his face in that tawny hair and breathe in the smell of Theo. Just to run a finger along the curve of Theo's mouth: the line that separated the rough afternoon stubble from the softest skin of Theo's lips. To peel a lip back and touch the blunt edge of his lower teeth. To feel what he could see daily. He couldn't allow himself to think further. There was a sort of terror in imagining even this much, and an even greater terror that one day he might respond to the dreadful hunger in himself.

"And *you've* got a friend who spends his days being something he's not," he said. "Who isn't sure there's a God. No, who's damn sure there isn't, yet who sits at an organ playing psalms and hymns, knowing his closest friend is infinitely, unimaginably better at playing the organ than he'll ever be."

Theo's face lit up. "Two days in London, one mad Russian," he said, "and you're a changed man."

The train shuddered over two sets of points. Theo gazed out of the window. He was like quicksilver, Benedict thought, his attention and ideas always changing shape and direction, his enthusiasms contagious. His hands lay limply on his lap, the book flat, the bony knuckles on boyish, long fingers that were capable of creating such beauty, the nails a little grubby.

"Are you going to get engaged to Agnes?" he said, more to focus his own thoughts.

Theo looked amused and rueful. "I think so. Though not yet. Soon. I mean, to be honest, I think I've rushed things a bit. It was a sort of joke, but Agnes doesn't really understand jokes and her mother certainly doesn't." He sat back again, sticking his legs out so his calf almost touched Benedict's. "I can't afford a ring and I haven't said to a word to Father. Mind you, a bishop's daughter—he'd not be likely to be against it. Might even give me some money. Or one of my poor mama's rings. If he hasn't given them to my various prospective new mamas."

"When are you going to tell him?"

"She's pretty enough, don't you think?" Theo went on as if he hadn't heard.

"She's very pretty. You're a lucky man." He wondered if Theo had ever spoken to Agnes about his plan.

"Don't laugh at me, Ben. I know you're a better man than me. But actually I'm beginning to think I just can't face another two years of Gloucester. I used to dream, sometimes, of signing on as crew down at the docks. Letting my lily-white hands grow gnarled and brown. Sail away to the South Sea Islands. *I must go down to the seas again, for the call of the running tide, is a wild call and a clear call that may not be denied,* and all that." He looked down at his hands. "But most of the boats were going to Liverpool. The longest journey was only taking pig iron to Antwerp. I could deny that quite easily."

He picked up his book again and opened it unconvincingly. He looked up almost immediately and, as he sat forward, as if about to admit Benedict to a great secret, finally their legs touched and Benedict could feel the warmth of Theo's through his trousers.

Theo's eyes were very slightly narrowed and the air of restlessness became one of suppressed excitement.

"But now, you see, I've got an idea. Things are changing. Every day. We're at war, or as good as. I don't want to miss out."

He eyed Benedict as if to gauge how his speech was being received.

"I like the organ, strange beast that it is, I like the music when I'm allowed to play anything halfway decent, but sometimes I feel like an old man sitting there. In ten or twenty years' time, my life would be just the same—thud, thud, thud, cold, stiff fingers on Christmas Day, slippery and sweating in July, except with Agnes grown stout and a brood of squealing infants we couldn't afford. As soon as we're at war, I'd rather join up, rather be part of it than spend decades with Stainer or banging out *Ur-bide with Meeee.*"

"Your father—"

"My father. My father—if I took a commission, I wouldn't be in thrall to my father. I'd be paid as a subaltern."

"Are you serious?"

"Of course I am. You can't think of one thing against it."

"Actually, I can. Though I can see what you're saying. But who says any regiment will take you?"

"*Us*, Benedict," he said, and his smile was so transparent, so hopeful, that Benedict was silenced, in anger and excitement. How dare Theo think that he, Benedict, would go to war just because he asked? How dare he?

And yet. And yet.

CHAPTER THIRTEEN
Harry, England,
August 1914

FOR THE LAST FEW DAYS, he and Marina had been traveling just ahead
of war—or running away, really, Harry thought—but at Abbotsgate
they had come to a standstill while the war moved inexorably toward
them, gathering speed. The British ultimatum had been sent and gone
unanswered; at eleven o'clock this evening, there would be a formal
declaration of hostilities. Politicians and military commanders were
poised over their long-devised plans. Everybody knew it.

At Abbotsgate, time was briefly suspended. The rituals were
observed: the obituary in *The Times,* a crowded funeral in the
ancient church, the heartfelt obsequies: his father had been much
liked, his death premature; but even back at the house, as they
held their delicate cups of tea, the black-clad guests talked, quietly
at first, of little else but the approaching conflict.

118

The Lord Lieutenant stood on the terrace, talking to Harry and a neighbor. "The local militia is ready," said the Lord Lieutenant, "and there's been a surge in recruits."

"While we were in Paris we watched the French mobilization," Harry said. "It was quite . . ."—he searched for a word—". . . quite quick. And quite chilling."

And it had been, in its simplicity. On every street corner, posters went up in hours. Men had left their jobs. Dinner was chaos with too few waiters; banks remained closed, despite the clamor of Parisians and foreigners at the doors, but the bank workers had gone. There were queues at recruitment offices, and men marching badly in their everyday working clothes, led by corporals in caps, red pantaloons, and blue jackets.

"It's their territory that the Germans will invade within hours, of course," said a neighboring landowner with connections to the government. "I imagine we British would be pretty keen to keep the Kaiser out of our country. And the French were humiliated by the Germans in living memory. But there'll be a bill before parliament here in days. Recruitment. We're not up to strength even with the territorials. The Germans have every man under forty-five in their reserves, every one of them trained as a soldier."

He was blunt and weathered; even as a very young man, Harry had thought he was cleverer than he let on.

"You'll stay?" the Lord Lieutenant said to Harry, and it was just barely a question.

"If there's war?" Harry was surprised.

"To take over the estate. Your estate. But yes, to war too. Will you take a commission?"

"I hadn't thought about it," Harry said. It was not the entire truth: the possibility, vague enough not to be too unsettling, had crossed his mind when he was talking to Wilding. "Anyway, I doubt they'll need me and I don't think they'd want me. I'm not very young, I've been living in America a long time, my wife is American."

"It depends on how many volunteers we get and how long the war goes on."

In the word "volunteers," Harry felt the slightest reproach. "Your father was a great cavalry officer in his youth, of course," said their neighbor.

"He'd have been sorry to miss this fight," said the Lord Lieutenant.

Harry looked for a way to deflect them both. "A friend of mine, a military man," another half-lie, although Wilding was indubitably some kind of expert, "says it will be an infantry war."

"Our cavalry and navy are the best in the world," said the Lord Lieutenant.

Harry was going to speak, but then his neighbor said, more firmly, "And artillery can destroy a cavalry charge in minutes. But yes, we have our expensive dreadnoughts. If the war stays at sea."

Marina and Teddy materialized at his side and the whole awkward conversation was diluted by their presence, although not before the Lord Lieutenant had said "My dear Lady Sydenham," taking Marina's hand and then holding it for slightly too long. "What a superb addition you and Harry will make to local society."

The long day faded. It was exhausting, Harry thought, just responding to polite condolences, overhearing local gossip that meant nothing to him, or being taken back to his childhood by the well-meaning and the curious. He both longed for and dreaded their departure and being alone with his wife. All the time, Marina was perfect: kind, serious, interested. Again and again, friends of his father's and their wives told him how lucky he was. She was the same to him. No more intimate than with the mass of strangers she was confronted with. Teddy was helping the cook, Marina said she wanted to lie down, and Harry wandered back to the church.

The family graves were together by the main door. His grandparents, a sister who had died in infancy, and his mother, her grave bordered in granite. A bunch of yellow roses had been laid on the plot. Under a weeping angel, the letters spelling out *Maude Alice Sydenham, 1855–1887*, were softening now. The lichen on the stone measured the distance since her death. Finally he stood by his father's grave, the fresh, warm earth half disguised by a bank of already-weary wreaths. He wasn't sure whether or not he was praying.

He felt as much as heard footsteps and looked up to see Isabelle. She was bareheaded, her wiry black hair loosely gathered at her neck. She came and stood next to him and was silent for a while. Looking down, he focused on her feet, the black stockings and buttoned shoes just visible below her dark hem.

Eventually she said "I'm sorry you had to return like this. But glad you could be here."

"Did he really have no idea?"

"No. I would have said he was in good health and spirits. We planned a big party for his sixtieth birthday. With dancing." She looked amused and sad all at once. "He was a little tired, perhaps, but then he wasn't as young as he'd been."

"Has Teddy taken it all right?"

She shrugged slightly. "Who knows with twelve-year-old boys?" She gave a small laugh. "But I think so, although he loved his father and brought him great happiness, I think."

"Whereas I brought him nothing of the kind." It was a statement, not a question, but she answered immediately.

"What do you want me to say? That it was all right? That he didn't miss you, want to see you? That he understood?"

"No, of course not."

"You were his heir," she said. "His first-born. Of course he was sad. But it was superficially comprehensible, even admirable; you'd shown initiative, gone to America. It was the sort of life he might have dreamed of himself. And you wrote from time to time, to start with, anyway. . . ."

He flushed.

"But he knew you could come back. That was the hard part. To start with, he expected it would be in a year or two. But he always made excuses for you, even to himself, I think."

"If you want me to feel guilty," he said, "I can assure you that I do."

She touched him briefly on the arm. "Don't," she said.

"You think it's an indulgence to talk of guilt now?"

"I think it's pointless." After a further silence when she looked into the distance with her eyes screwed up against the setting sun, she said "I know about guilt, Harry, believe me. I lived with him for well over a decade. And you think I betrayed you, too."

"It's all history," he said. "Ancient history. I expect you loved him—"

"No," she said, her voice slightly raised. "I didn't. Not at first, although I liked him very much. He was a good man, an amusing man, and, in time, especially when Teddy was born, I came to love him."

"But you didn't love me."

"For heaven's sake, you sound like a petulant boy. Yes, I loved you. But you were twenty; I was older than you."

"By four years. Nothing."

"I'd had a life by then," she said. "I'd been married, widowed. Life was very difficult."

He remembered how exotic he'd thought her difficulties. A woman with a past. Isabelle was an actress, classically trained in Paris. He'd been introduced to her by a friend who'd met her at an after-theatre supper party, and all three of them had spent a foolish afternoon in Hyde Park on the Serpentine, rowing in circles and noisily showing off for this woman of the world. They were both a bit scared of her, he thought, neither daring to see her alone. She always wore the same dress, with black dots on white and a blue sash, and it had never entered his head that this was because she had no money. Nor would she tell him exactly where she lived, waving her hand and laughing when the subject came up. Finally he'd followed her home from the theatre to a grim street. She was embarrassed, even injured, he thought, when he'd caught up with her. But she'd invited him in and he'd seen how she'd turned two tiny rooms into a retreat. A photograph of a man, evidently playing Hamlet, was, he assumed, her late husband. Another, less formal pose revealed him to have had a splendid moustache.

She had followed his glance. "He was ill for so long," she said. "He didn't look like that in his last year."

She poured him a brandy, then sat on a footstool, and they had talked and talked. She had no close family—only a cousin who was another widow, "even poorer than I am, and she has a child to support, poor woman."

When her current run at the Lyceum was finished, she would need to decide whether to return to France or not. It was entirely a financial matter. Then he'd thought, clumsy with youth, that he could give her money. His mother had left him a substantial sum, and it had been well invested.

Later, she'd read to him from Molière. She'd agreed he could return, and the next time he had read her Lord Tennyson's *The Lady of Shalott*, and she'd clapped when he finished, and she had recited French sonnets from memory. The next time he arrived, she looked solemn. She took his hand—he remembered the marvelous feeling of her cool, soft fingers—and led him not to the usual chair but to the bedroom. He sat on the edge of the bed as she very carefully removed her boots, her belt, her stockings, and then indicated that he should unhook her dress. It fell to her waist and she stepped out of its skirts. She looked at him, briefly, as if to check that what was happening was all right, then unlaced her chemise and folded every article carefully and with excruciating slowness, it had seemed to him. Finally she'd pulled two or three pins out of her hair. Naked, she was—like her dress—all contrast: very white and very dark. He had never seen anything so beautiful, or so thrilling, in his life.

She had given him a smile—not a confident one. "Do you like it?" she said.

123

And when she had finally helped him take his own clothes off—an everyday task at which he was suddenly all clumsiness—and pushed him down gently, she said, very politely, "You are a virgin."

"No," he'd lied. "Not really."

As he explored her with delight and a desperate curiosity, he was astonished by how much pleasure he seemed to give her. He was nervous that it would all end too soon, but she guided him inside her almost immediately and seemed to encourage him to reach a climax, but then she held him and murmured "How I've missed this." He supposed they slept a while before he felt her touching him and he took her again, much more in control but just as excited and amazed by her. She cried out in French as her thighs tightened around him, which he found unbearably arousing—she was somewhere else, in her own world—and that made their intimacy all the more thrilling. His face was buried in her hair and he kissed her, feeling that he wanted to become part of her.

Later she had gone to her tiny kitchen. He could hear her splashing herself with water. When she returned with a drink for him, she said "I miss my husband very much. You made me very happy."

Now, a mature man, he realized that it had been a warning; but then he had had no idea that a woman might long for a man or that love might not be equal or straightforward, and he had just laughed in a sort of nervous relief. When he stood up, naked before her, he had echoed her words: "You like it?"

This time she had given him a broad smile, her cheeks dimpling, and nodded. When he was dressed, she put her hand over his. "Soon I shall go back to France," she said.

"No. No!" he almost shouted. "Why?" He felt a sense of panic.

"Silly boy," she said. "Because I need to work. There is a part possibly for me in Lyons. The theatre there is very good. If not, I have an offer—a less good part, it is true—in Paris."

He was on the point of telling her he loved her and saying he could support her, but realized just in time the crassness of either comment. To offer his love as a reason for her to stay in poverty was an insult, and it would have been even more of an insult to offer her money when she'd just given herself to him. But eventually, he'd thought, as he walked back to Hyde Park, he would declare both of these things. He was filled with terror at the idea of her going and delirious with how she moved and smelled, and her appetite for him.

He'd invited her to Abbotsgate because she didn't seem to have many friends. His father was unconventional in his friends and infinitely welcoming. It was, Harry sometimes thought, partly because he was bored in the country.

She hadn't wanted to come at first. "Don't be silly, Harry. Your father will think you intend to marry me and will have apoplexy."

But he'd persuaded her by pointing out that she was about to leave England and, just as he'd seen her home, he wanted her to see his. And by asking three other friends, all of whom she knew. "See. Uneven numbers," he'd said. "And my father will have friends down too. Probably dull ones, but you'll enchant them."

What he'd not considered was how potentially cruel it was to flaunt the vast inequality of their circumstances by taking her there; but if she was humiliated by this, she didn't show it. She was, he thought later and ruefully, an actress. There was no question that she'd amused his father, and he remembered feeling proud that his father had taken a friend of his seriously. They'd ended the evening singing and playing the piano. At one point his father had played, rather badly, and Isabelle had sung, rather well, a French ballad, *"Auprès de ma blonde."* After applause and some table-thumping, from his friends and from a visiting couple his father had met the year before in Baden-Baden, they had all sung songs from *The Pirates of Penzance.* At one point, Harry had thought that the four years Isabelle had on him made her seem

125

closer to the married couple than to his younger friends, two of whom were now quite drunk.

"Why don't you recite some poetry?" he'd said. And then to his father, "She's awfully good."

She'd demurred but had finally been persuaded to do one speech from the play she was in. His father's friends, who had seen the production and loved it, were thrilled.

"What are you appearing in next?" Mrs. Daubeney had asked.

"I am returning to France," Isabelle said with slight awkwardness. "I have a part there. In a very good play."

But his father had jumped in and said "Oh, we can't let you go. It's years since we've made proper use of the piano and it's always impossible to lure Harry home. Surely a woman with your talents would make a perfect Shakespearean heroine here in England?"

She had smiled, but Harry felt embarrassed by his father's ignorance of the world of the theatre or even of what it was like to be poor. He lay awake afterward, wanting her badly, wondering if he dared tiptoe up to her room, or whether she, who so often took the initiative, might come to his, but eventually he must have fallen asleep and was awoken in the morning by a maid knocking on the door.

Isabelle had been hard to reach over the following two or three weeks. He had even gone to her lodgings, but she was never in. He'd left a note at the theatre, knowing that the play's run would end in days. She answered, affectionately, but explaining that she was very busy with arrangements for her departure. He longed to see her, but his dreams were of her body and her magical transformation from her usual modest demeanor to an almost wanton pleasure in making love. Was it because she was French, he had wondered? Were there English girls like her?

A month after their evening in Abbotsgate, his world fell apart. His father wrote to him, a letter shot through with happiness as well as his customary enthusiasm. He was going to remarry. He had been lonely for so long, he said, and Harry felt a twinge of guilt. But, his father had continued, although he must seem very ancient to Harry, he was not an old man. Now he had met a woman who had changed everything, and they were to be married as soon as possible. Harry was astonished. He'd had no idea his father had a woman in his life. His father had, he said almost boyishly, never been so happy—a slightly insensitive reflection on his time with his own mother, Harry had thought—but he was still amused by his father's impetuosity. He turned over the page. So, his father concluded, he had Harry to thank for introducing him to Madame Isabelle Dessonnes, and he knew that Harry would welcome her as his stepmother and the new Lady Sydenham. They both hoped they would see him at Abbotsgate as soon as he could get away.

He had raged. For three nights he had drunk until he felt sick. He felt like a fool, utterly betrayed by his father and his lover. He wanted to cry to relieve the massive tightness that knotted his muscles. It was obscene: she was young; his father was in his late forties. She must have seen an opportunity for protection and wealth, and for that she'd sing to the old man and let him paw her. Well, that was only what she deserved. That was the tradeoff. He could have given her money himself. But not a title, of course: what an extraordinary elevation for a young foreign widow and struggling actress. He wrote accusing letters to his father, revealing everything, and burned them all.

And so it had gone on in misery, in jealousy, and finally in coldness. He eventually wrote to his father, wishing him well, without warmth, and regretting that he could not come to the wedding as he been an offered a position in America. His father had written back, anxiously, saying he realized it was difficult for Harry with his understandable loyalty to his dead mother, and the speed with which they had made their decision, but he was not a young man and he hoped Harry still wished them happiness. Harry had not replied and had left for New York ten days later, by which time his father and Isabelle were man and wife. Not long afterward, his father wrote to say Isabelle was pregnant; but only a little later a further letter followed, announcing the arrival of his brother. "Far too early, far too small," but, his father reported, "a game little chap who struggled through after worrying us all for a few weeks." He was, his father said, the very image of Harry as a baby.

Harry counted the weeks. He knew to the night when he had last possessed Isabelle in the hours before they left for Abbotsgate, and he knew of propriety preserved by claiming a miraculously short pregnancy yet a viable child. What a fool his father had been. What a fool Isabelle had made of them both.

Now, yet again a widow, she stood beside Harry in the cemetery and wept.

"What will become of me?" she said. He knew in that instant that she had indeed loved his father, or come to love him, but he chose the easier answer.

"You and Teddy must go on as you are."

"You mustn't leave us," she said. "I mean, yes, your life is in America. But this time you must come back often. Please, Harry. If anything should happen to me, Teddy would be quite alone. I beg you, if you want no relationship with me, please start one with Teddy."

He felt ashamed, not wanting to deal with this now. She added, smiling now, but still with wet cheeks, "He already hero-worships you from the tales your father told of you. A naughtier, braver, more mischievous son never lived, the way your father told it."

"Teddy seems a very nice chap." He cursed himself for his clumsiness.

"We were lucky," she said, and happiness returned briefly to her face. "He's a jolly, uncomplicated boy, full of curiosity, friends with everybody. He wants to be a gamekeeper when he grows up, or be very rich and breed horses."

"I will do my very best by you and Teddy," he said. "My very, very best. With this war—it may not be easy here."

"This hateful war," she said, and he could still, just, hear her French accent. "But America will not involve itself; you can come to us on American ships and be safe; and besides, a war, however bad, does not last long, whereas Teddy will live for many years, I hope. Write. Tell us of New York. Bears. If you see bears, I think Teddy would be very happy."

"Perhaps you would both come and visit us?"

She nodded.

"Not many bears in Central Park, but I could arrange a camping expedition into the mountains," he said, finding that the idea of showing Teddy the hugeness of the American wilderness was suddenly exciting. "Sleep under the stars by some great rapids. See bison, bears, yes, rattlesnakes—"

Now she was at least trying to laugh, but she paused. "Does Marina know that we were once, that we . . . ?" She was unembarrassed and looked at him steadily, although it had never been mentioned between them since the last, vile letter he'd written to her.

He shook his head. "Better not," he said, hoping his reaction wasn't just pragmatic. "Too late now. Too complicated."

And probably fatal for his marriage, he thought. He looked up. The long day was turning into a fine, soft evening.

War

Owing to the summary rejection by the German Government of the request made by his Majesty's Government for assurances that the neutrality of Belgium would be respected, His Majesty's Ambassador in Berlin has received his passport and his Majesty's Government has declared to the German Government that a state of war exists between Great Britain and Germany as from 11 P.M.

FOREIGN OFFICE STATEMENT,
AUGUST 4, 1914

CHAPTER FOURTEEN
Benedict, England, September 1914

BENEDICT HAD NOT NOTICED THAT autumn was coming until he leaned out of his bedroom window on that last day. It was a hazy, golden morning: swaths of cobwebs on the vicarage shrubbery, the thick grass damp and the leaves of the horse chestnut edged in rust. The view had been the same as it had every year of Benedict's life, but the certainties of those earlier autumns had now been put aside. It had been a difficult weekend at home, yet he had felt elated by the tension, as if the distance between him and his family was widening and in that breadth was freedom. His father had been perplexed, angry, and then, obviously, frightened. It was enough that the small, safe world in which he lived had been threatened by good German Protestants, now that his only son—whose musical accomplishments had made him so proud, whose place at the cathedral was something he thanked God for, daily, in his prayers—was throwing away all he had achieved.

"There won't be any organs in the Army," he had said. "You won't be able to practice, you know. All this God-given talent thrown aside. What kind of a soldier do you think you'll make? Do you think this is God's purpose for you?"

And so it had gone on: the pointless conversations in the cold study after church, his father's insistence that they pray together for guidance, and later, at tea, his mother clinging to him as if his death was certain. As they walked in the yard over wet yellow leaves, his sister had given him a rueful smile and a little squeeze of the arm.

"Do you know when you'll be going?" she said.

"I'm volunteering with Theo. It was his idea."

"Of course. It has the feeling of one of your friend Theo's grand schemes." But there was light observation, not harshness, in her words. "What is he escaping this time?"

"Gloucester. Organs. A woman called Agnes Bradstock. God, for all I know." He laughed, as he only ever did with Lettie. "Or for all God knows, I suppose."

"Miss Bradstock? The bishop's daughter? Goodness." Now she too was amused. "He'll need to be sure to be sent overseas. India, at the very least."

"We're planning on joining the artillery. I can't ride a horse; I think I'm seasick, so no Navy. The Gloucesters were a possibility, but Theo is desperate to get his hands on machinery. A big gun would do. It seems somehow. . . ." He paused to think just what it seemed. "Better. More important. It seems more important now, to me, to be useful, and I think I might be quite a good gunner."

He also wondered whether it would be easier to fire at targets he didn't have to see.

"I'm glad you will have a friend with you," Lettie said. "You can watch out for each other. And who knows, you may just do a bit of training in a camp and then come home, war over, and even if you aren't awfully good at shooting, you're bound to be the best at marching. And very handsome in uniform." After a long pause, she added, quietly, "I wish I could go too."

He surprised both of them by reaching out and holding her close for a second, yet feeling, deep down, that there was a terrible dishonesty in the gulf between what she thought she knew and loved about him and what he knew about himself.

Theo was delayed in returning because of some unspecified crisis at home, so Benedict went alone to the Army interview, accounted awkwardly for Theo's absence, given that Theo had actually fixed the appointment, and emerged from an office in a camp near Salisbury to find he had signed various papers and was now, subject to a medical, a second lieutenant in the Royal Field Artillery. A junior officer in Kitchener's New Army.

"Well done, young chap," said the interviewing major. "We need more like you. First class."

He was to await a letter of confirmation and further instructions, allowances for uniform and so on—the major waved a hand as if Benedict knew what was involved, and the sergeant major standing behind him clearly did, as he nodded approvingly.

Benedict hoped Theo's training would still start at the same time as his, but at least the school of gunnery wasn't far away. The major, a cheerful middle-aged territorial, came around the desk and shook his hand enthusiastically. "Do your best by us and we'll do our best by you. *Ubique.* The regimental motto. You'll know what it means."

"*Everywhere.*" Benedict wondered if it was a test.

"Ha. Right. But for you, my boy, mostly the firing ranges on Salisbury Plain." It was obviously a joke he used a lot.

Benedict wrote to his father and had a far easier interview with Dr. Brewer than he'd expected. "Ah, yes," said Brewer. "You and Theodore, I gather."

135

Benedict must have looked surprised, because Brewer went on: "In here not half an hour ago with the news. Well, hard for the cathedral but good for the country. We all have to make sacrifices. Some of us are too old to fight, but 'O that I had wings like a dove, for then would I fly away,' eh?"

Benedict could hardly wait to get back to Theo and share Brewer's rare lapse into sentimentality, but Theo was nowhere to be seen. When he eventually showed back up at their lodgings in the Close, he smelled of alcohol.

"Been down the docks celebrating with Captain Ahab," he said, lying prone on his narrow bed.

"I thought you were stuck at home."

"Didn't want to tell you the splendid news until I was certain."

"Your father let you have the ring for Agnes?"

"Good God, no!" Theo raised his head and looked almost shocked. "Of course not." He seemed to lose his train of thought for a minute. "No. I've been accepted. For a commission."

Benedict found himself beaming, and a certain nagging worry slipped away. "Why, that's marvelous. When do you start? Do you know? I don't yet. Perhaps we'll go to Salisbury together, brother gunners—*Ubique* and all that."

"I saw a very good friend of my father. He fixed it. I'm going to be a pilot—well, once they've trained me, but I went up and showed aptitude, they said—probably from years at the organ."

His head was sunk into the pillows, but his hand came up in a snappy salute. "Meet Second Lieutenant Theodore Dawes-Holt, Royal Flying Corps. War is here and I am ready."

It would always be the same, Benedict thought. To be Theo's friend was to be alone.

1915

CHAPTER FIFTEEN
Frank, London, 1915

FROM BAD TO WORSE.

Poor François Faber the outsider, the furniture mover from Luxembourg. I expect he thought that his triumph in the Tour de France six years ago had been as hard as it would ever get: cycling 3,500 miles in snow and gales, digging out his bicycle, getting blown to the ground, being kicked by a horse, wading through potholes, sometimes all alone as others around him fell. He ran the last stretch to the finish, carrying his cycle with its broken chain. The next day he went fishing. If I could have been any man, I would have been François Faber, the Giant of Colombes.

I read in May that poor Faber had joined the French Foreign Legion and been mown down by the German guns. I could understand how he would have felt that France, which he'd conquered with his Peugeot-Wolber, was a land to fight for; but I was so angry and upset, I couldn't even speak of it. I devised a new system for storing gloves until I was calmer.

It was becoming impossible. At the Institute, I went to classes once on the Greeks. The speaker looked like a dry old stick, like he might have lived in ancient times himself. He had been a professor at the university up in Bloomsbury and he had this way of making it all come alive, and for a while we were in a world of monsters and pagan gods who were up to all sorts of things. So my situation, I thought now, was like Odysseus choosing between Scylla and Charybdis. On one side a monster, on the other a whirlpool. The professor had said, and you could tell he liked this bit: "So, which would you choose if you were Odysseus, captain of the ship?" No one answered, though I thought I'd choose the whirlpool, seeing as how I had learned to swim in the Dart as a lad, so stood a chance, and I didn't like the thought of being dinner for some octopus; but it turned out that Odysseus chose the monster and risked losing a few men, rather than the whirlpool and risk losing the ship. Later on, I realized that he had been what they called "officer material," whereas I was a typical soldier in seeking only advantage for myself.

It seemed that Mr. Frederick Richmond was Charybdis and Connie was Scylla. As Mr. Richmond's long arms were picking off the men and sending them to their fate, Connie was all seething passion for the Cause. Mr. Richmond expected every able-bodied man to join the colors. Connie demanded that every man of conscience turn away from war. For Mr. Richmond it was all *King and Country*, for Connie it was *Thou Shalt Not Kill*.

In time, two things came to change my view. First, one of the senior hands volunteered. Dick Wilson was in the luggage department and in the way of being a friend of mine. He had a Hercules bicycle that was his pride and joy, and he had sometimes let me ride it around St. James's Park. We planned trips we might make when I had bought my own machine. Our first was to be a place called Box Hill in Surrey; but we hoped, one day, to follow the Thames from Henley to the source. This was, of course, a dream, but the hours we had spent on it! We had a map and had worked out timings on trial runs around the Serpentine.

Dick had said nothing about his intentions to be a soldier, and the first I knew of it was him coming to say good-bye. Mr. Richmond publicly gave him and another man, a young lad from stores, the five guineas he'd promised. Florence kissed him, confirming the view I'd formed of her excitability, not that Dick looked anything but embarrassed.

"These men are heroes," Mr. Richmond said. I knew it was wrong of me but, after my course on the Greeks, I thought there was more to being a hero than signing your name, being kissed by Florence, and saying good-bye to a world of gentlemen's trunks, valises, and Gladstone bags.

Dick looked a bit proud, as well as a bit awkward, when he came to shake my hand, knowing, I think, that my own position had just gotten a little harder.

"If you should ever think of joining," he said, "the Bedford-shires seem a good lot. Infantry. Horses make me chesty." Then he shook my hand again.

"By the by," he said, "I'm giving up my lodgings for the dura-tion and I don't have any family, so I was wondering if you'd take the Hercules, look after it until I come back?" He must have mis-read the expression on my face, because he added quickly "Only if you want it, of course. It might be useful. I mean, you could ride it around. Even go to Box Hill." He tried a smile.

So that's how I came to have a bicycle for my own use, although I'd have needed a heart of stone not to feel some unease and I hoped the lads of the Bedfordshires would do all right.

About this time, my old father fell ill. Mr. Frederick Richmond gave me leave for one week, and I traveled back to Devonshire. My landlady let me leave the Hercules in the shed. I cleaned and greased it, sad that I had taken it out only once since Dick left but full of ideas for what I might achieve on my return.

The old man had gotten through the worst by the time I arrived, though it was a shock to see the years on him since I'd last been there. What was troubling him most, I thought, was spleen. The news was that soldiers who had fallen in battle were being buried where they lay. Without coffins. Or not buried at all, but left in fields to rot in their boots, one of the brothers from Leafield Farm had told him. I tried to reason with Dad. If there wasn't a war, I said, they wouldn't be dead, so they wouldn't be in his coffins anyway.

"But they would have died sooner or later," said my father. "And needed coffining then."

I didn't like to point out that these dead soldiers were lads of twenty and that in the normal way of things by the time they were of a dying age, he'd himself long have been six foot under. But then it turned out that even those locals who, in his words, "died like good Christians" (by which he usually meant paying his bill promptly) were, in respect of the war, seeking simpler service than in times past. Now even the magistrate, the gentleman farmer, and the lawyer's widow wanted no display in matters funereal, no silk-lined coffins, no fine woods, no marquetry. So suddenly I did feel sorry for the old man, though at least his being irked at the War Office meant he wasn't after me about volunteering. In fact, quite the reverse. It turned out nearly all my boyhood pals had gone. The 9th Devons had swept them up, and they were even now on their way to France.

"You won't go, son, will you?" Dad had asked one evening. "You're all I've got."

Two feelings hit me hard. One was that I was fond of the old man, for all his curmudgeonly ways, and two was that maybe this war business was bigger than my own inclinations.

I got back to London and spent a while in the shed with the bike, buffing the saddle and easing the bell. I oiled the gears. The spokes shone like new; only a little wear of the tires revealed that it had been ridden at all. It was a fine evening and I had intended to ride to the Institute, for a talk on Alpine Beauty which Connie had been eager to catch, but I had the beginnings of a headache and things on my mind. Since I had tried to explain my predicament to Connie, there had been a cooling in her manner and, every time we met, Nancy was with her and talking nineteen to the dozen. Connie must have become deaf to it, because Nancy was forever spotting soldiers in the street and imagining how they would be with their sweethearts and comparing Army uniforms with those of Navy lads.

The next Monday, I was off to Messrs. Lord and Stevas, military outfitters of Duke Street, St. James. I would take a cut in pay, I would be more junior, but, in using my knowledge of selling goods toward military ends, I could do my bit for the war. Or so I thought. Mr. Frederick Richmond—any doubts about my patriotism having been assuaged by his wrongly held belief that my father was trembling on the brink of the final abyss and I was, with proper filial respect, sacrificing my own longing to serve my country until he was beyond my attentions—had provided me with a splendid reference.

Duke Street was a very different place from Regent Street, and Lord and Stevas was an immeasurably different establishment from Debenhams. Masculinity dominated the street and the outfitters. The shop itself had an aroma I came to associate with war before I knew what war really smelled like. The shop was all leather, chalk, polish, tobacco, and hair oil. It was, I suppose, the smell of gentlemen, and I had not known many gentlemen. On one side of the shop was a life-sized model of half a horse, and on this cavalry officers could test the cut of their breeches, but John Quickseed, the head tailor, had a trick

143

of writing down a man's measurements having simply looked him over and only then confirming his dimensions with a tape. In a back room, which smelled of oil, steam, and wool, was a cutter, a Pole, Jakob Rozenbaum (who, Joe, the junior assistant, told me, had once had his own workshop in Stepney, but people had taken against him on account of his German-sounding name and burned it to the ground the year before), and an old chap, Albert, who acted as a finisher.

I had thought that khaki was khaki. But this was not so: there was every combination of styles and combinations, or weights, of rolls of cloth from brown to green, from buff to gray to cream, that Mr. Nugent (his Christian name, I discovered later, was Montgomery) indicated with a wave of his hand. Linings and buttons and twisted silk cord and stiffeners: barathea, viyella, twill, tropical lightweight wool, worsted, serge, drill. Mr. Nugent explained that some officers came to be outfitted knowing in every detail what they required, but others needed assistance, so that every one of us must know exactly what the requirements were for his regiment and rank, and judge what further, more personal embellishments he might care to make and how far he might exceed the basic allowance he was allotted.

"Pockets," Mr. Nugent said; "some gentlemen are very keen on pockets." He paused and I could have sworn a look of distaste crossed his face, but then it was gone.

"Some junior officers may even need our invisible guidance: yellow shirts have been one such area. Cavalry officers are also a law unto themselves. We have, currently, a most eccentric officer commanding the 29th Division, for instance. One more point," he said, fixing me with a stern look. "When an officer has but lately joined his regiment, he may, in anxiety or excitement, be inclined to purchase every single item that he believes he could conceivably need. It may not seem like good business to constrain him in his expenditure, but the officer who goes to join brother officers who are regulars can easily find himself a laughingstock. We do not want Lord and Stevas associated with his feelings of humiliation."

This was just the start: officers were, of course, just men going to live abroad, to the colonies or to the Continent, and they needed the collars and handkerchiefs and socks that any gentleman might require, plus cased clocks, stud boxes, binoculars, and hip flasks; these were, said Mr. Nugent, a great favorite with many a subaltern's mama and could be engraved to choice. These were to be my province, my predecessor having joined the Rifles a month earlier. I was quite impressed by our cigarette-case covers, canvas or wool in dull tones.

"For," said Mr. Nugent, "what if an officer opened his case to offer a brother officer a cigarette and the sun, reflecting off the metal, alerted the enemy to his position?"

"What about spectacles?" I asked. "Might they similarly catch the light?" I had read this in a book when I was young. But Mr. Nugent continued as if I had never spoken.

One afternoon when we were quiet and Mr. Nugent elsewhere, the junior, Joe, beckoned me. We went down a short passage and he opened a door that swung back as silently as everything else here. As my eyes adjusted to the light, I saw long racks, covered with white sheeting, from under which hung khaki tunic sleeves and trouser hems.

"The waiting room," said Joe. "It's for unclaimed orders."

When I didn't appear to react sufficiently, he said "Them as has ordered new stuff but never lived to wear it." He would have suited well as an undertaker's mute in the old days.

The day I started, I had written to Dick and told him how things had gone for me and the bike, and said I hoped he was getting along all right. From time to time I bicycled to work, leaving the Hercules in the park, as Mr. Nugent thought only butchers' boys rode bicycles.

Then, weeks later, on a fine June day, I bicycled a different route and who should I see walking up Regent Street but Florence. I rang the bell at her and she jumped in a gratifying way, but she seemed pleased enough to see me. At least she smiled, which Connie had rather given up doing. But it turned out that her main pleasure in seeing me was to tell me bad news.

"Did you know Dick got it in Flanders?" she said and, from her expression, clearly judged I didn't.

"Wounded?" I said.

She shook her head. "Fallen." Then when the word didn't quite provide the drama she required, she said, wide-eyed, "Gassed. We just heard, but it might have been a while ago. Not that he's been a soldier long. Hard to think of Dick dead, isn't it?"

Sentimental girl that she was, her eyes filled with tears and she got out a very small, clumsily embroidered handkerchief and pressed it to first one eye, then the other. "He was so reliable and decent, you wouldn't think he'd have let himself be gassed." She paused and screwed her eyes up. "It's a terrible death, they say: you go blind and your lungs fill up with blood."

My knuckles were tight on the handlebars and I found myself glancing at the bike, as if waiting to see a reaction. My throat tightened, thinking of gas, like at school how you'd imagine an itch when one of the other children had lice.

"But I've got his bike," I said, and she said "Well, he won't want it where he's gone," and she gave a sort of laugh. Which was in slightly bad taste, I thought, but she was upset, probably remembering she'd kissed him.

It preyed on my mind, and I found myself polishing Hercules every evening. Polishing away, as if Dick were coming back the next week. Before I went to work, I'd look in the shed to make sure Hercules had not been taken in the night. I had saved no more money, given that my landlady charged sixpence a week for the use of the shed, and I suppose having the use of the bicycle had dulled the urgency. But all the time now I was thinking it wasn't my property. I'd heard it said that soldiers made wills before they saw active service, and perhaps there was someone somewhere who should by now be riding Hercules.

While I was agitating over these matters, Mr. Nugent came in holding his newspaper one day. He had acquired a habit of standing at the center of the shop, when it was empty, to proclaim news of battles or the King, like he was a town crier from the olden days and we peasants unable to read. John Quickseed always made a point of absenting himself. Today the news was that they were drawing up a list of all single men between eighteen and thirty-five who were fit for service. Mr. Nugent shook his head, looking not at Jakob or old Albert or Joe but at me.

"Mark my words," he said: "it's a list today, but it will be conscription tomorrow. Just as you're getting the grasp of the business." He looked sorrowful. "To think we made a uniform for the Kaiser when he was a young man."

Then old Jakob spoke, and direct to me. "So, you vill be in invantry?"

"The poor bloody infantry," said Mr. Nugent.

"In var," Jakob said, using "V" for "W" and "F," as he did, "invantry soldier eating rat and each other body."

Mr. Nugent looked quite put out. "Not in *our* war," he said.

Later on Joe said to me, "No British soldier would be a cannibal. Have the Russkies had any other wars?" Neither of us was going to ask Jakob. He wasn't right in the head, and it wasn't just a matter of his neighbors burning his workshop down.

But I thought that if Mr. Nugent's newspaper was correct, it was, like as not, the "bloody infantry" would have me. I thought of old Dick and thought he'd been proud of the Bedfordshires— which was just as well, as he'd had to die for them. And I thought of Hercules and was bothered.

The afternoon was busy; three officers came in, one after the other. One officer was scarcely more than an excited boy about to join his regiment and was whisked off to be measured by Mr. Quickseed. Cavalry men were always high spenders. Then an older officer of engineers. We didn't see many sappers in Duke Street; most of our gentlemen had private means and the Royal Engineers, as a rule, did not, but Mr. Nugent obviously knew him and I noticed he wore a purple-and-white ribbon, very small on his tunic. He too was taken through to the back.

Seconds later, a tired-looking gunnery officer came in. Much my age, I thought, and in some way, I thought at first, familiar. He wasn't there for full equipping; he just wanted more shirts and gloves and to inquire about a cased compass he'd seen in the window.

"It's for my friend," he said. "He's in the Flying Corps, and I thought it would be useful."

I didn't like to say that they would be standard issue, but anyway by the time we'd added up the shirts, gloves, and a dozen of our best India cotton handkerchiefs, he couldn't afford it. He didn't say it, but I knew; and, at that moment, I knew where I'd seen him before.

He bought the compass anyway.

Then, when I was wrapping up his packages, I caught him looking at me, as if he too thought we'd met before. He frowned slightly and then looked embarrassed.

"Before. You were at Debenhams?" he said.

And then I was awkward on account of my reasons for leaving being not entirely creditable.

"I'm sorry," he said and I could see he was feeling awkward too. "You were once very kind to my friend," he said.

He waited to see if I was making a link.

"It was over a pair of gloves for his fiancée."

I always knew it was his friend who had stolen the gloves, and always knew that the man now in front of me had been quite unaware of it until I accosted them in the street. But he was in uniform, and an officer, so the less said, the better.

"I think I remember, sir," I said; "what a coincidence." Folding the paper neatly, as I'd been taught. Then, to change the subject, I said, "Are you on leave for long, sir?"

He shook his head. "Back to my regiment tomorrow. We've taken a great many losses," and he looked toward the window as if ghostly gunners might be trundling by.

"If there's anything—" he said.

An uneasy silence fell—the sort of silence that is full of sounds: rain on the windowpanes, faded discussions in the back room, a motorcar idling outside the shop, even, I fancied, Jakob's sewing machine, though I had never heard it before from out front.

Perhaps it was the silence or because we'd met before, in a manner of speaking, that I blurted out: "Well, excuse me for asking, but do soldiers make wills in case they might die?"

I looked behind me for Mr. Nugent, who had strong views on talking out of turn to customers and had even drawn up a list of approved subjects on which we might engage them. It was short.

"It's just that my friend left his Hercules in my care and now he's been killed and I don't know what to do."

He thought for a minute. "And Hercules is . . . a dog?"

"No, sir. It's a bicycle."

"A bicycle." He looked puzzled. "Is it hard for you to store it?"

"No. No. It's a fine bicycle, compares with the Raleigh Superbe, the Resilient Royal Centaur, or even the French machines, though it's more for straight roads than agility, but that's the point. It's very fine and it's not mine."

It all came tumbling out. Mr. Nugent would have had a fit.

"But my friend had no family, you see." And then, to my surprise, I heard myself saying, "I'll probably be joining up soon. I want to have things straight."

He smiled a little. "Well, that's splendid," he said, though he said it without the conviction of Mr. Richmond. He looked at me again as if assessing what kind of soldier I'd be.

"Are you a West Country man?" he said.

It was a small blow—I had hoped I sounded like a Londoner now.

"My own father is a clergyman in Devon," he went on, though I noticed he had no kind of West Country tone to *his* voice, but then it aways seemed to me that all officers spoke the same.

"Yes, sir. My father has a business near Totnes." That was overstating it a bit, but I hoped he wouldn't ask.

"Splendid," says he. "The Devons. Fine old regiment. You want to join the infantry?"

I shrugged politely.

"You obviously like bicycles, so I suppose you might consider joining a cyclist's battalion?"

You could have knocked me down with a feather. A cyclist's battalion. I must have looked surprised, because he said "I'll tell you what: there's a good unit I know of, and the adjutant's an old school friend. If you report with a bicycle in good working order, then I think you get an allowance. I'd say that would be quite a good use of your deceased friend's machine, wouldn't you? If you aren't set on the Devons, that is."

I was hardly able to reply. If I had to go to war, to take Hercules would be like taking a friend. "Is that an infantry unit?" I asked.

"More like cavalry, I suppose," he said. "Mounted troops, you see." And then he really did smile.

"Do you know where Huntingdon is?" he said. "They were a territorial outfit before the war. . . ." He hesitated and looked less confident. "Anyway, if you would care for an introduction, I could give you details."

I hardly knew what to say. In the end, I just said yes. "Yes, please. Thank you. Thank you very much, sir."

He wrote down a name. "Go to this recruiting office in Huntingdon, or write direct perhaps to see if it's worth the journey. And what's your name?"

So I told him, and he wrote it down in his pocketbook (officer's, pigskin), and while he wrote he added, in a nonchalant way, "Mine is Chatto, by the way. Benedict Chatto. If they take you, with any luck all your service will be at home. Patrolling the eastern coast and so on. A lot of birds, I'm told. Flat roads and wind."

Then he looked up and shook my hand, as if we had a bargain. And I said "Thank you, sir."

Then he said "Good luck," cheerily. I think they taught them that, because I was to hear a lot of officers speak in that tone.

A while after Mr. Chatto had gone, Mr. Nugent came out with the officer that he'd taken for measuring and opened the shop door for him.

"You know who that was?" he said. "My officer?"

I shook my head, and Mr. Nugent shook his as if he was shocked.

"Captained the MCC. Wonderful fast bowler. Military Cross."

He looked back to the door where the spirit of cricketing manhood still lingered, this hero having just passed through it. I had never been one for cricket, so I nodded again, up and down this time, thinking how I would have felt if it had been François Faber on his bicycle.

Despite Lieutenant Chatto's good wishes, in matters of luck I had both sorts. Connie, once I said I was going to be a soldier, would have nothing more to do with me; no matter that everybody knew we'd soon be conscripted, she wanted me to be a conchie, a conscientious objector, a martyr for her cause incarcerated in Wormwood Scrubs.

I went to tell Florence, and she said "Ooh, I hope you don't end up like poor Dick." But she didn't kiss me.

Nor was Mr. Nugent the type to hand out guineas. For a start, he was too inconvenienced by my leaving and, anyway, going to serve King and country was no novelty now, even with a bicycle. So I was surprised when, just as I was leaving, he held up a hand.

"Wait!" he said and pulled open a drawer. Out came a box holding a cigarette lighter, our basic model, with khaki cloth, which hadn't sold well, which was odd as it was good value. He handed it to me, looking embarrassed and surprised at himself.

"Good luck," he said.

I walked home, thinking I would start smoking as soon as I took the King's shilling. I stopped on Lambeth Bridge, gray as the water and the sky, and I looked toward parliament in its haze of drizzle, and what I felt was quite different from what I'd expected. Not fear, but a sort of relief in a decision. Now I was part of things; now I would know what other men knew. So I was grateful that my path had crossed twice with Lieutenant Chatto, as if the second meeting had made good our first.

The recruiting office acted like they were doing me a favor in taking me, given that the cyclists were mostly territorials.

"But we have been sent a recommendation," the officer said, as if that settled it. Good old Lieutenant Chatto had been as true as his word. Fate is a funny thing: "It's who you know" was a phrase I'd often heard but never grasped until now.

The sergeant said that my bicycle would need mudguards and front and rear lights and handlebars that did not curve down. I was all right regarding the handlebars, but the lights were a cost. Still, I was to get a 2s. 6d. allowance for the bicycle. I walked home and was thinking how I'd give Hercules a run on Saturday evening so he'd be ready. Then I nearly bumped into a young lady, very pretty with soft curls and a rather pert little hat. I had become so much the hero of my little daydream that I must have smiled. Her hand came toward me, touched me, so fast that I was caught off my guard. But then I looked down and saw she had tucked a white feather in my lapel.

"You should be in the trenches," she said. "My brother died at Gallipoli so you could loiter enjoying the view."

Then she was gone; I had a sense she was scared to linger in case I laid one on her. After all, she had no idea what sort of man I was; just because I was a coward in her eyes didn't mean I might not also be violent. The feather had fallen to the ground, but I picked it up; it seemed only polite. There was grit on it, and I wiped it away. There it lay, across my hand, perfectly white. I wondered where these young ladies found them. It was probably a goose feather and from a butcher's. I kept the feather, but as I walked across the bridge I thought about Gallipoli and Meso-potamia, Egypt and places in Africa where men were fighting. I wondered whether I might be cycling through deserts or jungles and whether I'd be good at it and whether Hercules had the right tires for sand, and I thought I would buy a bigger map than the one I'd had when I dreamed of bicycling on the Continent. For who knew where this war might take me?

In three weeks, I'd had my medical and received my initial instructions for the 7th Hunts (Cyclists) Battalion and could claim a train ticket for Hercules as well as myself, and so we set off to do our bit.

CHAPTER SIXTEEN

Harry, England, August 1914-Winter 1915

Teddy was full of questions about the war.

"I hope it goes on until I can join," he'd said. "I'd like to fly an aeroplane and drop grenades on the Germans."

"Well, I hope it doesn't," Isabelle said sharply. "It's not a game. France has already seen its boys killed—they all have to fight. Not like here, where they can choose whether to join. My cousin's boy will be a soldier now. She has nobody but him, but he'll still have to go."

Teddy had sat, half subdued, for a while; but then he said, with a glance at his mother, "Will you go, Harry? You'd look awfully good in uniform. You could use Papa's sword—the one he killed Russians with. Wouldn't you like to fly an aeroplane?"

"No, I'd be hopeless," Harry said. "And no, I shan't be joining up, whatever the allure of the uniform." He smiled at Teddy. "I have Marina to look after, and our home isn't here in England."

"But you *are* English," Teddy persisted. "I mean, Marina's American, but you can't change if you're born something, can you? And why aren't you coming back here to Abbotsgate for good, now that you're Sir Henry? Cook says the estate needs a man's hand. Anyway, you could be in charge and tell everybody what to do."

"Teddy," Isabelle had said, in mock outrage, "stop interrogating your brother, or he won't come back at all."

"I'm sure you can be in charge on my behalf," Harry said, "with your mother's help."

He had already appointed a good land agent who would come to live on the estate, but a little bit of him hoped that, in time, the adult Teddy might take it on. He had promised Teddy that he could come out to see them in America next year.

"Your mother too," he'd said. "When this war's over."

And so they had returned to New York, different people entering a different world. Marina had been dutiful and not at all unpleasant to him, but it was like living with a considerate stranger. At night she curled away from him and went to sleep, and although he drew some comfort from resting his hand on her hip and was glad she didn't move to dislodge it, there was nothing more. Until she specifically told him otherwise, he could only hope that she still loved him.

The Atlantic journey had seemed endless. After four days of waiting in the Adelphi, they had eventually departed from Liverpool in a second-class cabin and on a ship teeming with extra passengers. Their steward, apologetic, told them the crew was short-staffed because so many of the men had been called up by the Naval Reserve. The women and older men they had taken on to replace them had never really had time to learn their duties, and service was haphazard.

They had passed a recruiting office on their way to the docks, where a queue of seemingly good-hearted, jostling lads and men stretched for a hundred yards. Some had brought children with them, and one man was playing a harmonica. They seemed a jolly crowd. On the dockside, soldiers were checking manifests, and at the far end a warship was docked with sailors drawn up on deck. He felt—and, in the old days, would have told Marina that he felt—irrelevant. There seemed to be so many men of his age in uniform, and those that were not were busy and serious. Having left their luggage in Paris, he had a choice only of summer clothes suitable for a wealthy man on a leisurely European honeymoon, or the formal dress he had worn for his father's funeral.

As an RNR officer checked off his name on the passenger list, he gazed at the anchors on the man's gleaming buttons and felt like a lightweight fool in his blazer and boater.

"You're British, sir?" the officer asked. "Leaving for America?" and Harry had perceived it as a condemnation, but it also irritated him. That night, as Marina pretended to sleep, he made a compact with himself. He would not use his title, and if in time America joined the war, he would join the American Army. What better statement of his commitment to his new country? But he was troubled by a feeling that he was, yet again, running away.

The following months seemed unreal to him, and the distant war was always present. They spent a week in Nantucket, where the wind grazed the skin and whistled through the coarse grasses and the sea was dark and marbled. They returned to see newspaper photographs of the bombardment of the medieval city of Ypres. The city had been destroyed; human casualties were terrible on all sides. The grinning, skinny soldiers with bad teeth, whose pictures had accompanied headlines a few weeks ago, were now weary, knowing faces under muddy tarpaulins.

Back in New York, the majority view—and Harry sympathized with it—was that America should stay out of a purely European war. But among their friends, there were different levels of sympathy. They could discuss it intelligently, although at times it seemed obscene to reduce the suffering of a continent to the level of a Harvard debate.

Among those with German or British roots and interests, there were certain conversations one avoided at dinner. Once, when he was in the company of friends complacent about America's geographical distance and political wisdom, he had made some observation about war sometimes coming to find you even if you didn't choose to go to it. A man had turned to him and said "Well, of course, you're British; you would say that," and he'd retorted "Personally, I thought Britain should have stayed neutral" and realized from Marina's face that he had spoken too sharply. They went out less, by tacit agreement. Over a decade ago he had remade himself as a content, forward-looking American; now, through no choice of his own, he was being unmade again.

Britain was blockading German ports; Germany had declared British waters a war zone. Harry's business was booming as imports from Europe dried up, but it could only be a matter of time, he thought, until the markets he sold to faltered. He started buying the London papers and reading them each day. The situation in Europe was grim and relentless. After a quiet Thanksgiving, Christmas was upon them; they exchanged modest presents. Marina let him make love to her, but he was left with the feeling that, even in her pleasure, she was self-contained; the moments of abandon they'd once shared had been left behind in Europe. They saw the Ballets Russes and heard Caruso sing in *Carmen* at the Met. Meanwhile, uncertain of his own motives, Harry interviewed three men for the job of managing his business.

News came of setbacks in the Dardanelles so severe that even the British papers couldn't disguise the strategic miscalculations. Walking unwillingly to a concert later that day, one that Marina had told him excitedly would be the talk of New York, he knew he was increasingly acting a part, but he had no idea how to break free. He owed so much to Marina that her interests had to be paramount.

Yet the evening turned into something extraordinary. Carnegie Hall was crammed, the atmosphere electric, the audience curious or preparing to be shocked. The music was by Alexander Scriabin, but included what he called a clavier of light, an instrument of his own imagination. Even at the Moscow première, they had not attempted to provide such a fantastic instrument; but now, here in New York, a machine had been constructed that projected color onto fine screens in harmony with the notes. Harry understood none of it but had a sense of music escaping into another kind of expression, a new world of possibility; even the name of the piece, *Prometheus: The Poem of Fire*, seemed right for the music and the times. Listening, he knew that where once he had been grateful to escape the conflict, now merely to watch was becoming impossible.

A Christmas card arrived from Isabelle in late January 1915, enclosing a letter from her and one from Teddy. It had taken ten weeks to reach them. The autumn colors at Abbotsgate had been wonderful, she wrote, but high winds made the house cold and the roof needed repairing. The father of one of Teddy's closest friends had been killed in Flanders, and Teddy was very troubled by it. Jeremy Hope, the estate agent, was having trouble replacing young workers on the estate as they left to join the local regiment.

Teddy had sent a photograph of himself on his pony, Venables. His letter was short—an account of rugger scores, his Common Entrance examination for Eton, and a talk they'd had at school on diamond farming in Bechuanaland.

Harry had come home tired that day, forgetting that they were expected at a soirée, and was irritable as he dressed in a hurry. A harpist, wearing a spangled green gown and looking, he thought, like a rather stout lizard, played at one end of a fine drawing room. At dinner he sat next to an almost silent and blotchy debutante; he found himself hoping that she was accompanied by a large fortune. On his other side was the considerably more interesting wife of the editor of a leading Boston newspaper. She was, he had been told, a cousin of Andrew Carnegie.

Amid all the small talk, she was refreshingly frank. "It must be hard," she said, "watching your country suffer from so far away."

"Yes."

"I hear that your government will bring in conscription within months at this rate—my husband has heard that the losses have made this inevitable. Do you think it will apply to you?"

While he considered this matter, which had been hovering just outside his consciousness for days, she added "I mean, would you want it to?"

"I certainly wouldn't try to avoid it," he said. "But the truth is," and as he spoke, he realized that it was, indeed, an absolute truth, "there would seem to be something undignified about waiting until I'd been tracked down and forced to do my duty."

She smiled, mischievously, but evidently pleased with his words. "So you do feel it is your duty, then?"

"How would you feel, seeing pictures of your countrymen being slaughtered every day and then going out to—to listen to some—harpist—play Celtic folk songs?"

She touched his sleeve. Her voice was low. "I am so sorry. That was abominably insensitive of me. I was interested, genuinely, but it is not a good topic for dinner-party talk."

"No. No, I am very glad you asked me. I should have been asking myself. And I rather hate dinner-party talk."

On his other side, the debutante's knife grated on the gold-scrolled dinner plate, and she stared at it as if trying to pare it back to china clay.

"Are you enjoying the evening?" he asked her. "The harpist was rather good, wasn't she?"

The girl, with a mouth full of sole, stared at him, panic-stricken and chewing earnestly, her fork brandished like a weapon on the end of her chubby forearm. He put his hand up. "Sorry. I always ask questions at the wrong time!"

He turned back to the editor's wife.

"What would you do, if you were me?" he said with what he hoped was levity.

"Do you have children?"

He was caught by surprise. His eyes flickered across to Marina, who was in polite conversation with an elderly banker.

"No. No, we don't." Then he added, as if it were an excuse, "We haven't been married very long."

It struck Harry that he had thought very little about children. He knew of Marina's longings, but she was healthy and young: presumably children would come. For himself, he had taken it for granted that Teddy would be his heir—at least to Abbotsgate, his home—in his own right. Yet Marina had every right to expect that any son of theirs, if they had one, would inherit the estate. He thought again of what an inadequate husband he had been, isolated, detached from real life; even in his passionate exploration of this great city, he had been a spectator; his pursuit of Marina had been like selecting a particularly beautiful, interesting souvenir. If he had had the simple courage to explain his circumstances to a woman who had trusted him enough to become his wife, then these things could have been discussed. Now, it was impossible.

He was startled for a second when his neighbor spoke again.

"I would talk to your ambassador," she said. "Informally. He will know how things stand. You could see about taking a commission without committing yourself yet. Perhaps they won't want you. But your position is to either wait until they drag you off to fight, or to stay here and gawp from afar at horrors facing your childhood friends."

He nodded very slowly. "Thank you." Then he told her that if America joined the war, he'd enlist as an American.

She looked unflatteringly amused.

"I'm sure they'd be glad to have you. But President Wilson is quite determined that we should merely watch and stay well away."

"And you agree?"

"Of course. It's terrible. I hate war. My grandfathers were generals on different sides of the Civil War. North, South: we burned and destroyed each other, and we planted deep roots of hatred and distrust. I don't even know why you—Britain—are involved in this war. Truly, I don't. I'm not a religious woman, but as the saying goes, 'They have sown a wind but shall reap a whirlwind.' I hope that whirlwind doesn't engulf my country too."

"Of course—" he began.

"But do I think it will be possible for us to stay out?" She didn't let him interrupt. "No. The money says we'll be drawn in. Business interests have kept us out so far; and now that there's a blockade, it's proving impossible. . . . Maybe Mr. Roosevelt is right and we should be preparing ourselves."

"You talk like a man," he said, attracted to her forthright views and her passion, and conscious too of her dark eyes, her white neck and curls of dark hair in which nestled tiny diamond stars.

"And you like an Englishman," she said, briskly, but then laughed loud enough to make the couple opposite her look up. "I'm surprised you didn't ask me what my husband thinks. Or my notoriously pacifist relatives."

"I'm sorry, I didn't mean to patronize you. It's been a great help to talk to you." As he said it, he felt disloyal. What was stopping him from revealing his doubts to Marina?

"But, you know," she said, "your country's right in there. They're beyond choice. If I were an Englishman, even a legitimate exile, I might just want to see what kind of soldier I'd make."

She was watching him, perhaps to see if she'd gone too far. His eyes met hers.

"You mean what kind of *man* I'd be."

She inclined her head minutely, then looked around the room, taking in the company. He became conscious of a hubbub of voices, metal on china, clinking glasses, murmurs filling the silence when she stopped speaking. He realized how warm it was, noting that the skin of the black footman standing on the far side of the table was beaded with sweat. He could smell the gardenias. Yet outside, New York was frozen.

Finally, after a minute, she turned back to him.

"A wealthy man, a comfortable man," her smile softened any mockery, "a well-connected man. Clearly a thinking man. But what else might you be or not be?"

That night, he wrote to an Army friend of his father's who was currently commanding the Somersets. And the next day, he spoke briefly to a rather perplexed secretary at the British Embassy.

Over the next month, spring officially came closer but the weather got colder. He was restless and left his office early one day, intending to be home before Marina returned from her weekly painting classes. The air hurt his lungs as if particles of powdered glass were suspended in it. It was only early afternoon, yet the sun was beginning to set. He bought the papers and read them while stamping his feet to keep warm. An already out-of-date *London Illustrated News* had a cheerful picture of Australian soldiers training in England before departing for France. They looked healthy and happy: farm boys tanned by a recent southern summer. He read that Australian volunteers had overwhelmed recruitment offices. Boys looking for adventure, something outside the narrow confines of the world they knew, of sheep or mining, and on his home turf now, ready to fight. It had begun to feel as if America was the only nation not at war.

On the inside pages was an account of the battle being fought between Austrians and Russians in the snow and bitter cold of the mountains and forests of the Carpathians. He had no real idea where this was, nor could he envisage the two forces. A new atlas of the imagination was required for this war. The first photographs of Austria's armies parading as they went to war had looked somehow exotic, like the early nineteenth-century prints of men in shakos and gold-frogged jackets that his father had hung in his study at Abbotsgate. There was nothing of this here. The soldiers photographed in *The Times* were unidentifiable: dark, crouched bundles of despair or death in churned-up, dirty snow.

As he turned for home, he glanced back toward the park, a favorite view of his in summer, and saw something extraordinary. Between the bare trees rose a column of misty colors: indigo, pink, and green, a frozen helical rainbow rising from the ground until it vanished into the sky. He looked around to see if anyone else had seen it, but he was alone in the white expanse of frozen grass, with the shimmering prism of light an unknown distance away.

He left the park, turning his back on it. It was, he was sure, a combination of sunlight, temperature, and perhaps humidity. The sun would set in half an hour and the effect would not survive that, he thought. But he was still full of the wonder of it as he sat in the drawing room, gazing out into the New York evening: a darkness that never was dark, a wilderness of light, it had seemed to him when he first arrived.

Then, standing at the window, about to draw the curtains, he saw Marina's father's car pulling away from the curb, his driver at the wheel. When she came through the front door, he had turned on the lights and was waiting in what she called the vestibule and he still called the hall. She was still in her dark vicuña coat and a velvet hat trimmed with white fur, colorless strands of hair curling onto her pale skin. The tip of her nose was pink, but otherwise she was a picture in monochrome. Feeling a surge of love for her, he put his arms around her and, for the first time, felt reciprocation in her embrace: her chilly cheek against his, her lips on his neck, her fur hat tickling his eyes.

"This is purely in pursuit of warmth," she said. "Life-saving."

He pulled her closer, spun her around. Pushed her before him toward the bedroom, then unpinned her hat, set it carefully on the table, unhooked her coat, sat her on the ottoman at the foot of her bed, and, kneeling, unbuttoned her boots from ankle to calf. He ran his hand under her heavy skirt and up her calves, then stopped and glanced up, suddenly uncertain, and she returned his unspoken question with a look of such beauty and tenderness that he felt a vast sense of relief, enough to make him fumble for a second in loosening her stockings.

Later, he told her what he was going to do.

Looking back, he thought it had been an overly dramatic gesture, but he no longer wanted to exclude her from any part of his life, in mind or body. Even as the British Embassy was making its ponderous inquiries, his father's friend, a former colonel of the 2nd Wiltshires, had written back with enthusiasm, having misread Harry's inquiries as a direct request, and offering suggestions for his return. His fare would be paid: "Second class, I'm afraid."

Clearly, the colonel said, Harry would wish to see his family and the estate; but if he could let him know of his arrival, they could then arrange for him to be met at regimental headquarters. There would be the matter of a medical and a few other minor administrative chores, but he looked forward to welcoming Harry to the regiment. He would explain then about training, likely deployment, and so on. Plenty of time for that. He ended by saying "I know your father would be tremendously proud of your decision."

Over the next few weeks, green spikes of new growth emerged from the mud and grass of the park and a foam of almond and cherry blossom filled the front gardens of Fifth Avenue mansions. He thought that, despite everything, or perhaps because of it, he had never been happier. To his astonishment, Marina had supported his decision and, she explained, clinging to him, her tears were of pride as much as in anticipation of a long period apart. It was her father who was astounded and seemed to be unsuccessfully concealing his puzzlement. To him, this rash and unnecessary response to a nonexistent call to arms was evidently the act of a negligent husband.

Harry's first impulse was to not tell any of his friends, but of course this was unrealistic. The news didn't just slip out, it ricocheted like a bullet around their social circle. Some people clearly thought he was mad; some verged on almost perfectly concealed contempt.

"Well, of course, you're an Englishman with an island to protect," said one.

Some were amused; some ardent tennis and golf players seemed to think soldiering was a kind of demanding, if not very exclusive, sporting event. But others shook his hand.

To his regret, two of their heartier friends insisted on throwing a farewell party and, although it was a jollier affair than he or Marina had imagined, he was relieved when at last he could slip away, wanting to spend his last hours in New York with his wife. The next day, after very little sleep, he woke with a pounding head. He stood in front of the mirror in his silk dressing gown, tipping a headache powder into water. He drank it with a shudder and then, in the mirror's reflection, saw Marina still curled up on her side, asleep in a tangle of sheets and blankets. If only she were pregnant, he thought. How he hoped she might be. The strength and suddenness of his longing surprised him.

Hours later, he stood on deck, his face already sticky with salt from the Hudson breeze, the ship leaving on an ebb tide. The last cargo appeared to have been stowed; the nets, which had been busy swinging crates into the hold when he had arrived with Marina and her father, now hung limply from the cranes; and his arm ached from waving, his face from smiling.

The crowd was less jolly, yet no less frantic than when he had embarked on his honeymoon so short a time ago. It was not surprising: this was a British liner and, as there were threats regarding German attacks on shipping, few travelers now went to Europe simply for fun. A yellow streamer rose up from the crowd and landed gently on his shoulder, breaking his concentration for a second so that he could no longer find Marina's face in the mass below.

Even when the huge hawsers were freed and the great ship began to move away from the dock, she had not reappeared. The vessel vibrated under Harry's feet, the noise of its massive turbines drowning out the shouts from the crowd. Harry felt a rush of panic as his eyes scanned the throng in increasing desperation, trying to find his wife, but the waving arms blurred his vision. Eventually he fixed on the Manhattan skyline. The expanse of dark water opened wider and wider, the churning river smelled and moved more like the sea it was becoming, yet the dense buildings of the city seemed to stay immobile, with no sense of the distance growing between ship and shore for a very long time.

In the week's journey across the Atlantic, he had had little time to absorb the vast change in his circumstances, to take in how much he missed his wife, nor even to write a letter to her without interruption. His early notion—that there might be some justice if the ship was torpedoed and he went down with it—was soon deadened by the tedium of daily lifeboat practice.

He had decided not to stay overnight at Abbotsgate, but merely to join his stepmother for luncheon. Teddy was home on a temporary leave from school. Harry had bought him an antique, but reasonably sharp, trapper's knife. He had found it in New York's Italian quarter and suspected that if it had ever been used for hunting, it was more likely to have been in the Appalachians than the Apennines. Teddy was delighted and brandished it between his teeth like a pirate.

"When will you have a uniform?" he said. "Will you be a colonel? My friend Walter's father is a brigadier. Have you got a revolver yet?" Harry helped himself to more molasses tart.

"Will you go to France?" Teddy said, still chewing. "I'm really half French, of course, because my grandparents were French but it doesn't show." He darted a look at his mother. "Though all my grandparents are dead. Will you kill Germans, do you think?"

Isabelle raised her eyebrows, then said, calmly, "Don't talk with your mouth full."

She had been very controlled throughout the day. She was, Harry thought, well aware that the brevity of his stay was a conscious decision, not a necessity.

Abbotsgate looked well cared for despite a reduction in manpower, although the gardens had already been simplified, he noticed. He spent an hour with the agent in his small office in the stables, discussing national demands for wood and the Army's requisition of horses. But it was like visiting the house of a good friend rather than one that was, rightfully, his own.

All in all, it had passed off better than he'd feared. When he came to say good-bye, Teddy had gone riding with a friend. After Phillips had put his case in the car, he and Isabelle were left alone in the great hall, which, despite the warmth outside, was cool. He kissed her on the cheek, his eyes moving inexorably to the portrait of his father, and then he turned, rather awkwardly, to go before looking back one last time.

"You'll let me know. . . ."

"You'll be busy," she said, with a half-smile.

"Letters will get to me."

"Of course."

"I'll take care of you both."

She nodded.

He held her gaze for a second and stepped out into the sunlight. The car was on the gravel, Phillips at the wheel.

"Harry," she said, stepping out with him and putting her hand on his arm, and, ridiculously, he drew back at the unexpected contact.

"No, it doesn't matter," she said, looking embarrassed. "But go safely."

"Of course."

With immaculate timing, Phillips got out, opened the door, and said "Good afternoon, Sir Harry."

"Isabelle," he said, suddenly without words.

"Harry."

He settled into his seat and looked out of the rear window, his eyes not on Abbotsgate but on the slender figure in gray who stood motionless on the steps, her hand raised in a frozen wave. Eventually his neck ached too much, and he turned to face forward.

"Trowbridge, sir?" said Phillips, out of courtesy. He knew perfectly well where they were going and why. The car gleamed, fit to pass a sergeant major's scrutiny.

"Bad news from Turkey," Phillips said, as if they were talking about a day's racing. "Wouldn't fancy my chances there. Never been one for hot weather. And the Turks are devils when they're roused."

Somewhere between Abbotsgate and Taunton, as Phillips chattered on and the car brushed through narrow lanes, both his earlier lives were ending. The layers of what he had been—a son, a brother, an only partly honest husband, a selfishly happy exile, an absent landowner—were all stripped away now, and he was left just as a man like any other.

All the skills and weaknesses that he had known or discovered in himself, used or hidden, all the advantages he'd been born to and the deceits he had pursued, meant nothing, faced with the unknown question of what kind of man, what kind of soldier, he would be. But then he reflected that it was much more likely, now that he had made his grand gesture, that the war would be over in six months, and he would be stuck in a Whitehall office in the country he had worked so hard to leave, stamping requisition forms eight hours a day.

CHAPTER SEVENTEEN
Frank, Huntingdon, Winter 1915

THE ARMY HAS MORE FORMS than it does bullets. Forms to say you haven't got a squint or a crooked spine or an undescended whatnot. Forms for next of kin, forms for summer uniforms (other ranks, cotton, medium), and, eventually, when they'd taken Hercules from me, regulations having changed, a form for Machine, Folding, General Service, Twenty-four-inch, Frame No. 211567. I called her Nora.

I set off to a new life in September 1915—my second new life, really, London having been my first. Hercules went in the luggage compartment. There was nothing to see from the train: good flat cycling country north of London, but not much else. So my mind turned on this and that, including a bit of guilt that I hadn't gone home to see the old man, but I told myself it was only training, there was no actual fighting yet.

I arrived feeling tired and a bit blue, and a bit of a civilian when I saw all the lads in khaki drilling on the square. But then a soldier approached and you could have knocked me down with a feather. It was Isaac, holding his cycle upright and firmly, not clutching it as I did, saluting the sergeant in the approved manner. I had yet to learn this, and it took me a while. Hercules would always wobble the minute I held him with one hand and raised the other. Nora was worse. The more senior the officer, the greater the wobble.

"You never said you were a cycling man," I said first thing.

"You never asked," said Isaac. "And you never said you were either." But ours had been a friendship of minds and of aspirations, so perhaps it wasn't so surprising.

"You went away pretty fast," I said. "Nobody knew where you'd been sent."

He looked a bit shame-faced. "I couldn't face those women," he said. "That Connie was the most belligerent pacifist I'd ever heard." And, unexpectedly, he smiled at me. The first I'd ever seen on him, I think.

"And my brother was carrying on night and day," he continued. "Saying our parents were Russian and if I had to fight, it should be for Russia. Despite the fact that I'm sending my pay back home."

"Blimey," I said. "Do you speak Russian?"

"No. My brother does, but he's against the officer class on principle and he won't fight—not in any army. He'd go to prison first. I could have coped with the Russians, having Esperanto, but I don't like the cold."

"I'm glad to see you," I said. "I feel a bit useless, to be honest."

"You'll feel better in uniform," he said. "Though they're a bit short; you may only get a cap and a badge. And they'll swap your rig for a standard machine. BSA, folding bike. New regulations."

I felt a bit funny about that, seeing as Hercules had been Dick's, and I hoped they'd keep him safe, but I was curious to see a folding bicycle, although to the end I was worried that Nora would suddenly fold at a crucial moment.

Nora was a bit of miracle, I thought when I first put my hands on her handlebars (unfolded), but Captain Porson, the adjutant, thought folding bicycles were a liability and a handicap. He'd been a semi-professional when he was young. Now he'd point with his stick to the pivots, which allowed you to fold them on the order "Machine, FOLD!" and he'd say "Weakness at the crucial point, d'ye see? We need cycles that are robust: to cope with all terrain from the tundra to the veldt, from Dar es Salaam to the pyramids of Egypt, from the plateau of Troy to the clays of Flanders or the rivers of Picardy."

Captain P was very keen on geography, and also on what he called "machine versatility." He was forty-five if he was a day, had been injured in the war against the Boers, and would never leave England to fight again.

"And here some genius," he'd say, in full flow, "has devised some toy engineered to be light, undoubtedly at the cost of strength, and to collapse under stress."

It didn't seem likely to me. It was more of a problem getting them to fold at all if any grit had gotten in the pivot. Once they were folded and hoisted on your back, it helped to have a chum to get them off again. The first time I stood up with Nora hanging on to me, I very nearly fell over backward with her unexpected weight. But it was all a matter of getting to know her. In the end, she was part of me.

Captain P was always writing letters about "design iniquity" to the higher-ups and to magazines like *The Gentleman's Tourer* until he got told to stop. Though what advantage Jerry could ever have had from knowing we had folding cycles beats me.

The weeks of basic training were a surprise. The things I thought I might be good at, if I thought at all, which I soon learned was not encouraged, had me struggling, and the ones I thought I'd struggle with, I could do pretty well.

I had learned to shoot as a boy, my appearance was always praised, and I was punctual to a fault. The British Army was much of a mind with Mr. Nugent on punctuality. I was fitter than a lot of Kitchener's lads and even some of the Terriers. We did this run, lie prone, fire position, jump up, run down routine. Isaac trailed behind. He'd run, lie down, cough as he did when he was anxious. Find his handkerchief, struggle to his feet, blow his nose, and stand there rolling his eyes.

"Fritz has just blown your head off, Meyer," Mr. Pierce, the most junior of officers, would shout, trying to sound tough. He had a slight lisp, bad luck for him.

Isaac never remembered about firing positions, didn't really want to believe in them, seeing as how he was going to be riding a bicycle to war and just pass on messages, but he was a tremendous map reader. I liked maps, but nothing like him. Isaac could also look at any map and see how the terrain, as we now called it, lay.

"You'd need low gear and a lot of puff there," he'd say, stabbing at the paper with a finger. Or: "It would probably be easier to take the longer road, given the valley."

It was odd: he hated open spaces and loved cities tight with highways and alleys, but on a map he was master of the land. What's more, he could strip and rebuild a bicycle like it was a magic trick at Maskelyne's Hall.

"I used to work in a repair shop as a boy," he said, adding: "Bicycles are the future for the common man." I could almost hear myself speaking and was proud he was my friend.

Things I still had to learn: marching, stripping guns, army etiquette. What I found hardest was cycle maneuvers. Of course, the other lads almost all had their own cycles, and I hadn't been entirely clear with the officer who'd given me the tip back in the shop. I'd only ever ridden down a few London streets. The rest was polishing the bike while I dreamed of touring holidays. Of us new recruits, one was a grocer's errand boy, one was a country postie, two or three belonged to cycling clubs, and there were twin brothers who had worked in a factory making bicycles. They'd all been cycling practically since they could walk. I had an image of their fat little baby legs pedaling in their cradles while mine were just kicking in the air.

The training NCOs had this thing you did, weaving between posts.

"Call yourself a cyclist?!" the training sergeant bellowed.

I wanted to say "No, I never did, not really. I just thought about it a lot."

I was humiliated when I fell off; and just when I'd grasped the weaving with Hercules, they gave me Nora, the regulation Army cycle, and I fell off all over again. Then they mounted the gun, which shifted the balance, and it was right back to the beginning once more. I was nervous that if I didn't grasp it, they'd send me to the infantry.

But Isaac was a true friend and when we had half a day's leave, we went off into the countryside nearby and he laid out some stones and I practiced all afternoon. It was a kindness, because he detested the countryside with such a passion that I had doubts whether he had ever left London before: "Green, green, so much green and no houses, no one wants to live here, all that nothingness and buzzing things trying to get in your throat."

After, I bought him a couple of beers in a public house and we came back a bit squiffy. I fell off Nora, twice, but even Isaac was all over the road and giggling. He was most unlike himself.

The relationship between bicycles and me was quite different before I had Dick's Hercules, and it was different again now that I was training to be a professional. I expected that it would be different again when I was, in my way, a weapon.

Winter was coming: the wind and rain blew in from Russia, they said. Our new caps had flaps for our burning ears. What with the flaps and the wind, you couldn't hear an order, which was either a disadvantage or an advantage, depending. At last we learned that some of us were to be attached to serving regiments and would be sent off to France.

"We're looking for the *cream der lah cream*, as they say where some of you are going," said our sergeant, with a wink. "Our reputation is at stake."

He looked at us all as if we were potential saboteurs.

But when the list went up, there was one officer—our young Mr. Pierce—with a sergeant, a corporal, and twelve men, and two of those were Private Isaac Meyer and Private Francis Stanton. We had our photograph taken, all fifteen of us, holding our machines and with all our equipment neatly stowed as per King's Regs. Underneath the picture, it said *Hunts Cyclists Batt.*, with our badge. It was a stag rearing up, and one lad said it was like me and the bike in my early days, but I ignored him. I wrote to Dad and sent him the picture and hoped all was well in the coffin trade and said that when I got leave, I'd come and visit him.

Deep in my heart, I thought what an outcome: I, an Englishman, would be pedaling in the tracks of those French and Belgian heroes of the Tour de France. But as things turned out, I was very glad I'd kept that thought to myself.

Isaac held on to his picture, as he said he had no one to send it to. His brother would tear it up in the name of world peace and international brotherhood. Isaac was in an altogether dejected mood.

"Anyway," he said, "some of us may not come back. And I can look at it and remember our comradeship." And he coughed.

There was a smoking concert in the canteen the evening before our departure, and everyone was in a very merry mood. The sergeant sang "When Maiden Loves, She Sits and Sighs" and nearly brought the house down with his sighing and quivering moustaches. The lads ended the evening with a rousing performance of the famous "Song of the Hunts Cyclists." Every verse, many of them more than once. When it got to the verse about France, we boys who were actually heading off there got a lot of nudging and even free beers coming our way.

> *We've signed to go to France,*
> *And we hope we get a chance,*
> *For we've all come out for duty and for fun;*
> *We're the Hunts Battalion boys,*
> *And we're all our mothers' joys,*
> *But we're also sons of Britain—every one.*

Isaac whispered "Except me, who's Russian." Then he added "And you and me not having mothers. Not that we weren't a joy to them once, no doubt."

But I could see that he looked excited as well as entertained by all the carrying-on.

> *Cheer Ho! Cheer Ho!*
> *Do we dream this thing? Oh, no!*
> *We have waked from simple slumbers by the gun,*
> *And the thing that we're about*
> *Is to wipe the "Germ–Hun" out*
> *Or to die like British Soldiers—every one.*

I'd never thought the last verse was the best. Even we recruits knew that if you slumbered by your gun, you'd be up on charges; and it was noticeable that those who were being sent off to Scarborough to cycle around, looking for spies at railway stations, were the most enthusiastic about dying like British soldiers every one.

1916

CHAPTER EIGHTEEN
Benedict, France, 1915-1916

BENEDICT HAD TAKEN A COMMISSION in the Royal Field Artillery and continued with the plan Theo had once laid out for them both. The winter of 1914 was spent in the mud on Salisbury Plain or in the schoolroom, being taught math. Theo had gone from Brooklands, where he'd learned to fly, straight to training at Hendon.

Theo was sent out to Ypres almost as soon as he had finished training, while Benedict had a home posting in a garrison manning the southern defenses. The two short letters Benedict received from Flanders were of tales of derring-do that were hard to reconcile with the photographs of devastation that appeared weekly in the newspapers, or with the early casualty figures—or, at least, hard if you didn't know Theo.

Each of Theo's letters ended with a few musical notes instead of a signature. The first one had puzzled him until he realized it was the opening bar of "The Battle Hymn of the Republic." The second was in response to his reply, telling Theo he was finally being posted overseas—to France. These notes were more recognizable, not least because the bar end was a tiny soldier. It was Gilbert's "The Soldiers of Our Queen." Theo scrawled across the bottom, "I'm to France as well. Shall we meet?" And then he quoted from the song: "Upon the battle scene they fight the foe together."

It seemed unlikely. When he'd gone home and told Lettie that Theo was now a pilot, she had looked puzzled.

"Weren't you and Theo going to join together? In the same regiment?"

He'd come close to lying, to providing a reason that wasn't about Theo's inability to think except in the moment. A promise, made by Theo, was not a binding commitment, more a measure of his current mood.

The next letter began with with a small angel with a cockade, blowing a trumpet with fat cheeks: B♭. B♭. B♭. E♭. E♭—"La Marseillaise."

I know where you are, you secretive, virtuously discreet son of a gun, and I'm billeted near you chaps. Based at Doullens. Kept meaning to write again but you know how it is. Flying all hours. There's a sort of joy in it that's like playing Bach when Brewer's away. A good machine, a good plan of operation, and then skill and luck. Found this bijou residence—Harmony Cottage we call it. But the two chaps I was sharing with have left. One's back at H.Q. with promotion and a staff officer's job, the other's got chicken pox. Now we are one—or however the rhyme goes. I was dreading some starchy fellow being foisted on me. How do you fancy moving in? Might not be for

long, but we could shift your stuff stat. It's practically a palace. Well, actually it's a one-roomed
hovel, but we live in great style. We've got a well.
Cabbages, more or less. We've even got a bedstead: what they call a *"matrimoniale."* Took it in
turns. But you and I could share, being old friends.
I'll fumigate it. You won't catch the dreaded pox.
And I can show you my masterwork. Seriously.
It's a cantata. Or will be. On aeroplanes, on flight.

A moment with your guard down and happiness could catch
you just as unexpectedly as a sniper's bullet, Benedict thought,
and was full of fear.

Yet he had settled into a billet with Theo at the cold, single-
story farmhouse; and with a third man, a pilot called Dougie
who also stayed from time to time, they made a strangely happy
household. One of them had a hammock, one took the iron bed,
and one slept on a horsehair mattress laid on empty ammunition
boxes. Dougie had insisted on planting seeds he'd brought from
home and promised a garden next spring. To Benedict's surprise,
Theo really was writing a cantata, although there was nothing
religious about it. Read on the page, it was strange and brilliant,
sometimes lyrical, sometimes almost violent. Could it be played?
He wasn't sure. When he had any hours free, Theo would sit and
work at it, the oil lamp catching him in its halo of light, tapping
out the rhythm with a pencil held in mittened hands. If Dougie
wasn't there to observe him, Benedict could lie, half sleeping in
the hammock, watching him with wonder. Theo. Theo. Theo.

Theo was injured at Christmas.
    It was a rare occasion that they were all there, so they made
something of a party of it. On that evening, Dougie had brought
a friend along, a dour Scotsman. Benedict didn't get the feeling

that Theo had known him that long, but he brought some good whiskey with him and they had some French *pinard*, the rough red stuff all the *poilus* carried, and some brandy. By the time they decided to cook something, they were all pretty drunk. The Scotsman had spent time in India and insisted he could make the standard-issue bully beef into some exotic Indian dish.

"It cleanses your gut," he'd said. "They'd all be dead of gut rot, those Indians, without it." He had packages of bright-colored powder he waved at them. "You can smell the spice on them. Those women—fine, fine-looking lassies, and what they don't know about pleasing a man could fill a book." He looked happy for the first time since he'd arrived.

"You've got that wrong, old chap," said Dougie. "You mean what they *do* know could fill a book."

The Scotsman seemed put out by this. Some of the yellow powder trickled out of the package. Theo bent down, scooped it up, and threw it in the skillet, licked his fingers, made a face, and laughed. He was enjoying himself. With Dougie and the Scot, Theo was a different man: a coarser, older man. Yet at one point he'd pulled out his half-written cantata and hummed the opening bars to them, conducting himself and an imaginary organ. Dougie had yawned and flapped his hand at him.

"Enough—you sound like McIver's bagpipes."

Benedict was sent to bring up onions from a string they'd found in the cellar. The smell beneath the house was rank, and his head was reeling as he levered himself up again through the trap door. With bright yellow hands, Theo started opening the cans of beef, digging in the tip of a bayonet. It was one they used to poke the fire.

"Bloody quartermasters," said Dougie, slurring now. "Sadists. The stuff tastes like excrement, and they seal it up so we can't even get at it."

Theo was trying to roll back the lid. The can's contents smelled nauseating. Afterward, Benedict was certain he'd felt the sharp pain in his own hand, had even lifted it to support it with the other arm, before he heard a sudden gasp from Theo.

"Blast it." He held his hand up, blood dripping from a cut in the web between the thumb and finger. The parting of the flesh was visible.

Dougie laughed. "Drip it in, man. It'll add flavor."

"It damn well hurts." Theo pulled out a cloth from under the bed and wrapped it around the injury. "*You* dig the bloody stuff out."

And they'd eaten the beef, which tasted rather better with the Scotsman's strange powders. But Benedict felt giddy and had a throbbing headache from the wine and the whiskey. He fell asleep on the floor. When he got up to be sick in the night, someone had removed his tunic and boots and put them tidily over the foot of the bed. But the tunic smelled of vomit even after he'd sponged it.

The next day, Theo had gone on duty early and Benedict left for two nights in Albert. When he returned, he was surprised to find Theo on the bed, sitting against the wall, flushed and sweating, his eyes bright. His shirt was open, moisture shining in the hollow at the base of his neck.

"For God's sake, you're ill." Benedict felt a slight sense of panic, and pain seemed to leap from his fingers. "And you smell to high heaven."

"My fucking hand," Theo said, but with no rancor.

"Let me see."

"No. If you see, I'll have to see, and I won't like what's there."

But he fell back, hot and exhausted, and let Benedict unwrap the layers of grimy cloth. The wound smelled. It was puffy and red, and bluish streaks ran up his arm.

"For God's sake, Theo. You need to see the M.O."

"No. I just need to rest it. I'm not having some sawbones take my arm off. I need to fly." His face creased in pain.

Benedict fetched some water, held Theo's head while he was sick, although only bile came up as he retched. He felt the fine, wet hair on the corded muscles at Theo's neck, and the tremors that occasionally ran through his body; he saw the mauve eyelids. And all the time his own hand, which was supporting Theo, throbbed and burned. Then he tried to rinse the cut, but Theo gasped every time he touched it. Finally, he fetched him a small brandy, and after a while Theo let him dab the injured hand. Eventually Benedict just held the suppurating hand in his own on the cleanest cloth he could find; it was actually his undershirt. The day got darker, Theo fell into a restless sleep, grimacing from time to time, and Benedict lay down beside him, occasionally propping himself up to wipe Theo's brow and always feeling the radiant heat of his skin down the full length of his body.

In the morning, Theo didn't even open his eyes. His hand smelled worse than ever. "I'm supposed to be at Doullens," was all he said.

Benedict left him, went outside and found a couple of soldiers from the tented billets down the road. One he sent off with a message. Then with the help of the other man, they half-lifted, half-dragged Theo to the nearest aid station. When he was eventually seen, even the tired young medical officer made a face.

"Septic case," he said. "We'll send him on as soon as possible. Find him a bed. He should be in the hospital." He put a clean dressing on the cut, then turned to another unconscious soldier.

"He can't lose the hand; he's an organist," Benedict said to the M.O.'s back. The doctor turned slowly and looked at him, as if he'd said something obscene.

Benedict thought, he *hoped*, no news was good news. Men died swiftly from septic wounds, but Theo was healthy. He lived as well as anyone could here; and there had been no filthy and fatal shred of uniform carried inward by a fragment of exploding metal. He had bled copiously—didn't that mean the germs were borne *out* of the body, not into the bloodstream? But it hadn't looked like that when Benedict had last seen him. He had waited with him until they loaded Theo onto a wagon. His eyes opened, apparently with effort.

"I couldn't go on without you," Theo had said, but his eyes seemed no more focused than his thoughts.

A fortnight later, Dougie was injured crash-landing and was sent back to England for good. Two subalterns from the Lancashire Fusiliers replaced him at Harmony Cottage but were hardly ever there. Meanwhile, Benedict had been promoted to acting captain, which meant slightly more pay and the responsibility of packing up his predecessor's effects. He returned to the cottage as little as possible. When he did, the roof was leaking, the stink from the cellar was worse, and it was warmer and not much wetter outside than in.

It was a slow and grueling winter; the losses were constant, and the recruits who came out to replace the dead or injured gunners had less and less training, and more and more of the shells seemed to be duds. The heavy guns being moved into position slipped off the tracks laid for them, shattering the ice over pits of mud, and the men were reduced to shuffling bundles of scarves, balaclavas, shaggy jerkins, and double layers of dirty puttees. Benedict looked no better and had a rash on his chin from the chafing of damp wool. He heard nothing of Theo and dared not ask.

In March, a parcel and a letter arrived. The large box appeared to have traveled all over France: Christmas cake, stewed plums, glacé fruits, some mustard-colored fingerless gloves, and a letter from his sister bringing news from home. She had become engaged. "Fancy that!" she wrote.

> His name is Robert, he is in the Navy. A naval
> surgeon. Before the war he worked at Plymouth

Hospital. He is a little older than I am (and I am hardly a girl!) and a widower. Father frets about that, but I think he's more worried I won't be here every day to care for Mother and him. I met Robbie at Abbotsgate. You know—the Sydenham place? It's a convalescent hospital now. The new baronet, the mysterious Sir Harry, whom no one's ever seen apparently, is, despite his mysteriousness, serving somewhere in France just like you, and his wife is American so is back there. But I've been helping out. At least, I hope I'm a help. One never knows. But now Robbie's rejoined his ship at its base in the North. I do hope you can both get some leave next time you are back, as I know you will like him. Dear Benedict, I am so terribly happy. I had long thought of myself as a spinster and I pray every night that such good men as you and Robbie will both be safe.

Her happiness was infectious. He was opening the other letter, not recognizing the writing on the envelope, while still imagining his sister as a married woman. With children, he thought. He would be an uncle.

The other letter was from Theo—and his writing had changed. It was large and uncontrolled.

Ben, Master Gunner,

The wanderer returns, dispose of the funeral meats.

Lost my finger—hence this writing like a girl—and the top joint of another and a bit of flesh around my thumb. Near thing, actually. Lucky to have the hand, the medics say. Apparently it was dying on me. But it died, I didn't, so seems a good swap. Don't remember much of it. Have a very passable claw—two and a half of my nicer fingers and some thumb. But the good news is I'm being returned to my squadron. It was touch and go, I can tell you. First with me, then with some knife-happy colonel who had designs on my entire arm, then with the RFC. I saw a long dreary life ahead using my good hand to stamp leave passes. But now they say I can still fly. Probably because so many other chaps have gone west. They need all the pilots they can get, even ones with one and a half hands. So if this gets to you at Harmony Cottage aka Notre Repos, tell Dougie to get some Scotch. Home is the hunter, home from the hill.

There was no cheerful musical notation to start or end the letter.

He felt numb where he knew he should feel happy. Theo had made it. Was coming back: coming back to do the thing he loved. He would fly. He would be Theo. With any luck, they would both return home one day. But Theo would never, could never, play the organ again. The pain and grief Benedict felt was all-consuming and at the same time ridiculous, because Theo himself seemed to have no regrets for the loss of his vast gift as long as he could fly.

Over the last weeks, the engineers had been building roads, wells, and railways, and soldiers of every regiment were, with bad grace, extending the trenches that might save their lives. The battalion drilled and went out on the hated patrols. It was hard to maintain discipline in these protracted periods of waiting. Men drank themselves into unconsciousness, went absent without leave, appeared daily before the M.O. with trivial complaints; they squabbled, fretted, stole, or became inert. To keep them battle-ready, whatever that meant (but it certainly didn't mean fighting each other), companies were moved to the rear to practice storming German trenches. All this they did with enthusiasm, at least at first. They were undaunted, knowing that no one was actually going to shoot them. There were football matches, a concert. There were pep talks from visiting High Command; these, at least, seemed to bring amusement. But little could be done to hide the fact that machinery and soldiers were pouring into the area hourly and that the end of the waiting was going to demand everything these men could give.

Benedict felt it was his duty to spend all his time with them but, in truth, without Theo, Harmony Cottage had become a lonely place. Nevertheless, when his own leave came—just four days—he chose to return to Harmony Cottage, hoping that Theo was back.

The Theo who had returned was not the same Theo.

After surgery, Theo had gone home to rehabilitate, then taken leave, seen his father, was vague about his meeting with Agnes. He said nothing at all about Gloucester. He spoke of spending time in London with Novello, going to nightclubs and meeting his famous friends. Novello, he reported excitedly, had also joined up as a pilot.

If it had sometimes been hard to get through to the real Theo, now there was something more frenetic about him. The hand was misshapen, although more or less functional, but it was obvious that it caused him pain. Benedict tried not to look it.

Theo had a medicine case he'd brought with him when they joined up, at the recommendation of a cousin who was a regular. It was a beautiful thing—dark polished wood with a moiré silk lining. Each amber glass bottle stood in its allotted place, and powders were stored in a drawer. They had laughed at the names on the labels, speculating on what the various drugs were for: Mist Pot Cit; Mist Asp; Quinine; Cocaine; Chlor. Squills; Ammonia; Charcoal; Tincture of Benzoin. "For piles from sitting in a staff car for hours at a time," Theo had suggested.

The only two Benedict could remember them using were iodine and syrup of figs. Now the powder wrappers were scattered about Theo's bed and the silver hypodermic was missing. They had once laughed at tablets called "Forced March," which, the label promised, "Prolong the Force of Endurance," but it was hard to miss the empty bottles in the fireplace. Every time Benedict came back to the billet, Theo was drinking or restlessly asleep. He was flying longer hours than ever. His face was drawn with pain. Another of the RFC lads had told him Theo was only back on flying probation, but he never spoke of it himself.

Then in June he came in to find Theo shirtless and washing. Benedict saw for the first time that Theo's right arm was withered and scarred way above the wrist.

"What are you staring at?" Theo looked at him as he might a stranger. "A freak show? All these weeks of you averting your fastidious eyes. Or are you some kind of nancy boy? Do you want to kiss it better?" He waved the damaged arm at him.

"I'm sorry." He looked away, hurt and ashamed. He could smell the drink on Theo's breath.

"You can be top boy in Gloucester now."

"I don't want—"

"You don't want to fight a war. That's it. You want to play hymns for old ladies until you smell of mice and mildew."

He didn't, couldn't answer. Then he started, stupidly, he knew, to defend himself, say something about beauty and having something to believe you'd go back to.

"Just a game, Ben. It was all just another merry, merry jape." Theo smiled, baring his teeth.

"What's the matter?" It sounded plaintive—whining.

Theo threw his metal shaving bowl across the room, his razor still held in his better hand.

"What's the matter?? For fuck's sake, are you blind, or is it all one great tinkling rainbow for you?"

Suddenly Theo punched the strip of mirror. It shattered. A thin streak of blood ran down his stump and then he seemed to ignite. He spun around, lashed out: a sick devil sweeping things off the old range, smashing the already handleless jug, tearing the faded picture of the Virgin, which had been their lucky mascot since they first saw it hanging there. There was so little to destroy, yet he destroyed it.

"That was you, Ben. Not me. You wanted me to live the life *you* longed for—pretty colored tunes in a pretty church with a pretty house next door—well, now I'm free. Of it all."

He leered at Benedict. Then he staggered away, reached under his bed, and pulled out a bundle of papers.

"Look! Agnes's letters."

He untied them, held them out, read a few anodyne sentences in a lisping falsetto voice, and then, and with pathetic difficulty, ripped them apart. There was gleeful savagery in his face, even as he winced with pain at each violent movement of his arm.

"And O, what do we have here? The cantata, the precious cantata. *Raise Me, Raise Me to the Stars.* You want it?" He tore the first sheet across, screwed it up, hurled it to the floor. "Why don't you wipe your backside with it?"

Benedict reached out, tried to take the pages from him. "Don't," he said. "Don't, Theo."

Theo wrenched them away. "Naughty Theo, don't," he repeated, mimicking, but then said "Fine, have it."

Theo scattered more single sheets, attempted to rip a thick wad of them, then suddenly had Benedict against the wall and was trying to force the paper into his mouth. He was still strong.

"Consume it," he said. "Become me." Then he had dropped the music and was pushing at Benedict's lips with his mutilated hand and one sheet of foolscap. "Take. Eat. This. Is. My. Body. Shed. For. Thee. Isn't that what you'd like? What you've wanted? My body? That's what Novello says."

Benedict turned his head away, choking, as Theo tried to force his teeth apart. Then, as suddenly as he'd begun, Theo reeled back and sank to the bed, weeping hoarsely.

"Fuck off," he said. "Find another billet. I'm sick of you. Stop looking at me with your great doggy, understanding eyes."

Benedict snatched up his immediate possessions, which were few enough; and, as he dipped his head to go through the low door, he heard Theo shout: "You were always so completely second-rate."

CHAPTER NINETEEN
Jean-Baptiste, France, February 1916

JEAN-BAPTISTE HAD COME TO EXPECT death. Probably the next day. Early on, he'd thought death would take other soldiers who'd been there longer. Since then, he'd learned that death was no respecter of natural justice, but was in fact a great practical joker of the nastiest sort, like Lucien Laporte at school. A bullet in the forehead: that was fair. Being blown into a hundred glistening bits of meat: that was fair, though not so good for your comrades. Being bayoneted was fair; gas was vicious but war. But dying from a septic foot or drowning in a puddle or being kicked by a mule: where was the glory in that? You didn't have to travel across France and sleep in a trash pile—death could have found you at home for that.

Everybody knew death was out there, and it seemed the higher-ups were currently making preparations to entice him in.

They were flaunting themselves. There had been a visit by little General Joffre and even the president.

Usually, officers were little seen from day to day and, when they emerged from their billets, were men of few words and no conversation, except with each other, somehow both focused and indifferent. The ones who wanted to save their own skins, just as their men did, only more elegantly, were as dangerous as the ones who were all "They shall not pass." Their own platoon commander, Aspirant Collinette, was scarcely more than a boy, a cadet. Some claimed to have seen him surreptitiously reading a book on how to fight wars.

The men around Jean-Baptiste put what remained of their trust in Sergeant Folz, a blocky, grizzled man who had fought the fuzzy-wuzzies and run two through at once on one of their own spears. He was a brute but a survivor, and his prestige came from bringing his men through. Captain Joubert, who was the section commander, wore wire-rimmed spectacles and reminded Jean-Baptiste of the schoolmaster back in Corbie. He was glad that, unlike the two previous captains, Joubert didn't have a saber. An officer with a nineteenth-century saber seemed to betray a worrying level of misunderstanding. Rather than telling them what the hell was happening or reciting the virtues of the Republic that had sent them to be slaughtered, Joubert trotted out little mottoes when he briefed them. Yesterday's was "Never overestimate your enemy."

Some men said the Germans were using the time to dig a wide tunnel right under the French positions at Verdun and attack them from the rear. For a while Jean-Baptiste found it hard to sleep in the burrow he'd cut into the trench side, thinking of Germans moving noiselessly below and behind him. Some said the British were coming to reinforce them. "Ah, perfidious Albion," said the captain when Folz asked him if it was true.

On February 11, they were ordered to prepare for battle. For months, Jean-Baptiste had kept a small piece of paper and a stub of pencil. Not for the first time, he looked at it for an hour, intending to write to his mother, but, finding there was too much to say, decided it was easier to say nothing. Most of the men around him were veterans; most had been wounded and patched up in earlier battles. In their last hours of being under shelter, three older men played piquet, with sous changing hands back and forth accompanied by grunts and occasional snarls. Another was making a ring for his girl out of a fuse cap. He even had a proper vise in his pack. He'd chucked out his cooking pan to lighten the weight. But most, like Jean-Baptiste, were silenced by the cold, the boredom, and the suffocating blanket of fear.

Two German deserters had turned up a couple of days earlier. They were Alsatians and narrowly escaped being killed as they approached, their hands up, shouting "Don't shoot! Don't shoot! Friends! Don't shoot!" They looked frightened. "Brothers," cried one. Which was a mistake. They insisted they had been forced to be Germans and wear German uniforms but, like all good men of Alsace, were French at heart. They both spoke good French, so Sergeant Folz had punched the one who'd called them brothers and broken his nose as some sort of compromise of justice.

"French, my arse," he'd said.

The other man had blathered that they'd only come to warn them that the Germans were about to launch their push and had a thousand guns trained on this sector. He clearly didn't want to be around, on either side, to see it and seemed relieved when the two of them were sent back to the rear for interrogation.

"They'll shoot them after," said Folz.

Jean-Baptiste imagined that tomorrow's death would be hot: fire or explosive, searing metal or the burst of warm blood. But instead, sometime in the night when he must, finally, have been sleeping, the snow came out of nowhere and with it came life. He woke up because he was even colder and wetter than usual. Thick flakes were falling, blown by gusts into strange shapes. Crests of ice formed on greatcoats like raised white seams, and every so often a soldier in an animal pelt shook himself like a dog. Even with their heads bowed down, snow fell on their cold cheeks and, melting, ran down inside the back of their collars.

Guinard came back from sentry duty and reported the disappearance of earth and sky as well as Germans. Nothing could be seen a meter from the trenches. The mood changed as it became obvious that there was going to be no attack in the next few hours.

Slowly men found their voices, stirred, shook off the small drifts on their uniforms. Joubert was nowhere in sight, but Aspirant Collinette was standing forlornly by Sergeant Folz, looking out into the whiteness. The slender officer cadet had his eyes screwed up and kept wiping his binoculars with his sleeve as the snow fell. Folz stood, legs apart, impervious to the conditions. In his shaggy sheepskin he looked half man, half beast. Jean-Baptiste imagined that any flakes that had the temerity to fall on Folz simply fizzled away. Somebody passed around some brandy. A few meters away, a soldier laughed. This tiny sliver of hope, the likelihood that it wasn't today that was marked for their death, had reanimated these living corpses. He thought that they were like starving beggars being thrown a single crust and felt something like embarrassment: suddenly they were revealing to each other how much they all really wanted to live.

Death, though, had always played a long game. Death could outwait any living creature; while their brief euphoria subsided under the weight of cold and ignorance, death, quite at home in snow, stayed close at hand, waiting for them to starve if they wouldn't fight.

Blizzards, fog, squalls, and gales attacked both sides for days. First one, then four, then twenty men got the runs; the latrines were running over, and only the cold saved the men from being made sick by the stink. The soldier in the hole next to him crawled out at all hours and sat outside, bent over, groaning and occasionally belching, his greatcoat open to reveal his filthy uniform, his fists thrust into his stomach. After a while, he'd stumble off and then, in another while, return to his place, holding his belly as if he'd been bayoneted and was trying to keep his innards from spilling out, his sparse wet whiskers creating black slashes in his white face.

It was odd that they had so much in their bowels to evacuate because, having stayed put longer than anyone expected, they had almost run out of food. Jean-Baptiste's own stomach was griping—but with emptiness, not emptying. He was giddy and his head was full of strange images, half-dreams. Those men who weren't ill drank to ease their hunger and their terrible hope.

For a week, the snow and the freezing fog camouflaged each side from the other, and still death waited. Perhaps he was hopping from one foot to the other, crossing his arms back and forth across his chest to keep warm, Jean-Baptiste thought. Or perhaps death wrapped the snow around himself, like the furs that comforted the ladies of the Faubourg St. Honoré; perhaps, like them, he gave a false little shiver and shrugged as he settled into luxury; perhaps he too wrinkled his nose rather sweetly with the contented warmth of being more fortunate than anyone else around. Death was not a bully, Jean-Baptiste thought. Not a cat-torturing, girl-pinching lout like Laporte, now Corporal Laporte, number one bully to the 165th. No, death was a smooth, clever performer, waiting, spying, like Dr. Vignon. Luring you into friendship. After the third night of standing to and after he'd had three glasses of *pinard*, Jean-Baptiste could imagine Vignon-Death whispering "Let's get out of this, let's go for one of our afternoon trips on the river. It's not far away. You could walk home. Sleep in a proper bed. Don't worry, I've got the very thing to keep the cold away."

Just when they were all wondering if perhaps the weather had set in for real and they might not have to die until May, a priest arrived and gave them all absolution. Aspirant Collinette had his eyes closed, his lips moving in prayer all the way through and crossing himself as if God might look kindly on sheer quantity of genuflection.

"Always bad luck, a holy man," Doré said, and belched. He was close enough for Jean-Baptiste to smell fish on his breath.

In the afternoon, perhaps for lack of anything to do, their guns had opened up from behind them, letting the Germans know they were ready. As night fell, Jean-Baptiste had not had so much *pinard* that he didn't notice it was colder than ever but frighteningly clear; puddles froze and the moon shone on the motionless earthworks, transforming the naked beech and oak trees; the residual snow and the encroaching mud had a black-and-white beauty. There was a silence in their lines, and because of it the rumble of distant German trains could be heard, moving to their depot deep in the Spincourt Forest, undoubtedly loaded with ammunition. As he was dropping off to sleep, his tight grave of a hole spinning when he shut his eyes and acid rising from his stomach, Jean-Baptiste could even hear Germans singing, a lot closer than the trains.

The next day, Jean-Baptiste woke with a sick headache; and when what passed for daylight came, they could—as he had feared—see. It was still freezing at first, but the fog had gone, the wind had settled, and the sun came out. There was a bit of a ruckus as Giseaux had disappeared in the night. Aspirant Collinette didn't seem bothered; he was nervous as hell, anyone could see that, and his guts were still playing up. He couldn't even get to the officers' *cabinet* but had to use the men's stinking latrine.

Sergeant Folz said "Giseaux's dead if I find him. I'll crucify him with my own hands." He made a strangling motion. Then he crossed himself, at which a massive explosion shook the ground and debris fell on them. Another, nearer, followed. Explosion succeeded explosion and the trees came apart with a terrible cracking and crashing. The ground trembled, and the hole that had been a bed for Jean-Baptiste caved in. Other men were still in their burrows when they and their holes disappeared after the big guns—210-millimeter shells, Doré said, field mortars—started landing horribly accurate fire along the wood.

"Under cover, men," said Collinette, almost politely.

"Move, you numbskulls!" Folz bellowed.

As they were running, bent double, to defend their broken defenses, they passed one of their own guns, torn camouflage fluttering from it, and a handful of artillery men fanned out around it almost in a circle, deader than dead.

A runner passed in a panic, delivering his message to anyone who'd listen: the sector to their left had taken a direct hit and they couldn't count on support. Jean-Baptiste stumbled on. After the next close shell, Jean-Baptiste thought he was deaf; but then he could hear shrieks, quite plainly and not far away.

So death had been waiting even closer than Jean-Baptiste had imagined. The alarm was sounded: a tiny bugle, as a spotter saw large numbers of Germans moving toward their damaged positions. A second soldier, badly injured, came tumbling into their bay, warning them some Germans had entered the trench system and infiltrated their defenses.

"Fix bayonets," Folz shouted and Jean-Baptiste fumbled, suddenly short of room. Despite the cold, his hands were slippery. Finally the bayonet slipped into place. He allowed himself to think of his mother as he crouched, certain that the discomfort of it all would soon be over. He chose to see her pulling up leeks by the canal with black earth speckling her apron and the clogs she still wore for tending her vegetables. She stood to see him and smiled, her eyes crinkling as she tried to make him out against the sun, and she mopped her face with her apron corner.

"Go! Go! Go!" Folz was shouting, waving them out to the left. He could see tiny gray figures moving in small groups toward them, rifles raised, and there was Aspirant Collinette, lying on his back, his head at the edge of the defile, broken twigs lying on him, his arms by his side as if he'd been laid out.

The trench here had been blown open. He ran, crouched low, directly behind another stooped figure. The ground was still residually frozen and uneven; he nearly fell into a fresh crater, but dodged to the side just in time. Simenon, level with him, had a grenade out and was pulling the pin. He wanted to tell him to watch out for the hole, but the noise made him mute; Simenon went head-first into the crater and blew up.

Jean-Baptiste jumped over a blue-uniformed back: somebody from the reserves who'd gotten ahold of the new uniform. Wasted. As he looked down, something massive hit him—blew all the breath out of his body. This was death, he thought. But it was the great weight of Sergeant Folz, thrown backward. They both lay on the ground, but Jean-Baptiste scrambled free, still fighting to breathe. Folz's whole leg was gone. Jean-Baptiste thought for a minute that it was folded under him but no, it was visible a meter away. Or, at least, someone's leg was.

Folz opened a remaining eye. "What are you staring at, you numbskull? Keep moving or you'll be fucking killed."

So he moved into the thin metallic thread of noise and the fatter, ground-shaking explosions, the surprised "oofs" of the falling, and sounds like seagulls and of pigs being slaughtered, and he could see some shapes ahead of him but were they French or Germans and the ground became more bodies than mud, and under his boots things cried out. Then there was a German, within touching distance; where the hell had he come from? Both of them paused but Jean-Baptiste's bayonet got the soldier in one of Folz's approved spots—into the neck. It sank in—not at all like into a sandbag—and ground against something solid. The man, old enough to be his father, gurgled and a hand came up and Jean-Baptiste pulled, then was frantic when the blade wouldn't come away. "Lunge, forward, in, out," Folz had shouted. "Easy! Clean!" The German soldier tried to grasp the blade and twisted on it, blood was everywhere, but then at last he fell back and off the bayonet.

To his far left Jean–Baptiste saw a small group of Germans, stationary, with some equipment. With a roar that he could hear, even over the exchanges of fire, a great spout of flame belched out and he watched it search for a target, suddenly remembering Lucien Laporte busy burning ants. The flame engulfed two Frenchmen, but he was too far away to see if the writhing, blackening soldiers had been his comrades.

And then, finally, it happened: he heard nothing, saw nothing, but he was on the ground too, a little shocked, not with a sharp pain but as if a great gust of wind had hurled him down. His ears were ringing and he felt that he was gasping like a landed fish. There was only a very little room for each breath. He tried not to panic, to take tiny sips of air. Either the sky or his eyesight was blurred, and he had a fancy that he was looking down on himself and that he had been blown right into the earth, planted into the mud. He blinked several times; his crotch was warm and his shoulder hurt but he reached down, gingerly, with tentative fingertips toward the fiery center of what he now was and found naked skin and the thick wetness he feared, and his fingers went into a sodden space that was horribly unfamiliar, then he looked to his side and there, next to him, was Doré, looking at him through slitted eyes, his mouth in a small "O" but no more exhalation of fish, and death had swept both of them to him in one loving embrace.

CHAPTER TWENTY

Frank, France, March 1916

ONE THING YOU LEARN ABOUT war is that, like most sports, it is more or less seasonal. Summer is the time for the big events. Winter is the slow season, mostly spent fighting the weather, and everyone gets back in training in spring. But this March was bitter. The French were dying in all kinds of hell to the southeast, but we Empire boys were, in a manner of speaking, waiting. It was exercises by day when we weren't digging, patrols by night. Fritz must have heard us crunching through the puddles of ice, but he obviously couldn't be bothered to come out of his cozy nook and shoot us. You could smell his sausages cooking.

They said that much of the war around the Ancre and the Somme was about mining under the enemy and blowing him up. And Fritz doing the same to us. Sometimes they ran into each other, scuttling around down there in the dark. *Überraschung!* Which is German for surprise.

But at its center, it was all about messages. The sappers had their underground army and its wires, set to create hell (a message of a sort, and just as likely to get an answer sooner or later), and we had ours, an army of signalers and messengers, passing info to and fro.

After a while, you'd notice that the moles were pale like city men who worked in shops, and the messengers were weathered like farm boys. But if you passed messages, you knew stuff and knew it first. Some liked to keep their expressions like stone: "You won't read any military secrets in *my* face." Others liked to give just a bit away. Others liked to give a lot away as they hurtled past, gabbing, on Army business.

The order of signaling usefulness went like this:

1. Linesmen. They mostly ran, squatted, or crawled through the mud, rolling their drums before them, and they were top of the heap because they *were* modern warfare and had to know how to fasten the wires up to field telephones at each end.
2. Signalers had lanterns and had to know Morse and liked to practice it with each other for a laugh: "Your girl's off with a sailor" and "I've pissed in Spook's water bottle." Very funny they thought they were.
3. The flag men stood on a hill and waved their flags. But the signals were read one way by our boys: "Range too short," and another by Fritz: "Shoot me now."
4. The rocket men suffered because Fritz and us had the same rockets—so when a flare went up it, could be ours, could be theirs. Could mean anything.
5. The runners were the backup boys—when every-thing else had failed. Like being a cyclist, it sounded

easier than it was—and like with us cyclists, it was the terrain that b*****d them up: there was no running through trenches and wire.

6. Dogs. They just upset people. They were impatiently enthusiastic, but nobody liked to see ours hurt and nobody wanted to shoot Fritz's. One corporal was killed trying to put an injured dog out of its misery. For a while, we had one dog of Fritz's we'd captured—well, he changed sides basically. Big chap; he'd lost his message, useless dog, though he had his service number on his collar. He came from Westphalia, but he was anybody's for a bit of corned beef and a stroke. We called him Kaiser Bill.

7. Pigeons. Sometimes they flew, sometimes they hid, especially if the weather was bad. Sometimes they were turned into stew. If pigeons weren't clearly on our side, I thought, who could blame them, given their treatment back home?

8. Us cyclists. Not many of us went to France, and who knows what they were thinking of who sent us. A few were switched to stretcher-bearing, but I thought of the others I'd known in training, still guarding the eastern defenses of England on long flat roads that roared like the sea as the tires covered the miles, the only enemy the wind.

Here? In the mud? Cyclists? Pointless. So I'm putting us last, after the pigeons even.

Back in Debenhams, Mr. Richmond liked to feed pigeons and see them cluster at his window, just as he was taking his tea. He'd crumble up Madeira cake and chat to them, claimed they knew their own names. "Look at their colors," he'd say; "who could ever say the London pigeon is gray?"

Meanwhile, Bert, the store handyman, hated them, said they spread filth and germs and were destroying the façade of his building. "Blinking vermin," he'd shout out the window, which would have startled the ladies if he wasn't five floors up at the time.

Mind you, he was cut of Isaac's political cloth and probably thought the customers were vermin too. Working men were his gods, and in his den in the basement he would show anyone who came by the plans he'd bought for making bombs. He couldn't actually make them, because the instructions were in German. Was he out here too somewhere, I wondered, finally blowing something up? I know for a fact Bert put poison out for the pigeons. He disguised it in crumbs. So the pigeons wouldn't know whether their next meal would fatten them up or kill them dead.

But sometimes I thought it was odd that cyclists and lantern-men and poor old flag-wavers were all reckoned equal now with a bird you could put in a pie. And sometimes I thought they were dead right. Every day out in France was like a pigeon's dinner: would it be Madeira cake or arsenic?

It snowed so hard that they canceled formations and the officers laid on a picture show and concert in the evening. Hundreds of us turned up, maybe just for the warmth. There was wine and women in town if you had a mind to it, but it was a freezing-cold walk back home. After the evening, we were in good spirits. Some lads were taking bets on the next day's rugby match: 1st Middlesex vs. the Liverpool lads.

"I want to bet they can't even find the field," I said. But they wouldn't take it.

The Middlesexes won 42-0. Thought we would never hear the last of it.

We still had on our winter sheepskins at night and scarves or balaclavas knitted by sweethearts or Red Cross ladies. Sweethearts tended to knit in a single color, very neat, sometimes with initials worked in. Red Cross scarves were like something biblical: scarves of many colors, made of oddments. So, plain says someone loves you, stripes says someone likes the idea of you. But after an hour cutting trenches or latrines, you'd be down to shirt and suspenders, loved or not.

Horrible work. I had lumbago from the start.

I wondered about Isaac. How would he manage? But I smiled to remember how in training he'd shown me a great dark fur hat that had belonged to his granddad, back in Russia, and that he now planned to take to the war. Great flaps you could tie under the chin and a furry peak to catch the snow. He put it on once and looked like a theatre bear; and then he took it off fast, feeling faint from heat and the weight of it. But now, Isaac should be smiling.

"Excellent," says Sergeant Oughtibridge, stamping on the ground with his boot that morning. "Like a racetrack. Off you go." More like a skating rink, I thought.

"Good show," says Captain Bolitho when I got there; "you'll be of some use for once."

Cheeky blighter—but I liked him. He was a cheery sort on top and serious underneath. He didn't just give orders, the lads said, but often explained what they were doing, like they could learn something. Some liked that, some didn't. When he saw me, he'd always say "Ah, here comes Hermes." I don't know why he called me that. Some of the other lads thought he'd called me Hermann, and I never heard the last of it.

The captain even spoke German and was quite happy to tell us he'd been in Vienna and Berlin before the war and what fine cities they were, in a way that didn't make anyone think he was soft on the enemy. One day a while back, I'd taken a message up to him where the sappers were digging wells. Suddenly some corporal tells us to shush and get down. We could hear singing— German singing. A fine voice and a marching tune. And then a whole troop marched by, above us but only yards away, singing cheerfully as they went off to kill our boys. We'd ducked down but they only had to look to their right to see us, yet Bolitho had a little smile on his face the whole time, and his head was moving like he was enjoying it.

"What's he singing?" says one lad as a second voice joined in, and the others gave him nasty looks for speaking too loud, though they'd passed well down the track by then.

"It's a traditional song about the Rhine," says the captain very quietly. Then he adds, "That's a river in Germany."

"Shall we take them out, sir?" whispers the corporal.

The captain shook his head. When the German and his pals had sung themselves off back to their lair, he said it was because it would simply alert Fritz to our position, which was far closer than we'd been told, but I think he liked the voice.

When things were quieter I asked "What was that German song, sir?" Most officers would have told me to bug off with my stupid questions. But he told me, and he wrote it down in German and English and I tucked it in my pack. *"Fest steht und treu die Wacht, die Wacht am Rhein."* "That means: one thing is certain and true—the watch on the Rhine," he said. Which seemed like something an Englishman might sing about the Thames.

CHAPTER TWENTY-ONE

L'Abbaye de Royaumont, April 1916

Je donnerais Versailles,
Paris et Saint-Denis,
Le royaune de mon père,
Celni de ma mère aussi. . . .

ONE SOLDIER SINGING DOESN'T DISGUISE the fact that it is another bloody morning in the Abbaye de Royaumont. The ascetic shades of medieval monks have fled before the Scottish ladies who have turned the abbey into a military hospital. The stern lady doctors, the prim and pretty lady nurses, the orderlies, cooks, drivers, managers of supplies, cleaners. All females. All from Scotland. The patients, most of whom are French, think this is part of their delirium. They wake from what they thought or hoped was death to find themselves in an ancient holy place with women toiling over their vulnerable and altered bodies. Some cross themselves. Some weep.

Auprès de ma blonde,
Qu'il fait bon, fait bon, fait bon. . . .

Fucking hell. By the Holy Virgin and all the saints. Fuckfuck-
fuck my fucking leg.

Fix bayonets.

Of your mercy. . . .

Maman. Mama. Aide-moi.

I'll show you murdering bastards.

My friend. Where is my friend?

Tu est un petit poisson . . .
sous un petit bateau. . . .

The smell. The smell. The bellies of dead fish are around like
stepping stones, and the eels are fat with meat.

"Don't worry, Jean, when the river returns to its proper place,
it will have left a gift of black earth and we shall have the fattest
onions you've ever seen. *Tarte à l'oignons.*"

Oignons, rognons.
Comme ça comme ça.

Don't worry, little Jean.

For some, silence.

"He's mute," the lady doctor said to Vignon. "Fusilier. Casualty
from Verdun. Came to us in February. Flesh wounds to the legs,
shrapnel to the chest. Right-side pneumothorax. Bladder tear,
one kidney ruptured. Has done surprisingly well, given how ill
he was when he arrived. But mute. We thought at first he simply
couldn't understand us, but most of us speak passable French and
the other invalids manage."

Her accent was, Captain Vignon thought, truly extraordinary.

"He's not deaf," the lady doctor said. "Indeed, he's very easily startled, but he certainly can't—or won't, poor man—speak. Not a word."

She pushed her wire glasses up her nose. A thin strip of dressing gauze knotted their two arms around the back of her head. On the right woman it might, just, have looked attractive, bohemian. She was not the right woman.

She was perhaps only forty, but her chin was downy; her thick sandy hair, streaked with gray, was lifeless, her body under its stained white coat shapeless. As a doctor Vignon could imagine it, but as a man he preferred not to try. These women who took on men's jobs must throw away their chances of ever knowing a man's loving vigor, he thought, although it was impossible to feel sorry for them: there was a kind of magnificence in their masculine inflexibility.

"Will he return to his regiment?" Vignon asked as they moved on to see three other cases, but in his heart was a sliver of fear.

"The fusilier? Perhaps. I don't know. He shouldn't. I doubt he'd survive another injury. But he probably will. You medical officers come and check the casualties, always convinced that as women we have soft female hearts and might hold on to them once they're relatively fit." She shrugged. "As if we had room for even half-fit men. And one case of typhoid can destroy all our work."

"But he's mute, you said?" and was ashamed at his need to confirm it. "Are you treating him?"

"We don't have mind doctors here," she said.

He wondered whether her feminine heart heard the pain and madness echoing around her any more. All military hospitals smelled and sounded the same, but here the cries ricocheted off arches and vaults that had once amplified the voices of monks praising God. If God was still listening, Vignon hoped he shared the capacity to suffer that he'd bestowed so freely on his children.

Captain Vignon, Surgeon-Militaire, had volunteered to come to the hospital at Royaumont to consider cases for transfer so felt himself implicated in the brutality with which sick men were returned to service. No doubt she intended it to be so.

He looked across at the iron bed. He had not been sure at first; the face had changed, but as the boy opened his eyes there was no doubt. Vignon's heart beat a little faster.

Vignon had been curious to see this hospital run entirely by women. It seemed entirely unnatural; but despite himself, he had to admit that they had made a good showing in this ancient and unsuitable building. Some patients were being nursed in the cloisters, most of them oblivious to the fresh summer air. Unlike the lady doctor, some of the nurses, he observed, were not unaware of a handsome French officer in uniform. Nor were their crumpled and straining aprons unappealing, and he had always liked to see a curl escaping from a woman's pinned hair. Were they Scotswomen too? He had never met a person from Scotland before, and he feared for their menfolk.

"I'll leave you with our administrator to look at the patients," she said. "Do you speak English? Miss McAdam's French is not yet fully honed."

He was shaking his head. "Small," he said in her own language. "A very small English."

"Ah well," she said and for some reason looked amused; "where there's a will."

What did she mean? It meant nothing. Where was there a will?

His gaze was shifting back to the bed a few yards away, set in the shade of a stone arch, when she turned round again, hands thrust in her pockets.

"You don't speak German, do you?"

He was already saying that he regretted that he did not, when she said, "We have this young soldier, no more than fifteen or sixteen, we've no idea of his name. We get them from time to time—prisoners. Occasionally one of the ladies can speak German, and I suspect one or two of your soldiers do, but of course they hate the Germans so can't be trusted, although we had a French surgeon visit, much traveled, and he was quite proficient. But currently—not a soul speaks more than an *Auf wiedersehen*. Which hardly seems appropriate here."

She turned away again and with some relief he watched her start to walk away.

"A shame," she said, half turning. "He's dying. The German boy. Very agitated for a while, but quiet now. He's had the priest— unfortunately Father Clément is a very patriotic Catholic, and for all we know the child's a Lutheran—but—" She made a small face of regret. "It would have been nice for him to have heard someone speak in his own language."

"I could try," he said, after a few seconds, and felt deep unease.

The administrator took him to the German boy. He was in a tiny side room, on his own but under no kind of guard, but then he wasn't going anywhere except to the angels. His head was bandaged, and his pallor and grayish lips gave him the look of a corpse, so much so that, not seeing any movement of his chest, Vignon reached out and felt for a pulse in his neck. The boy's eyelashes were long and black and his eyes sunk in deep purple bruises. As he felt the thready pulse under his fingers still just keeping the boy in the world of the living, his sticky lips moved. Vignon reached over to a bowl of water, took a square of lint that lay beside it, and dripped a little moisture on to them. He thought the boy might be trying to speak, and he said *"Wie heisst du?"*

The lips kept moving, but the response might well have been the last spasms of a failing system. There was a stool by the bed. Vignon sat down on it and took the boy's hand in his; it was very soft and young, hairless, almost a woman's hand. He looked behind him, but the doorway was empty. He could hear pigeons on the cloister roof. He rotated his shoulders in an attempt to ease his aching neck, but kept his eyes on the boy all the time.

"Vater unser im Himmel," he began. *"Geheiligt werde dein Name, Dein Reich komme. Dein Wille geschehe. . . ."*

He was whispering, the words taking him back to his own childhood, kneeling next to his mother.

The boy, the child, whose hand he held appeared to hear nothing, gazing at Vignon. How could one believe in a God any longer?

"Ihre Mutter soll sein . . ." he said. *"Ihre Mutti . . ."* Then as he started to form the word *stolz*, proud, he felt anger rising: his mother would be proud? No. His mother would be heartbroken. With her child dead—his mother would be finished.

And then he leaned forward, his fingers and thumb slowly massaging the boy's knuckles, as he sang, very low, *"Schlaf, mein Kindlein, schlaf. . . ."*

And the next time he felt for the pulse, it and the boy had left him.

Just for a minute he sank his head into his hands, abominably weary, abominably old. But he had work to do. He pushed himself up, using the metal bed as a support, and turned as he heard a noise. To his dismay, a nurse stood in the doorway. He thought she had tears in her eyes.

"I came to take over," she said hesitantly.

"Death has taken over, mademoiselle."

"Oh," she said, her glance moving to the dead boy. "I'll tell Sister." Her voice was uneven and she looked genuinely sad. "He was ever so young. Even if he was the enemy."

He bowed slightly as he left the room, but as he passed her she said "Where did you learn German so well?" And then as he felt a quickening sense of alarm she added, like an eager schoolgirl, "I know some words, but I can't put them together."

He was formulating an answer when she said, quite simply, "It was beautiful."

He returned to the ward, taking half a dozen files with their skimpy notes. Although he was unable to translate some of the words, the diagrams of injuries and procedures were as clear in

English as they were in French. He selected the injured soldiers who would be loaded onto the French hospital barge to transfer them to Abbeville. One further patient clearly had consumption and Vignon added him to the list, but for transfer to the sanatorium in Paris. As he signed the administrator's forms, she smiled at him for the first time.

"That was a great kindness, with our German boy," she said. "I'd quite misunderstood; I gather you have excellent German. Nurse Campbell said you were a great comfort."

He refrained from saying that the shattered soldier had been far beyond comfort.

Then he went back to the cloisters. He thought of the German mother who didn't know yet that she had no son. He wanted a long look at the French soldier. He stood at the foot of the bed and, this time, without an onlooker to scrutinize his reactions.

"Jean-Baptiste," he said and, unlike the dying German, the soldier's eyes flicked open immediately, although he looked blankly at the man standing nearby. Vignon moved to one side, so that he was more than just a silhouette against the light.

Jean-Baptiste's rudimentary beard made him look older than his years and had been the cause of the doctor's initial confusion.

"It is I, Vignon," he said. "Captain Vignon." Then, with a sense that he was hiding behind his rank and their changed circumstances, he went on, "*Doctor* Vignon. We used to go on the river in *Sans Souci*. My little boat." He paused, waiting for a reaction. He had almost said "I was a friend of your mother," but clearly that was territory best avoided.

Jean-Baptiste was staring at him. Was that recognition he saw in his eyes, or simply bewilderment?

"At Corbie. We used to have happy afternoons on the river."

Jean-Baptiste turned his head away in what seemed like a deliberate snub.

"Have it your own way," said Vignon. "I want to help you." But the young man just closed his eyes tightly.

Vignon walked off, signaled an orderly with less than his usual peremptoriness. It was, he thought, very peculiar to have women where he was used to seeing men.

"This man," he pointed to Jean-Baptiste. "I shall take him with me. We can speed up his treatment, and then he can join his brothers back in his regiment."

He could have sworn the woman looked at him with contempt. Her carriage was entirely ladylike, her green eyes, on a level with his, claiming them as equals.

"He's not strong," she said, her accent perfect.

"Nevertheless. . . ."

She shrugged in a way that any Frenchwoman would have been proud of.

As he waited for the men to be loaded, Vignon's pulse was beating hard. His head ached. The nurse who had interrupted him with the German boy went by, carrying carbolic and bandages.

"Auf wiedersehen," she mouthed at him with what he assumed was meant to be a conspiratorial smile.

The pulmonary case was being taken in a separate vehicle; one of the remaining men was well-nigh unconscious or drugged. A very pretty nurse, if a little freckled for Vignon's taste, was leaning over an alert young soldier with fine moustaches and a well-healed scar from scalp to chin, holding his hand. He whispered something and she blushed. A chasseur was muttering to himself, but one patient grasped at Vignon's hand as his stretcher was steadied, ready to be positioned.

"Doctor! Sir! Thank you. Thank you. Long live France!"

Clearly the soldier had misunderstood the purpose of Vignon's visit. Two weeks was the desired turnaround. Two weeks, and the man would be back with his section.

CHAPTER TWENTY-TWO
Frank, France, June 1916

A ROTTEN DAY.

Some Frenchmen were billeted with us on their way to join their section. I spent the evening talking bicycles with them. When I say talking, we weren't so much talking as gesturing. Isaac tried Esperanto, but it's not as good for communicating as it was as an idea back in London. Isaac insisted he'd been able to speak to all sorts using it—French, Belgians, Bulgarians, even a German prisoner, though the sergeant said he was shouting at the German in some lingo Jewish people know, not Esperanto at all. But it was obvious that what Isaac was really good at was gestures. He didn't even realize how naturally these came to him, so much so that he'd started to use them when speaking English to his chums.

I said to the Frenchies, slowly, that they had some good cyclists.

"Tour de France," I said very clearly. "TOUR DE FRANCE." I sensed Isaac pedaling an imaginary bicycle beside me.

One of the Frenchmen was nodding his head. "Tour de France," he answered back.

His friend was giving Isaac some clear liquid from a small bottle, patting his chest to make it clear that it was French medicine for coughs. Isaac knocked it back and his eyes watered and he breathed out hard,but in a while he stopped coughing and looked a lot happier.

So I said to the other man, "François Faber *mort*." Because I knew *mort*. You soon learned the word for dead when you were a soldier. *Tot* it was in German.

The Frenchman nodded. And mimed a machine gun.

I nodded.

His friend nodded too, and then he said something very quickly and I thought I heard the name Lapize.

"Lapize? Octave Lapize?" I said.

They both nodded.

"Mort," said one.

"Terrible," said the other, almost in English.

Not Lapize, I thought. Not after poor Faber getting it. Not the proud Lapize. I could have wept.

Once war came, that had put an end to the Tour de France. France was not the greatest of racetracks now but the worst of battlefields, and a bog to boot. The race was finished and the champions had become soldiers. Now it seemed like it was the end of those cycling men too.

"Lapize *mort*?" I said and, half-heartedly, made a movement like a firing gun.

He shook his head. Put his thumbs together and turned his hands into a bird, flapping them down across his body and making, although quietly, the noise of a screaming aeroplane.

"Pilote," says his chum. Which meaning I grasped. And it is obvious what happened to Lapize. Tried to master the air as well as he had the mountains, it seems. For a while, anyway.

It sickened me.

I'd been that glad to see Isaac again. Went back to billets one spring day and there he was. We'd been split up on arriving in France in late '15. He'd been kept at base in Étaples, I'd gone on attachment to the 30th. He sent a battalion Christmas card with Father Christmas riding on a gun carriage to say he was well and had done no fighting. He put in a cutting about striking factory workers back home. Connie had been arrested for "agitating workers." He'd written "Nothing new then!" on the top. So when I walked in, saw him and his pack sitting on a bunk like two orphans, I could have thrown my arms around him.

"Where's your hat?" I asked straight off.

"It's a *ushanka*," said he. "That's its Russian name. I could have sold it ten times over last winter. Including officers. But I didn't. If anything happens to me, it's yours."

He looked more sickly than ever. He'd been in the hospital for a while with a bronchial infection. Even the doctor had tried to buy the *ushanka*, he said.

For all that we were both glad being together, we found ourselves squabbling much of the time. He'd liked the training all right, and was good at it, but the active service didn't seem to suit him. The area was all countryside for a start, and what villages there were were half deserted or being turned into rubble, and Isaac had never been happy outside a town. But I couldn't cope with all the dramatics. When I called him on it, he'd give me this doleful look as if it wasn't even odds whether either of us could come to grief. But I'd soon had it with him carrying on like he was already done for every time he went out. It was bad luck.

For example, one evening, when things were starting to heat up, Mr. Pierce came along and took two cyclists to go forward to run messages for the Lancashires. One was Isaac. He put his stuff together on his bed, coughing a bit as he did. The tracts, his

Book of Thoughts, his Esperanto dictionary, his clippings and pamphlets, and his creased photograph of his father and mother, taken in the last century by the look of it. He suddenly got very formal and insisted on shaking my hand.

"Please write to my brother if I don't come back," he said.

"Don't be an ass," said I. "You'll get a grandstand view, see a bit of proper action but not be part of it, and you'll be back swanking and able to live off it for days." He would, too, in his pessimistic way. That was Isaac all over.

"His address is in my tin," he said. "But it's easy. It's the same as my name. Meyer Street. Number 14, Meyer Street. Stepney. If you remember fourteen, that's all you need. Samuel will get it. When he gets out of prison."

But I wasn't listening, because to hear would be bad luck.

Five hours later, Isaac came back in, pushing his machine. He nodded, in a sort of exhausted, sort of relieved, sort of proud way.

"All right?" I said.

He nodded again, breathless. "Sticky," he said. "It was, I mean. Out there. Very bad."

But as he put his photograph and his book and his dictionary away, something about him said Now I've seen it all and I didn't shirk it. That night he didn't cough at all. Very quiet, he was.

So, his luck held and my luck held for ten months or so from when we'd signed our papers right through to the next summer. But then as June unfolded, stuff started to go wrong. One of our best officers caught it just standing there lighting his pipe, one patrol went out and didn't return, and our colonel collapsed with a burst ulcer. Sent back to Blighty.

I went out with a message one foul night, thinking that if Nora and I fell in a shell hole, she'd drown us both, and when I got there—a trench overlooking Mametz—there was nobody wanting my message, just three dead men, sitting tidy, all with their throats cut. Even after everything I'd seen, it gave me the heebie-jeebies. I was looking behind me; someone had crept up on these three, unexpected; two hadn't even lifted their rifles. On the way back, I heard shouting and passed a wagon train with two soldiers, and they had slipped half into a crater of mud and they'd shot one of their mules, as it had broken its leg. They'd cut the remaining mule free, and it had pulled away and charged off to fall in the next foxhole. As I came past, one of the soldiers jumped on the other lad, knocked him backward, and looked fit to drown him too.

I was a bit iffy with Isaac when I got back. I shouldn't have been—he'd been a good friend to me, but he thought backward too much.

"Did you ever see men dead before?" he said. "I saw my mother and father, but they were neat in their clothes. I never thought to see bits of people. But yesterday—"

"I've seen thousands of the deceased," I said. "Timely and untimely. In all conditions of death." It was probably an exaggeration and less than a hundred was more like it and the worst I'd seen before France was an old farmer hanged himself. Isaac looked at me as if I was Jack the Ripper, so I had to tell him my father was a coffin-maker and I'd gone with him for the measuring since I was a young 'un.

"You never said," he said, as if we were an old married couple keeping secrets from each other. "Though I always thought your voice was a bit funny."

Two days it rained: bad news for battles and cycles alike. We all thought the big show was in days: June 25, some swore, definitely the twenty-eighth others said, but, like a creeping barrage, the day of reckoning (what the new colonel called "giving Jerry a good kick up the backside") seemed to march on ahead of us.

They'd been moving up men and stores for weeks: rolling stock, horses, and mule trains bringing it in, and there were more

219

gunners and guns than I'd ever seen in one place. Put your hand out and you'd touch a gunner. Not that you'd want to, they were a cocky lot and thought it was all about them. So did the sappers. We cyclists didn't. We *followed* war, we didn't make it. With no war, they'd be out of a job and we'd just be on a pleasant tour of the Continent.

There were exercises and patrols like there was no tomorrow, but unfortunately tomorrow was always what we were leading up to and—when we got there—was what some of us would have no more of. Everybody was exhausted and tense all at the same time. A random shell hit one of the latrines, blew it and its contents sky-high. The men in it knew nothing, I expect, dying with their breeches down. You'd feel safe like that, I thought, as if you'd stepped out of the war, but you weren't safe anywhere with guns that could fire from miles away.

What a stinking mess.

That waiting made some mute, made some peevish, excited some madmen, and made most of us damned fed up. I saw a man fly into a rage because he was doing a jigsaw and the last two pieces were missing. Sky was all they were, you could see it was a picture of Windsor Castle, but he was accusing this man and that in a fury. Another West Country lad was full of how his brother had helped a wounded French soldier; but when he'd unbuttoned the blue tunic, underneath it was a girl. "Short hair but two little titties," he said. "What do you think about that?" He told us the story three, four, five times over, holding his hands up in a double squeezing action on each telling.

But it wasn't likely anything special would happen while the rain kept coming down. At night the noise of it, on the sheets of corrugated iron that were called a roof, was almost louder than the exchanges of fire from the forward trenches and the thump-bloody-thump of our guns. The water trickled through, and no sooner had you moved clear of one drip than the rain found a new way in. The M.O. had given Isaac syrup for his cough a while back, but he'd still wake us up, hacking away, then keep us awake finding a spoon he'd lifted from a canteen and carefully measuring out the dose by the light of a torch, all the while, in case any of us, by some miracle, was still asleep, hissing, "Sorry. Sorry, boys."

"Just take a swig," I said one night. "It's not opium, it's sugar water. You don't need to measure it. Take too much, you're not going to die of it; more likely it'll fatten you up, which you need."

"It's got squills in it. It says syrup of squills," he said.

"What the hell are squills?"

"I don't know," he said miserably. "They don't seem to help."

One of the other lads had said they'd be better off ditching the medicine and giving everyone who had to be in billets with Isaac a double dose of rum.

"You're all bones, Meyer," he said. "Just go forward sideways and no Jerry'll ever hit you: all they'll see is a helmet and a kitbag and they'll think you're a spook."

"He's bonier than his cycle, en't he, Hermann?" one spotty boy said to me, hardly able to speak for laughing. "Your machine gets in the mud again, you can ride on Spook here."

After that, the names stuck, though for me he was always Isaac and I Frank to him. The next evening, we were polishing our equipment when he started coughing. Then, as he reached for it, he saw that someone had emptied his bottle. It lay on its side in a small sticky puddle beside his pack. The cork was nowhere to be seen. Isaac looked as if he was going to cry. His stifled coughs went on all night.

At one point, a voice from the darkness said "If you don't stop coughing, I swear I'll spike you on my bayonet."

And then another merry lad said "We could let Spook get captured by Jerry, and then he could drive *them* all mad with his cough. He'd be a secret weapon. Tire them to death."

I spent that night feeling low. It seemed to get light only an hour or two after darkness fell, and I got up and went out for a ciggie, though it was a habit I was finding hard to acquire. It was warm, but a fine drizzle was falling. All the time the guns. What hell they were laying down over there in Fritz's luxury trenches, with their electricity and cuckoo clocks, I thought. At least I hoped they were. Or mostly I hoped so, but sometimes I thought there might be some Manfred or Wolfgang over there as had worked his way up to the counter of a great shop in Berlin and thought he'd got it made and now, well, now was all he'd got.

It was edgy waiting, like it always was, even when it wasn't you going out. I wondered if the boys were in position ready to go all this time.

I went over and unfolded Nora, glad the ground was drier and I had a chance of getting messages through. Nora felt warm. I checked her tires, though I'd done it the evening before. Checked the chain, which was clean and oiled. Spun the pedals. Looked in my tool kit. As I was standing there, Lieutenant Pierce appeared out of the darkness. I held the handlebar with my left hand and saluted with my right arm. Not a wobble; the training sergeant would have been proud of me.

"At ease," he said.

Here we go, I thought. Let battle begin.

"Don't worry," he said, as if I might be feeling left out. "We'll be needing you a lot in a day or so. They're trying to run extra trenches across no-man's land, make it easier for the You Know What. I'm afraid you'll mostly be bringing shopping lists back; a bit of an errand boy. The wires are a mess there and the signalers have got other priorities."

We exchanged a look, man to man.

So here I am. Errand Boy of the Western Front. But tomorrow I have to cycle to Amiens, Mr. Pierce says, which will be a matter of real roads, fifteen miles of them.

Mostly I'd be better off being a runner instead of lumbering around with a heap of metal, but mostly in the Army if you're down as a cyclist you stay a cyclist until the end. Which I sometimes think will be sooner rather than later, slowed down as I am by poor old Nora. Sometimes I think of old Dick Wilson and how I came by Nora and her being at war and what he'd think of Hercules being swapped for Nora and a form with a quartermaster's moniker on it and a regimental rubber stamp.

Kitchener's been drowned while leaving Scapa Flow. His ship struck a mine. One up for Fritz.

CHAPTER TWENTY-THREE
Jean-Baptiste, Amiens, June 1916

HE WAS ON WATER. THAT was certain. The river had taken him back.

Before he woke up for good, Jean-Baptiste remembered bits of time. Men weeping and shouting. Pain. Smells. Foreign women: the first one, all in white, he had thought was an angel and wondered if fish-breath Doré was here too. The arches of heaven rose above him. Then a woman came and they held him down when he fought and put something over his nose and mouth and first his head and then his body spun as he died again.

Time had dissolved and everything became confused. There was his mother, but she turned and was a nurse in blue, hurried but kind-faced, and there was Godet being lifted from the bed beside him, his head wrapped in dark bandages. But it was not Godet, just another dead man. After that the doctor. Vignon. No, not Vignon but Wiener, Wiener, that was it, the German spy, in the uniform of a Frenchman. Of course, like all spies he was deep in their midst, and ruthless, and, thinking of him, Jean-Baptiste was afraid. But he closed his eyes tight and the doctor faded too and he was being lifted and the movement hurt and made him feel sick.

He remembered nothing of how he'd gotten to the hospital nor at what point he'd realized where he was. Once he was traveling in some kind of vehicle and strapped down. The movement had made him vomit. He was hot and confused and he had no recollection of being transferred from that bunk but some time—days?—a week?—later, he had come to. It was the middle of the night, or so he assumed, as it was dark but for an oil lamp and a woman with her head down, writing.

Around him were men, sleeping or groaning—sometimes the woman, a nurse, he now saw, got up and went to one of the blanketed heaps and offered water or a few soothing words. But he had known, instantly, that he was on the river. Beyond the smell of sickness and chemicals, he could smell river. He put out a hand and laid it flat on the wooden wall beside him. There was something like a shiver just detectable beneath his palm; he was in a big boat, a barge, he guessed, judging by its dimensions, but once you'd been on the water you recognized its rhythms.

In the following days, he discovered that he was right. The nurse was from Paris, she told him, undeterred by his refusal to speak, chatting on as she changed the bandages over the wound below his ribs, removing the tube from what she called his *pipi*, and applauding his ability to heal as if it were his own willpower that had kept infection at bay. This was a hospital barge, currently moored on the outskirts of Amiens, she told him, away from the reach of the German guns. "For now," an orderly had grunted.

His injuries would leave him with very little disability, the nurse said. When he urinated now, he could still see traces of blood, but it was not worrying, the duty doctor said. He had a limp where he'd broken his ankle, but he could walk without aid.

"Clever bugger," the orderly said. "As long as he keeps his mouth clamped shut, they won't send him back."

So then he spoke. Not a lot—what was there to say?

"Good news. Good news. Nearly there, I think." The doctor announced this as if he were bringing him a present. His face was pale and old. "We'll soon have you back with your companions."

Then, out of the corner of his eye, Jean-Baptiste saw the so-called Vignon. This time it *was* him. Not a dream. There was no mistaking it. The senior surgeon was pointing toward the bed and nodding and no doubt telling Vignon how they could soon send Jean-Baptiste back to be blown apart again and what a successful case it had been. Vignon stared at him, looking bleak, but came no nearer, and Jean-Baptiste heard the surgeon say "Talking. At last. Yes."

And Jean-Baptiste knew he was in danger.

As he lay in bed for weeks, months, his mind had returned all the time to Corbie and his childhood. But now there was Vignon. Flesh and blood. He had seen him again, twice. Once he was at the far end of the narrow ward. He had a feeling that this wasn't where Vignon normally worked. On the second occasion it was night. He woke from sleep and found Vignon looking at a chart right by his pallet. What had he been about to do? His instinct was to shout out for a nurse. Tell her that Vignon was not what he seemed, not what he said he was. But having been mute for so long, he knew that his mental state would be considered unreliable; and no doubt Vignon had long since destroyed any papers that revealed his true identity.

He knew that it was Vignon who had brought him here from Royaumont, a hospital in the old abbey dealing with acute cases and run by Scottish ladies. It didn't take much imagination to see why he had done that. Jean-Baptiste knew who he really was. With Jean-Baptiste alive, Vignon was in danger. The doctor knew he had recognized him, knew he had seen Herr Wiener hidden within Dr. Vignon's French uniform.

Here, at Amiens, Vignon could keep an eye on the invalid. Could make sure he didn't recover. With Jean-Baptiste dead, Vignon could continue his real work, and what a fine job he had for it: dealing with men straight from the front, from every kind of regiment, hearing where medical supplies were being sent and field hospitals were being established. Under the cover of his work, he would see the pattern of future campaigns, the success or failure of current ones.

The third time he saw Vignon, he was handing the nurse some tablets and nodding his head to indicate Jean-Baptiste's bed. He wanted to refuse to take them, but the nurse was his favorite, Émilie. The day before, she had whispered admiring comments about his body and his returning vigor as she washed him, lingering with her coarse washcloth, and the effect had been to exclude any doubts he had as to whether he was still a man. So he took the pills and later his fever returned, the ache in his loins made him vomit, and when he urinated the urine was brownish-pink. The next time he was given them, he spat them out the second the nurse had gone.

It was fear that drove him to write the letter. He couldn't say he had fought to live: he had simply been fortunate to survive; but now that he had survived, he wasn't going to let himself be murdered by his mother's seducer, a German spy. He asked for a pencil and paper and after a couple of reminders nurse Émilie brought them, looking a bit sour.

"Writing to your sweetheart?"

He shook his head. "Hardly."

She looked pleased.

He didn't yet know who he was writing to, but his words were plain.

227

The doctor who calls himself Captain Vignon is not what he seems. He is a German born in Berlin.

He looked down at his words; they could be the ravings of a lunatic or an aggrieved underling.

I have seen his documents. His real name is Wiener. He is a spy.

The nurse kept passing, easing her way down the narrow gap between the two rows of bunks. Several men had left to return to their regiments, but Émilie had told him something big was coming now. They were clearing all possible hospital beds.

"You'll be off in the next group, I expect," she said. "They need every fighting man they've got. We're going to blow those Germans out of our country once and for all."

He wondered what she thought they'd been trying to do for the last two years. Why did she think the hospitals and cemeteries were full?

It was intolerably hot, even with the tiny portholes open. Every time another motor launch passed, the barge moved slightly and a little air entered, but she fanned herself ostentatiously. He knew she was trying to see what he was writing and he tipped it away from her.

Eventually, the next time she rustled past, he reached up and tugged gently at her apron. She squatted beside him, plumped his unplumpable pillow.

"Is there someone in charge of these barges?" he said.

"Captain Allisette is the doctor here."

"I thought I saw Captain Vignon."

"No. Allisette. He's on another barge—Vignon. He helps sometimes if Allisette is called away, and vice versa. I prefer Vignon, although he is melancholy." Her voice dropped, and she said, coquettishly, "He's very handsome, don't you think? But then you know him from before, of course?"

He must have looked startled, because she said "Well, you suddenly arrived and he insisted on you having a bed. No space on his barge. Most men here are just being taken straight from clearing stations to Paris or Amiens. They've been injured a day or so before we get them. They're not like you." Her small hand slipped under the covers and like a hesitant small mouse moved down his body.

"You'd been at Royaumont for weeks. If anything, you should have been sent to a convalescent hospital. You were already almost in Paris. Why bring you back up here if he didn't want to care for you himself?"

He almost told her, but he didn't trust her to keep his secret. Her hand had reached its destination. The gentle efficiency with which she cupped her fingers around him still had something of the nurse about it.

"But there surely must be someone in charge of the whole set-up here?"

She made a face. "For heaven's sake." Her grasp tightened, more from irritation than trying to arouse him, he thought. "That'll be Colonel Marzine, I suppose. He inspects us from time to time. He's old. Finicky. But he's a real doctor."

"So where is he?"

"Now? Haven't a clue. At the old asylum in Amiens, I expect. Anyway, you can't go summoning up the colonel just on a whim." She gave him an indulgent look and kept stroking. He was hard now and longing for her to go on.

He smiled at her to put her at her ease.

"I just wondered." With his own hand he reached out and touched her breast which, even through layers of starched cotton, felt young and firm.

She looked behind her. There was one man propped up on an arm, in the far berth, smoking an illegal cigarette.

"Too much thinking," she said, pulling her hand out and straightening the sheet. She always did that to end a conversation. She stood up. "We need to get you back to the front."

That night he slept badly. The old dreams. Good times, terrible times, Godet's head, Doré's mouth, Émilie's hand.

In the semi-dark, there was Vignon at the base of the ladder into the forward ward. He was a silhouette: just a cigar tip alternately glowing brightly, then fading. Jean-Baptiste could smell it and he knew it was him and knew Vignon sensed he was awake. He stayed alert until the doctor disappeared.

A bit later, the night nurse came and offered him a powder to help him settle. He took it, but the fever, pain, and nausea he'd had a week ago returned. Had Vignon prescribed this little elixir, he thought? Of course he had.

In the morning, exhausted and still feeling sick, he knew he had to get the letter to somebody in authority. He had nowhere safe to keep it. He pulled it out when he thought no one was looking and scrawled a signature with the pencil, making sure it was entirely illegible.

Vignon might be responsible for the deaths of more Frenchmen, but right now he, Jean-Baptiste, was worried about himself.

There were two nurses, Émilie and Nurse Thibault, a former nun. The nun talked little but took deep and audible breaths a lot.

"She was in a sighing order," Émilie had giggled on one of her friendlier days.

There was Victor the orderly and, of course, Captain Allisette. Who could he ask to deliver his letter? Who could he trust? He didn't even have an envelope. Every one of them would read it, except perhaps Captain Allisette, who would probably just throw it away unread.

He could smell and hear Amiens. The remaining casualties were to be removed one by one on the next day. He was walking now, becoming stronger than he let on, and Émilie, cheerful as her duties came to an end on this trip, agreed that he could be helped up to the deck to walk by the quayside.

The light almost blinded him; he had to turn his head away. The firm land beside the river seemed to lurch, to move beneath his feet, and he was almost grateful for Émilie's possessive grasp on his arm. Soldiers and bargees passed him, carrying massive loads and scarcely glancing at the nurse and her patient. There was no way Émilie was going to let him walk away, no way he could find a senior French doctor to hand over the note in his pocket. With her hovering, he would look like a questionable informer. Then he saw the British officer, sitting on a bollard by the river, sketching. He was a major. It appeared to be the boats and, indeed, him and Émilie that the man was drawing. There was no alternative but to act.

The officer looked up as they came within voice range.

"You don't mind?" he said, in good French, indicating his drawing.

Émilie straightened her veil. Jean-Baptiste simply shook his head. Then, as Émilie tugged on his arm, an act of desperation, he pulled free of her, bolder now that he knew the officer spoke French.

"Sir, please. Could you deliver this for me?" He had it out of his pocket, thrusting it forward. "It is of the utmost importance. Please, sir."

He could see first surprise, then amusement, in the man's face. Clearly he would refuse. He thought he was being asked to post a love letter—Jean-Baptiste could see it in his face. He sensed Émilie's anger beside him.

The British officer looked down, his expression now puzzled, then grave. Where he had folded the letter, Jean-Baptiste had written *Colonel Marzine, Hôpital Militaire d'Amiens*, in his best writing.

"Sir. I have no one else."

The officer looked him straight in the eyes. He's seeing if I am mad, Jean-Baptiste thought.

"Is it a complaint? About your treatment?"

"No. No, I swear."

The major put out his hand without a word. He just nodded.

"How dare you?" Émilie asked as she dragged him back to the barge. She let go of his arm completely and he staggered. "How dare you. I should report you, using a British officer to deliver your *billets-doux*. What will he think of you? Of us French?"

"It wasn't—" he began. Yet as she pushed him back on board, he looked at the sun and the gulls, and then upward to the vast cathedral, and felt something like hope or joy. Something he hadn't felt for months. He dropped his gaze to the tall brick houses of the quayside, and then he saw the café table. There was Vignon, standing by the barges, staring back at him as he lit a cigarette.

Émilie had helped him back to bed, seeming to hurt him deliberately. He was sweating. He closed his eyes, exhausted. Either way, it was done.

CHAPTER TWENTY-FOUR
Benedict, Amiens, June 1916

LORD KITCHENER HAD BEEN LOST in the sinking of the *Hampshire*, the French were mired in their forts around Verdun, and the town of Albert was all ruin, nerves, and bad news. But Benedict thought that in Amiens, for a little while, one could pretend things would work out.

Some big push was coming, perhaps within days, but for now he had forty-eight hours of leave; and after days of rain, the sun had broken out, although there was a strong breeze. From where he sat, looking across the river, the great cathedral was half mountain crag, half ship. The eye traveled upward to it from the old city below, which was half land, half water: the river, the quayside, and the narrow waterways; the grid of tiny canals crossed by simple bridges. On the Somme itself, at its widest part, the river was clogged with barges, barge after barge with a red cross on almost every roof.

Men and women in uniform dominated the quayside, but a few bars and cafés were open; a family with three small children sat noisily at one. He'd heard that the city was being evacuated, but there were still plenty of citizens who appeared to be biding their time.

He took a table next to one where two English women—nurses, he guessed—were being persuaded by the proprietor to try local mussels.

He didn't dare order mussels, so he pointed to the dish in front of the French family and nodded and then, as an afterthought, asked for brandy. When the elderly waiter went back into the café without demurral, he assumed he'd asked for the wrong drink.

The bells rang the hour. Foreign-sounding and thinner than the bells at home, the twelve alternating strokes resonated in stars of pink and then pewter gray.

Tiny clouds were moving swiftly across a fragile blue sky and seagulls swooped down the quayside, strutting aggressively, perhaps lured by a memory of better times when barges held edible cargoes and café-goers had bread to spare. He watched them until something startled them, and his eyes followed them as they rose with heavy wingbeats into the air.

The river smelled slightly of drains, but the slight wind ruffled the lime trees and he could smell those too. From time to time as the wind changed direction, he thought he caught the smell of the hospital barges: sweat, carbolic, festering wounds, ether.

A French officer tapped him lightly on the arm. "Cigarette?" he said, holding a silver case toward him.

Benedict shook his head. *"Merci. Non."*

The officer smiled; his teeth were very white against his black beard, yet now that he studied the man more closely, he could see the lines of fatigue behind the handsome face. The man had already turned to offer cigarettes to the young nurses.

A brandy materialized in front of him. He looked away; a camouflaged truck drove past, followed by an Army staff car. He picked up his glass; the brandy was almost undrinkable. From behind him, he heard the French officer say "How do you do," in an accent that wouldn't have sounded out of place in the mouth of a comic foreigner on the stage, and the nurses burst into loud laughter. Chairs scraped, and the next time he looked, the officer was somehow between them.

He looked from the three of them laughing in the sun and then to the nearest barge and then down at the piece of meat resting on his meager piece of pickled cabbage. He cut it, and what looked like a fan of brown entrails sprang out.

When a hand fell on his shoulder, he expected it to be the Frenchman and dreaded being asked to join their jolly table; but then a voice said "Well, what a coincidence," and he recognized the greeting and his neck felt tight just as he turned and saw, to his astonishment, that it was indeed Theo. Theo looking dashing in an eccentric version of his Flying Corps uniform. Theo grinning, bonier and evidently excited to see him. Theo instantly opposite him, blocking out the view, trying his brandy and ordering one himself as well as a pot of mussels. Theo, and Benedict's eyes went to the hand and moved swiftly away.

"You look well," Theo said. "Are you well? Is life being at all kind?"

Benedict found himself nodding rather than speaking. "Leave," he said. "I go back tonight."

All at once he wanted to weep.

"Just the thing. How unutterably splendid. I'm off for the day. They say it's the last leave for a while."

Theo made a face: the same face he'd made at Gloucester when Dr. Brewer had rehearsed the choir endlessly. Benedict thought he was avoiding making more than fleeting eye contact. Had he always been like this?

"Have you been back to Blighty?" Theo said, as if they had known each other, vaguely, in the past.

"Not for months."

In truth, although pleased to see his sister back in March, and to wash regularly and have his uniform cleaned, Benedict had been bored rigid at home. He'd played the tiny, wheezing organ in the parish church, been admired by the old ladies, and spent much of the time asleep.

"You?"

"Went home. Saw Father. Current stepmother-to-be. All very pleasant, but nothing had changed. Which was odd, because *I* had, and yet nobody seemed to notice. Dropped by Gloucester."

"How was Agnes?"

Theo waved an arm. "Obliging. Let me kiss her. Terribly excited by the uniform."

Benedict wondered what Dr. Brewer had thought or said, seeing Theo's mutilated hand.

"Have you arranged a date? For the wedding?" he said.

Theo drank the brandy as if it were water, then shuddered.

"God, this is repulsive stuff. A man would need to be seriously committed to drunkenness to get in the habit of it. No, of course I haven't. She might be a widow in a month."

"But you are engaged to be married?"

"Oh, absolutely. Completely. Announcement in *The Times* any day now. Squeezed in between the casualty lists."

After all the years of friendship, Benedict still couldn't sense whether Theo was making the whole thing up, nor could he ever tell him how much he hoped the story of his courtship and his plans for marriage were another fantasy. More and more, he thought they were.

"Mind you," his friend said, "she'd look marvelous in black, don't you think? Trouble is," he went on without waiting for an answer, "I wouldn't be there to see it. Some other bugger would, and he'd be consoling her in less time than it takes to say 'staff officer.'"

The mussels arrived in a steaming pot and Theo, insisting that Benedict eat with him, set to, discarding some, tapping others on the rim, sucking out the tiny pieces of flesh as if he had lived on mussels all his life. His scarred hand lifted—it never fully unfolded, Benedict noticed; it was an implement, but one that had lost its fine movement—then set down the empty shells, and eventually he mopped up the liquor with a chunk of bread.

When he'd finished, he sat back contentedly for as much as a minute before summoning the waiter in passable French and paying the bill.

"No," he put the hand on Benedict's arm. Their khaki cuffs touched. "I owe you some mussels, for God's sake." Perhaps he hadn't noticed that Benedict had no shells in front of his own plate. "I owe you a mountain of mussels; every mussel from the Bay of the Somme. For being an unspeakable rotter. I'm astonished you'll even sit down with me."

Benedict thought how like Theo it was to overlook the fact that it was Theo who had sat down with *him*, embarrassed, perhaps, but assuming a welcome.

"For God's sake, old chap," Theo said, "you're my best friend, I'm feeling a bit blue, and suddenly here you are, always calm and cheerful. Nobody in the world I'd rather have bumped into."

He looked down at the remnants of Benedict's lunch, said *"Andouillette,"* reached for the sausage, and put it in his mouth.

"And anyway, I'm sorry. Again. I was drunk. I was vilely, horribly drunk. Mad. A lunatic."

Benedict was still considering a reply when Theo said "I mean, thank God you're not dead, or I would have expired of guilt and probably boredom. I should have written. But I couldn't even remember what I'd done, said. . . . Didn't want to remember, to tell you the truth."

Benedict watched Theo's eager, but slightly drawn, face. He had nothing to say. He nodded very slowly. He looked beyond Theo to the cathedral.

"So you'll come back to Harmony Cottage?" Theo said.

Benedict hadn't thought of it and was surprised to find that the idea, which had once given him such happiness and provided the illusion of a refuge, simply brought back all the wretchedness and violence of their last weeks there together. All he could taste was rancid meat.

But "Yes," he said. "Yes. Of course."

"I'm still flying," Theo said. "Thank God. Officially subject to a medical checkup every three months, but the M.O.'s never likely to get around to it."

Perhaps the flying would make it all right, Benedict thought. Perhaps if music could be kept outside their lives.

"My arm. . . ." Theo rubbed it. "It aches and it's clumsy, but it does the job. *That* job, anyway. I have to say Agnes was rather impressed." Then, "Let's walk," he said.

They crossed the bridge immediately ahead of them. A steep flight of old brick stairs rose over one of the narrow canals, took them past the watergates of tall houses, and then led them to a small green tucked below the cathedral. The grass was worn—a French soldier lay under its only tree, with a woman and a baby. They looked happy enough.

There was nothing but cathedral now: his gaze was drawn upward toward the disordered jungle of tiny spires and solid towers, of gargoyles, lead spouts, and tracery, which ended only with the sky. Gargoyles had been part of Benedict's life since he was a child. At Gloucester, the green men playing lutes, the snouted beasts, the great cats and winged dragons had been stone fairytales. But the Amiens figures were creatures of real horror: toothless, slobbering, clawing, shrouded or with empty eye sockets, created out of fear and probably drawn from life. From the ancient stonework rose one great shriek of pain and despair.

He knew the cathedral had a newly restored organ; he had seen pictures of it in that other life he had once lived. It would have been impossible to turn away without giving a reason, but all

Benedict wanted was to see it as a Gothic masterpiece and not confront it as a place where music was made.

His father had spoken of Roman Catholic churches as dark, gilded, elaborate caves for the worst kinds of popish practices: incense, glittering treasuries, relics, martyrs, superstitious locals bowing and crossing themselves. But as the heavy door thudded shut, what lay before Benedict was the embodiment of grace and light: pale, fine columns to either side of a narrow nave, rising unornamented to a great height. Only near the altar had the symmetry been interrupted. Rough-cut wooden struts braced the columns, and sandbags surrounded individual monuments. The largest window was boarded up. As they moved forward, mortar crunched underfoot. He looked down. They were walking across a black-and-white labyrinth, its pattern neatly filling the central nave and now covered with grit. Beyond it, the golden sun rays of the altar were screened by planks. Two old ladies sat, dark shadows in black hats, just below the pulpit.

Fighting had yet to reach this ancient city; yet the cathedral's message was that come it would and, too large to armor itself externally, it was defending its heart. Benedict felt ferocious anger, somehow more than he'd allowed himself to feel for all the damaged human flesh and shattered minds that had become his daily life. The destruction of so much genius, so much history: and for what?

"Benedict."

Theo was gazing up at the organ, its painted pipes high above the business of the church, almost to the roof. As he stood there, the door to the cathedral opened and a shaft of light sliced in; a dark figure, a man, Benedict thought, stood there before coming in and walking down an aisle toward a side chapel. Benedict could smell his cigarette smoke.

Theo called him. He had moved to the far right of the west door in front of what seemed likely to be the door to the organ loft. It was small and insignificant enough. Clearly it was locked, but Theo was feeling along the lintel above it. Then he moved to a funerary inscription a few yards away. He felt above the scrolls and carved urn. Shook off a spider.

He stood back. His eyes scanned the door and its immediate surroundings, then moved swiftly to a carved marble angel holding an open book. He stood on tiptoe, reached up, and then brandished a key.

"We can't go up." But even as he spoke, Benedict knew that they would.

"Oh, but we can." The key turned easily in the lock.

Benedict knew his face was full of doubt, and he hated himself for it.

"For God's sake, man. It was restored only twenty-five years ago, by Cavaillé-Coll, no less. And it's five hundred years old. You know it is. You're an organist: how can you *not* want to go up there?"

When Benedict still hesitated, Theo rushed on. "Look around. What do you see? They know what's going to happen here. Even if *you* survive all this, what might you never see again, hear again? This organ."

Benedict dipped his head to pass under the low arch and came to the stone steps of a spiral staircase. The treads were narrow and deep and, as he followed Theo upward, he held tight to a sagging rope handrail. At the top they reached scuffed floorboards. Theo was searching for a light. Eventually he found the oil lamp they both knew must be here and lit it with his cigarette lighter.

In front of them lay the marvel of pipes, bellows, and the mechanisms that revealed the secrets only organists saw. With another rasp of the flint, the light was lit over the console. It was stuffy up here, and the organ had not been played for a while, it seemed; there was light dust on the keys. He could hear pigeons on the roof, see specks of light through the timbers, but Theo seemed oblivious to anything but the organ itself. He unbuttoned his tunic and slung it to one side, sat at the console, legs extended, and eventually looked up at Benedict.

"You play it," he said, after a pause. "It needs playing." His gaze moved to the old bellows. There was no electricity here yet. "Five minutes. I can still do the bellows." But he didn't move. He was biting his lip.

Benedict just watched on, his breath slowing. Looked at Theo, his half-suppressed excitement, his creased uniform, his posture, slightly bent over, the cross of his suspenders; the way they buttoned to the center-back rise of his breeches. The pale cream shirt tight over his shoulder blades, the dark, damp patches under his arms. Finally, his hands, which had been capable of creating such worlds, turning noise into beauty, writhing in his lap. His healthy fingers moved slightly over the strange curvature of the damaged hand.

Benedict ached. He felt as if his heart would burst or shrivel. If he could only touch. He could touch, of course. There were a dozen reasons why he might touch, and just one why he never could.

Theo stood and moved over to the bellows; and as Benedict took his place at the unfamiliar console, he could hear Theo waking the creature sleeping in the roof. The rumblings, the wheeze, the inhalations of air into the bellows and regulators; each big organ had its own unique sound. Its coming to life was always a moment Benedict loved. Even here, illicitly, in Amiens, in wartime. Even where Theo would soon exhaust himself doing the work of two or more men. Benedict wondered, briefly, if Dr. Brewer had ever felt any of these things. Then he thought of the possibility of this monster being slaughtered by men of either side armed with high explosives.

He peered at the stops, just visible in the unsteady light. They were different, of course. In Gloucester he would see *Choir, Great, Swell, Solo*. Here they read *Pédale, Grande Orgue, Positif, Récit*. The arrangement of the stops was different too, and he moved his hands over them, a few inches above the keyboard, as if trying to understand them. He reached down and unlaced his boots, freed his feet to play.

To one side of the organ was a small, newish plate with the name of the restorer: *Aristide Cavaillé-Coll, 1889.* How little the old man, perhaps the greatest organ-maker ever, could have suspected what was to come as month after month he worked on this wondrously ancient organ to create the best possible sound in the last years of his life, in the last century.

He nodded to Theo. Tried an arrangement of chords. Tried to get the feel of the organ, knowing that had Theo been in his seat, he would have experimented with confidence. Would once have done that, would never do it now.

Then, he played. Bach, because Bach was what he knew best. He could hear Theo moving heavily from bellow to bellow and yet, there, immediately, was blue, purest blue, then mauve, like a morning glory they had seen on a wall in the hot summer five years ago. Now he began "By the Waters of Babylon" and created green, falling over blue. He made a few mistakes. Started again. Stopped. He looked back at Theo, who was mopping his brow and counting the bellows.

"Am I stoking up rainbows?"

Benedict shook his head.

Theo was gasping, slightly, but Benedict's hands were already moving again, and with the opening chords the blue filled him even as the familiar music filled the cathedral below him and his heart beat so fast that he could hardly breathe and for a brief time Theo and the pain of Theo was lost to him, as he focused with utter intensity on the notes. He had no sheet music in front of him, was out of practice and on an unfamiliar organ, yet on this second pass he was nearly note-perfect. His feet moved securely across the unfamiliar French pedal board as though he had known it all his life; keyboards and draw-stops obeyed his hands as if being offered to him. His head and shoulders moved minutely with the music. Theo would soon reach the end of his physical ability to step from bellows to bellows, but for Benedict the purity of the color, the astonishment that, so out of practice, he could still draw all this out of a strange organ, and the longing for his old life, almost consumed him; and the Bach, the music, was his, could only ever be his.

After a few minutes, Theo said "Enough. Enough, I think." His voice was very quiet, though he was breathing fast from exertion. His expression was unreadable. He stood, leaning against the wall by the bellows. Benedict stayed sitting, absorbing every detail, trying to commit the organ to memory.

Theo walked up to him, put his hands on Benedict's shoulders. Benedict stared ahead at the console.

"It was quite beautiful," Theo said. "What a fool I've been. Always a fool. There's something wrong in how I'm put together. Something mad or cruel in there. Perhaps that's why I'm good at this war thing. This," he lifted his claw and stroked Benedict's cheek, "this is what I'm really like all through. And you know it."

They had only just come down the stairwell when a priest appeared in front of them, rushing across the nave with another man, a civilian in his forties who wore a thick dark coat and was holding a Homburg in front of him like a shield. Both men were clearly in a fury.

Benedict caught only the word *orgue* in their fast and enraged French; but from the gesticulating upward at the organ pipes, then at the braced walls and sandbags, the shaking fingers, and the priest's sour expression, he grasped quite well what he already knew. That they had trespassed in the organ loft and played the organ without permission.

Theo answered in French; he had traveled in France in past summers as a boy, and his French was far better than Benedict's. Benedict recognized the name Bach when the priest said it with anger, but the conversation moved too fast for him to keep up. Theo was shaking his head and looking nonplussed.

"Ah," he said, still facing his interlocutors as if conversing. "The priest believes, he's not sure, mind you, that we might have been playing enemy music. I assured him that, there being no sheet music at hand up there, you were merely using your musical genius to improvise."

Then he turned to Benedict, his face benign. "I can't think of the right word for pompous ass. Help me out here, Benedict. What's 'pompous ass' in French? And surely the priest's chum is young enough to be in uniform?"

Theo could hardly get a word into the flow of complaint.

"He says that we have violated his great house of God and the noise we made may have alerted the enemy. I've just pointed out that the enemy can hardly have missed the fact that there's a great hulk of a cathedral here. The enemy has very good maps, as we know, and has a reasonable claim to have produced the greatest musicians in history, so they'll know more about this organ than the cathedral director of music does."

Now the priest spoke, clearly trying to control his voice. Theo answered gravely and slowly; Benedict understood much more. He caught the name Cavaillé-Coll, and, later, London in England, and whatever Theo was saying seemed to bring down the fever of the argument. At one point he placed his palm on Benedict's back, as if to introduce him. Both Frenchmen turned and scrutinized Benedict. Eventually the layman, now with an expression verging on respect, put out his hand and shook Benedict's. Then he shook Theo's.

"The priest said we might have ruined this venerable old instrument by our sudden violation. That it isn't being maintained these days. So I explained that you were the chief organist of the famous St. Paul's Cathedral and I your pupil until I was injured in battle. That you had played for the King before departing for France and that in a break in hostilities we had hurried here to see the wondrous instrument of which so many great men had spoken."

Now the older man spoke directly to Benedict.

"He wants to know if you found it as you hoped," Theo said. The priest added another apparently earnest statement.

"Say something, for God's sake," said Theo.

Benedict's mind was blank. "Say the organ was beautiful, then," he finally managed to say. "Apologize. Thank you. I mean, thank him."

Theo spoke and then translated. "I've told him that you will return to the battlefield strengthened in fortitude and vigor to assist in the liberation of the great heritage of France. The priest is going to pray for us, although he very much regrets that we are not Roman Catholics."

The four men stood awkwardly and then, with a slight bowing of heads, the two Frenchmen walked away.

They moved to follow them, with Benedict saying "Why on earth did you—?" when another figure rose from his seat in the side chapel. As he eased himself between the pews and moved in and out of a shaft of light, Benedict could see that it was a French officer who had obviously been listening to the exchanges.

The officer put out a hand.

"Vignon," the Frenchman said. "Captain Vignon, military surgeon. How do you do?"

Now the officer held Benedict's hand with both of his, almost as if pleading.

"Thank you," the Frenchman said in English. He cleared his throat and then again, "Thank you," still holding Benedict's hand. *"An Wasserflüssen. . . ."* For a split second Benedict's mind struggled to grasp why he was being spoken to in German, and then he realized that it was simply the name of the piece he had been playing: "By the waters of Babylon, there we sat down, yea, we wept."

The officer released Benedict's hand to shake Theo's, spoke briefly in French, then fell silent; but his gaze strayed back to Benedict.

"He's a surgeon," Theo said. "He works on one of the hospital barges out there. They are moving today, making space for more barges with expected casualties. He says he first heard the piece as a boy, when he sang in a cathedral choir, and finds it very moving."

Benedict wished either his French or the doctor's English were better.

The man spoke again.

"He has to return to his duties," Theo said, and then, with very un-Theolike seriousness, he added, "He says, whatever lies ahead, he will treasure the single moment of comfort—I think that's what he said—and perfection, of hearing that music. Of light in the darkness. Of *you* playing the organ, Benedict."

The Frenchman gave a half-salute, put on his cap as he stood in the doorway, and walked away.

"Me too," Theo said. "I felt it too. Here we all are in a strange land, all weeping by the bloody river."

CHAPTER TWENTY-FIVE

Harry, Amiens,
June 1916

IT HAD BEEN THAT RARE thing, a happy day, Harry thought at the end of it. He had gotten up early and packed his things, knowing that tomorrow a new man would have his job behind the lines. Tomorrow he would move forward to rejoin his regiment and take over a company that was already at the front. A driver had dropped him in Amiens before midday, and he had only to deliver some papers and pick up a book for his colonel before the Eton dinner at 7 P.M. He had loitered, knowing what lay ahead in the next few days. The empty hours seemed a great luxury, for now he could walk and sketch and breathe fresh air.

The happiness was more precious because he knew it was finite. The evening before, he had gone to the last big meeting at H.Q. The attack was set. They had pored over the maps: confident lines curving, sweeping around rising ground or following rivers.

If you looked at it one way, it seemed a triumph of surveying and of control; another way, and it looked like the scrawlings of a maniac. He had realized early on that he needed glasses: was he getting old? But he focused on the portion of map nearest to him, the northern sector—there was the French landscape and there were the ancient and evocative names: Foncquevillers, Le Breyelle, Beauregard, Sailly-au-Bois, Chateau de la Haie; and there the superimposed new British geography, so homely and so deadly: four small copses: Matthew, Mark, Luke, and John; Watling Street, Rose Cottage, Waterloo Bridge, Blackfriars Bridge. Running north to south down all the maps, the serpentine broken blue line, which meandered like a river but which marked the British front-line trench. "The Styx," he'd once said, early on, and was met with looks of determined incomprehension. Each inch of blue a temporary home, a last home perhaps, to hundreds of men. Behind them were other trenches, thousands more men; three waves; hundreds of thousands of soldiers waiting to turn the plan they were so busy refining on paper into flesh and bullets.

The Somme in Amiens ran in a businesslike way between wharves, warehouses, and quays, lined by a long row of barges. No doubt there had always been barges, Harry thought, but these all had red crosses on their roofs. A few French nurses and orderlies had been chatting by the moorings, and women came and went with armfuls of crumpled linen. Since last winter, the rumor was that the French losses at Verdun were running at seventy thousand casualties a month, and the fighting went on and on.

He had sat down on a bollard and started to draw: quick pencil lines. The barges, the swooping gulls, and the fluttering headscarves: he had wanted to catch a moment of movement, when things were alive. Two British officers rose from a café table and crossed the river, near his stakeout, nodded to him. Then a nurse had helped an injured French soldier down the short plank onto the shore. He was young, wan, and unsteady on his legs. But then he had

THE FIRST OF JULY

looked up at the sky and across to the cathedral, and in a few
minutes he let go of the nurse as if with every breath of river air
he was drawing in strength. Harry had begun drawing the pair
of them but then became conscious of the soldier's gaze and, not
wanting to be intrusive, he laid his pad down on his knee. The
soldier started crossing the short distance between them, and just
when Harry had thought there might be some sort of altercation
coming, the young Frenchman had reached into a pocket. What
he had brought out was a folded and slightly grubby piece of paper.
Harry looked down, puzzled; the writing was quite neat: *Colonel
Marzine, Hôpital Militaire d'Amiens*. The young man gabbled something, but too fast and in too strong an accent for Harry to pick up.

"*Lentement*, slowly," he said.

The soldier had pointed at himself and then the barge. "*Péniche*,"
he said, pointing. Harry did not know the word.

Then the soldier had mimed an injury to his side and said
something about Germans; as the nurse hovered, he had slowed
down and, curbing an evident urgency, asked Harry to pass on
his message. He regretted that he was himself too weak to reach
the colonel; but it was a most important letter.

Harry had considered whether the man was serious—he was
still wondering much later in the day; so many soldiers were sent
at least partly mad by fighting and injury—but the young man had
steady gray eyes, and his agitation appeared to reflect intensity,
not insanity.

Eventually Harry had put the message in his pocket just as the
nurse reached forward trying to intercept it, and then, failing,
turned to argue with her charge, hands on hips. The boy wasn't
listening to her but gazing, his face almost like stone, at a spot
beyond her, and for a moment Harry had doubted his wisdom in
becoming involved. How would he pass the message on?

Before letting himself be swept up by the evening and the bra-
vado, or arrogance, of a school reunion at the heart of war, he had

continued his walk, taking a steep cobbled street up toward the basilica, past a small hotel and some fine medieval and eighteenth-century clergy houses, coming out into the Place de Notre Dame. He was staring up at the fine spire of the cathedral, which seemed to tip toward him out of the fast-moving sky, when a British Army messenger swept around the building on a bicycle and looked as surprised as he was by the near-collision. The corporal gave him something between a salute and a wave of apology. Harry put out a hand to stop him.

"Sorry, sir." The soldier had dismounted and was having trouble holding his bicycle and saluting at the same time. "I didn't see you exactly, sir."

"No matter. I need you to deliver a message for me. Is that possible?"

"Yes, sir. I'm all finished here, sir."

"Please take this to the French military hospital. It's on the east road, I believe. Hand this message to an officer."

The man nodded, putting the message into his bag. He had an intelligent face.

"Only to a French officer. You understand?"

"Yes, sir."

"And your name?" he said, as the cyclist mounted again.

"Stanton, sir. Corporal Stanton, Hunts Cyclists."

Two nuns walked away from the cathedral, their high coifs bobbing. A French officer had come up the steps behind him and was lighting a cigarette. Harry held back for a few minutes. He had taken out his pad and sketched a quick impression of the scene, not of the cathedral, which he could no doubt find in photographs, but of the square and the people in it. Recalling the fate of Ypres, he had simply wanted to capture it, right now, on this midsummer day.

It was only once the Frenchman had gone ahead into the building that Harry walked up the steps to the great door and stood there, looking outward. It had rained on and off for days, delaying the long-laid plans for the attack right along the line. But now that they had a time and a date, he felt an odd, strange relief, and the sun was out and the smell of damp stone and grass was wonderful. Long ago, in that school by the Thames, there had been a smell like this in summer. He felt the sun on his face and then, as if he hadn't been lucky enough to have one sense indulged, there was another tiny miracle.

He had suddenly heard the organ, faltering at first and then being played with more confidence. For the five minutes or so while it continued, he had just stayed put. He had no wish to move from the pale sunlight into the darkness or see religious paintings of death and suffering, but out here there was both joy and sadness in the music.

After a few minutes the organ fell quiet again, and he'd moved on toward the mess, the evening, and whatever appalling jollity lay ahead.

Now, nearly twenty hours after the Old Etonian dinner, Harry still had a lingering pain between his eyes and a stiffness in the back of his neck. The photograph in his hand reminded him of his wife. The woman had fair hair, white skin, and a look of mischief, as if her stillness concealed possibilities. Her thighs were plumper than Marina's, her nipples darker, as was her pubic hair, and there were holes in her stockings, her only item of clothing apart from a ribbon around her neck.

The photograph was French, found among the effects of an officer who had died of appendicitis in the hospital a few days earlier. The task of writing letters to the families of dead or wounded soldiers was a thankless one, and this was a man he didn't even know. His nib caught on the rough paper and spat ink on the page as the words came out, stilted and inadequate and kind. Every soldier's end was courageous or at least dutiful, all their deaths were instant, all the men were much liked by their fellows. It was harder when a man had died while inhaling chloroform so that his appendix could be removed. The man who had secretly owned this photograph and possibly enjoyed the woman, "Marie," whose signature was on the back with a loving dedication in French, had, according to his brother officers, been an insistently devout Christian who had held back his men's ration of rum before attacks. He had turned out to have a wife and child in Hove. Harry allowed himself to consider, very briefly, whether one day Marina might get a letter like this and what it might say.

This evening, there was just the one letter of condolence. Harry thought back over the strange, unrelated fragments of his twenty-four hours in Amiens and how much he had to tell Marina for once: of the brief exchange with the young French soldier, the organ playing in the cathedral, and then the ridiculous dinner. There was an almost impressive admirable folly in assembling Old Etonians for dinner just days before they all knew the big push was coming. You didn't need to have the ear of High Command to know it; on the way to Amiens, the road had been clogged with wagons, guns, trucks, officers on horses, and company after company of soldiers. High above the road, aeroplanes kept watch for German spotters. The staff car that had picked him up in the morning—and he had an image of a Bairnsfather cartoon of this surprisingly shiny car scouring the lines to bring in recalcitrant Etonians—had to stop at times to let pass all the traffic coming the other way. There were a few sour looks and fewer grins from the marching men, as well as a few times when the driver, grumbling, had to pull off into the mud beside the road, to allow a heavy gun or a mobile canteen to pass.

Nearly a hundred and seventy of them had made it. "Floreat Etona," one brigade major said under his breath as they climbed the stairs and were shown the seating plan. There were subalterns who had undoubtedly been on the famous playing fields last season and some gray-haired generals with straining mess dress, whose memories of their stripling selves must reach back far into the last century. There were a great many regular officers in addition to the men, like himself, who'd taken commissions in the New Army.

Among those present were a handful of chaps he'd known at school and was glad to see, although nobody he'd considered a really close friend. But there was a sense that they were all trying to avoid a roll call of the dead and if this drove them back to hazy school memories—cricket matches and pranks and the eccentric geeks who had taught them Greek or Latin, or rowing on the river or playing the wall game—well, it was just an evening on which the past seemed more compelling than the immediate future. The claret was good, and he wondered what Parisian hotel had been persuaded to surrender some of the treasures of its cellar. He sat next to a talkative RFC man to his left; across the table from a likeable regular, Reginald Bastard, who had fought in the Boer War and was now commanding the 2nd Lincolns.

General Rawlinson, "Old Rawly" the buffers called him, had given a rousing speech: without Eton the officer corps would be much depleted, not just in numbers but in spirit; it was the values of Eton that this war sought to uphold. At this point, Harry had looked around the sweating faces, the pink cheeks, the dazed young newcomers, and noticed, with no great surprise but a degree of amusement, that there were significantly more staff officers here than there were proportionately in the officer corps as a whole. Some excellent port and brandy fueled loud cheers. This encouraged Old Rawly to give an impromptu performance of a song from *Carmen*, but it all seemed to go down well. More cheers, applauding fists hammering on the table. From a small group of very drunken subalterns came the opening bars of "The Eton Boating Song," but he was glad they were told to pipe down.

They had been returned to base late in the evening. It was still just light. The driver decided to take the side roads, but they were met by an extraordinary sight, something that in the violet semi-darkness might have been a scene from a medieval tapestry: there, avoiding the endless trail of troops and guns on the main road, were the cavalry, their tall lances upright, bobbing up and down as they rode between the fields, a slender new moon above them, and the only sound the horses' hooves and the jangling of bridles.

Their car went slowly past them: the Dragoons, the Lancers, the Hussars, the Royal Horse, and the Life Guards, even the Indian Cavalry—for a while they were caught in the middle of dark-skinned turbaned troopers from the Deccan Horse, and he thought he identified a small group of mounted Canadians. The sight had moved and disturbed him where all the modern machinery of war he had seen earlier—the great guns, the wagons carrying rolls of barbed wire, the canteens and field ambulances; the parade of metal and men heading inexorably to the front—had failed.

CHAPTER TWENTY-SIX
Jean-Baptiste, Amiens, June 1916

HE WAS WOKEN BY A hand shaking his shoulder. Vignon was standing over him. He struggled to sit up, his heart racing.

"It's too late," he said. "I've told them who you are. You're finished."

Vignon sat down, squeezing himself with difficulty between Jean-Baptiste's feet and the foot of the bed, his head bowed.

"And who am I?"

"You're a German. A spy. A poisoner."

A smile flickered across Vignon's face and was extinguished.

"A German? Yes. My father was a German. I was born in Germany. But my mother was from Alsace. When the Germans were handed Alsace in 1870, they were handed my mother's family."

"You never said anything about a German father." Jean-Baptiste suddenly felt defensive.

"I don't think I actually mentioned my father at all. Any more than you told me about *your* father's violence." Vignon looked angry but then held out his hand. "I am sorry. I shouldn't have said that. Let us agree that we both had difficult fathers?"

Jean-Baptiste nodded, very slowly, uncomfortable that Vignon had always known how things were at home in his childhood, either through his mother or village gossip.

"My mother," Vignon continued, "was a very young, naïve woman when she met my father; he was a military doctor." He put his hand up as Jean-Baptiste tried to interrupt. "Yes, a German military doctor. Charming, I'm told. He took her to Berlin. Once married, he was rather less charming. His family loathed this wife with French roots; she tried to be more German but was very unhappy. She had only one child, me. My father sent me to medical school, then he died quite suddenly and my mother returned to Alsace. Once I finished my training, I too returned to Alsace. I was a Frenchman by nature, with German nationality and a love of both cultures. My mother resumed her maiden name, as did I. I didn't want anything to do with my father's family, who had rejected her."

"You lied about where you came from."

"I don't think I did," Vignon said. "I think if you're scrupulous in examining the evidence, you'll find I was rather . . . vague."

"Why?"

"Vengeance. That foolish, meaningless word. Revenge against the Germans for a war forty years old that the French started and then lost; it was in their blood. Even decent men like Godet. German-haters—long before the war. Them and their goddamn 'Vengeance.' It was easier to believe myself French.

"So, no, I am not a spy. I am a victim of revenge, of arbitrary borders, of long-ago struggles. I wanted to do everything I could to help my motherland. It's what my own mother would have wanted."

Then, perhaps steering away from the sensitive topic of mothers, he added, "But yes, I am a poisoner."

Jean-Baptiste had felt the first stirrings of anxiety as Vignon pleaded his innocence, but now, strangely, he felt reassured rather than vindicated.

The doctor was silent for a while. He'd taken out a cigar but he didn't light it, just turned it between his fingers.

"Do you know how army medicine works?" he whispered. "Very simple. Three categories. One: hopeless; two: might survive in some shape or form but not as a soldier and scarcely as a man; three: could be patched up and returned to combat—'conservation of effectives' is the official designation."

He leaned so close that Jean-Baptiste could feel his breath on his cheek and opened Jean-Baptiste's shirt. Took Jean-Baptiste's own hand and guided it down the wide, lumpy scar under his ribs.

"Which do you think gets the medical attention? Which group were you placed in when you were brought in?"

When Jean-Baptiste didn't reply, Vignon repeated himself, then continued: "Which? Eh? You were 'might survive.' *Might*. Hence the diabolical surgery. Not worth too much effort. You were lucky you didn't get gangrene or typhus. Most do. But despite the doctors' best efforts, you did rather better than they'd ordained. They moved you to Royaumont with life, albeit a short one, probably, ahead of you. But the ladies did a good job. Fed you properly. Gave you fresh air. Cleaned up your scar. Put in a proper tube for you to piss down and let the one God gave you heal. You fought off one infection after another. The only thing wrong with you was that you wouldn't open your damn mouth.

"All this time, I've been trying to keep you from being sent back. I removed you from the terrifying Scottish ladies. When you and I met that day at Royaumont, do you know what had been written on your chart by the visiting doctor ten days earlier? 'CdE.' Conservation of effectives. You'd been upgraded. You were good to be sent back as soon as you were on your feet. You were worth their resources."

His eyes never left Jean-Baptiste's.

"So I took you with me. It was impulsive—but if I'd waited, you would have been sucked back into service. I brought you here: the only place I could keep an eye on you. Yes, each time you improved enough to be discharged, I gave you drugs to ensure that you had a new outbreak of worrying symptoms. But you got better all the same, and you refused the cure I was providing for the almost certainly fatal disease of being returned to your unit."

He looked almost resentful. "I put myself at risk. Why? Because all I do is save broken men and send them back to be broken again. It disgusts me." His expression reminded Jean-Baptiste of Godet in a spitting mood.

"And, mostly, I just want your mother to have a son when all this is over."

Jean-Baptiste had started off not believing it; but slowly, and with horror, as Vignon had been speaking, he saw it all.

"But I thought . . . I've told. . . ."

"I know. I know. I presume it was the British officer, from the appalled look you gave me. But I've had a little walk, considered our problem. Your note will take a while to reach the French authorities—although it is possible, I suppose, that they'll ignore it. But it's a dangerous time for us both. You, because they're emptying the boats; me, well, because—" He leaned forward and patted Jean-Baptiste on the leg. "Because no doubt like all British gentlemen, your major will be scrupulously reliable."

He stroked the untidy beard that had been so black, so sleek, back in Corbie.

"You addressed it to?"

"Colonel Marzine."

Another smile. "So. Marzine. The Germans killed both his sons at Douaumont." He sighed. "Ah, well."

"What will happen—?" Jean-Baptiste couldn't go on. He thought of his mother. Vignon had continued to care what happened to her when he, Jean-Baptiste, had fled in childish rage—and now he had, unwittingly, betrayed the man who was loyal to her.

"What will happen to me is that I'll probably be shot. I might get prison. But my money is on a firing squad. No time to sort out the little question of my change of identity, nor the matter of my lack of papers; no matter that I have been a good doctor. The army is full of criminals and bigamists with false identities but, as you have so vehemently pointed out, I am a German."

"I'm sorry." The words were so unequal to what he felt. At first he had thought or hoped it was a trick, but now he had no doubt. Vignon had tried to give him life—and he had probably brought about Vignon's death.

The doctor continued as if Jean-Baptiste hadn't spoken, pulling out a letter. A proper letter in an envelope.

"I have had a little walk. Time to think. These are for you." he said. "They're your medical discharge papers. All correct and proper. They say that you have a bladder injury, kidney damage, disease, probably renal consumption, exacerbated by an injury in that area, and are unfit for further service. The last part is almost true." He held the envelope for a while, tapping it on his knee, then handed it to Jean-Baptiste.

"Now get up and leave. Leave Amiens. Follow the river. You're a web-footed boy"—he paused, with a little smile; "you know ways where other men won't go. Tomorrow the British have something under their hats, so get as near to home as you can tonight. Stay on the north side and mingle with the British traffic. On the south side you'll meet your own soldiers walking back toward Verdun. No point in looking for trouble."

"But I have papers. You said—"

"And they need soldiers and you are, clearly, able to walk." Vignon felt his pocket again, brought out a small, corked, brown-glass bottle. "If your wounds weep or open up, apply this. Don't ignore them. It's strong stuff."

Jean-Baptiste looked at the label. *Solution Carrel-Dakin,* it said.

Vignon made a flapping motion with his hand. "Now. Off with you." He eased himself upright and looked at Jean-Baptiste. He smiled; but behind it was, Jean-Baptiste saw, an unspeakable sadness.

"Dr. Vignon. . . ."

"Walk."

"I'm sorry I stole your boots."

Vignon nodded. "Start walking."

The Plan

CHAPTER TWENTY-SEVEN
Theory

THE PLAN IS LOZENGE-SHAPED IN transmission. In London, the War Committee has communicated its wishes in outline to the Chief of the Imperial General Staff; he in turn has passed on the resolution to break through in northern France to the Commander-in-Chief; and he has conveyed this to his generals in France.

The British generals, situated at the widest point of the plan's progress, argue about the date with the hard-pressed French, who are struggling at Verdun; under pressure, they choose June 29. The generals draw up the detailed plan and relay its relevant objectives to the divisional commanders. These meet the battalion commanders, who communicate the basics of the plan to the company commanders and, the plan becoming simpler and narrower in the process, so on down to the private soldier at the lowest point. He has one task, one field to cross, and nobody else to tell.

The plan envisages a British attack on an unprecedented scale on a front stretching from a diversion at Gommecourt in the north down to Montauban in the south, with the French Sixth Army providing a subsidiary attack from there down to Foucaucourt. The attack, thrilling in its ambition and deployment of resources, will be preceded by five days of shelling of the enemy positions. Nearly two million shells are to be fired. Troops have gathered in Picardy. Railway lines have been laid, wells sunk, roads built with stone ferried from Cornwall and Jersey; hospitals are equipped, mass graves dug. In Britain, the Whitsun holiday is canceled so there need be no interruption to the flow of munitions.

This is a British plan and, almost inevitably, rain delays the attack. But the men are ready, the bombardment has begun, and eventually the rain will stop. On June 28, General Rawlinson hands down the new date: July 1.

At 0551 hours, the sun will rise. At 0720 hours, the biggest mines ever laid will be detonated under the German front-line positions. At 0730 hours (well into the clear, warm light of a summer's day), the troops will leave their trenches and advance in waves: thirteen divisions; over half a million men. They will move slowly, on foot, not bunching up, safe in the knowledge that, after what has now become a week of shelling, there will be little resistance from the enemy. A hot meal will be ready for them when they reach their objective. The details are all in the plan.

CHAPTER TWENTY-EIGHT
Benedict, France, June 30, 1916

THE MEN WERE DRINKING FRENCH wine, and who could blame them, Benedict thought. An illicit bottle or two had kept his battery in good spirits over the past week. The division was so far to the south of the line that several of the soldiers had made friends with sections of the French Sixth Army and various items of food and clothing had been swapped. When he returned to camp, they were diverted by a can of French rations that they were daring the youngest lad to eat.

"It's monkey, sir," said Smith. "That's what they get, the French. Canned monkey meat, they say."

The boy was pulling out something solid from the brown jelly and staring at it dubiously.

"And the wine, sir. It's part of their rations."

"They need it to wash down the rest." A bombardier, whose name Benedict had forgotten, laughed, but then waved a can at him. "Chicory coffee, sir. Disgusting. No tea at all."

"They've got some mighty big black infantrymen, sir. Six foot tall. Red caps. They say the Jerries shoot themselves rather than fall into their hands. Fearless. Never take prisoners. Wouldn't like to run into them in the dark, sir. Wish we had some."

Most of the division was comprised of northern regiments, the majority volunteers still up for a fight. The accents around him had been unfamiliar, sometimes incomprehensible. Initially, the problem had been neutral.

They were good lads, but Benedict had to stop the flow of wine now. The colonel had finally talked his junior officers through the detailed plan of attack. The front line was shaped like an L. Its aims were to secure territory from Gommecourt in the north, where they would stage a diversion, down to Montauban, which Benedict could see through his binoculars.

He had returned to his battery to tell them that the date of the infantry attack and cavalry follow-through had been changed to July 1. "Z" Day. Zero hour. Not that the next morning would be any different to them. Their field guns had started the run-up to the attack over a week ago. The infantry grumbled at the noise and worried that the shells weren't hitting the barbed wire. The shelling seemed relentless, but the gunners were actually firing on a schedule of two hours on, two off, plus one session of eighty minutes every day. Howitzers and eighteen-pounders. Four days. Five days. Six. Who knew what it was doing to the three German lines, apart from alerting every man of them that something big was coming.

He had seen the effect in their own trenches: men crouched with their hands over their ears, grimacing, mere gargoyles of flesh, but it made no difference. The ground itself shook with the barrage; earth fell into the trench. The Germans fired back from time to time, but the British troops were quite adequately numbed by their own artillery. It was making sleep well-nigh impossible, as well as deafening the gunners.

On and on it went, day and night. The first night there had been a sort of glory to it in the darkness—the sky lit with man-made and lethal shooting stars, fiery planets, phosphorescent flares shooting up. After that, it rained and then became so misty that they were hurling missiles from a limited world of guns, sandbags, and tree trunks into the unknown. Spotters were useless, so they had no idea whether they were succeeding in destroying the wire. The pounding was colorless, apart from the close detonation of a shell, which would create a purple veil of light that Benedict alone could see.

The gun he was standing by was a beauty, as guns went. New, still shiny in places. The horses had pulled the limber up a slight incline, and it had been set up in a small wood. The infantry had put a Lewis gun on the perimeter to cover their positions. They were all exhausted. When active, the gun crew had stayed half naked; it was hot work despite the rain. But waiting, as their own gun fell silent, listening to other guns firing in sequence, they were hunched together in shining waterproof capes as implacable as a coal face. The branches above them offered no cover; when it stopped raining, the leaves dripped constantly and the sandbags were sodden, so to lean against them to rest was to be sodden too.

After the main attack—"the infantry breakthrough," the colonel had said, confidently—it would be the turn of the cavalry. Benedict's gunners would lay down a final barrage on the wire and then shift the range farther to allow the attack to follow. By then, the first and second waves would be moving forward to seize the German positions. But had his guns destroyed the wire? He had a good team, but they had been hurried to the front with very little training. One of them still winced every time they fired a shell.

The wire, he thought, and knew his faith had been finally obliterated when he couldn't pray.

"July 1," said Corporal Smith in a lull in the firing. "Who'd've thought it?"

"Why?" He liked hearing Smith's Lancashire accent, and the man's common sense steadied the young gunners.

"It's my birthday, sir, and it's Saturday tomorrow. Has to be good luck. Last year, Saturday night, the big excitement was going for a pint of ale with the lads."

Benedict was surprised to find tomorrow was Saturday. Had lost count somewhere.

"I expect we all had something better to do," he said. "It would have been a lot quieter, anyway."

"To my way of thinking," said Smith, as if it were something he'd thought about a lot, "it must be worse for you. You officers. Blokes like me—hold down a job if you're lucky, marry a girl from the next street, a pint of ale in the pub of a Saturday, that's it. Nothing wrong with it, mind, good laughs. But you—you'll have expectations. For all kinds of things. To see the world. Meet people. Read books. Learn stuff. I'm missing out on my pint, but you're here missing out on everything."

When Benedict didn't answer, he went on: "I didn't mean to talk out of turn, sir."

"Not at all. No. Let's hope we all get back home soon. Get this business over with. Though I don't think my life was quite as rich as you think. Mostly I played a church organ. And I liked a pint too."

Smith made a face. "Well, you'll have to come and have an ale with the lads, then. One day."

Behind them, the gun started firing again. Benedict moved forward. On the accuracy of their fire depended the lives of thousands of soldiers, spending this last hour of daylight waiting in the trenches. Soldiers whose waiting was tempered only by the knowledge, for those who believed it, that the wire would be obliterated. It was torn apart at Loos the year before, the colonel had said, hitting his boots with his swagger stick for emphasis. Shredded. Men had sauntered through the German defenses. As every soldier would have noticed, the ordnance here was on a vast scale. Thwack. So much greater than Loos. Where it had torn apart the German defenses. Thwack. Thwack.

The adjutant had raised his eyebrows.

If the gunners had failed to cut the wire, soldiers would die as dancing men, trapped and twitching in its coils, so it had to be true.

CHAPTER TWENTY-NINE
Harry, France,
June 30, 1916

IT WAS ALL WIRE TALK at dinner, with the C.O. making no attempt to stop them. Harry was with his new company, replacing a man who'd been killed two weeks before. Dinner, with the battalion commander and three subalterns, consisted of some kind of fatty pork stew. It was all a long way from Amiens.

Their new colonel was trying hard to be in good spirits. He was short with a reddish moustache, recently promoted from major. A scared man, out of his depth, Harry thought and, for a few seconds, felt sorry for him. They had been ready to go on June 29, but the foul weather had delayed the attack and the C.O. had to cope with over a thousand men and officers, few of them very experienced soldiers, all tensely waiting for what they knew was coming. The continuous shelling of the German lines by their own artillery was, in the colonel's view, a mistake, and now it had stretched out a further forty-eight hours.

"Impossible to sleep," he'd said when he welcomed Harry. "They'll run out of ammunition if this goes on much longer. Which would be something of a relief." He gave a short, loud laugh.

"The first of July," the C.O. said. "Thank God."

He poured out some brandy and handed each officer a small glass.

"The wire's not cut, of course, not all along, and the Germans will be ready and waiting after our week of explosive announcement with those bloody guns."

He poured himself another drink. It was increasingly obvious he'd had several before they arrived.

Despite the mood in the room, it was clear that the company commander and two of the platoon commanders couldn't wait to go. The third, a boy, looked apprehensive. He was eighteen, no more, and had joined his regiment only three weeks earlier. He had gone on exercises with the whole division at the rear and been out on patrol a couple of times, he explained, as if accounting for a misdemeanor to a housemaster, but the second time had been a fiasco and they had lost three soldiers. He blamed himself, he'd said miserably; they were good men. Harry thought what he was sure the boy was also thinking: that such an inexperienced subaltern shouldn't be here. But now that he was, he must at least act the part and reassure his troops.

"Do you think they've cut the wire? sir?"

"I think the gunners know what they're doing," Harry said, in what he hoped was a persuasive tone.

As he walked back to his billet to ready himself for the morning, he could hear the men, out of sight but shuffling like tethered horses in the darkness. Then, a single voice singing an old tune, "Oft, in the Stilly Night." Instantly and achingly, it brought back his night walks in New York and the ever-wakeful Irish of the Lower East Side tenements.

There were two letters waiting for him. One was from his lawyers, confirming his recent instructions. The other was from Isabelle. His servant, a new man, Welsh and efficient, brought him some strong tea and he sat down to read it. Abbotsgate seemed so very far away.

Dearest Harry,

I hope all still goes well with you. Here we follow the news in the paper and hope that you are safe and not in the thick of any fighting. Too many local boys are killed or injured and I was glad to hear you are at headquarters because I always imagine that to be out of the reach of the Germans, but of course I know little.

To see the photographs of destruction in the newspapers is very shocking and for me painful. As a Frenchwoman by birth I weep for my poor country and hope this time the Germans can be kept from reaching Paris. Who would have thought, when we first knew each other, that you would be there, defending my country, and I would be here, caring for your estate?

I don't like to think of you carrying unnecessary burdens at such a time so I must speak now. I have your recent letter and it goes beyond saying that I am so very grateful that you have left the unentailed part of Abbotsgate to Teddy in your new will. This removes all fear that I had for Teddy's future should anything happen to me. Thank you.

But then you say that you want to make it clear that this *is not because you assume he is your son,* but because it is the right thing to do, and this I was horrified to read. No. No. You have made a terrible mistake, Harry. Of course Teddy is not your son. He was a very early, very frail baby, who fought for life, I was seriously ill and the doctors said we would lose him. His early birth was not some device to deceive your father, if that's what you somehow came to believe. He was, is, your *brother,* your father's son. Not yours. I cannot bear it that you thought this for so long. Why did you not ask me?

Did your father know about us, whatever it was that we were? I think he did not. I came to love him very much. But I married him, as you guessed so angrily, all those years ago, because he had position and wealth and could take care of me.

Yes, I lured him into my bed. Yes, your rage was not misplaced, although I had no idea that you would then turn your back on us, on Teddy, on Abbotsgate, on England. I did not mean to hurt you. It never entered my head that you thought Teddy was your son. But you never let me speak to you, never came back to Abbotsgate again, or all this might have been made clear in an instant. No. No. He is your brother—so very much like you. Dearest Teddy, the greatest gift I ever had, the son and brother of brave men.

Thank you for providing for us both.

I pray for you, and Teddy and I both send you our love. He has a photograph of you by his bed at school.

Isabelle

"Jesus." He heard himself say it aloud and his orderly, who had just returned with a top-up of tea, looked startled.

He was bone-weary yet overalert; the barrage would test the patience of the most pacific saint; he had nearly three hundred

273

frightened men under his command, an attack tomorrow—and now this. A simple piece of information, which, when his tired brain could process it, would change how he viewed himself, how he had led his life, how he had treated other people.

His first, slow response was a mixture of relief, all-consuming regret, and then shame. He had run away because his lover had chosen a man over a boy; he had assumed because of his youthful virility that the child was his, yet he had refused to confront this, had hidden rather than find out the truth; he had abandoned his father, treated Isabelle with icy reserve, and ignored the little boy who was guilty of nothing and who was, in fact, all the time, his brother. All he could grasp at now was that clearly his father and Isabelle had been happy, and that Teddy was much loved. He was determined to survive these weeks and months and get to know this brother properly.

How could he have been so stupid about so much? The answer was his utter self-absorption. With his obsessive jealousy over Isabelle, there had never been any time for anything or anybody else until Marina. How incredibly lucky he was, and how undeserved his happiness with his wife.

He put Isabelle's letter in his pocket. He would think what to say to her when tomorrow's attack was over. He looked at his watch—*today's* attack. He owed her an apology so great, he hardly knew how to begin it. He longed to return to Abbotsgate, all guilt behind him.

For now, he picked up his pen to write to Marina. He had saved up much to tell her, but in the end it took no time at all to set down everything he needed to say. When he'd finished, he handed the letter to his servant to post, sat back, and drank a single measure of brandy from his hip flask. It had once, in some other war, been his father's.

CHAPTER THIRTY
Jean-Baptiste, France, June 30, 1916

AT FIRST JEAN-BAPTISTE HAD STAYED north, making his way between soldiers and heavily loaded horse-drawn wagons going in one direction and refugees going the other. He kept his head down, tried not to look at the men who were walking alongside him, and dropped back often so that he was not with the same group for any length of time. It was not hard, but after two or three hours he was already tired, muscles he had not used for months aching, his scars tight. His bladder burned, and despite the warmth of the day he shivered in what were now damp clothes. He ate some bread, drank from his water bottle. Everything was hazy as he walked on into the low afternoon sun. The river—which, when he had known it, changed from one stretch to another; sometimes green, sometimes clear to the bottom—was now all one murky brown.

As the sun set, the air smelled of explosive, the noise was loud and continuous, but it was difficult to judge how many kilometers away the guns were. Sometimes he thought he recognized the landscape, but new roads had been dug, small farmsteads flattened. The smell was getting worse along the bank. A few meters on, he saw a dead horse that had been swept downstream and had lodged in tree roots where the bank had been undercut by water. Its belly had burst open and greenish intestines were drying on its upper flank. He put his arm up over his nose and mouth. Flies were crawling over its head and the leather bridle that was still attached. So many flies that he could hear them. The horse's yellow teeth were bared in a snarl around the bit. He thought of Godet and the forge and the beautiful bay that had killed the old man and then been shot, after which one calamity after another had seemed to follow him. He would get back to Corbie and he would make it up to his mother. He wouldn't even tell her that Vignon was a German, that she had been deceived in more ways than she could imagine. He would tell her Vignon had saved his life.

"Of course they'll go through the motions of a trial, they're not barbarians, but, no, on reflection, I shall certainly be shot," the doctor had said, in that last conversation. He had been drawing on his cigarette. "No matter what my sympathies are, no matter my service for France. In the end your country chooses you, not you your country. I'm a German by birth and medical training, and once a German always a German to your fellow warriors. They'll shout 'Remember Verdun' as the volley rings out." He looked contemplative. "I'll have no chance to say 'my good chaps, I do. I do. I have spent days and nights and my health and vigor reassembling your countrymen just to send them back there to be dismembered again.'" He exhaled a ring of smoke. "I don't expect they'll even let me wear my uniform."

Jean-Baptiste hadn't known what to say. Vignon was probably right.

"Why did you come to us? To Corbie?"

"It was nowhere. I liked that. And I liked fishing."

CHAPTER THIRTY-ONE
Frank, France,
June 30, 1916

I WAS WRITING A NOTE to Dad, full of jolly stories, when the major came to tell us that after all the chopping and changing, the big June push was in the morning. Which would be July, in fact. He said it tapping the side of his nose as if he was sharing a big secret, as if we didn't know anything was in the air. There had been a long buildup, he told us (in case we were blind), and tomorrow we would take over German trenches. In case we were deaf too, he added that we might have noticed a heavy barrage— "Ha, ha, ha," he said—well, this barrage would have torn the wire apart and, undoubtedly, most of the Germans too who might otherwise not be too happy to have us in their trenches slicing their Battenberg cake. This was a joke. The major was keen on jokes, although it turned out he had only another day to get them all out.

One of the lads made a noise—halfway between a snort and a laugh. The major gave him a hard look.

"There's been a great deal of planning by a great many first-class military minds," he said.

"Sorry, sir," the lad muttered, but you could see by his face that he was trying not to laugh at the thought of this, and even Mr. Pierce wouldn't catch anybody's eye.

I often thought that when they'd run out of the right-size boots, or half the shells were duds, or they were short of medics or tea or plans or, basically, ideas, they tried to draw you into some big scheme in which fussing about small things made you seem less of a man. When I look back, the Reverend Mr. Tudor Williams was much the same. Once you were in search of salvation, wanting to hang on to a florin you were saving for a £9 17s. 6d. bicycle seemed niggardly.

Our big distraction was going to start with some pretty mighty fireworks, so they promised. The sappers were so excited, they couldn't resist the odd hint, the odd wink. Not that, given it was war, given there was going to be an attack, there was much that would surprise anybody. All the sappers could do was produce more and louder of what they'd been doing all along. One of them crept up on another while his pal was drinking tea and clapped two metal plates together behind his head. The tea drinker threw tea all over himself. Oh, how the other sappers laughed.

First thing the next day, it was all going to happen. The sergeant major said the lads up front would be able to saunter over, Fritz would be jam and our boys could take all the glory. The newer men were all keen to up and go, and disappointed to be held back until the third wave, and comforted only by being told they'd be going forward soon enough. They were the ones going to win the war, they'd been told. But they knew that this time tomorrow, one way or another, some of them wouldn't be here.

That was a fact, although nobody said it. All they didn't know was how many.

So, what was I thinking? I didn't sit there knowing what was ahead. Not the whole measure of the thing. I didn't care much. June had been a washout. So, one more month was coming; perhaps it would be drier. One more attack; perhaps we'd push forward half a mile. One more half-year of war; with any luck it would end by Christmas. Like they'd said last year and the one before. Fat chance. That was the future now: nothing like the plans that had once driven me on. The saving, the dreaming, the working hard in order to climb, all that "this time next year," the finding a girl or a Sturmey-Archer gearbox, going to the Institute, keeping accounts and getting fit to cycle the length of the Thames with Dick. Now the future was always more of yesterday or it was nothing. Oblivion. A new word I'd learned from Lieutenant Pierce when he'd had a bit to drink one evening.

I was all over the place with messages that last day; Isaac too. I could even see the shells whizzing over Nora and me to Jerry's lines, and I could get a smell of the coming battle. I was whacked by the time it got dark. The major thanked me. He was good like that and the men liked him, despite his little ways.

He said, in his reciting voice:

> his state
> Is kingly: thousands at his bidding speed,
> And post o'er land and ocean without rest;
> They also serve who only stand and wait.

I must have looked a bit puzzled because he added: "*They also serve who only sit and cycle*—what?"

I could see I was expected to smile, so I did. We were all going a bit barmy.

The Day

CHAPTER THIRTY-TWO

Benedict, France, July 1, 1916, Morning

BENEDICT LOOKED AT HIS WATCH: 0728 hours. Two minutes to go. Instinctively he looked out toward the invisible wire: the barbed swags and webs and coils of it.

The gun fired again, rolled back. The air shook.

"Do you think they'll give us a a pension later for being bloody deaf, sir? 'scuse my French," Smith shouted now.

Then, as if Smith had created it, an explosion of silence, and in the silence an immensity of fear.

The wire.

CHAPTER THIRTY-THREE

Jean-Baptiste, France, July 1, 1916, Morning

HE HAD SLEPT IN THE ruin of an old stable. At dawn, he was rested but stiff and bitten all over by insects and more nervous than the day before, when his mind had been full of escape. It was warm and gray, and he was thirsty and knew he had very little water left. He moved off slowly, a little giddy when he first stood up.

North to the British, Vignon had said, south to the French, east to the Germans, but he could hardly stumble upon them without crossing the British lines first, or at least not if the line was continuous. But who knew whether he might run into an early-morning German patrol probing into enemy lines? He ducked down twice as he heard voices from the towpath. He sat down again after an hour or so, with his back to an old oak, already weary. The sun had come out and, astonishingly, there were butterflies on a small patch of dandelions. He put his head back, shut his eyes.

And then, suddenly, there was an explosion, an eruption that sent tremors through the earth beneath him, and he found himself curled up on the ground, his hands over his ears, back in the hours of terror that had been his last memories of Verdun. Two other vast explosions followed; to the northeast and also some distance away, but so violent that he almost expected to see cracks run along the ground. Leaves and half-grown acorns fell from the tree. He sat, clasping his knees tightly to his chest, and retched. He mustn't succumb to fear now. He looked down and saw fine chalk dust on his sleeve; it was falling like powdery snow. Two aeroplanes crossed the sky, humming, almost innocently, and then there was—nothing.

A great hole of nothingness. A great silence.

Yet just as he had started to absorb the silence, the almost reassuring noise of shelling returned and the machine guns opened up. Something big was happening, an attack: from what Vignon had said, a British attack across the Ancre. Assuming that it had some success, it should push east away from him. He moved behind the tree, half camouflaged by brambles, and there he stayed for a while, until his breathing steadied, listening to war but hidden within it.

He began to calculate: he thought he was about halfway along the fourteen kilometers from Amiens to Corbie. If he followed the river, soon it would make a great loop north before returning to his home town. But he would reduce the distance if he made his way south, crossing over the river and then the lagoons and fens that spread south of Corbie. It was going against Vignon's advice, but Vignon was not—as he'd so often said, and Jean-Baptiste felt a small knot in his chest thinking of it—web-footed. Jean-Baptiste had been born to this landscape; he knew the hidden throughways, could weave his way through the shortcuts, could tell solid land that looked sodden from apparently dry land in which a man could sink and be lost.

An hour or so later, he had crossed the canal along the one remaining plank of the half-demolished Fouilloy footbridge. Now he was on the south side, the side Vignon had told him to avoid, walking into the waterlands toward the fighting, on the far side from Corbie and nearer the French positions.

The reeds and mud of the southern river bank stretched as far as the eye could see, and patches of water shone between mis-shapen willows. The path ran through pockets of yellow grass and sedge, and the turf was soft under his feet. He stooped to loosen his boots. A lake loomed ahead, a finger of land projecting into it but not, apparently, reaching the far side. He picked his way along this spit, hardly glancing at the opaque green depths to either side, except to notice that the placid surface he remembered was now bristling with lance-like rushes. He hoped the water at the far end was as shallow as he remembered it. It was, and he arrived on the opposite bank, momentarily triumphant, with almost-dry boots. Two other small lagoons, connected by deep ditches, lay ahead. He took a slight detour to avoid the marsh between them, though it seemed smaller than he remembered; a rotting fishing hut, now abandoned, stood several meters from the water's edge. A large duck rose up shrieking from behind it and he stumbled back, his heart hammering in his chest.

He went on more slowly, inhaling the familiar stagnant smell of summer. A rotten coracle lay on the edge of what he had expected would be the next large open expanse of water, but instead half-dried gray mud filled a large bowl in the earth. A few decaying fish lay on the surface. He suspected the British had extracted so much water for their needs that the levels had dropped, drying up the shallower pools. He considered whether to try to cross the depression; it would save him time, particularly desirable since he was already tiring again. He stood on the edge, picked up the largest stone he could find, and threw it. It thudded down and skidded a short distance, scattering up dust. He took out his knife, cut a long pole from an alder, and, testing the ground ahead of him, stepped forward tentatively.

He continued to move slowly, prodding the surface to either side like a blind man. As the pole found only solidity again and again, he became more confident, and the ground held under his feet as he edged out. He looked behind him: one footprint had dented the surface and filled with water. He was wondering about the wisdom of continuing when, about two meters from the bank, his right foot cracked the clay surface, went through, and found nothing: no purchase, no bottom at all; just the waiting lake that he could feel pouring into his boot.

His left foot started to sink too, albeit more slowly than the right. Trying to extract it, he sank farther to the right and almost toppled over. He lay down, pushing himself backward—they always said you should take your weight off your feet, spread it over the surface. He threw his arms back behind him, his scars burning as he stretched. He could feel the edge of dry land but couldn't extricate his right foot; each time he attempted to lever himself free, the weight of the lower half of his body seemed to sink farther. His right leg was in mud up to the calf. His left heel was touching something solid, but he was frightened to put any weight on it in case it lost this fragile purchase.

One hand grasped and lost a tuft of vegetation and then, flailing, the other found coarse grass. He pulled. Nothing but pain—it felt as if he were tearing his old wound apart. He felt panic growing; the watery mud was rising around him. He was going to drown here, slowly, after so long, so close to home. He pushed down hard with his left foot, grasped the reeds; and as one tuft came away, cutting his palm, his bottom lifted and his feet slid out of his boots.

He scrabbled backward and sat gasping, giddy, on the bank. Because he was exhausted and hungry and afraid of man-made danger, he had been stupid in a way that would never have hap-pened when he was a boy. He had always respected the river and the land it lay claim to. He was proud of the landscape and had never taken it for granted. Everyone around here knew someone who'd drowned. Drowned and been eaten by eels, they said. It was Godet who had told him that if a man wore boots, not sabots, he should untie them before walking in the fens. The marshes swallowed up boots, but a man without laces could slip his feet out of their hungry grasp.

CHAPTER THIRTY-FOUR
Frank, France, July 1, 1916, Mid-Morning

IT WAS A NICE DAY, July 1, in weather terms.

We were back in support. After breakfast, a handful of big bangs went off, just like the sappers had promised. Then the infantry must have gone forward. We could hear the machine guns open up. Isaac made a face at me. The firing went on and on. And we just sat. Some lance corporal was playing with a kitten. He looked up and said "Them Germans sound pretty lively, truth be told."

We had tea. We watched our aeroplanes taking off from the base at Doullens and heading south toward the big balloons. We didn't see any of Fritz's. We were bored, and it seemed all wrong when other men were out there fighting for their lives. The morning got hotter and we moved into the shade.

"What's a Battenberg cake?" said Isaac.

"Search me."

They said the cavalry would follow through after the initial attack, but the horses stayed behind the front line the whole time. Beautiful, they were, so I was glad.

When did we see it? The signs? They crept in. An hour or so in. The officers as had working telephones were getting news. You could see it in their faces and see it wasn't good. Just after lunch, there seemed to be a lull in the fighting. Men who should have been in new positions came back: a mass of them. The walking wounded and the convoys of ambulances, and some said the attack had failed and yet not half the men that had gone forward came back. Some said, well, they wouldn't have; they'd be having their hot dinner, as promised, at their objective. Others said the Ulsters at least were well forward.

There were rumors flying like bullets, humming overhead with no fixed target. The wave had broken and here was its vicious undertow; with the casualties came all shades of truth and speculation. The unbroken wire, the broken promises (this was mostly the young ones who still believed in such things). All those shells, they said, the crossfire from machine guns that had never been taken out. Men had been mown down as soon as they left the trench, or were left dying on the wire; they'd tried to hide in foxholes but found them stuffed with corpses. They said an upturned rifle stuck in the ground to mark an injured man had been used as a target by Fritz. They said brigadier generals and even full generals had died; that one had killed himself right there—or right somewhere else that someone had told them of—and whole regiments had been lost; the 7th Green Howard—probably the Green Howard, probably the 7th, but maybe the 1st—had attacked by mistake; the Londoners were through but unsupported; that it was hand to hand and slippery and the Scots using their knobkerries; that the 30th had done all right but in the northern sector it was a disaster. That the Devons, poor boys, lads I thought I might know, had gotten through but with terrible casualties; that ambulances were driving from one dressing station to another and being turned away while the men in the back slipped into death and the ambulances themselves got blown to kingdom come from time to time.

In the north, the second wave had run over fields of corpses, no avoiding it. There was a third wave, but it broke on a shore of disaster. Better in our sector, they said. "Considerable success." We kept repeating it. But better in war is always relative. And still we messengers waited.

"Do you think it's true?" said Isaac. He was so pale, his lips looked blue-gray like slate.

I shrugged. I was tired from watching and hearing, and spooked, I must admit.

"Well, sounds like it was pretty even-handed," I said. "Higher-ups mown down with everyday Tommies, so I suppose you would approve of that."

He gave me a hurt look with those great dark eyes of his and his face all bones these days. He didn't look good. It was a hot day, but he seemed clammy rather than sweating. That cough of his was getting him down, although I felt more sympathetic about the cough by day than at night when I was trying to sleep near him. I'd lie there imagining what it'd be like to press a pillow over his face. But we didn't have pillows.

"Why don't you go back to the M.O.?" I said, by way of making up. "You really look rotten."

"Now?" he said, his voice getting higher as it always did when he was agitated. *"Now?"* He flung an arm out. "With all those guys blown to bits? I'd have to have my lungs blown clean out of my chest before I could see a medic now." He looked exhausted even from speaking.

He was probably right. The Army doctors always liked things they could see: missing body parts, rashes with pustules that might be contagious, raging fevers. Things that didn't depend on a soldier's say-so. Corporal Byers said he'd had to shit blood on the M.O.'s floor before he'd been sent to the rear with dysentery. What chance a man with a nervous cough? Not that I thought it was all nerves now.

There was something happening. Looked like the reserves were moving up. There was a piercing whistle: not an officer's silver whistle on a chain, but a two-fingers-in-the-mouth common soldier's summons. Isaac looked up wearily.

"I don't think I can do it again," he said. "Not after yesterday. I was on the go all hours. Not if they ask me today. I'm finished, Frank."

I eyed him over.

"If they send you out," said I, "just take it at your own speed. If a message is urgent, they'll send a runner. Don't try to ride the bike—it'll slow you down and you'll only be a higher target. Don't put it on your back on your own—you're not strong enough."

It was true; I had visions of him snapping backward.

"Use the bike to lean on, to take your weight."

He looked at me as if I was doling out the wisdom of Solomon.

Then he reached into his pocket. "You've been a friend," he said. "Before the Army I had comrades, but not many I'd call a friend." He handed me a page from a message pad. "This is my brother's address."

"We've done this. I'm no more likely to make it than you," I said sharply.

He just looked at me. "Read it," he said.

"I've read it," said I, making to tuck it straight in my pocket.

"Aloud," said he. "If you read it aloud three times, you'll remember it."

I was about to tell him to stop all this now when I caught the expression on his face, and it was the look of a man who'd given up.

I opened it up. "Samuel Meyer, 14 Meyer Street, Stepney, London East," I said and then, feeling a bit of a fool, repeated it two times more, rather more quietly.

"Tell him," he said, "and he can say Kaddish for me. Tell him I did all right."

I just nodded. Couldn't bring myself to look straight at him.

Then we heard a shout that had our name on it. It was Mr. Pierce. There was an NCO next to him. Pierce thought he was staying in the rear, but now he was taking some men forward to support a bunch of Wiltshires who'd gotten cut off. I got up quick, Isaac more slowly. I straightened my uniform, picked up Nora, and wheeled her toward the officer.

"Two messages," said he. "From H.Q. One for the gunners in Sherwood Forest. And one is for the C.O. of 17th King's."

"Blimey," said a Pioneer Corps private who was hauling one end of a box of ammo, "I wouldn't want to go down there. That's right in the thick of it."

"That's enough, Perkins," said Lieutenant Pierce. "Things are much quieter now, as you can hear if you actually listen. And get another man to pick up the other end of the fucking box or you'll do Jerry's work for him."

Mr. Pierce never used to swear when he first came out. When Mr. Summerskill, his pal, called him on it, his mess servant heard him say, "I blame the soldiery. Salt of the earth, but rough-and-ready ways." He should have worked with Mr. Nugent back in Duke Street.

"Sorry, sir," said Perkins, in a voice that made it clear that Mr. Pierce was, despite the influence of the soldiery, wet behind the ears, and everybody knew he was scared of the new colonel.

Brave now, though. Tugging at his Sam Browne. Standing up straight. Looking five years older and every bit the officer about to lead his men where other men have failed and no bit of schoolboy left in him.

Pierce looked at Isaac. "There's been considerable success in the south," he said. "The 30th has met nearly all its objectives. The Liverpool and Manchester pals have taken a whole sector of the German front line. They're through and into Montauban, or as good as. You'll need to put on a bit of speed to catch them, Meyer. Wires have been cut by shelling."

"Not so good farther north, though?" I said.

"It's not clear," he said. But his eyes were moving from side to side. My old dad used to say you could always tell a man who was lying about his means to pay a bill, by if his eyes was yessling about like that.

"I'll go to the pals," I said as we pushed off. "You go to the gunners."

Sherwood Forest was a piddling little copse with a big gun sticking out of it. It was much nearer us and farther from the front, whereas the pals could be anywhere, judging by Summerskill's reports. I thought Isaac might just get to the copse, but in his condition he'd never make it as far as the front line, with or without being shot, so what would be the point?

Isaac took my message, I took his. We followed each other out onto the track. I rode in front, slow enough that Isaac could keep up until we got to Shadow Corner where we'd go our separate ways. Shadow had been *château,* which was French for castle. There wasn't any castle left now, of course. Not so as you'd notice. We stopped once we were beyond the junction, which was a favorite of Fritz's for shelling, and Isaac showed me on my map which was my best route.

"It's longer but safer," he said and cleared his throat thickly; for a minute I thought he'd choke right there, but he spat to one side. "Sorry," he said. "I can't breathe with it. There's a gentle slope and you'll have some cover. If you turn *here*, you'll be straight in the back of the trench system. Let me mark your map."

Which he did. He didn't seem keen to move on. "Be careful you don't go too far south, or you'll be joining the French Foreign Legion." He gave me a weak smile as he traced the line of the French sector with a grubby finger. "Or get stuck in the Somme marshes. Listen out for ducks." There was a sweetness about him when he smiled. Even with his glasses taped up. Even now.

It was a lot quieter, but that was saying nothing after the racket this morning. I looked around me—it was too exposed—and Isaac started in on one of his coughing fits. Some wounded men passed between us, and none of them gave either of us a glance. Not that far down the road a shell exploded. I hadn't seen any Manchesters; did that mean they'd gotten through? Or were they all dead?

A shell screamed over us and exploded behind us somewhere— someone else's bad day, and not far away.

Isaac mounted, riding so slowly that the front wheel wobbled and I thought he would fall off, though eventually he got going. But only fifty yards away, the road had been hit. There were dead horses, parts of them, and dead men; one of them, his head, at least, looked Chinese. But there was no road, just a crater.

"We're going to have to carry the bikes," I said, and wondered, not for the first time, what cyclists had ever done to the top brass that when the going got tough, we had to be burdened with a bloody bicycle on our shoulders. If you were in the cavalry, you didn't have to heft your horse about, piggyback, if it was injured or the ground was too muddy. It was clear: you rode the horse, never the other way around.

I struggled to help Isaac with getting his machine on his back. I hardly dared let go of the two of them. He swayed. We walked on, bent slightly forward, going far too slowly for my liking, but there was all kinds of human traffic coming against us now, all of it dark and weary and stained. Clumps of men. We turned into the better cover of a so-called sunken road, where the remains of thorn bushes provided some meager shade. Isaac had to stop to cough, one hand on the side of his chest, the other to his mouth. I held him by his arm, as I thought him likely to fall, and helped him unscrew his bottle, and he drank. Wiped his hand across his mouth. Where his hand had been was a brown smear.

I put a hand out as two men from our division came past, their arms around each other. One was from the Lancashires. One had a head wound, the other a bloody arm with a rough tourniquet.

"Manchesters?" I said.

I thought he wasn't going to answer, but then he nodded and said "I reckon as some made it through. If they can hold on."

The other looked angrily at me, the whites showing all around his eyes.

"Scots dead on the wire, bare arses in the air," he said. "Caught by their fucking skirts." They moved away.

I knew his anger was at the whole world he'd found himself in, not me. I turned back to Isaac. He was pulling at his shirt around his neck as if trying to loosen it. His thin shoulders rose and fell jerkily, as if he were laboring to get his next breath.

Soldiers, northern lads mostly, were draped along the bank, filthy and bloody. Some staring into space, some asleep or maybe dead. They were usually a talkative lot even if you couldn't understand much of it, but now they had nothing to say and eyes you didn't want to see. The most communication between them was one private lighting another man's cigarette. I was trying not to watch Isaac, and instead I saw how the hand of the man with the flame trembled so much that his companion had to steady his arm and guide the match to his cigarette.

"All that racket and they didn't cut half the wire," I said, but Isaac wasn't listening.

Isaac had blood on the back of his hand. He simply seemed to have stopped. He was wasting the breath he had worked so hard to suck in by muttering something, and not in English.

"Don't," I said. "If you talk like that, it sounds German. You'll get yourself lynched." Then I took him by the elbow. "Come on. It's not far."

But he went on muttering, and I was half glad I'd be splitting off toward the front line in five minutes and Isaac could be someone else's responsibility. We came up toward a bank. I was to circle south toward the entrance to the trench system. Isaac would only have to cross a small piece of ground and then find the battery in the wood that we could see straight ahead. No sign of the battery, and it wasn't firing, but that was his orders.

"Good luck," I said, and meant it. But when I turned, he was fumbling at the straps holding the bike and was standing with his cap off, looking puzzled and wiping his brow. I knew, just like that, we had to get the weight off him. I eased the bicycle off. It fell with a metallic protest, the top wheel spinning. Slowly Isaac's knees bent and very tidily he folded up, almost like the bicycles themselves when they were being folded for carriage.

There he lay, knees drawn up, his eyes slightly open and unfocused, his breathing slow and noisy. A longer gap. Then another breath. I patted him on the cheek, but there was no response.

"Isaac," I said, "get up. Bloody well get up."

Nothing. I lay on my front on the bank and crawled up it. There was firing, but not toward our current position, although plenty where I was supposed to be delivering my message. I thought the ridge would allow me enough cover for a while, though after that I'd be in the thick of it.

I looked back to Isaac. I'd have to leave him and hope the first-aiders picked him up. His face was waxen. I took his legs and pulled him, as smoothly as I could, into a tiny patch of shade and then moved his cycle. It was hard work, for all that he was light. Plenty passed us, but nobody helped me.

But then I thought, what about his message? Possibly I could deliver both, but I needed to know which was more urgent. It was an offense to read them, but I had to make a decision. I presumed mine was the priority, as it was going to the front line. I opened Isaac's message and it was about altering the gun elevation to give cover for a late-afternoon advance, the morning's having stalled. I thought of the poor b*****s who couldn't get through the wire and who'd be having our own shells land on them if the message didn't get through. Then I saw that the battery commander was a Captain Chatto. Of all the times to remember a name, now was not the best, but it was an odd one and "my" Chatto, who had sent me off on the cyclist's path, was a gunner too. Would I have thanked him for my present position? Well, he wasn't to have known, back in Duke Street, how it would turn out.

I opened the other message. The one that was sending me to the front line. It was from the quartermaster's office:

To Whom it May Concern: Please draw outline of Corporal Johnston's foot and confirm size thirteen boot required.

Isaac's occasional breaths sounded as if they were drawn through thick liquid. His lips were sticky with what looked like blood and mucus. His bright eyes were just glistening slits through almost-closed eyelids. I unscrewed his water bottle and tried to give him a sip, but it just ran away. A handful more soldiers came from the direction I was supposed to be going in. Two were dragging a third, whose tunic was dark and wet. The others were pale, and the last, who was trailing behind, had lost most of his uniform as well as his helmet. The group had to part to walk either side of us. One looked down at Isaac.

"Can't you move him?" he said. "He's plumb in the way."

"He's ill."

"He's blithering dead."

I put my hand up to Isaac's mouth. I couldn't feel or hear a breath. I touched the side of his neck, wondering if that was a faint shiver of a pulse but knowing it was my own heartbeats I could sense.

"Isaac," I said in a whisper. "Isaac. Please."

I pulled on his hand as if to wake him from sleep.

"Isaac," I whispered and put his hand back across his chest. My jaw ached and my eyes burned as I looked down on my friend. Thinking that he had, in his way, fought to the end. Thinking that really he'd had enough of it. Maybe he'd turn out to be the lucky one.

I would have said a prayer, but who knows what words his people used. So, with my hand on his arm, I said:

Samuel Meyer, 14 Meyer Street, Stepney, London East.

And I said it three times.

Then I took his red tag from around his neck. He had the six-pointed star that they wear too, but that he kept with him. I left him with his cycle, the two of them curled up, facing each other, and looked back only once to make sure it was true.

I stood for a second. I touched my bayonet, then found myself stroking Nora's crossbar because I knew now, for certain, that I would abandon her sooner or later. Then I shrugged Nora back into place. I thought of dumping her once and for all. I could say back at the depot that she'd been blown off my back, but it didn't seem right. Not yet.

I set off as fast as I could, because the message of Isaac's that I was carrying seemed likely to save other men's lives. If I hadn't been in the Army, I might have thought the other message was some secret code, but I knew for certain that they simply didn't want to issue a pair of large boots. They'd have to make them specially. They'd cost. I expect Private Johnston was hobbling his way toward Montauban and the Germans, his monster feet crammed into size tens even now; judging by the size of them, he'd be a nice big target. For all the supply section knew, he'd already be dead and they'd wouldn't have wasted money on a pair of size thirteen boots.

So I set off toward the trees, but by an indirect route. I don't trust open ground, and I didn't like the silence from the wood. So this is it, I'm thinking, I'll get this over and then I'll get back and have a think about Isaac. Now I'm just François Faber and it's 1909 and I'm carrying my cycle to the finish.

But somewhere between the two—between the lane and the woods, out in the sunlight, somewhere not far from the river, Isaac had said, but a long way from anywhere you'd want to be—I see the German and he sees me and when it counts I can't disentangle myself, or the rifle I haven't fired since training, from Nora's embrace. There's just time to think you've had it this time, Frank Stanton, and so I do.

CHAPTER THIRTY-FIVE
Benedict, France,
July 1, 1916, Midday

THE CYCLIST BOUGHT IT WITHIN minutes of them seeing him emerging where the track broke off. Their gun far back, deep in the trees, was silent; Benedict had given the order to cease fire at 0728 hours to allow the infantry to move forward. The infantry boys were, for a while, blasting away with the Lewis, drawing German fire on the copse, which severed the telephone wire.

It had been gloriously cool under the trees but hot in the clearing where the gun stood in freshly dug chalk. Two of the gunners had taken their shirts off, their backs oily. These were thin, sinewy men, and every time they lifted the shells, you could see every muscle working. Their bodies were young, perfect machines, every action coordinated. He let himself see the beauty in them.

He'd been about to send one of them back for further orders. He could easily spare a man, and it could only be a matter of time, he thought, until the next shell came closer. He'd noticed German spotter planes coming toward them, but on every occasion RFC pilots had scared them off. They'd been even quicker with the German balloons, which were hardly in the air before falling in a mass of flames. Were any of these planes Theo, he had wondered?

That's when he saw the messenger through his field glasses. The cyclist. The ridiculous cyclist, carrying his cycle on his back. He was emerging from a track that was protected by a raised bit of earth and a stunted hedgerow. He looked to either side before coming out slowly into the open, his body bowed. Smith had seen him too. He moved forward slightly, though still within cover of the trees, and waved to try to show their position.

"Stupid fucker, 'scuse my French, sir," Smith said. "He's still got his blooming rifle strapped to the machine. What the hell's he thinking?"

The man came on, stumbling a bit on the uneven ground, looking up once as a small plane came over. It was only fifty yards between the track and the edge of the wood.

The messenger paused—he'd obviously seen something he didn't like. He was fumbling around with the gun clips.

"Keep going," Benedict said, as much to himself as anyone else.

The cyclist stepped forward, warily now; he was within hailing distance and had obviously seen Benedict and Smith, as he altered direction down into a slight declivity; but then, from the far side of a single crater, a handful of gray shapes appeared. Germans, carrying their rifles, and looking momentarily surprised by the single figure in front of them. Perhaps they had come to silence the gun, and here was a madman, standing still in the middle of the field with the protruding bicycle, looking like some Indian god with extra limbs. Benedict took out the nearest German with a single revolver shot. Smith's rifle fired beside him and two more went down.

"Christ," he said. "Down!" he shouted to the messenger. "You're not a bloody scarecrow." Shots were being fired in their direction now.

Two Germans were crawling to the shelter of the crater. Smith fired again and the Germans kept their heads down.

"Get down!" he yelled to the cyclist. "Don't just stand there, you blithering fool!"

It was as he shouted, or he thought it was then, that suddenly everything about them, the wood, the gun and the half-naked gunners, the Germans, the hapless messenger and his message, disappeared in a rush of sucking wind and falling earth and a numbness that slowly became a terrible, roaring pain in his ears and chest, and burning in his arm.

Later, his face stinging, he was aware of his nose and mouth being full of earth, and he coughed to clear them, his tongue clearing grit off his teeth. He couldn't have been out long, as while he began to realize what he was and where he was, there was still a patter of falling earth and leaves and, as he tried to turn, he was covered by a layer of twigs.

A hand touched him. It was Smith, squatting beside him, his mouth moving. His words were distorted. Smith's face was cut and scratched, one eye closing already, but he looked substantially uninjured. He was feeling for Benedict's pulse, turning him over.

Benedict winced. The pressure on his chest was reducing—it had been a shell, he was certain, and must have been very near to have blown the wind out of his lungs. He coughed up some phlegm. Spat onto the grass. He propped himself up on his good arm; the other didn't respond, and distantly he felt a deep ache below his shoulder. Tried and failed to see the gun. Where the barrel should have been was nothing at all. It was very quiet and strangely light.

"The gun?" he said, and his own voice reverberated oddly in his head.

Smith shook his head. "Gone," he mouthed. "All gone."

Benedict lay back and looked up to see that the canopy of trees, which had protected them in the morning, had been blown away, transformed into a landscape of shattered branches and savage spears of wood, and above that the sun, burning down on them.

"Germans?" he said, remembering the exchange of fire immediately before the big explosion.

"Gone. A mine, I think. Home goal." A grim smile from Smith.

"Messenger?" Again the word echoed around his skull.

Smith shook his head.

Benedict got up with difficulty, leaning heavily on Smith's arm. Once standing, he could see through the blasted tract of what had been woodland: there was nothing left of the men from his battery, the men he'd been working with, around the clock, for the last week. The gun barrel had been dislodged. The shells, piled under the trees, had, amazingly, not exploded. Perhaps they were all duds, he thought. There would be an irony in that. But the shell in the breech had clearly gone off. What might be a decapitated and shriveled man sprawled close to his position. A single gunner lay some way away, pinned under a massive fallen tree, only his legs protruding, and grisly fragments of the others hung from nearby branches.

Slowly Benedict felt his nerves starting to deliver messages to his brain. Blood was running down his right hand and dripping down his uniform, and he was ashamed to feel faint, yet he couldn't raise his arm. He must have swayed, because Smith held him and lowered him to the ground.

Smith gazed down at him, studying the injured arm. Benedict examined his side; he couldn't get a clear view, but he could see flesh and, he thought, bone, as well as fragments of uniform and welling blood. His ears were singing and his head spun: red blood, a mash of green vegetation, and that blue sky. He turned his head to avoid the dazzling light and the heat of the sun. When Smith had fastened a tourniquet around Benedict's arm, he gave him a sip of water. Benedict turned away, feeling slightly sick, but Smith mouthed "Bleeding. A lot. Must drink." He undid Benedict's tunic and looked relieved that there was no other injury.

He spoke again. Benedict could watch his mouth moving and guess at a few words, but still only one or two syllables were clear.

"Back. Way. Luck," he heard. Smith pointed. Then he sensed Smith's arms around him in a sharp smell of sweat. The corporal's legs braced as he pulled Benedict to his feet and, supporting him, his arm around his waist, started to walk.

Benedict experienced only a moment's anxiety as they left the cover of the trees and he looked south to where the bodies of the Germans lay. Then he turned his gaze toward the messenger: he and his machine lay crumpled in the sunlight in the center of the strip of pasture. Smith shook his head. Benedict pulled away slightly in the direction of the cyclist, and Smith shook his head again, resisting Benedict's efforts. He made a slicing motion across his throat.

"No point," his lips said.

But we must check, Benedict thought or perhaps said, knowing he was being obstinate. Still Smith held his ground, and Benedict struggled to detach himself.

Eventually Smith, looking anxiously down the field toward the distant German lines, relented and they altered their path to pass the dead soldier.

"Jesus," said Smith.

The man was not dead. Benedict felt the pain leave his own injured arm and fill his body. The messenger was alive, his eyes open, blinking as their shadow fell over him. He was bent backward over his folded cycle. He looked very pale, a little puzzled, and, from the movement of his heels and the fingers of one arm spread to the side scrabbling in the dirt, he was trying to get up. But two spokes protruded clear through his body and one handlebar was partly embedded in his side. Freckles of blood spattered his face. The metal spokes quivered with his every attempted movement, and blood seeped around them. There were already flies feasting on it.

"Lie still," Benedict said. "You've been hurt." Was he shouting? He could no longer calibrate it. "We'll send stretcher-bearers." He wanted to kneel down and help the injured man, but extracting the metal from him, or rather, as he looked down, removing him from the metal frame on which he was impaled, would probably cause him agony as well as hasten his death.

The man was trying to focus on them, his eyes squeezed up against the pain or possibly the sun.

His lips formed one word: "Nora."

"It'll be his girl, I expect, sir," said Smith, turning his head aside to speak directly in Benedict's ear.

"Don't you worry about her," Smith said in a loud, clear voice. Even Benedict could hear his words. "We'll get a stretcher out to you just as soon as we can. You keep thinking about Nora and how you'll soon be home with her."

Something about the injured man reminded Benedict of somebody. Another of many soldiers he had known and would watch die?

The man was trying to speak, trying to lick his lips. Smith kneeled down and, more tenderly than Benedict would have thought possible, said "Don't try to speak." He supported the man's neck with his hand and gave him a little water.

"Message: Alter range. Wire intact," said the dying man with a terrible clarity.

Smith stood up slowly and was silent.

The wire. Benedict felt his face contort. The wire. After all that time, all those shells, they'd got it wrong.

He took out his handkerchief. Smith tipped water on it and covered the injured man's face to give him some protection from the sun. Apart from a smudge of blood, the handkerchief was as beautiful, as stupidly well-ironed, as crisp and unused, as on the day Benedict had bought it in Duke Street a year ago.

They moved away, lurching like a pair in a three-legged race. They had reached the edge of the sunken road, when simultaneously he heard the crack of a rifle and Smith fell away from him. Benedict collapsed, sickeningly, onto his injured arm. Smith was on the ground, a hole visible above his ear, blood pooling under his head. He was clearly dead. Benedict looked back across the field, seeing one of the Germans rising from the crater halfway across. He picked up Smith's rifle, fired it unsteadily with his left hand, and, to his surprise, the German went down. He felt for a pulse in Smith's neck. Nothing. The corporal's pupils were fixed.

"Thank you," he said softly, and remembered pointlessly that it was Smith's birthday. Then he staggered on, joining a trail of walking wounded but very alone.

By the time he was seen at a first-aid post, he was light-headed and could no longer feel much pain. He tried to get the orderlies to send out stretcher-bearers to the young soldier, impaled and roasting in the sun all on his own in the middle of a field, but it was chaos. The stretcher-bearers were overloaded; injured and dying men were being carried in from every direction—some on the backs of men only marginally less damaged than those they bore. He could no longer even give clear directions, no longer remember the coordinates of the field-gun position.

His hearing was improving. A blood-smeared doctor told him he'd lost a great deal of blood. His right wrist had been shattered and would need setting, and a piece of shrapnel had taken a large swath of muscle from his upper arm. They would put a pressure bandage on but leave it unstitched to reduce the risk of infection. It looked clean, he said, but time would tell. A nurse strapped up the arm, biting her lower lip. Dark shadows shaped her white face, and ginger curls escaped from her crumpled veil.

"What's your name?" Benedict said, just for something to say. She didn't look up.

"Louise."

An orderly gave Benedict two cups of strong tea, filled his water bottle, and told him to walk back to the rear.

"You won't be doing any more gunnery for a while, sir. If ever. One for Blighty, I shouldn't wonder."

He was lucky and got a lift, squeezed on the tailgate of a lorry, where he held on with his good arm and tried not to be sick. He reported to an unfamiliar and distracted C.O., before going to an aid post. Again he asked for help for the cyclist, but the C.O. didn't even seem to hear him. "Jesus Christ. What a bloody mess," he kept saying.

At the casualty clearing station, there were more doctors but so many men waiting, so many almost-tidy rows of injured lying on the ground, as if abandoned, as gray as the blankets covering them, so many soldiers staring into space, that all he wanted to do was run. Pain, his and theirs, eddied around him, searing his flesh and crushing his joints. He heard himself groan. Then he turned away. He was going home, to Harmony Cottage. If Theo was there, well, they were now equal. He just wanted to be back at the filthy shack where he had once been as happy as he had ever known. The pad on his arm was getting wetter. He touched it and his fingers came away sticky. He wiped them on his breeches. It was hot, he was hot, the air smelled purple. He thought of the man in the field and hoped he was dead by now.

CHAPTER THIRTY-SIX

Jean-Baptiste, France, July 1, 1916, Afternoon

BY LATE AFTERNOON, THE OVERHEAD sun was hot, a blue-gray haze lying at lower levels to the east. Jean-Baptiste considered his situation, wondering if it would be safer to wait and travel across the kilometer or so of field by darkness; but on balance he thought he might be less likely to be shot by day than by night. Night patrols were always twitchy. On his first patrol, a man named Dubois had nearly gotten them killed when he shot at a rat—drawing German fire on them. The lieutenant had hit Dubois across the face.

He was barefoot on the sharp, dry grass, covered in mud and without food. The river reappeared; water swirled past, pieces of debris rotating slowly in the current. He had swum in it more times than he could remember; once he could work out exactly where he was, he could pick a relatively narrow spot where the current was in his favor. But then to his surprise, not far ahead, set back from the water by fifty meters or so, was a good-sized farmstead, or what remained of one, a ruin, but substantial nevertheless. He watched it for a while from behind a stump of blighted bushes, hoping no one was inside. Even so, as he finally stood up, he raised his hands in the air. He moved toward it slowly, stumbling across a wide strip of weeds, sorrel and bright-yellow groundsel, half expecting to hear the crack of a rifle. As he got closer, he saw broken paving stones sprouting buddleia, alive with butterflies—tiny Citron, Vulcain, and the patterned russet one the schoolmaster had called Robert-le-Diable. One misshapen apple tree survived in what he thought must once have been an orchard. It was as if he had stumbled into an oasis, the memory of how things used to be overwhelming the evidence of how it was now.

The farmyard was chaos: broken pallets, carts without wheels, a well with its handle missing. He guessed the Army had taken all the iron. If he could find a bucket and a length of rope, he could let it down for water. But when he threw a stone over the rim, it took several seconds to hit water. Too deep. He went up to a stone trough and peered at the flies and the decaying barn owl floating just below the surface. Finally, by the ruin of a wash-house, he found a pump that delivered a small amount of rusty water to fill his bottle.

He stood up. Better to approach the house openly, as if he had nothing to hide. The front door had been removed, and part of it lay on the ground. As he walked up to it, he hesitated, then halted. He looked upward above the splintered door frame. The collision of his old life and the one that had sucked him up hit him like a shockwave. The entwined initials of Godet's nephew and his prize of a wife were still there. He turned around and, as he gazed across the yard in the direction he'd just come from, he recognized exactly where he was. He had stood on this doorstep before.

He entered the dark hall, avoiding clods of ceiling plaster and broken boards, and passed into what must once have been the kitchen. The range was full of debris: straw and mummified starlings and broken glass. There were empty tin cans on the floor and a stained horsehair mattress with a single battered metal bowl beside it. A solid-looking table top lay on its side by the low window. He was reassured by the dust that no one had been there recently. The shelves were empty, some shards of earthenware pots scattered on the flagstones. At some point, someone had lit a fire in the center of the room. He was not the first person who had sheltered here.

He went through into the back room. It was empty but for a truckle cot, a filthy blanket, and some rags. He decided that if he could find clean water, he would rest there. The stairs looked safe although damaged, and he climbed them, thinking that he might get a view of his surroundings, might even see Corbie from an upstairs window. When he reached the landing, he understood why the departed occupant had had a bed downstairs. Clearly the house had been hit by a stray shell that had taken off the upper rear of the building, or possibly it had been destroyed deliberately to act as a lookout post or a gun emplacement. He had seen cottages used that way on the Marne, the villagers weeping as their homes and their lives were torn apart. Perhaps a thousand meters away, there might be a road with vehicles and horses and gun carriages moving unevenly up to the front line and, shuffling the other way, wounded men.

Then he turned around. Scraps of floral wallpaper hung from the walls, and a prim iron fireplace was all that was left of a chimney, bar some sooty brickwork. There was a smashed washbowl on the floor, decorated with forget-me-nots. Extraordinarily, he could stand among these fragments of domesticity, remember the soft lips and the delicacy of young Madame Godet, and think that she had slept up here, once, right here, with her hair loose, sharing a bed with her pale, pompous husband. Yet just a few kilometers away, he could hear the unmistakable sounds of a continuing attack, and he shivered. He slid down the wall to the floor. Maybe he could stay here. Maybe he could wait out the war. A month, a year: however long it took. He could fish by night, catch eels and snare rabbits. He could eat sorrel and blueberries and apples. He could lie curled up in the corner, centimeters from where she had lain; he would watch the wallpaper roses by day, the stars by night, and go downstairs only when it rained.

He can see himself from above: a speck on a map. There he is; around him, like armor, is Godet's house. This is in clear focus. Beside that, the river, then Corbie; to either side, the waterlands. He pulls back: there is Amiens. Around the edges of his map, the detail gets hazy: somewhere east, tiny figures fighting; somewhere west, lines of breakers rolling.

A single large explosion. This one was closer at hand: loud enough for him to put out a hand to brace himself instinctively against a wall, and for dust and plaster to float down from the broken brickwork. He could see the road that had been hit. A plume of smoke rose upward. All traffic in either direction had stopped. Tiny figures were spreading out into the fields, and a lone horse galloped wildly away from the damage. He walked into a smaller bedroom, keeping to the shelter of the wall. This room, although also roofless, was less damaged than the one he'd just left, and it faced south. The window frame was still in place, though missing all its glass, and he stood beside it, listening. He could hear the sound of an approaching barge, coming downstream. He saw the red cross on its roof and then the stretchers. It was low in the water, moving slowly, the foredeck crammed with wounded men. Some covered, some half naked, they made a dismal sight, as if the vessel's freight were corpses.

He was so focused on the boat that, when it had passed, it was a shock to see that in midstream, to his left, was a long, thin island, some willows and long grass still growing upon it, and just visible on the far side another small farmstead and beyond it, unmistakably, the rooftops of Corbie. It overwhelmed him: he felt a tightness in his chest, and he squeezed shut his stinging eyes while the world around him reeled. For a second, he didn't dare open them—was Corbie just ruins? Had his imagination seen what it once had known, not what was there now? But when he looked again, the stone mass of Corbie's ancient abbey, and the gray and red roofs, were still there.

He walked down the stairs, keeping to the wall, then through the kitchen and on out into the yard. When he saw the man standing just a few meters away, leaning against the farther arch, he jumped back. The man was facing the river and seemed to be armed with something that Jean-Baptiste could not at first identify but feared was a flame-thrower; various bits of metalwork were visible on either side of him. From the back he looked like a strange sort of insect. He wore the uniform of a British corporal. Jean-Baptiste straightened his muddy cotton jacket. He called out, not wanting to surprise an armed serviceman, even one of France's allies. He had heard of deserters shooting civilians on their own side.

But the man gave no sign that he'd heard him at all. Was he waiting for something on the river? Eventually Jean-Baptiste moved toward him; but even when he was only an arm's length from the man, he did not turn around. Instinctively Jean-Baptiste moved to the right so that he could approach the soldier from the side, again seeking not to startle him, letting himself appear in his eyeline rather than tapping him on the shoulder.

He drew level and finally stood in front of him. The corporal looked like a dead man. He held his body like a monster in a children's story, his face strangely immobile, his eyes unfocused, his pupils huge. His lips and nose were blistered with sunburn and he was covered in tiny cuts, dirt, and, farther down, dark blood. Jean-Baptiste put up a hand in greeting but withdrew it immediately, realizing that the apparatus he had taken for a weapon was, in fact, part of a damaged folding bicycle strapped on the corporal's back. As he drew closer, he could also see that both of the man's hands were behind him, clasping the sides of the cycle, taking its weight, and were covered in blood.

He approached him slowly. Talking, all the time. "Let's get this off," and "Don't worry. I'm here now."

Meanwhile his own heart missed a beat. Parts of the machine were embedded in the man's flesh: he could see that now. People said that if you were stabbed, sometimes it was only the knife staying put that kept you from bleeding to death. But until the bicycle was off him, this man could not lie down. Sooner or later he would collapse and the metal be driven farther through him, and until then he was condemned to stay upright.

But how to part them? He uncurled his fists and undid the holding strap. The machine began to fall away with its own weight, and he could imagine it tearing at the man's flesh. The soldier gave a terrible groan as if his entrails were coming out and sagged, heavily, into his arms. There was no return now. The machine crashed to the ground and the sight of clots of blood on the brake handle made him feel giddy for a second. The cyclist's legs finally folded under him, and Jean-Baptiste caught him around the waist. He dragged the man across the yard, feeling a burning in his own damaged muscles. As he did so, he became aware of warm, wet blood and the smell of urine. He laid him on the mattress on the kitchen floor. The man was trembling but unconscious. Jean-Baptiste fetched the soldier's pack from outside. He opened the man's tunic and blood-sodden shirt, then took out his knife, cut through his vest, and looked down. The blood was coming from small puncture wounds: one, to the left, looked deep and had penetrated under his ribs. He turned him partly on to his side, though it evidently caused him pain. The edges of the wound caused by the bicycle had rolled inward and the cut was thin, slender enough for a bayonet.

He took the metal bowl out to the pump to get water to clean the injuries, and when he returned the soldier's eyes were flickering. He set down the bowl, wiped the blood off the man's mouth, and poured a little water into it. The man retched almost immediately, but Jean-Baptiste was relieved, and quite surprised, that there was no blood in it. The second time he lifted the bowl, the man actually drank a little. His eyes opened and then closed. He muttered something incomprehensible. Jean-Baptiste shook his head. Military cyclists usually had their machines strapped on their backs when they weren't using them. But then what? A shell, he guessed. A massive blast, at that. Why hadn't the shock killed him? How far had he walked in that condition, how much dirt was in his wounds? Émilie had told him it was the dirt, not the shell fragment or bullet, that made your leg go black and stink; that was what killed you. Dr. Vignon's hands were raw from scrubbing.

He turned to the man's pack, hoping it would contain a field dressing or something that he could use to cover the deeper wound, which continued to ooze black blood. Then he remembered Vignon's lotion. The one he was to use if his own wounds opened up. It was, miraculously, still in his pocket and unbroken; but what he pulled out with it made his stomach lurch. Next to it were his papers. Sodden. He eased them out of the envelope. They were legible only in one corner. Vignon had written in ink, and Jean-Baptiste had fallen in the marshes. He stared down at them and realized that his sole officially justified reason for returning to Corbie had as good as been eradicated.

The soldier was watching him, he thought. His eyes were certainly open. Jean-Baptiste pulled the cork out with his teeth. The smell took him straight back to the hospital at Royaumont; it reached the back of his throat. He looked at the label: *Solution Carrel-Dakin*, it said. *For wound irrigation*. He poured a little into the deeper injury, which made the soldier start, and patted it on the other injuries until the bottle was empty. Then he gave the man a drink and was glad when he took a mouthful and swallowed.

Once he'd done all he could, he sat back on his heels. He was tired and his side ached; his feet were already cut and sore. It was all very well getting the injured man under cover, but he urgently needed help. If he set out to Corbie now, where the British were, if he could get across the river, he could fetch assistance. If the man lived that long. He looked at the soldier's wrist for identification but, finding nothing, remembered his sergeant saying the British wore their names around their necks. Feeling slightly awkward, he felt for a plaque and found a cord, but nothing hung from it.

Jean-Baptiste slipped his hand into first one pocket of the corporal's uniform and then the other, but all he found was a small notebook, its pages crammed with writing—handwriting, mostly in pencil and in English so it might as well have been written by a pharaoh. He turned to the pack. Empty water bottle, a waterproof cape, rolled-up bindings. In a side pocket there was, finally, an identification disc. Isaac Meyer, it said.

He touched the corporal, who appeared to be asleep, put the man's own rain cape over him, then the grimy blanket, and left him. He walked back across the yard, remembering the last time he had left, with old Godet muttering under his breath following him to the cart. He thought of stolid old Mabelle, the chestnut who had pulled it. Long since eaten, he assumed.

He headed toward the river bank, looked carefully upstream and downstream, then walked to a spot a hundred meters south where the waters divided briefly to pass on either side of the small island he'd spotted from the window. The island where Vignon, poor Vignon, had spent a few stolen hours sinking into Madame de Potiers's welcoming white flesh. Jean-Baptiste remembered returning to the island to see the flattened greenery after the couple had left; it was an impressively large area and showed the passion of the doctor's lovemaking. He had been excited and angry and ashamed at the thought of the power that had crushed the long blades of grass.

Now the island would provide a place of rest, dividing his swim into two parts. He sat on the bank, his bruised and scratched feet cooled by the water for a few moments, then he fixed his eyes on the island and slipped into the water. He was nearly home.

CHAPTER THIRTY-SEVEN
Marina, New York, July 1, 1916, 9 A.M.

MARINA SYDENHAM SETS OUT FROM home just to buy flowers. She has had a restless night and woken with a slight headache and a stiff neck, but it is a beautiful day: the first of July, the doorman of her apartment reminds her. She thinks of Harry, his day coming to an end on another continent, just as hers begins. It is just nine o'clock and another fine, hot morning, and she stops momentarily at the shock of it, absorbing the early warmth and enjoying the sight of Central Park, where the trees have yet to take on the darker shades of high summer. Here she is at the start of a summer's day and there, more than three thousand miles away, Harry's day moves toward mid-afternoon. He is, she thinks, not so very far away in hours.

It is unusually quiet; so many have left the city for the beach in fear of the poliomyelitis epidemic. She had promised her father that she would go away, but she knew that Harry's letters would come first to New York and she didn't want to worry him with the city's hysterical response to the epidemic. He could not run away, so she would not. So many restaurants and theaters are shut, invitations are few, and she has found that she likes a less social city: prefers it when most of her friends intrude only by letter. She thinks Harry would love it too. She is painting a lot. Not now of imagined wilderness, but of scenes around her: places she learned to see properly through the eyes of a stranger in love with the city.

Ornamental lakes have been drained: some say, loudly, that water is the danger in the epidemic. But she often walks to Battery Park, mostly because it is where Harry first took her and where they had stood looking out across the Hudson, to Ellis Island.

"In different circumstances it could have been me. Herded toward the sheds and the baths and the doctors," Harry had said. "Petitioning or easing in. Rich or poor, English, Irish, Italian, German: we're all immigrants to a country vast enough to absorb us."

Despite war and epidemics, she feels happy today. She thinks she will buy a bunch of delphiniums as blue as the sky, and she turns left toward the small flower stand. She knows that the flower-seller is too poor to close up or to leave the city, despite poor trade; and anyway probably the safest place the woman can be is away from the disease-ridden tenements and out in the fresh air.

She walks slowly because of the heat and because the whole day is hers. The early newsstands no longer show headlines and grimy pictures of faraway battles, but of rows of polio-stricken children in high-sided hospital cots right here in New York. But she has, anyway, long since stopped reading of every advance and setback in France. The stories are mostly distorted: exaggerated for pathos, or lightened so as not to lower morale among those with European connections on either side. Beautiful, ancient Europe. It was hard to imagine it: the little countries, civilized countries, that had centuries of literature and music and ideas, and, yes, cruelty and violence and poverty in their history too, as Harry insists on reminding her, now all tearing each other apart. Their sons gone, their unimaginably old monuments and churches pounded to rubble. She never wants to return, even if it becomes possible, to see those places brought so low.

She shivers slightly as she moves into the heavy shade of the trees as she rounds the corner. She is chilly despite the heat of the day. It occurs to her that in some ways she is better off than her friends. In time, she thinks, America will be sucked into this European war. It's inevitable, or so she hears from friends whose husbands are close to the President's circle. It will not take much. One more *Lusitania*. One more secret channel exposing German hostility to American interests. A few months. A year. So married girls and mothers with handsome sons were anxious now, seeing their men differently: not as absolutely theirs but, already, on a different path. The men themselves behaving in subtly changing ways, excited, apprehensive. It was almost like suspecting your husband had a lover, her friend Nancy had said. Wondering if he'd be with you next summer, wondering what he was thinking about.

They might petition highly placed friends, but their menfolk would be plucked from them eventually, just as they had been last winter in Britain. Conscription. American women live with that fear. Whereas her Harry has chosen to go, and the two of them have been through it all, and yet here they still are: her a married woman, waiting, and him her husband and a soldier. It is an old, old story, and it is behind her, the sick anticipation and the leaving and the first selfish loneliness.

Harry's letters, sketches, his roughly drawn caricatures, his anecdotes and regrets, his dark moments often followed swiftly by an apology and reassurances, are all she needs. Sometimes she thinks that she and Harry have become closer, now that they communicate through letters, than they had been when their every day had been spent together and either they had been too wrapped up in each other, or unable to talk of war and fear and weakness because it all seemed too fragile. She is stronger, more independent now. Around her the city turns, but she thinks of Harry and the unfinished letter on her desk. She feels, very suddenly, an overwhelming pride in her husband and, equally suddenly, she understands. He had not chosen a cause he didn't believe in over a marriage that he didn't quite believe in either. She had known instantly, on that first visit to Abbotsgate, that he had once loved his stepmother, which was why he'd arrived in New York and in her life. She had come to realize only much later that he no longer felt as once he had.

She is glad her husband is fighting, that he believed he should because other men he'd known a long time ago were fighting for the country where he had grown up. A small lump rises in her throat and tightness radiates across her shoulder blades. Harry, she thinks. I do love you so frighteningly much.

The sweet smell of the blossoms reaches her before she turns the corner to where the old Italian lady stands behind her flowers like a woodland creature hiding in exotic shrubbery. Marina decides that she will press one perfect bloom and send it to Harry to explain all the thoughts of her summer day.

CHAPTER THIRTY-EIGHT
Harry, France, July 1, 1916, Early Evening

MY BROTHER, HARRY IS STILL thinking. He tries to retrieve that earlier summer's day, when his father died, war began, and he first saw Teddy standing in the hall, in mourning, yet looking at him curiously. Teddy was always just my brother, he thinks. But he cannot hold on to any thought for long.

He had looked up at blue skies a few hours earlier, astonished by the birds, faltering in their song but still there. Now he lies back, his face to the sun, his eyes closed. He imagines it is any other July day in his thirty-four years when he might have thrown himself carelessly to the ground. A picnic. The end of a hard set of tennis. Being lifted off his father's shoulders. He tries to ignore the fact that his legs no longer respond to his will. Just for a short time he is out of this foxhole of seven men, one minus his head and one with his intestines leaking out of him and with it the stink of feces. He tries to remember grass and laughter and lemonade, and just for a second he has them.

He struggles to make sense of what has happened since he led a much larger number of men into action. They got through the wire, but the Germans were more than ready for them. It is only the fact that the surviving soldiers seem as numb as he feels that allows him time to try to work out where they are now and to decide what to do next. He knows they will have to wait until dark to move back. He is gripped with thirst; but when he feels for a water bottle, he finds it missing. Corporal Jones appears beside him, his face bright and shining red with blood. He sits with his back against the raw earth, with one great sigh but without saying a word, and hands Harry his own. As Harry drinks, his uninjured leg keeps trembling and he tries to still it with his hand.

The ragged edges of this small world seemed blurred and insubstantial like the shimmer of any hot day. Time, too, seems to be playing tricks. He closes his eyes against the sun that is hurting them and wakes to find that it has almost disappeared from his view and he is now lying in shadow, the lower rays just skimming the broken chalk at the crater's lip. He is shivering with cold and nausea. He thinks of his men—boys, many of them, scarcely more than half his age—who had also believed what he told them. Then he reaches for Marina, but pain and shock make memories too hard to assemble.

Eventually he feels strong enough to crawl to the edge of the crater, dragging his useless, disobedient limb. He looks for a spot that provides cover, pulls out his binoculars, and scans the disturbed ground around him as quickly as he can. The day is ending. Within a foot or two of the crater is Pickard, staring at him like a gorgon, eyes and mouth open, flies at his lips, hair corkscrewing outward. He forces himself to shift his gaze away. Turns his head slightly, although every movement grates, to see over the corpse. Beyond him is a landscape of sleeping figures, some graceful, some ugly. His vision is hazy. He screws his eyes up and releases

323

them a few times, then moves the binoculars as fast as possible from side to side. He can't risk holding a position for more than a few seconds in case some lucky German sniper gets his head in their sights. But something catches his eye, and he turns again to identify the movement. It is a first-aider, virtually on his stomach, the red cross visible on his sleeve, dragging a pack as he crawls from one man to another, apparently feeling for signs of life and not finding any. A couple of puffs of chalk rise to either side of him, but he crawls on, unhit.

"Bloody lunatic," says Jones, who has appeared next to him.

Harry sees Jones put two fingers in his mouth and whistle. The first-aider goes flat, then raises his head and eventually changes his direction. They duck down. Waiting. There is nothing except distant machine-gun fire, much more sporadic now. Perhaps all sides are finally glutted. Eventually Harry thinks he can hear a dragging noise: it might be hope, or it could be something worse; his revolver is in his hand. A few more small explosions of earth along the crater edge and the crack of rifle shots. Then the man is over the rim and rolling in to join them, his bag coming to lie a foot or so away from his body.

But then he moves, blows his lips out and says "Champion." And Harry almost laughs, except that it hurts. The man lies winded for a few seconds but then sits up and retrieves his first-aid kit, brushing it down carefully.

"I am the first-aider. How many alive and injured?" He scans the crater.

"Four," says Harry. "Hutton"—he points to Private Hutton, who lies with his head in his brother's lap, legs straight, feet pointing outward, bleeding from nose and mouth; then to young Pierce, who is not one of them, who has a name only because Jones looked at his identification disc and who, in truth, he is not sure about.

"Lieutenant Pierce. Jones here. He's in bad shape. And my leg's been hit."

"It's nothing," says Jones, touching the long cut down his head and neck. "Cuts on the head; everyone knows they're buggers."

The first-aider stoops to get to Private Hutton, shakes his head. Hutton's brother continues to stroke his brother's hair. Harry can't remember which brother is which. Is it Albert or Stanley who's dead?

"What's your name?" Harry says to the newcomer.

"Higgs, sir. Gordon Higgs. I'm a searcher. I am a first-aider," he says, unnecessarily. "I search and bring aid. That is my job. Wherever God takes me, which is always unexpected. For instance, I saw a man today who had been attacked by his own bicycle."

Jones exchanges a glance with Harry, a glance that says: that explains it, the man is actually mad. They are stuck in a crater with dead men, parts of dead men, injured men, and now a madman.

Higgs moves, shakes his head too at Lieutenant Pierce, who ends the day as he began it, eyes open, gazing upward.

Harry lies back as Higgs touches his leg, preparing himself for pain, but Higgs's hands are strangely gentle, almost anesthetic as they pass over his immobile limb. He simply says "Right, we'll keep this boot on, sir. Boots make good splints. I've run out of morphine, I'm afraid."

"I've got a mint, sir," says Jones and brings out a crushed paper bag of grubby sweets. "We stay put and wait for stretcher-bearers, I reckon," he says, wincing as Higgs probes his scalp for more than the flesh wound Jones admits to.

Despite Jones's protestations, Harry pulls himself up to the ridge on the edge of the crater. It is dusk, becoming safer; the explosions are dying away. What takes his eye is the little church steeple across the fields. Was that their objective? Was that where they were supposed to be? Just there?

Jones is pulling, hard, on the hem of his tunic, like a bored child. "Too long, sir. Too long. Get down."

Six hundred meters away, Gefreiter Werner Franck, armed with a Mauser Gower 98, fitted with an optical sight, has been waiting for the officer's head to reappear. He nearly had him last time. He waits and he waits. He is tired and thirsty, and soon it will be dark and too late. He traces the words on his belt buckle with his fingers—he does that every time, for luck. *Gott Mit Uns.*

The first star comes out like a sign, because then the British officer's head rises up right in the middle of his field of vision. Franck curses when just as he fires the officer jerks his head and his binoculars to one side, so the clean head shot doesn't find its target, but the man falls back silently.

The bullet hits the binoculars. Harry feels the blow ricochet down his hand, followed by the shock of finding himself down and fluid filling his throat, choking him. He puts up a hand and there's a terrible lack of contour in his jaw, everything wet and sharp. Between him and the greenish sky, dark heads now loom like gargoyles, and black specks—birds? missiles?—whirl around above them.

"Fuck," says a stranger.

"Dressing pack—get a bloody pack." It's Jones, sounding more Welsh than ever in his panic. "Oh, bloody hell, his face."

"Keep calm," another voice shouts, unsteadily. A hand is exploring his neck and chin. "His jaw's smashed."

Harry's mouth is full of blood and fragments. "Turn him on his side," he hears a voice say. "Keep the pressure on. Keep the pressure *on*!"

Am I fainting?, he wonders; am I dying? He wants to scream as they rotate him onto his broken leg. He can hear gargling and coughing, right there. His ears are ringing, the dark lines spread inward, and he's bitterly cold. His legs and arms are dancing, he thinks.

"Sir."

The movements make him feel sick. He heaves, vomits. Can't clear his throat of blood and debris. Jones seems to be pressing down on him, preventing him from breathing. His legs are shuddering, something has trapped his arm, and he has, in the end, only a brief moment of panic before the roaring darkness, while Gordon Higgs tries to maneuver a dressing pack on the devastation of Harry's lower face, muttering "I am a first-aider, I bring aid. I am a first-aider. God is with me."

Harry is not thinking, in the approved style, of Marina, or Abbotsgate, of Teddy or his father, nor even of his regiment, his country, or of an all-encompassing regret; those are the fancies of dying men with time on their hands.

The animals in the winter zoo are restless; they squeal and gibber in this secret place; clouds of frost obscure the trees.

CHAPTER THIRTY-NINE
Jean-Baptiste, France, July 1, 1916, Late Afternoon

THE SECRET OF THE ISLAND was the all-concealing greenery and, as Vignon had discovered to his advantage, unlike most islands it dipped rather than rose in the middle. For a while, Jean-Baptiste lay flat on his back in that hollow, getting his breath back. Only a solitary willow remained where once the small glade had been surrounded by a palisade of vegetation. He heard barges pass as he lay prostrate and invisible and the boum, boum, boum of shelling tolled across the fields. His ribs ached and he was very stiff, his mouth sticky. He spent a few minutes easing his limbs before returning to the river. This time, having looked in both directions, he jumped. The bank was sheer, the water deep where the current scoured and undercut it. The roots of long-dead trees still twined like monstrous serpents just under the surface. As a boy he had worried that they would trap and drown him. He sank

328

into the water, his eyes stinging, and then he was heading for the far bank, though it was more of an effort than he anticipated and he was swept some way downstream. He reached the other side, pulled himself out, struggled to his feet.

He looked around to make sure the area was clear, and there to his astonishment he saw a survivor, a familiar friend, peering out from under two willows that grew more in the water than on land. He blinked twice to clear his vision in case what he was seeing was just the product of hunger, wariness, and wishful thinking. He edged forward, and the regular shape of the obstruction made it obvious, or obvious if you knew what you were looking for. It was a mound of greenish canvas, weighted down by rocks and mud and half-covered by rotting vegetation. He swept the branches aside, his heart beating as if at the sight of a long-lost lover. He moved a rock with his foot, pulled hard at the canvas, and there was Vignon's boat. He rolled back the cover with some difficulty; it had become stiff and heavy. There was *Sans Souci*. She was on dry land, although holding water and dead leaves. The rowlocks, amazingly, were in place, and the blades of the oars were visible inside the boat. The bailer still hung on its hook.

He crawled over to the boat. The varnish had peeled a bit and a moorhen had nested in the prow, but it seemed sound. He stood up, bent under the overhanging branches, and clambered in. The boat rocked slightly in the earth. He sat down, noticing that the rowlocks had moss growing around them, and sat there for a while, feeling absurdly safe. He shut his eyes. The dappled light, the sound of the river breaking over some submerged obstacle, the birds, and even, in the thin fringe of dried grass, a cricket. With his eyes shut, the grumbling and explosions were the sounds of a summer storm. With his eyes shut, it was all right.

But then his thoughts cleared. What was he doing sitting, his thoughts drifting? Every minute he sat gathering his strength, the injured British soldier's life was seeping away.

329

He didn't want to take the towpath, but the fields proved too rough going for his bare feet. River craft passed him and soldiers were visible from time to time on both sides of the water, but he soon realized they had no interest in him. Soon he was following the canal through a broken avenue of poplars.

Jean-Baptiste felt simultaneously sick and ravenously hungry; it was hard to remember what he was doing. He thought about the food he might find. The people of Corbie would be short of food, everywhere was the same, but his mother would have something. Her tiny garden abutted a narrow waterway that ran down to the river. Every inch was covered in growing things, mostly leeks; he had teased her about the leeks, always her most successful crop, but he remembered red-flowered climbing beans too, the green pipes of onions, and the ferny carrot tops. Her pear tree bore little fruit, but she always believed in next year's yield. Her hens pecked among the greenery, and an old chair caught the sun's rays on spring afternoons. The privy was perched precariously on the bank. It was never a place to linger.

Now that the prospect was becoming more of a reality, he allowed himself to think properly of his mother. He wished he had written, wished he had at least told her he was safe. Had he died, she would have gotten his pension, but he had lived. She must have assumed he was a soldier—what man wasn't? He thought, uncomfortably, that she had wanted him to be one, but that was when there hadn't been a war; he doubted *any* mother would have wished the last two years on any son. But she would have liked a picture of him in uniform. Other men had laughed about how their mothers had cherished the pictures they had left them: of awkward poses and pristine uniforms. But his mother had never had a chance, and all because he was so furious with Vignon and with her for giving herself to him. Even the memory of it stirred uncomfortable feelings, even now that Vignon had saved his life.

The sun was still warm, but he felt clammy in his damp clothes. He walked along the edges of the fields, pressing his ribs with his hand. Eventually the river narrowed and across the canal Robisart's mill came in sight, just where it should, though its glass was broken and it looked deserted. Had Captain Robisart survived?, he wondered.

The outlying houses of Corbie appeared; in the few small orchards between them, unripe apples hung on the trees, though the grass was thigh-high. The first house was ruined; nettles grew immediately around it. A word had been painted on it, but it was a word he didn't know. A scrawny pig nuzzled in the earth. He tried to remember who lived here. Was it the widow Morisot? A skinny girl sidled out of the house and stood between Jean-Baptiste and the pig, staring at him as if he might try to steal the animal any second. He called out a greeting, but the girl just went on staring.

To his left the first river gardens appeared, their neglected crops nothing more than a tangled mass. A few lines of cabbages showed that somebody was still trying to nurture his allotment, but it was mostly just yellow columns of decaying sprouts and rusting metal. There was one incongruous sight: Monsieur Petit-bon's rose bower with its seat that nobody had ever seen him sit in. Made out of old planks and wire, it had always looked mad in winter but now, rising out of rotting vegetables, it was covered in red roses. He walked on. The edge of the towpath was deeply rutted, invaded by dark weeds. Rather than go into the center of town and to the lock, which he was sure would now be guarded by soldiers, he turned toward the Remparts des Poissonniers and up the narrow cut of the Rue du Four Perrache. To his far left was the Mairie, its fairytale turrets and spires like a chateau on the Loire, Vignon had said.

As he came out on the corner of the Place de la République, he could see that the place he was returning to was not the one of his two-year-old memories, although its buildings were mostly intact. He leaned against the wall, tired but suddenly apprehensive, gazing at the British trucks drawn up from one side of the square to the other, at the sawn-off stumps of trees that had once brought shade to the town, and at the soldiers and female nurses milling about. But whom could he tell about the soldier? He was still trying to take it all in when there was a loud shout. The tone was of command, but he didn't understand the meaning.

Two soldiers were coming toward him. They were clearly British soldiers. One gestured to him to put his hands up. He did so, realizing that in his wet clothes, with a cotton jacket over his army breeches, his own identity was hard to discern. As they reached him, one of the soldiers reached out and turned him around quite roughly. He stumbled. One felt his waistband, presumably checking for weapons, and then said something to him that he didn't understand. He shrugged. The man spoke louder, but he shook his head.

The same man turned him back toward the square and gave him a firm push in the small of the back. As he walked on, both of them close behind him, he sensed their guns still on him and thought how ironic it would be if he were shot by France's allies and in his own home town. He was shivering, from his wet clothes, from fatigue and hunger, and now from fear. Around him, the whole town seemed subtly changed. It was like a bad dream, its very familiarity making it appear stranger. It was not just the air of watchfulness, the pockmarked stone of the fine houses on the square, the half-boarded windows and sandbags around the doors, nor even the British flag entangled above the ancient gate to the abbey: the town's whole character had changed. The sense of euphoria he'd felt on seeing Corbie at a distance from the ruined farm and the weary relief that he'd felt on crossing the river had both faded now, to be replaced by anxiety.

They passed along the Rue Pichet. Many of the shops were closed and boarded up, a handful with smashed windows. One of them, a draper's, had belonged to a distant cousin of his father's who in his lifetime had always done his best to put distance between them. Now his shop appeared to have been burned out, reduced to a black cave. More soldiers passed them, marching in loose formation, heavy packs on their backs, looking clean but tired. They reached the abbey, where the great studded door was shut against them. The Virgin in her little shrine had lurched to the left, clutching her child as if she might drop it. Diagonally opposite on the corner, Armand's bar looked much the same as it had when Jean-Baptiste had left, with its peeling paint and grimy windows, but then Jean-Baptiste's mother had always said both the bar and Armand himself needed a good cleanout and setting straight. They used to laugh at the priest, who could have crossed the ten meters of the square separating church and bar after mass but instead took a route right around the back and behind the cottages before coming up Rue Pierre Guinard and emerging on Armand's worn steps, as if he were somehow a different person and surprised to be there at all.

The ancient abbey buildings were scruffier and much, much smaller than he remembered. He knew this was probably due to his time in Paris rather than because of the war. The Boche could blow men and houses into so many bits, or incinerate them to a cinder, but they couldn't yet shrink them. Vignon came into his head again and he understood the man's air, which had once irked him, of seeming to find everything in Picardy rather undersized. Vignon came from a city, and cities made men bigger but they also diminished the places men had come from.

The abbey church was much the same, its tower intact, unlike so many he'd seen that had made convenient targets for gunnery crews. And there, in front of it, stood the priest and, even more dreamlike, he was talking to Armand, out in the street, which would never have happened before the war. But the soldiers were hurrying him on, and although Armand and Father Lefroy looked across at the tiny drama, neither seemed to recognize him. The next shop was open, although it seemed to be selling nothing but onions, and then the *tabac* too, and across the square several small shops were doing business. Smoke rose from the baker's chimney. It was as if all the life of the small community had been sucked into its center.

Jean-Baptiste had begun to see what sort of place it had become. Because Corbie was well behind the lines and of reasonable size, the British were obviously using it as some kind of headquarters, which was hardly surprising. Some of the town life still continued as it always had. Two women in aprons and an old man stopped to talk on the street. One was Madame Didot, who took lodgers, her reputation suffering because of it. His mother had sometimes helped with the laundry. The younger one must be her daughter, Angeline, only grown from a lanky child into a young woman while he had been away. Both looked in his direction, and he wanted to wave but didn't dare make a sudden movement. If only he could explain to his current guardians that he only wanted to be home. The two women continued to stare. Had he changed so much in two years?

They had reached the old schoolhouse, from where Jean-Baptiste had turned his back on his birthplace, not as he had dreamed in Vignon's boat but on the schoolmaster's bicycle. Would they have realized it was he who had taken it? Would his mother have looked for him, or would she have felt too ashamed at having to explain the reasons he had left so suddenly? Perhaps they'd think it was old Godet's death that had somehow unhinged him and sent him running off to Paris. He'd seen plenty of men since go stark raving mad, faced with smashed heads and raw blood. But *she* knew why he'd gone; she knew because he'd left his father's boots and taken Vignon's, which were more elegant and much better fitting.

The older soldier had reached the foot of the steps to the schoolmaster's house and barred his way before entering himself. The younger still had his gun at the ready. Did he look like a dangerous criminal? a German? a spy? But then he thought that he probably did resemble one of these: a pilferer or a deserter at the very least. Someone who might be shot.

The soldier came out again and beckoned him in. The hall was nothing like he remembered. A British sergeant came out and barked at him, then repeated the gobbledegook more slowly and more loudly. He was no different from Folz, Jean-Baptiste thought. All stripes, voice, and red scowl. The sergeant pushed his face up close. It was bristly. He shouted so loudly that it hurt Jean-Baptiste's ears, and as he drew back from it he noticed the two soldiers grinning at each other.

The noise had obviously attracted attention. At the back of the hall a door opened and an officer came out, frowning. With his pale face and dark hair, he looked a bit like the schoolmaster, but he was a British captain. He said something to the sergeant and the man saluted sharply. The captain looked at Jean-Baptiste as if taking stock of him.

"God save the King, how do you do," Jean-Baptiste said, and one of the soldiers sniggered.

The officer went on looking at him, and especially at his bare feet. He was conscious of dried weed on his sleeve.

"You're French?" he said, finally.

Jean-Baptiste nodded, nodded so fast he felt dizzy and had to blink to clear his head. The captain pointed toward the back room and gestured to the soldiers to go.

The room had once been the schoolmaster's dining room. It still had the same brown wallpaper, now with light patches where the pictures had once hung. A grimy lace curtain drooped at the window. A large table had been placed diagonally across a corner, its surface completely covered with maps and papers topped with an overflowing ashtray.

"I am Captain Bartram," said the officer once he had sat down. "And you are?"

"Trooper Mallet, sir," he said. "One of your men is injured, just across the river. He needs help. Quickly."

For a second he watched the British officer's serious face. The man was not French, but he spoke French like a Parisian.

"Commendable. But there is a war on and you are dressed, more or less, like a soldier."

"I've been discharged. I was injured. I have come to see my mother. She lives here. In Corbie."

His hand went up and touched his ribs. "And then I had—I *have*—a disease. Of the kidneys. From before, I think. I was in a hospital and then on a barge, but Dr. Vignon said that as we were near my home, I could leave."

The officer looked thoughtful.

"Do you have permission to leave your regiment? Do you have papers?"

"Yes. Well, no." Jean-Baptiste felt in his pockets. He must have swayed, because the officer got up, held him by his elbow, and guided him to a chair; then he went to the door and shouted down the corridor.

"They'll bring you some tea," he said.

Jean-Baptiste's fingers were trembling as he pulled out the papers from his wet trousers, the envelope lying in his hand like little more than a slab of porridge.

"I was in the river," he said.

"Unfortunate," the captain said. "The water seems to have dissolved your alibi."

Jean-Baptiste nodded miserably. He had been so careful, but it was as the schoolmaster had told him long, long ago: the river could never be trusted. It could scour a bank away, pour over the fields, drowning whatever lay in its way: a package of paper was nothing.

Suddenly the officer asked him: "Are you a deserter?"

"No, sir. I served at Verdun and was commended, and then I was injured. They thought I would die."

The officer looked almost sad. "I'm afraid plenty of deserters have given honorable service before they decide they have given enough."

He got up, walked over to Jean-Baptiste, and picked up his wrist. For a second he thought the captain was going to take his pulse, but he simply turned his identity bracelet around. "Well," he said, reading it, "at least that seems to agree on who you are."

There was a knock on the door. An orderly came in with a mug and a plate of bread. Jean-Baptiste had been ravenous earlier, but now his appetite had gone. He picked up the solid mug, almost too hot to hold, and drank. He had never tasted tea, but it was the British national drink and he had no wish to offend the officer. It was terrible—bitter-sweet with an oily surface and the color of chestnuts—but he drank a little more and felt it spread its warmth through his body.

Then he remembered his other mission and put the mug down.

"Sir, the soldier," he said. "He's at Monsieur Godet's farm. I mean, it's ruined now, but it *was* his. It's just over the river. Up from the island. Up from Robisart's factory. He's injured. Quite badly, I think. I tried to help."

The captain picked up his pen.

"A British soldier?" he said.

"Yes. He is with bicycles. He had a bicycle. On his arm—a stag." He could feel himself tapping his own arm to demonstrate where the badge was, nodding like an idiot, to emphasize his words. The captain nodded back.

"He might be asleep, but he might be unconscious."

The captain stood up a second time. This time the bristled sergeant came to the doorway. He was like a great hog, Jean-Baptiste thought. He and the captain exchanged words.

"My sergeant thinks it could be a trap," the captain said, turning to Jean-Baptiste. "If it's the building we're thinking of, it's within range of the guns. We have thousands of casualties already."

"No," Jean-Baptiste said, surprised at how much he wanted them to find their wounded countryman. "Please. He is hurt. He will die if nobody goes. His name is Isaac, I think. I said I'd send someone." He felt in his pocket and brought out the disc.

337

The captain turned the identity disc over in his hand.

"It has been a very bad day," he said and looked somber. "We are only beginning to find out how bad. I don't have time for this. My sergeant would quite like to see you shot, just to save time." There was a hint of a smile. "So I hope you aren't giving him any reason to press his case. My own thoughts are that quite enough men have died today already."

"No, sir. I just said to the cyclist that I'd get help." Then he added: "But I don't know if he could understand me."

"All right." The officer's attention seemed to flag. "We'll see in good time anyway. Usually we'd simply hand you back to your own people, let them sort it out. But even you can't have missed the fact that we're in the middle of a major action." He waved vaguely to indicate a world that they both knew existed not far from this room.

Jean-Baptiste nodded.

"I'm not risking men we don't have just to take you south. Of course, we could lock you up." He stopped, walked to the hall door. Turned. "Where does your mother live?"

Jean-Baptiste felt faint hope.

"Here," he said. And when the officer looked surprised, he added "A hundred meters from here. On the edge of town."

"Right. Here's what we'll do. I'll have a medical orderly look you over and see if your story holds up."

"Sir, thank you. Thank you."

The orderly made a face at the sight of his scars. Put one hand behind and one in front of the tender area beneath his ribs and squeezed. Jean-Baptiste gasped. The officer looked up and waved the orderly away, but Jean-Baptiste kept ahold of the man's arm.

"Please," he said. "Please go to Godet's farm. On the other side of the river. No distance at all. One of your men is there—he will die. I put the solution the doctor gave me on his wound. His bicycle was stuck into his stomach."

The orderly looked up, though he made no attempt to pull free. He gave Jean-Baptiste a blank look and then turned to the officer. After a few seconds, the captain spoke to him in his own language, and the man replied. The orderly looked at Jean-Baptiste as though assessing what kind of man he was dealing with. The tone of his conversation with the officer sounded like a series of questions and answers. The orderly patted Jean-Baptiste on the back.

The officer said "The first-aider confirms injuries to your kidneys. For now you can go home. And he is willing to try to find your patient. He has volunteered. So now it's up to God and Higgs. Here's some paper and a pencil. I want you to draw me a simple map of the farm. Then write your address down. Then you may go." He sat down and returned to his papers, looking deathly tired.

"Thank you," Jean-Baptiste said, as much for the cyclist as himself.

It was strange taking the usual road toward his mother's house, but when the lane curved and he finally caught sight of his former home, the upper windows were roughly boarded up. Soldiers in shirtsleeves sat on pallets in what was now just a yard, where she had once grown vegetables.

He slowed down, trying to make sense of it. She must be staying with friends in the town. It was not so strange; it was already clear that houses in Corbie had been commandeered by the British soldiers. But how would he find her?

For the first time, the enormity of what he had done back in 1914 hit him. He had abandoned her. It was a much bigger sin than anything his mother had done. It was not his fault the Germans had come, but she would have guessed he had gone to fight and would never have known whether he was alive or dead. He felt his face twitching. Maybe with every bit of news, every French defeat or ferocious battle, she would have wondered. Was her boy alive or dead or horribly mutilated? He blinked hard and swallowed with difficulty. This was the house where she had given birth to him, where she might have read his letters and been comforted. If he had sent her any. It was here that she had sat when he had gone away and, later, when Vignon had gone too. And what did her neighbors think of a woman whose son left her without a good-bye?

He walked to the edge of the low wall. None of the men in the garden looked up. He didn't know what to do. He took a deep breath, and it set his cough off. He had to wipe his mouth with the back of his hand. The sun was in his eyes and he squinted to the bedroom windows. Then somebody tapped him on the arm, their approach so quiet he jumped.

"Jean-Baptiste?" It was Madame Petitbon. She had been old when he had been a child, and she seemed not much older now. She wore the remnants of traditional local dress, and her lips had disappeared into the cavern of her mouth.

"Is it you? My poor boy," she said. "Poor child."

She looked down at his bare feet, puzzled. He found himself struggling not to be overwhelmed by emotion. Somebody had welcomed him.

"We all thought you were dead," she said, reaching up and stroking his arm.

He shook his head.

"And grown so tall. And a soldier?"

"Injured," he said, his voice ragged. He wanted to touch her in return. "My mother?" He willed himself to ignore the expression on her face. "My mother must have gone?"

She was silent, her black eyes never leaving him. "My poor lad," she said in the end. Her hand reached out again. Then, wearily, "She's gone, yes. Gone to our Lord and his blessed mother and all the angels. Nearly two years ago now."

The muscles of his face were pulling it in directions he couldn't control. For a few minutes he could think of nothing to say. "My mother," he said, finally.

After a few more minutes, he said "Why? She wasn't old." And then without meaning to, he said "Why?" again, like a small child.

"She died with the nuns," the old woman said and pulled her gray shawl around her, her eyes sliding away from him. "She was not a bad woman. Always a good neighbor." She patted him on the arm a few times. Then she took his hand in her tiny dry one. "She always missed you," she said. "She'll be looking down, glad you came home."

But what home *was* there? No mother, no house, the town full of the British and at war? Now tears filled his eyes. He screwed them tightly shut but still felt tears escape.

"Talk to the nuns," she said. "Talk to Father Lefroy. He buried her. November '14. Leaves everywhere. Cold. She's in the church-yard." Her face brightened. "You can go and see her, tell her all about it. No cross there, but she's on the right near the gate. Next to old Godet." He felt her move away and looked up to see her shuffle off across the road.

He wiped his face on his sleeve again. It was filthy. He was filthy. And it had all been for nothing. He might as well have gone back to fight. Vignon hadn't known, and the thought of Vignon's act tightened around his heart. She'd died only months after he'd left. She had looked well, seemed so strong, but perhaps he had never really looked at her? At least she had never heard of Verdun, of the losses and the lives of daily horror. She never had to imagine that or imagine him there.

He was gripped by a pain of regret that almost stopped his breath: not just his chest, but his whole body was tight and frozen, as if fingers were digging into the back of his neck, paralyzing him. He tried to stop the trembling by wrapping his arms tightly around himself, but felt dizzy and lowered himself to a squatting position. But at that moment, Madame Petitbon reappeared with Madame Laporte at her side. The older, smaller woman seemed to be supporting the raw-boned, black-frocked Madame Laporte, who held out a pair of well-worn sabots.

"My Lucien's," she said. "He won't be needing them."

He leaned against a wall; there was a faint smell of baking bread. Out of nowhere, there was his mother making him a bowl of hot chocolate for breakfast on his saint's day. He thought that had been before his father died, before times got harder though happier. The memory of her patching his blue school pinafore, of her watching him from the doorstep, the doorstep just across the street, as he walked to classes: the same route he had just taken. Keeping him safe. Another image hit him, each one like a blow. Perhaps the last time he saw her before Vignon. Before it happened. She was squinting as she read a book, leaning toward the oil lamp. Now he thought it was a new book. Remembering the poetry he'd found in the doctor's boat, he wondered whether Vignon had given it to her. She had been the only daughter of the mayor's chief clerk in Amiens, and she had been properly taught to read and write. Her favorite cousin had married a rich Englishman, she'd told him when he was a boy. It was then that he'd gotten it in his mind to row to England and find her.

His mother had once told him that her parents had tried everything they could to prevent her marrying his father. "Oh, but he was so handsome," she'd say, "such a manly man." This was after his death, when other aspects of him could be forgotten. The day after the wedding—"Where grandemère was dressed for a funeral," she'd said laughing—his grandfather had died of apoplexy while drafting leases for *hortillonages* on the Somme. "He fell on his big bottle of ink," she'd said, "and ruined six months' work, and when we saw him, the side of his face looked bruised. But it was ink, just spilled ink. The women had scrubbed and scrubbed but they couldn't get it out. Even when they practically rubbed his skin to the bone."

She was gone. Only he now knew these things, and he had nobody to tell. Nobody cared.

He rubbed his eye with the heel of his hand. Someone coughed. It was a priest. Looking harder, he could see it was Father Lefroy, an anxious, thinner-looking Father Lefroy. He and his mother had thought the priest rather pompous, but now he was just grateful for a familiar face. Another wave of emotion swept over him.

"My child. My child," said Father Lefroy, putting a hand on his head as if for a blessing. His lips moved silently for a second. "A son of Corbie returned. But to a tragedy. We all thought that you were dead, and you thought your dear mother was alive. What terrible misunderstandings. What sorrow God asks us to endure."

"Why did my mother die? Was she ill? Was it an accident?"

"My dear boy, it was God's will. But I shall take you to the nuns. They can tell you all about her end. But first, a restorative?"

"No. Please. I want to know about my mother."

The priest, whom he remembered as so voluble, seemed to have little to say now. He looked tired and old. His cassock was fraying and dusty.

"My mother—" Jean-Baptiste began.

"The nuns will tell you."

The convent had always struck him as a miserable place, even before old Godet's accusations. A high flint wall hid all but its steep roof. He had peered at the orphans through padlocked gates from time to time. The village children liked watching one particular strange boy who made animal noises and flapped his hands. He dribbled too, and once he'd taken his trousers off and waggled his private parts and all the village girls had squealed. A nun came out, furious, slapping the boy with both hands and shouting at his audience. Later, when Jean-Baptiste was in Paris, he went to the Menagerie and realized that watching the idiot boy was a bit like seeing animals in the zoo.

It hadn't changed. But this time, he and the priest passed through the gate and rang the bell of the great door. After a long and silent pause, it opened. A young maid in drab dress and apron listened while Father Lefroy explained that they had come to see the Mother Superior. They stood in the hall, gazing at the portrait of some violent martyrdom. Eventually a nun appeared, looking flustered, and they followed her down a corridor, her coif nearly brushing the ceiling. Despite the sunshine outside, it was very dark, and Jean-Baptiste became aware again of the distant explosions.

She ushered them into a room where a middle-aged nun, with a bony face and raw red hands clasped in front of her, was standing waiting for them. "Father?" she said, in a irritated tone of voice and then, looking to Jean-Baptiste, nodded.

"Jean-Baptiste Mallet. The boy wants to know about his mother," the priest said.

The nun looked weary. "Madame Mallet," she said with the emphasis on Madame. Her look was not of sympathy but of calculated indifference, somehow tinged with pleasure, Jean-Baptiste thought.

"Your mother," she said, "was brought here for her confinement."

He didn't understand. Why had his mother been confined? What had she done that made Father Lefroy look embarrassed and the nun look stern?

The priest interrupted. "The midwife was delivering two other babies. The doctor had left to join the Army, and the elderly physician who replaced him was unwell. So she was brought here when things became—difficult."

"It was a complicated delivery and unfortunately she succumbed, although not before receiving final unction," said the Mother Superior, and she dipped her head toward the priest.

His heart was pounding and he hated the fact that his cheeks were on fire and that he had an audience watching his every reaction to this enormous news.

"The child survived," the nun said, and this time he was sure her tone was one of regret. "He has been here ever since. Your brother is now nineteen months old and surprisingly healthy."

His brother. A brother. His mother had had a baby. Another lurch as he realized the father must be Vignon. He was torn between wanting to run out of this grim place to somewhere where he could take in all that she had told him, and wanting to see the child.

"Well?" the nun said.

"What is his name?"

"Leo," she said.

He must have looked surprised. "He was born in November, on the feast of St. Leo," said the priest. He lowered his voice. "Your poor mother succumbed the following day."

"She had lost too much blood," the nun said, curtly.

Standing there with a single shaft of sunlight cutting a diagonal line across the floor, he had a sudden vision of blood. Not the blood he had seen everywhere in the last two years, but that of his father. In his memory, his gaze traveled once more from the soles of his father's boots up to the red halo spreading outward from his dark head as it lay in his mother's lap, staining her white apron. And he heard again the screaming—not at the end, as she was cradling his father's body in her arms, but as he hit her and as he fell down the stairs.

And then, years afterward, there was Vignon. Kind, clever, fastidious, full of stories—not all of them true. Smelling of violets and reciting poetry. Had Vignon known he was a father, or had he, too, left her, never knowing his fate?

"Now I'd like to see my brother," he said.

"He'll be asleep," said the nun, dismissively. "It's hardly convenient."

Father Lefroy looked anxiously from her to Jean-Baptiste, nodding his head as if hoping he might be seen to agree with both of them.

"All the same," Jean-Baptiste said, "I wish to see him."

CHAPTER FORTY
Benedict, France, July 1-2, 1916

THEO WAS WHIMPERING IN HIS sleep. He lay on his back in his gray undershirt and drawers, one arm thrown back, his hand loosely closed, his stubble dark against his white skin. Benedict watched his chest rise and fall, each exhalation seeming to catch briefly. The fingers of Theo's bad hand hung over the edge of the iron bedframe. His leather jacket, gloves, balaclava, and boots had been discarded on the floor, and his bottle of Macallan, the top off, was just within reach. Benedict reached down, picked up Theo's drooping arm, and laid it across his chest. The hand was cool, the scar from the lost finger and the puckered one up his forearm quite healed and neat. He touched the web of ivory ridges very gently with his finger. Then he turned the hand and, with a single finger, stroked the tributaries of blue veins running under the fine skin of Theo's inner wrist. The fingers opened very slightly, but Theo slept on.

He stood there for a second, remembering Theo's long fingers moving over the notes or reaching to pull out or depress a stop, his feet in control of the pedals, his face utterly focused. Yet it was aeroplanes that had given Theo a happy war; and despite fear, discomfort, horror, Theo had survived. To be near him was, briefly, to share his armor of euphoria.

Benedict had a swig of the whiskey before putting the cap back on, then made up one of Theo's powders. The liquid stung his mouth ulcers, but he swilled it around his mouth, hoping it might be some kind of cure for the pain and nausea of his broken arm. He was very thirsty, but he lay on his back next to Theo on the bedstead, gazing through the hole in the roof as the threads of clouds and smoke blew away and the stars came out, while the noise, which had become part of him, rumbled and crashed and wailed like a departing storm.

When he opened his eyes, it was morning. Theo, his uniform, and the bottle were gone. Benedict was due at H.Q. at 1000 hours, and he thought he could probably get that far and have his wound dealt with properly. He got up, feeling abominably weak. There were bloodstains where he had been lying, but the bandage seemed to be dry. He needed a bath, he thought, and looked for a paper spill to light the Primus stove. He picked up some torn paper from under the discarded bottles in the long-dead cottage hearth. It seemed to have been a letter, and he could see at once that it was in Theo's strange new handwriting. While his mind was still casting about for some justification for looking at a discarded private letter, he was already starting to read it. While the water was coming to the boil, he walked outside. What he was reading was more of a journal entry, but by a Theo who had become a stranger.

We were on the first patrol today—those parasols—sometimes they're clumsy things, but I felt like a great bird soaring among others of my family.

347

In all that chaos and death, the people having fled, their animals having gone or perished, the birds stayed—thrushes, skylarks, blackbirds singing their hearts out. And I was privileged to see what no man was born to see—the map unfolding beneath me, the whole salient with its fields and hills, marshes and forests, traversed by trenches, blown apart by man, the fine threads of rivers running like veins and blocked with death. Yet where we would all cease to be, in an hour or a week or in half a century, this would all return. Oxen would pull the plow, trees would bear blossom in spring, fruit in autumn, enough villagers would return to repair their violated cottages, women would hang linen on a line, priests cling to a faith undented by shrapnel, uncorrupted by gas. The river would flow clean and fill with fish. But now it was as if, having become a bird, I was transported into a dark fairytale. Giants walked the earth, the pounding of their footsteps reverberating horribly. Banshees wailed, and silver razor rain fell incessantly. There were no princesses in towers: the towers were long shattered and the briars around them barbed metal. I flew on, higher, 4,000 feet. I was seeing the greatest unleashing of power man had ever created, in a machine that could itself, like God, deal death from above, and then, after dawn, I turned south and saw a world end as even that land ceased to exist.

The earth seemed to rise into a hill, so slowly that it was if I were giddy, and I probably blinked, assuming it was my eyes that were seeing wrongly, but then the hill burst with pressure from its very core, a sheet of light flashed and the ground came up to meet me, fast, for a second I thought I'd misjudged it and yet I exulted to think my end would be part of something so magnificent; there was nothing like it since God first created the earth and man upon it. It was almost an act of blasphemy, that we should hurl this world back at him. For the air itself developed an extraordinary force and my little plane rocked in the mightiness of its thrust as a beautiful column of earth and trees and men rose and went on rising upward and then, after a long moment's suspension, fell back on itself, forming a ring of dust moving ever outward and, when it cleared, beneath it a bright, new-born crater of chalk, innocent, pristine. A grave or a womb?

But then, as he turned the page over, it was as if, in the next few lines, Theo had caught him red-handed.

Oh Ben, what have we seen? How can we ever return from it? If this should ever come to an end are we doomed to go on for ever, longing to return, longing for just one second more of this exquisite terror? This cleansing of the world? How can I speak of it at home, what can I say to Agnes? Who is Agnes? Who am I? How can I talk of poetry, hear music, or make the right noises when she shows me her pressed flowers, or tells me of the Mission or her father's elevation or her mother's nerves? After today I am done with that. Marriage, obligation, nations—all exploded into nothingness.

There were meteor showers this last week— natural wonders, Ben, that man has gazed at in awe since time began, and we saw nothing because we were blowing the sky apart, showing God what man could do without him.

Benedict let his arm drop. The last sentence seemed to combine elation with despair, and the writing traveled upward along the line, the letters becoming successively wider and less finished. He had never known a Theo who wrote like this, never thought him capable of such thoughts. Yet he was overwhelmed with misgivings.

He turned to the Primus, where the water had nearly boiled dry, and did a poor job of shaving without a mirror. Dabbed blood spots off his chin and looked around for his boots. But all the busying about had not distracted him enough, and he picked up Theo's letter, if that's what it was, and turned it over. His heart sped up. There was only one further short paragraph:

> Oh Ben, patient Ben, who suffers for others, who can be so quietly angry at my awe, and, yes, sometimes delight, in destruction and my fascination with the means by which we ensure it. Loyal Ben, who knows me to be a liar and a thief and a boaster, who has seen me behave like a beast, and still loves me. You are wasted out there in the dry desert of lost faith because you would make such a very good Christian—of the quieter, more pacific sort, the turn-a-cheek sort. Ben, stay with me, I shall need a friend, a warrior-companion who was with me at the beginning and at the end of the world. Then we won't be alone with it all. We can go forward together.

And then, more neatly, the old Theo suddenly reappeared: "Don't worry, old chap. I haven't gone off my rocker." Below these few startling sentences there was the usual small drawing; this time the tiny aeroplane had feathery wings and its nose pointed upward. These were musical notes drawn in the cloud below it: e, d, c, f, e, d, f. He smiled, and the tension slipped away to be replaced by warmth.

"O, for the Wings of a Dove," Mendelssohn's anthem from Psalm 55.

For a few seconds Benedict sensed his heart beating erratically, and his cheeks burned even as he knew Theo's were the fleeting thoughts and emotions of fatigue and hunger and fear, not helped by alcohol and the contents of the medicine chest. Despite himself, he read the page again, yet with more apprehension than the first time. Theo had shown him a future, and all he needed was to trust and be brave: was that it? Was he missing something? His brain moved slowly, perhaps from loss of blood; his arm throbbed.

He heard someone coming: footsteps moving heavily and fast toward the house.

"Captain Chatto, sir. You need to come. There's been an accident, sir." The soldier hadn't even paused to knock but had burst into the room, apparently not registering the officer's state of semi-dress.

"One of ours, sir, it's come down. Just returning, sir, it's on the field and smoking."

Benedict frowned. "Our what?" He imagined some unexploded missile aimed at the enemy had failed and was now threatening to blow them all to kingdom come.

"A plane, sir. And he's moving. And it's like to catch fire. Two lads say he's alive but his leg's caught. They've gone for a surgeon." The soldier's eyes showed that he knew that this meant they would amputate a limb to get the man out. And they both knew the plane would have gone up long before then. "But the smoke's getting worse and Sergeant Laughton pulled them back."

When Benedict made no response, the soldier looked at him, uncomprehendingly at first and then, seeing his blood-soaked arm, said, with less certainty, "Are you all right, sir? I thought you'd want to come, you see."

Benedict sat to pull on his boots with his good hand and the soldier added: "Seeing as it's Captain Dawes-Holt, sir."

He froze for a second.

"No," he said. "No." Theo shouldn't be flying at all. "Captain Dawes-Holt? Are you sure?"

"Yes, sir. He was up first thing yesterday, saw them blow up the ridge. Said he was off to test the machine now, sir. Running ragged, he said, but told Sergeant Laughton he'd been too close to the mines when they blew them and the balance was off."

Then he was up and pushing past the soldier, his tunic still unbuttoned. His clumsy steps turned into a run; he held his bad arm in his good one and stumbled on uneven ground. He ran on. A single shell whined and burst to his left; he heard its bright greenness edged with orange. He ran on without his usual instinctive ducking down. One of three soldiers saluted—he noticed they were dirty and one had a bandaged hand. His chest hurt. And then he saw it. Behind some broken trees. A mean stretch of what had once been meadowland. The plane was nose-down, almost comical with its tail up and one wing broken. But he saw this through fingers of smoke, which came and went. White smoke mostly, but as he drew closer he could see more ominous darker billows.

"We need a fire chain," he said as the soldier caught up. "Tell the NCO."

"We tried, sir. Shell's broken the pipe. The sappers are at it now. We only got the stream and a bit of fire water. In the tank. Sar'nt says we're not to go too close."

He could hear shouting as well as crackling now. What the devil was the sergeant thinking of? Men were running up the bank with individual buckets, but it was going to be hopeless. They needed to get Theo out. He reached a small zinc cistern; buckets were almost thrown into it, clanging in sparks of pink and blue against the side, and the opaque water gathered up and spilled as each soldier ran to the flames. But it was too slow; almost worse in its pointlessness than nothing.

"Tonge thought he was moving, sir, a few minutes ago." Hall was at his side. "Just for a minute when the smoke cleared enough to see him. He must have had a problem with the rig because he can only just have took off. He wasn't hit," he added, as if it were relevant. "He just went up high and came down like a bird as been shot. Clipped the trees."

He almost pushed him away. Then he smelled more than smoke at exactly the second that the significance of Hall's words hit home and he understood why the sergeant was holding them back. If he'd only just taken the plane up, it would be full of fuel.

Now that he was closer, he could feel the heat and see the thickening oily clouds and, on the ground, more debris and the flicker of small flames. Hall and the sergeant caught up with him as he hesitated.

"Where's the bloody M.O.?" he said to the NCO.

"They've got thousands of casualties. They're overwhelmed. We're trying to find an orderly."

"An orderly?" He could hear his own voice rise, its desperation. The smell was nauseating. He moved forward and was halted by the heat. He ducked, brushed a spark off his shoulder. Bits of burnt canvas blew in the air. A handful of soldiers, some with buckets, were standing back, hands raised to protect their eyes from the heat. There was a piercing purple haze of metallic crackling in his head. A noise: almost perfectly B minor.

He heard the sergeant say to Hall, quietly and all in a rush, "Sooner it all goes up, the better."

When the sergeant realized he'd heard, he said "Sorry, sir. I know he's your friend, sir, but it's hopeless if he can't get hisself out."

The pain consumed him. He burned—he felt blisters and his scalp a halo of fire, his eyeballs sucked dry, he felt his flesh melt like candle wax, but looked down to see that he was untouched.

"Dear God, Theo. . . ."

And then he was moving and, feeling someone's hand on his arm for a second, shook the man off and he understood it all. Said or read or thought Theo's unspoken words, not Mendelssohn's music, but the Psalm itself and all its truth.

My heart is sore pained within me and the terrors of death
are fallen upon me. Fearfulness and trembling are come
upon me, and horror hath overwhelmed me. And I said,
O that I had wings like a dove! For then would I fly
away, and be at rest.

He began to run; although he felt a tug on his arm, he shook it off.

"Don't you understand—I love him," he said, and then shouted "I love him," and he could feel his eyes weep with the smoke. Then it was hotter than ever, as his feet pressed hard downward and fast and the rainbow of war colors and smells hurled around him and the everything was alight and the wreck wailed and he heard a shout, "Wait for me," and perhaps it was Hall but then he knew it for his own transparent voice shouting. Wait. Theo. Wait. And he felt first a terrible pain and his body curled away instinctively, shoulder up, arm across his face to ward off the fire, but then he was through and going forward with ringing in his ears, a pounding, his face stiffening, somehow growing smaller while his chest seemed to balloon outward. He had a white-hot vision of his lungs, their delicacy perfectly illuminated, but then came surprise as the colors went out and then the sound died and he was for the first time free of it all and he was not running, he was flying and his legs were not his and he cried with sealed eyes and lips that would not move toward the heat and the heart. Fly away. Fly, Theo, fly. And he was carried forward—not alone— never alone—and his arms so wide and feathers from them now and he was in snow: white and black and very cold and shouting out I love you I love you I love you I love

CHAPTER FORTY-ONE
Jean-Baptiste, France, July 1-2, 1916

THE LITTLE BOY HAD BEEN in a cot in a small room with four or five other infants. Most were small bundles and asleep. One wailed—a thin animal sound. The room was on the ground floor along a gloomy corridor. It had a small empty fireplace, two windows and narrow glazed doors to the outside, and a small courtyard. None of the windows was open and the room was airless. A fly buzzed against a pane. A young nun was reading her breviary, sitting on a hard chair in the corner. She stood up as they entered and brushed down her apron. She looked nervous but said nothing.

"We've come to see Leo," Mother Superior said. There were two older children as well as the tiny babies, but Jean-Baptiste knew which one was his mother's child immediately. The little boy, dressed in a faded frock, was sitting up and looked at the newcomers but did not cry. The crumpled sheets around him were gray.

The three of them walked toward the cot, with the younger sister behind them. The priest made some strange clucking noises, and the child continued to gaze at them.

"You may pick him up," said Mother Superior to the sister and the young nun passed them, leaned over the chipped metal bars, untied what looked like a bandage from the little boy's wrist, and swung him onto her hip. His legs and arms were thin and his head seemed large; he had dark hair, which had, Jean-Baptiste thought, been shaved to the scalp, a very pale face, and a rash around his mouth. He clung to the sister's habit.

"He can stand," said the young nun. "Even walk a little. And he can say 'amen' and 'thank you.' He's no trouble."

"He seems a little thin, perhaps?" the priest said, hesitantly.

"We're *all* a little thin, Father," said Mother Superior. "There's not enough for the sisters to eat, let alone feed the children. It's not safe here. The Germans could come any day. We have petitioned to have the children moved to our mother house in Paris. There are promises, plans. But these things take time and travel is difficult and nobody wants the babies. Their care is too onerous. God will provide, no doubt." Her tone, however, suggested doubt.

The priest nodded, apologetically, as if it had been rude of him to ask.

Mother Superior gestured across the room. "That one"—she nodded to the crying baby, whom nobody seemed inclined to soothe. "A decent family." The priest's head bobbed in agreement, his mouth pursed. "It's a mercy the grandfather is dead," she said, "and the child like to follow him. It won't eat. And the mother? Run off to Paris. These girls, they see a soldier, and all their modesty and decency is put aside. Then they expect us to pick up the cost of their shame."

Jean-Baptiste wasn't sure if the look she gave him was because he was a soldier or because his mother had set aside her decency and had not had time to settle her account.

"We're turning them all away from now on," she said sharply. "If they can't pay, they can't leave their fatherless children here. We'll take good Catholic orphans from respectable families and that is all."

Jean-Baptiste could hardly take his eyes off the little boy. He was watching them, but he didn't respond to the priest's smiles, nor to the young nun jiggling him on her hip. His linen dress was crumpled around his hips and his small legs hung free. Jean-Baptiste held out his arms and the child turned his head, briefly, to the nun. But he let himself be taken, without a murmur. He was heavier than Jean-Baptiste had expected, but felt like a small animal in his arms.

"Hello," he said, self-consciously. The boy smelled slightly of urine and there was a warm dampness where he was pressed against him. Jean-Baptiste smiled, and just when he thought the baby would not react at all, the child put out a small hand and reached toward his face.

He sensed Mother Superior signal to the priest and heard his cough. "I fear we've intruded too long," he said.

"What will happen to him?" Jean-Baptiste said, turning around to face the older woman. "To Leo?"

There was a moment's silence. "He's a pretty child" she said, almost grudgingly. "In normal times he might be placed with a good, devout family. But now . . . too many men are away. Too many families have orphans related by blood."

"So he stays here?"

"Unfortunately, yes. Until he goes to Paris."

"I could have him. I'd like to have him." He found himself holding tight to the small body, the child who was his. Who was all that was left of his mother's life and of Vignon.

"You?" The Mother Superior's voice was loud in surprise.

"It's impossible . . ." the priest began. "Quite unsuitable. You're an unmarried man. . . ."

"And neglecting your duties," the Mother Superior said, bitterly, with all the implications that carried.

The priest looked at her apologetically. "The British are sorting it out," he said. "They will return him to our army as soon as it's safe."

"I'm not a deserter," Jean-Baptiste said; and at his raised voice, the boy clung harder, but began to whimper.

"Take the child," Mother Superior said to the young sister and then almost hissed at Jean-Baptiste: "You have no idea how to handle a baby. How could you? You're a childless man. You need patience, discipline."

Jean-Baptiste resisted the sister for a minute but, seeing the anxiety in the younger nun's gray eyes, released his brother. The little boy began to wail.

"See, you've upset him," said Mother Superior.

Father Lefroy cleared his throat. "It seemed only fair that he should see the child. He will be gone in days and, with his mother dead, is unlikely to return."

Jean-Baptiste looked at the priest, the reality of his position suddenly hitting him. Where would he go? All his plans had been of return, of seeing his mother, of explaining. Telling her about Vignon. Perhaps she would have explained things to him too. He would give her his back pay, she would take care of him, he would get strong again, he would work and look after her. The question had only ever been of his own survival; he had never considered that his mother, so healthy, not old, would die and he would live.

Mother Superior opened the door and stood back as if to ensure that he left. He looked at her. "I have a little money. My pay, saved while I was in the hospital. I shall let you have it for my brother."

Mother Superior inclined her head. She seemed interested though unconvinced. Then, as if deciding he might be in a position to make good his offer, her features softened a little.

"Once this war is finished, we may find a home for the boy. Who knows. He is a good child."

"That would be the best possible outcome," said the priest, who had been nodding as she spoke. "A good home with a good Catholic family."

Jean-Baptiste found himself unable to speak and left the room quickly, his brother's thin cries following him down the corridor.

In the street, a convoy of Army ambulances was coming slowly from the marketplace. He could see stretchers of immobile figures being unloaded, as well as seated, less badly injured men but bloody and desolate-looking, drawing on cigarettes. Nothing surprised him. Not the ease with which men died, apparently untouched, nor their extraordinary capacity for lingering with limbs missing or a crater in their skulls or bicycles blown into their flesh. Nor losing a mother and finding a brother on the same day.

The priest stared about him, as if disoriented. "This is the worst," he said, "the worst it's been. This must be a bad day." His expression was grave, his mouth turned down. "All we can do is pray. God understands his plan for us."

Jean-Baptiste thought back to the massive explosion that had rocked the banks of the river and the dark plume of fast-moving darkness and debris he had seen pushing up into the blue dawn sky toward the north. Was this carnage the result of that? They had finally blown apart everything they were fighting for, he'd thought. Who cared if the Germans took what was left.

"You had better stay with me tonight," the priest said, and they started the slow walk back to the presbytery. The sky was turning violet as the presbytery loomed, as dark and forbidding as he remembered it.

Father Lefroy poured them both a brandy. Having seen the nuns, he clearly felt there was no further need to speak of the misfortune. After a while, a stick-thin woman came in, but not the housekeeper who'd been in residence when Jean-Baptiste was last in Corbie. That one had been considered too young and too pretty, first by the townsfolk and then by the bishop. Or so his mother had said, laughing.

"Do we have any potted meat left?" Father Lefroy said.

She nodded.

"Bring some through, then, there's a good girl." She turned to go, and Jean-Baptiste noticed she had a twisted spine.

After a few seconds, the priest said "She doesn't speak. She's not a mute; she chooses not to. Except to cats."

Jean-Baptiste put on what he hoped was an interested expression. "She was a convent child," said the priest. "An orphan."

They sat in silence for a few minutes. The sounds of war entered the room, accompanied by a single shaft of gold-pink light. The sun was sinking. Would the shelling stop at nightfall?

"Poor Madame Laporte. You remember Lucien? He was shot. For assaulting a woman. A French woman. And he was such a popular boy." He looked puzzled. "A terrible thing."

When Jean-Baptiste didn't reply, he said "You had a bad time?" Then he added, rushing his words at the end of the sentence, "No need to speak of it if you'd rather not."

Jean-Baptiste nodded. "I'm still here," he said.

"Injured, you say? But not dead. Unlike so many of your schoolfellows. Unlike Lucien."

Then, not knowing why he did it, Jean-Baptiste lifted his shirt, smelling his own body as he did so, revealing the broad, purple, puckered scar that curved untidily from near his spine to his loin. He was conscious of the stiff resistance of the scar tissue, saw the priest's gaze slide away, and felt diminished.

"I'm sorry," said Father Lefroy. Jean-Baptiste wasn't sure whether he was sorry for the wound or for not believing him without proof.

"I was discharged because my kidneys are bad," he said after he'd tucked himself in carefully, as much to ease the tension as to provide information. "It was Dr. Vignon who discharged me."

"Vignon? He enlisted as a surgeon, of course."

"He saved my life."

"So you saw Vignon. I am glad to hear it. Not a perfect man, but a good doctor. He is all right, then?"

"No," said Jean-Baptiste. "He's dead."

He said nothing more, thinking that if Vignon was not dead by now, he would be soon, and why should all Corbie know that a good man had died because he had told a lie a long time ago, a long time before the war? A good man and his brother's father, he also thought, and made a decision.

The food came on a wooden platter. They ate; and when the woman returned to bring them a minute quantity of stewed apple, Father Lefroy indicated a little gristle he had left on his plate.

"For the cats," he said.

She gave him something like a smile and her hand went up to her mouth, but not quite in time to hide the missing teeth. During the meal, Jean-Baptiste had gathered up bread and cheese and the remaining meat from his own plate, storing it in his roomy pockets. If Father Lefroy had noticed, he didn't say.

"Are you tired now?" the priest asked, and Jean-Baptiste nodded. It was true; he was bone-tired.

The priest looked tired himself as he climbed the stairs to a room on the third floor. It faced away from the street, its view down a sloping roof, presumably with the kitchen below. The bed was not made up, but gray blankets were folded neatly on top.

"We weren't expecting—" the priest began.

"No, thank you, thank you very much."

"Thank you," he said again when the door closed, though to what or whom he did not know. Despite his exhaustion, he doubted he would sleep but was glad to have some time to himself. Now he could lie on the bed, gazing at the eaves of this attic room and out to the sky, still light and under which, he knew, other men lay in agony or resignation or simply without hope.

His mother's face, which for so long he had fought to not recall, was now lost to him when he wanted it. He had a powerful sense of her but, as with all ghosts, when he tried to grasp her, she was gone. Except her hands—he could recall her long fingers, her touch, the skin; unlike her face, her hands were older than her

361

years. He experimented with thoughts of Godet, of Pierre Duval, of Marcel and young Pierre who had both died at Verdun, even of Lucien Laporte, and it was the same with them: he could easily remember the idea of them, but their faces and even the pitches of their voices had gone. Vignon was clearer, but no doubt he would slip away too. He thought again of his mother's hands. Had she ever held her new baby son?

He slept for an hour or two and when he woke it was, finally, night and the new moon sharp as a wire in the clear sky. The shelling had died down, but the grumbling of lorries up the main street continued. After what seemed like a long time, the church bell started to chime. He was surprised that the bell had not long since been taken for melting down, but now it rang twelve peals almost in rhythm with the distant guns. He found he was clutching the edge of the blanket, but he forced himself to swing his legs out of bed and pick up the sabots.

CHAPTER FORTY-TWO
Teddy, Eton,
July 2, 1916

TEDDY SYDENHAM SLEEPS RESTLESSLY IN his small school dormitory just a short distance from the Thames. It is just past midnight and his fourteenth birthday. He has been Sir Edward Sydenham for four hours, although it will be weeks before he will know this.

Teddy sleeps off and on, dreaming of boats, worrying about his Greek unseen, and hoping his mother has arranged for a birthday cake to be sent to school as he has boasted so confidently that she will.

The dark river, midway on its journey from a muddy field in the Cotswold hills to the cold estuary in the North Sea, fed by twenty tributaries and interrupted by more than eighty islands, is peaceful. Punts are drawn up on the bank, pleasure boats are moored on both sides; some have remained there, without once making a trip to Oxford or Maidenhead, since the outbreak of war. Away from the lights of Windsor and Eton, the new moon casts much of the scene into darkness, but a careful listener might hear the watery noises of nighttime: water rats, jostling ducks, a soldier on leave with his giggling girl crossing the Brocas. Deadwater Ait, a green islet by day, is a crouching monster by night.

It is hot and stuffy and he has kicked off the tartan blanket that has fallen across his trunk on which his initials have been painted over those of his brother Harry. Harry's picture, with Harry in uniform, is by his bed, next to the one of Mama and his father. The house dame had commented approvingly how alike the two brothers were. Teddy has kept to himself the fact that he doubts he would recognize Harry easily in a Windsor street and certainly not in uniform.

CHAPTER FORTY-THREE
Jean-Baptiste, France, July 2, 1916

JEAN-BAPTISTE CLAMBERED DOWN THE ROOF outside his window, clutching his sabots and the water bottle and hoping the roof was sound and that nobody would wake. When he reached the gutter, the drop was slightly more than he'd guessed; but directly below him was a row of what were probably onions, so he thought he would have a soft landing.

He looked back at the two windows next to the one he'd left and was surprised to see a pale face at one. He started for a second before realizing it was the mute girl, the maid, and she was only staring, not moving to raise an alarm. He dropped to the ground, landed heavily but continued, limping slightly, through the bare garden onto the back lane and then on down between the houses, always aware that there might be a jumpy British soldier with a gun somewhere in the shadows. The town was noisy: lorries grinding their way up the main street behind the houses he was passing. Shouts and metallic clatter offered a useful cover for his own movements.

He reached the outer wall of the convent easily. It was in darkness. He went up to the front gate, attempting to open it soundlessly. It was possible that the sisters, with all their praying, might be about, but it occurred to him that there were hardly enough of them to be everywhere in the big building and at night they were likely to be either in their beds or in the chapel. But the gate was locked. Not surprising, with soldiers in the town, *Protestant* soldiers, he thought, and the idea pleased him. He took off his, or at least Bully Laporte's, sabots and placed them, neatly together, at the gate.

The side walls were the same height as the gate, but he remembered from childhood that an oak tree grew so close to the wall that one boy had dared climb up it to look in and reported that he had seen two nuns in their drawers. They had all believed it at the time. Would the tree still be there? He saw almost immediately that it was and that, if anything, the branches seemed closer to the boundary. Nor was it hard to climb; but once he was on the wall, the drop on the other side onto a paved courtyard was intimidating. He sat astride the wall, glad the moon was not full, and checked to see whether there was any change in level, where the drop might be lower. Some sort of structure seemed to stand in the farthest corner.

As he eased himself along, it became clear that a shed was indeed tucked away there, but he couldn't tell whether the roof was sound. But he had no alternative way down; so when he reached the spot where the wall passed behind it, he braced himself and lowered himself onto the roof. It held. From there it was an easy scramble to the ground. Still nothing stirred. He looked up. He was on the northern side of the building; two windows were open on the second story. How many nuns were in there? Did they have a night watchman, as they used to before the war?

The babies' nursery was around the corner, he thought, and the doors to the outside were shut. He reached out, fearing that they too were locked and wondering whether babies were woken easily by breaking glass. But the latch opened easily and he peered in, just in case a nun sat up with the little ones all night. There was nobody—he could just pick out small sleeping forms; one was snoring gently. The room was stuffy and smelled of ammonia. He walked quietly but quickly to his brother's cot. The little boy was fast asleep, lying on his back, one arm thrown up. Jean-Baptiste went to another cot and picked up a blanket the baby had kicked off. He then picked up his brother, held him close while he wrapped him, clumsily, but without rousing him.

The child started to wake up as he crossed the yard. He prayed that he wouldn't cry and that the front gate had been locked only from the inside, leaving the key in the lock. Someone must have heard his prayers, because he was through the gate in a second. The little boy struggled a bit but seemed to want to be carried sitting up. Even in the near-blackness, Jean-Baptiste could see that his dark eyes were wide open now and watching him.

"It's going to be all right, Leo," he said softly. He picked up the sabots, and they were off into the night.

They walked out of Corbie, not along the main road, which was heavy with traffic, but back down the track to the river. It was dark and rough going and Leo was heavy. Jean-Baptiste stumbled a few times, but he could soon hear the water. The little boy occasionally muttered syllables that Jean-Baptiste could not understand, but he seemed to take this nocturnal adventure in his stride. Only once, as an explosion sounded close to them, less than half a kilometer away, Jean-Baptiste judged, did he worry about the great responsibility he had taken upon himself. It was hard enough contemplating a dangerous journey alone; but with a small child, how could he keep them both safe? But what was the alternative for either of them? Once on the river, he felt, they would be safer. The river would take them with it.

He had to stop and put the boy down a couple of times, and Leo clung to his knees while he drank from the canteen. How did the young, slender mothers he'd seen before the war cope with their babies on their hips all day?, he wondered.

He followed the river west until he saw the island. He set Leo down with some relief and walked over to the willow that had harbored *Sans Souci* while everything else in his life had fallen apart. He unhooked the bailer and emptied the boat of black standing water and its mulch of leaves. Before the war, it had been a matter of a few minutes to launch it, almost skimming the grass as if to return it to its home on the water; but the boat had settled into the mud and vegetation for at least two years now and wouldn't budge. He crawled around it on his knees, suddenly desperate to free it, tearing at the most obvious obstructions. Then he reached up, lifted out a rowlock and dug around the keel with its metal prongs, careful not to damage it. It was still dark now, but he needed to be well clear of Corbie before the nuns woke the children. By dawn, anybody might see him.

He pulled again, bracing his feet against the roots of the tree, and the boat creaked. He had a sudden vision of it all falling apart, into a pile of planks; but just as he was having serious doubts, it started to move and, once it started, he found himself trying to keep hold of the gunwale to prevent it launching itself and floating north without them. He couldn't risk putting it into the river and leaving it for an hour to make sure it was sound and had no leaks. He had to chance that even if it did, he could bail more quickly than it would take on water. Behind him, Leo was becoming restless. He kept moving away, or picking up dirt, so that Jean-Baptiste had half his eye on the boat and half on the child. He gave the boy a little drink of water and handed him some bread. Leo gnawed at it but seemed as interested in playing with it as he was in swallowing it. He said something that sounded like "bread."

Jean-Baptiste smiled. "Yes, bread," he said. "Clever boy, bread. You eat it so that you're strong."

A single flare shot into the air to the east. He had no choice; he couldn't control the boat on the water and the child on the land at the same time, so he threw his sabots into the boat, then reached forward, scooped the boy up, lifted him in too, and, standing with one foot in it and one against the bank, he thrust it away from the shore. With a last creak, the boat made a final splash into the water, some of which broke over the prow, and was immediately pulled into the current. Again, he felt a surge of anxiety, but he knew this boat, this river. Picking up an oar, he pushed *Sans Souci* free of the obstructions that projected from the bank and into the side channel down the length of the island.

He moved his brother onto one of the two blankets on the duckboards of the boat, where he thought he would be safest, and tucked the other blanket around him. The boy was alert, watching him continually. He made little noises from time to time, but was strangely unperturbed by this sudden change in his fortunes. The boat had left the midstream island behind it now, carried smoothly on the current. He wasn't sure if the sky was lightening to the east, or whether the strange color of the night clouds was simply a byproduct of the fighting, but he hoped to have made some distance by daylight. Tomorrow they would reach Amiens. They could rest by day, find food, perhaps. Every kilometer he rowed was farther from the battlefields and farther from the sisters. His brother would never return to the orphanage. He owed that to his mother and to Dr. Vignon. The Somme would take them northwest. Laporte had said it was impossible to reach the coast, but Laporte was dead and nobody knew the habits of the river like Jean-Baptiste. It might be impossible for a heavy barge, perhaps; but with a light, shallow-bottomed rowing boat, over many weeks, surely it could be done.

Once they were clear of Corbie, they would travel through the locks and the river gardens, the marshes and the eel ponds.

Maybe the river was unnavigable, maybe there would be military guards, maybe he would have to abandon the small craft and carry his brother overland, maybe he could rest and get stronger until he found another boat and another way north to the great bay and the roar of its breakers and the wail of seabirds. Then, maybe, one day, they would go to England and find Cousin Isabelle. But meanwhile the sea air would be good for his chest, he could do odd jobs and the boy could play on the sand and get some color in his cheeks, and they could both paddle in the shallows as the tide sucked the Somme out to sea.

Afterwards

Deeply regret your husband, Major Sir Henry Maurice Bourne Sydenham, the Somerset Light Infantry, killed in action in France, July 1. The Army Council expresses sympathy. Unfortunately during the morning's engagement very few of the Company got back without being hit. However, such is War, and it is the memory of these gallant deeds that must remain to us for our consolation. Assuring you of our deepest sympathy in your sad loss.

It is my painful duty to inform you that a report has this day been received that your son 145083 Cpl Francis Percy Stanton 1st Huntingdonshire (Cyclists') Batt'n, is missing, believed killed, in action, July 1.

There was fierce fighting in the area at the time and there are as yet no further details. The Army Council expresses sympathy and regrets the loss you and the Army have sustained on the death of your son in the service of his country.

Any application you may wish to make concerning the late soldier's effects should be addressed to the War Office, Whitehall, London SW.

It is with the deepest regret that I have to inform you that your son, Acting Captain Benedict Arthur Chatto, was killed in action on July 2, while attempting to save the life of a brother officer. His death was that of a fine soldier and a brave man and he has been mentioned in a Dispatch for his courageous action.

The King and Queen deeply regret the loss you and the Army have sustained on the death of your son in the service of his country.

Sad news has been received by Mr. Reginald Dawes-Holt of Avalon Court, Bristol, on his return from honeymoon in Scotland. A telegram awaited with notification of the death of his only son, Captain Theodore Reginald John Dawes-Holt, Royal Flying Corps, who was killed in France during the opening hours of the Battle of the Somme. Many casualties were sustained during this heroic action, we hear, and sadly this popular young officer was among them.

Captain Dawes-Holt, whose late mother was the celebrated singer Mrs. Serafina Dawes-Holt, was engaged to be married to Miss Agnes Elizabeth Bradstock, daughter of the Right Reverend the Bishop of Gloucester.

Before taking up his commission, Captain Dawes-Holt, who was educated at the King's School, Gloucester, was an organ scholar at the cathedral and his early promise had been much remarked upon in musical circles.

—*Bristol Courier,* July 28, 1916

CHAPTER FORTY-FOUR
June 30, 1916

I love you more than life itself. Never forget that.
Your Harry

CHAPTER FORTY-FIVE
Frank, Devon, 1917

THERE WERE THINGS I LEARNED from that war. Too many to list. One is: just because it's written down and looks official, don't believe a word of it.

It nearly killed my old dad getting the telegram, but I don't doubt he had got into the way of enjoying a bit of sympathy. There was plenty who lost their boys and their husbands, but he had no one left at all, of course. Then, six months later, it nearly killed him all over again seeing me turn up. I thought it would just be a pleasant surprise, not knowing the Army had, in the matter of telegrams, let off its barrage too early, which, as we'd learned to our cost, was the usual way with them. I'd been out of it all for weeks, they told me in the hospital, and all that time down as Isaac Meyer, whose name tag they had found on me after Nora had ripped mine off my neck that day. Every week, the rabbi came to sit with me; even when I didn't know who I was, he stayed, holding my hand. Even when I did, he still came.

Now Dad was as pale as if he'd seen a ghost, which in a way he had. The War Office nearly had the death of the old man on its hands on top of all those young ones.

It was two heroes who saved me from certain death, they said. A French lad, nobody knew his name, who found me, wandering, stuck through with bits of scrap, which was all poor Nora was by then. The French boy cleaned me up, laid me down, and got a first-aider to me. The story followed me, no doubt growing in the telling. Wherever I went, they said you're the one made it because the French lad swam the River Somme, in the middle of a battle, to get help. Then when nobody wanted to come out and fetch a single soldier who looked like he was a goner, least not on a Frenchman's say-so, one first-aider volunteered. My second hero. His name I do know: such an ordinary name—Higgs. A searcher who found me, a nurse told me. I could never thank him or have him tell me how it was, as by then he'd disappeared. No record, they said. They'd all disappeared who'd been part of my story; all except me.

So I can't say for certain what happened. Sometimes I thought I could remember a stranger coming and going, talking gobbledegook. But then most of that, before I finally realized I was in a hospital bed, came to me in bits and really I didn't know what was real and what I'd been told and what I just imagined.

There was the sun, burning, taking up the whole sky, falling fit to crush me and I thought I was poor Prometheus, who I'd learned about back at the Institute, from the old professor who told us all about the ancient Greeks. Pinned on a rock and every day his liver pecked out by a great bird, and every day it grew back, every hour more agony and he could not die. Nora was that bird. Water. I was that hot and my mouth shriveled up. Scraping through the earth. Couldn't lie, couldn't sit. Peck, peck, peck. The bird never left me. Trying to get to the river. Isaac says it's close. Waterbirds, he says.

Was I in a boat, or was that on the Serpentine, before, with Connie and Nancy?

Somehow, there was always Nora and if I held her close, the pain went, and if I let her fall, the pain shot through me.

One strange thing haunts me. When I was better, when I was in the hospital in Blighty, they gave me my belongings, not that they were many or serviceable, but among them was a handkerchief, officers' quality. It was one of ours, from Duke Street, that is, with our tiny label, our hand-rolled edges and of the very best kind.

Sometimes I saw that German rising up behind the spoil at the edge of a crater like through a trapdoor in a music-hall stage and both of us staring like we were each other's nightmare. Him pointing his rifle, but Nora had trapped mine. Do I remember turning my back so the bullets would hit her first? Was that just a dream? Did Nora, who'd done nothing but drag me down ever since I left England, save my life? And what happened then? The medics said it was blast from a shell that blew Nora and me together, as it were. For a while, I was Mr. Longfellow's iron centaur.

After a day or so, I showed Dad my scars. It's like a miracle, says he, gazing at the lines across my back; it's like a resurrection. I looked at him sharpish because he wasn't a great one for God, but his eyes were fixed on the dark little crater in my side and his hand hovered as if he did and didn't want to touch it. I tucked my shirt in quick.

That deep injury was the one that had nearly done for me, caused by a brake bar piercing me under my ribs like a blunt bayonet, tearing through muscle and sliding past my liver. The fine lines were spokes that had slid in as easily as giant needles. But on my other side was a greater wonder: the big scar there was in the recognizable shape of the pivot of the BSA Folding Machine. If you knew one well, of course. Bits of Nora were still embedded within me as well as leaving the pivot scar. The Army surgeons said as how they might start finding their way out and not to be unnerved if I felt hard lumps of metal emerging here and there. Poor Nora. Along with that French soldier boy, a deserter, they thought, and the vanishing Higgs, she probably saved my life and all of them left to rust in France.

Dad had tears in his eyes, but I thought that he would soon have me down the pub, lifting up my vest to all and sundry for the price of a beer if he had a chance.

It was hopeless from the start: a waste of machines and a waste of riders.

In the whole time I was a soldier, I bore Nora ten times farther than she bore me. It was an offense to abandon equipment, of course; but although I was tempted, I would never really have left her, not for Fritz to have her.

CHAPTER FORTY-SIX
Frank, Devon, 1919

I WANTED TO LEAVE DEVON but didn't know how I might live in London again. So I lingered on with Dad. I had wanted to emerge as a different man, but the man I was now was no good any more for heavy work, nor for standing serving in a shop.

The months went by and the war seemed to be drawing to an end, and I seemed to be slipping back into the mire of the life I'd been so proud to leave years ago. Nobody was interested in my time in London or what I had learned. Most seemed to think I was as lucky to have escaped the big city as to return alive from France, both being, in their eyes, places where the enemy lurked. I gave a hand to Dad, trying the fine work on the coffins. The heavy stuff was too much for me now, and we had a strong lad in for that. Jim. He hadn't got any kind of eye, just brawn, and I'd have to hold my tongue when he heaved in the wrong wood or ruined a beautiful bit of timber by not thinking before he went charging in at it with his chisel. I wasn't unhappy all the time, but I longed for London like some man might long for a girl, and what I wanted most was not what you'd expect, not the great domes and spires and galleries, nor even the amusement parks and Sunday bands and music halls, but the ordinary things: the smell of gas in the Institute, the rush of people crossing Westminster Bridge so sure of the city that they didn't even look at it. I missed the tang of smoke and the noise of hansoms and drays and cars. The bells, the shouts, the rattle and roar of coal down the chute. You'd think after France I'd want the peace of Devon, but I longed for noise.

Dad and Jim were all right together and the business was surviving, though never what it used to be. The old man was tetchy because even though folks were still dying and doing it at home and even though some other coffin-makers had failed in the war, he worried and fussed and spent hours over his books as if by adding up the same figures again they might suddenly show a different truth. Yet he'd take no suggestions for expanding, nor even for letting me do the figures in the modern way as they did in London shops. I tried to tell him business was business, no matter what goods it dealt in, but he wouldn't have it.

I sometimes wondered what had happened to Connie. But what did Connie know? She'd have had me in prison like Isaac Meyer's brother, being taunted by warders and attacked by prisoners while other lads died for me. Thinking of Isaac, I remembered my promise to write to his family and I remembered it with shame. As I was identified as Isaac for a while, as I *was* Isaac in the rabbi's eyes, perhaps they had been told, at first, that he was only injured. My resurrection was his end. How its significance had escaped me, I do not know—thinking only of myself, I expect.

I remembered the simple address, of course. So I took my time on a letter and I was careful to leave out a lot and add a lot more and, by the time I'd finished, Isaac's death was the best you could hope for. Almost glorious, but not so as they'd wonder why he'd been passed over for a medal and make inquiries. But he *was* a hero, really, in his way, but not as anyone who'd not been there would think. I said as how I'd been injured and was not fit for work and if I'd been in London as I'd hoped, I'd have come to see them and told them face to face. It was probably true, that bit.

And so things went on in the coffin corps. Low morale. The C.O. failing, the crippled adjutant exasperated and drinking, the trooper a general dogsbody dreaming of his sweetheart. Sometimes I felt pretty desperate. I was useless, unwanted, really, and, to tell the truth, lonely, as I never had been in London.

It must have been the end of 1917 we got two strokes of luck. The first began with the old vicar of Thaxton. He was a widower who'd never recovered from when his boy—an officer in the artillery—had been killed on the Somme around about the same time I'd been injured. He'd sacrificed himself for another officer. "Greater love hath no man than that he lay down his life, etc." It was all very biblical. He'd gotten a medal.

But there was no consoling the father, and a rumor at the Arms said after that it had been nothing but hours of Old Testament, death, and destruction and the flightier members of his flock had gone off to neighboring villages or even Chapel for all they were sorry about his boy. At which point the bishop intervened. Still, the reverend was past all his woe now and to be buried next to his wife, who'd died two years back.

Dad and I went to see the daughter, Miss Chatto. She was a nice young lady, very sad. Then it hit me. Chatto was the officer who'd come to Duke Street and had got me in with the Hunts cyclists. He'd said he came from Devon. It wouldn't have been right to ask if he was "my" Chatto, so I didn't. Anyway, he didn't make it back.

Miss Chatto was talking about how she didn't want anything showy for her father, him being a modest man of the cloth, but she said it should be nice. So nice we did: polished elm, and a good bit of wood, with a touch of mitering and handles in the classical style. There was no money in it: you could tell she had little, so we did it almost at cost and out of respect. Poor Miss Letitia Chatto had lost her father and her brother and her fiancé as well, Jim heard, a Navy man.

But it was as if God was watching and judging, because a few weeks later we got a good commission from the widow of the mayor, who, it turned out, was in the way of being the Reverend Chatto's sister-in-law and had heard good of us from the daughter. Only the best would do, she said, even if the old man had heard down in the Arms that she was part German, though you couldn't tell.

"Guilt," said my dad. "It's always guilt when nothing but the best will do."

The coffin would lie in state in the town hall (Dad snorted on hearing this; he'd never been one for the mayor), then borne through the streets. The whole of Totnes would see it. Trouble was, we didn't have much of the best left.

"Where's that fine oak we had way back?" I said. "We had a whole lot of it we bought off a timber merchant back in '09 or '10." When things were going well, was what I didn't say. It was lovely, fine-grained, seasoned timber. When Mother died, he'd used some for her coffin.

"No," said Dad, a bit too quick. "Long gone."

But I didn't see as how it could be. Even then, rich customers, or guilty ones by Dad's reckoning, were few and far between. And he looked shifty.

I let him go out drinking down the Arms by himself. And no sooner had he gone than I went out to rummage through the sheds. I was damned if I wasn't going to find the oak, though I had my suspicions that he'd gone and sold it. At a loss, no doubt.

Moving the planks of cut lengths was hard work, where once it would have been nothing, and I didn't find anything but elm and pine. There was a lean-to right at the back, but I didn't see that he would have put valuable wood in there. It was just used for offcuts and logs and bits of old rubbish he could never bear to give away. But he used to keep a couple of made-up cheap coffins in there in case of emergencies. It was worth a look. Ivy hung down like curtains in front of the doors, and I could get only one fully open. But I slipped inside, glad I'd brought a lamp. There was a coffin shell standing upright without its lid, a flimsy thing, and a stack of planks. I moved the coffin and took down the top planks and directed my light behind.

The light found oak almost immediately; I could tell by the color and the grain even though it was half in shadow. I could see that this was a coffin. Made up, finished. I lifted the lamp higher. A perfect, beautiful coffin. I took more planks away, getting out of breath, and then squeezed past the remainder. The coffin was carefully balanced on trestles. I touched it, and it was smooth and waxed. I could see its pale shape clearly, but I set the lamp by it to stare at the delicate inlay, the lozenges set into the side, the hand-cut beading, and the chamfered lid edge. The handles were splayed in the shape of acanthus leaves. I touched them; they were solid brass. It was a masterwork.

What on earth was such a piece doing stored in here? Why on earth hadn't Dad said? And when had he made it—if it was him, and who else could it have been; nobody had these skills now—and how on earth had he ever afforded the materials? How the hell long had it taken him? Longer than any corpse might wait for it, I thought. Then as I ran my hand over the lid, so pleasing to touch because of the layers of wax and polish, I touched the edge of a coffin plate and bent over to see it in more detail. It was brass, too, and I saw it had a name on it, and dates set within a finely etched wreath of laurel. I lifted the lamp and leaned forward, feeling my skin tingle a little.

Francis Percy Stanton, August 18, 1891–July 1, 1916
RIP

The lamp went out, and I stood there in the darkness for a long while. Nothing is ever as you believe it to be.

So we soldiered on, Dad and I and the lad (who learned to make good, basic coffins in the end). Dad got older and more tired, and I got older and more resigned. Anyway, the old man liked us living together, and I liked it well enough; or at least I had grown used to it and he needed me. I saw that now. I never said a word to him about what I'd seen that night.

The Armistice came and went and I was trotted out with all the other village lads who'd served. Even poor Wilf Gates, whose brother brought him to the Arms in his chair. They'd carry him in and there he'd sit by the bar, dribbling a bit and having his special drink in his old mug. It looked like ale but wasn't, on account of his light-headedness. Now they pinned his campaign medal to his chest, over his bib. There was bunting in the church hall, and tea and music and kissing.

All the while, there was another enemy creeping from the Continent. Not so long after the Armistice, we both caught the Spanish flu, Dad and me. It was a bitter thing that just as there were plenty of deaths and all close at hand, he should fall ill himself. Jim nursed us both, sometimes with his girl helping: an odd sort of family we were by then—and I came through, but Dad slipped away at Christmas. He was sixty-eight years old, and he'd probably had enough.

I went out the next day and found the coffin. My coffin. In daylight, it was as fine as I remembered, and I found I was shaking a little. This time I lifted the lid and found it lined with quilted ivory silk and tiny silk-covered buttons and the top edge fitted with brass studs. A pillow in the same silk. I levered off the nameplate and took it to keep as a testament. Then I took one of our stock plates and I cut a new one for him, though his one for me had been far better work. Then I called Mr. Rook the undertaker.

Jim was set to marry at Easter, and his girl's father was a farmer in need of a strong hand, and I was fitter every day but at a loss with Dad gone. I had no interest in the coffin business, and anyway these days you could buy a coffin from Manchester or Bristol, ready-made, for half the price. That was the dark shadow that had lain over Dad in his last years. The great funerals were a thing of the past, the coffin was soon in the ground and the demand for bespoke wasn't there.

One summer morning I sat with my beer, with nothing to do as usual but rub at the tender lump that had appeared under my armpit, knowing it was one of Nora's steel ribs pushing through.

I had read in the newspaper the day before that the recent Tour de France, the first since the war, had been a shambles. A Belgian, Firmin Lambot, had won it in the slowest time ever. It wasn't Lambot's fault. They said it was the roads, blown apart by the war, but it wasn't the roads, it was all that had happened. Where were the gods? Where were Petit-Breton, Lapize, and Faber? Gone. Lambot was racing against ghosts.

There was a knock at the door. I got up slowly; even if it was for a coffin, I could scarcely be bothered. But it was the postman with a single letter. It was postmarked London, and the writing was black and untidy. Early on, I'd had a letter from Mr. Nugent. He was sorry to hear of my injuries, he said, and said Mr. Quickseed and Jakob sent their regards. Albert had retired, as his eyesight was too poor, and Joe was gone, he said, but it was hard to tell if he meant to the Army or the hereafter or another position in men's outfitting. They had two young ladies who'd taken our positions, he continued, and they were most satisfactory. The weather was very fine. Mr. Nugent's letter had made me depressed; how many uniforms were hanging under dust sheets in "unclaimed" now?

There'd not been a word from anyone since then, and the writing I was looking down at was certainly not Mr. Nugent's elegant copperplate of which he was so proud. It was more like a lunatic might write. But the letter, two pages of it on thin paper, turned out to be from Isaac Meyer's brother, Samuel. Now that the war was over and he was out of prison, he had been grateful to know the details of his brother's death and my comments about him and knowing that he had not suffered. Isaac had written of me several times, said Samuel Meyer, and our ideological exchanges had been important to his brother in keeping a wider vision of the world and the greater struggle even as it sank into an abyss. He didn't know how I was fixed for work, having been injured, but though he could offer me no money to speak of, he and some comrades had a house in Stepney that had once been his parents', where several young men and a few women now lived together, sharing what they had, be it money or abilities. They had a small printing press. He would be happy if I would join their community. They were working to change the world through public speaking, political action, and international understanding, he said. We would educate each other and then educate the masses. Wars such as the war just past were possible only because of ignorance and distrust between working men—and women, he'd squeezed in above the line—who should be brothers. The enemy was not Germans or Hungarians or Turks but the conspiracy of the privileged, the rich and the powerful across all our countries, and that fight was only just beginning.

In truth, though I went along with the first bit, I didn't really go along with the second. Some of the best officers I'd known had been sons of great families, and you'd only relish a further scrap if you hadn't been part of the last one. Nor were my times with his brother exactly conversations. As I recalled, apart from in London when I'd heard him deliver his talk on "The Conditions of the Working Man in Russia" (so nobody gives a fig about the women, I remember Connie saying), we mostly talked about cycles and the weather in training, and in France we just looked out for each other. He was my friend.

But still, I felt my heart beat fast; it was a life and it was London and I was used to Samuel Meyer's sort of tone from the days when I was walking out with Connie. A cause seemed a good way to go forward and, who knows, in time, I might reach the masses by bicycle.

Postscript

"As I was one of the lucky ones, I still say I was glad I was there."

Lieutenant Corporal C. F. T. Townsend, 12th Middlesex Regiment, quoted by Martin Middlebrook in *The First Day of the Somme*

"I have come to London to-day to take my life. I have never had a moment's peace since July 1."

Letter read at the inquest into the death of Lieutenant Colonel E. T. F. Sandys DSO, Commanding Officer, 2nd Middlesex Regiment, September 6, 1916

The first day of the Battle of the Somme, July 1, 1916, was the middle day of the year in the middle year of the Great War.

That day remains the worst military disaster to have befallen the British Army in terms of losses. The final returns showed 57,470 casualties, of whom 19,240 were killed, 35,493 wounded, 2,152 missing, and 585 taken prisoner.

The Somme campaign was finally brought to a close by bad weather after 143 days. By that time, there had been few territorial gains but over one million casualties on all sides.

Similar numbers of casualties were sustained by the French and German armies during the Battle of Verdun, which was fought in appalling conditions, from February to December of the same year.

Acknowledgments

My thanks, as ever, are due to my agent Georgina Capel: guide, advocate, and tactician for many years. Writing any book begins in solitude and becomes a collaboration, and I have been enormously fortunate to have had the same team at Virago for all three of my novels; and I am delighted that *The First of July* will be published in the fortieth anniversary year of this remarkable imprint. I am very grateful for the continued support and sensitive editing of Victoria Pepe and the input of the wise Lennie Goodings. The invisibility of Celia Levett's painstaking copy-editing is its triumph. This is the first of my novels to be published by Pegasus Books in the U.S., and their enthusiasm, which matched my own, and their meticulous work in preparing it for publication have made this a very happy experience.

Of the vast number of books about the Somme campaign, Martin Middlebrook's *The First Day on the Somme* has been the one that I have returned to most often. By contrast, there are very few books in English about Verdun; but Alistair Horne's *The Price of Glory: Verdun 1916* is a gem, still in print after forty years, that recreates the rich culture and the turbulent politics and mindset of pre-war France as well as the horrors of Verdun itself. Three other books were invaluable: Henri Barbusse's 1916 novel *Le Feu* (*Under Fire*); Maurice Corina's *Fine Silks and Oak Counters, Debenhams 1778–1978*; and Mary Schaller's *Deliver Us from Evil: A Southern Belle in Europe at the Outbreak of World War I.*

I first became interested in writing about synesthesia, as experienced by Benedict Chatto, when hearing a friend, Dr. Maria Scholfield, discuss it with Michael Berkeley on Radio 4's *Private Passions.* Jamie Ward's *The Frog Who Croaked Blue: Synaesthesia and the Mixing of the Senses* and John Harrison's *Synaesthesia: The Strangest Thing* are fascinating accounts of the experience and scientific understanding of this condition. I am also extremely grateful to several individuals who responded to my requests on Twitter to provide vivid descriptions of living with synesthesia.

About the Author

Elizabeth Speller lived in Berlin, Rome, and Paris before reading Classics at Cambridge. She has written for publications as varied as the *Independent*, *Financial Times*, *Big Issue*, and *Vogue* and was a Royal Literary Fund Fellow at Warwick. She divides her time between Gloucestershire and Greece.

Her debut novel was the bestselling *The Return of Captain John Emmett*, which was both an Orange New Writers pick and a Richard & Judy Summer Book Club selection. This was followed by *The Strange Fate of Kitty Easton*, which also featured Laurence Bartram.

ML   12-13